MIDNIGHT AWAKENING

KISS OF CRIMSON

"Vibrant writing heightens the suspense, and hidden secrets provide many twists. This dark and steamy tale ... is a winner and will have readers eager for the next Midnight Breed story."
—Romance Reviews Today

"Hot sensuality with emotional drama and high-stakes danger ... [Adrian] ensures that her latest is terrific supernatural entertainment."
—*Romantic Times*

"[Adrian] pens hot erotic scenes and vivid action sequences."
—The Romance Reader

ASHES OF MIDNIGHT

"*Ashes of Midnight* will scorch its way into your heart."
—Romance Junkies

"Lara Adrian continues to kick butt with her latest release. . . . *Ashes of Midnight* is an entertaining ride and as usual kept me riveted from page one."
—The Romance Reader Connection

VEIL OF MIDNIGHT

"Adrian's newest heroine has a backbone of pure steel. Rapid-pace adventures deliver equal quantities of supernatural thrills and high-impact passion. This is one of the best vampire series on the market!"
—*Romantic Times*

"*Veil of Midnight* will enthrall you and leave you breathless for more."
—Wild on Books

MIDNIGHT RISING

"Fans are in for a treat. . . . Ms. Adrian has a gift for drawing her readers deeper and deeper into the amazing world she creates. . . . I eagerly await the next installment of this entertaining series!"
—Fresh Fiction

KISS OF MIDNIGHT

"Evocative, enticing, erotic. Enter Lara Adrian's
vampire world and be enchanted!"
—J. R. Ward, bestselling author

"*Kiss of Midnight* is dark, edgy and passionate,
an irresistible vampire romance."
—*Chicago Tribune*

"Lara Adrian delivers a fast-paced, sexy
romantic suspense that . . . stands above the
rest. . . . A gripping, sensual love story."
—The Romance Reader

"Gritty and dangerous, this terrific launch book
sets up an alternate reality filled with treachery
and loss. The Midnight Breed series is poised
to deliver outstanding supernatural thrills."
—*Romantic Times*

By Lara Adrian

KISS OF MIDNIGHT

KISS OF CRIMSON

MIDNIGHT AWAKENING

MIDNIGHT RISING

VEIL OF MIDNIGHT

ASHES OF MIDNIGHT

SHADES OF MIDNIGHT

TAKEN BY MIDNIGHT

DEEPER THAN MIDNIGHT

Deeper Than
Midnight

MIDNIGHT BREED SERIES
BOOK NINE

LARA ADRIAN

DELL

NEW YORK

2011 Dell Mass Market Edition

Copyright © 2011 by Lara Adrian, LLC
Excerpt from *Darker After Midnight* copyright © 2011 by Lara Adrian, LLC

Published in the United States by Dell, an imprint of The Random House Publishing Group, a division of Random House, Inc., New York.

DELL is a registered trademark of Random House, Inc., and the colophon is a trademark of Random House, Inc.

This book contains an excerpt from the forthcoming book *Darker After Midnight* by Lara Adrian. This excerpt has been set for this edition only and may not reflect the final content of the forthcoming edition.

ISBN: 978-0-440-24611-4
eBook ISBN: 978-0-440-33991-5

Cover design: Jae Song

Printed in the United States of America

www.bantamdell.com

9 8 7 6 5 4 3 2 1

Dell mass market edition: July 2011

For all the readers who have been asking me for a story about Hunter since he first walked onto the page four books ago. I hope you enjoy the ride!

ACKNOWLEDGMENTS

Thank you, first and foremost, to my wonderful editor Shauna Summers, for patience and guidance, for championing my books from the very beginning (and I mean day one, thirteen years ago in the slush pile!), and for continuing to shape me into a better writer each time we talk about my work.

Thanks also to my fantastic literary agent Karen Solem, for counsel and encouragement, for deft management of all the details that would otherwise make me crazy, and for believing in me and my career at a time when I had needed it the most.

To the rest of my publishing colleagues, both in the United States and abroad, thank you so much for the care, attention, and support you give my books. It's a privilege to have you all in my corner.

To my assistant and friend, Heather Rogers, a growing debt of thanks for undertaking the challenge of keeping me organized while also ensuring that there is always something fun and creative going on at my Website or Facebook community.

And to my husband, John, for more than I could ever adequately express in words or on the page. Everything, always, because of you.

Deeper Than
Midnight

CHAPTER
One

The club was private, very much off the beaten path, and for damned good reason. Located at the far end of a narrow, ice-encrusted back alley of Boston's Chinatown district, the place catered to an exclusive, if discriminating, crowd. The only humans permitted inside the old brick building were the stable of attractive young women—and a few pretty men—kept on hand to satisfy the late-night clientele's every craving.

Concealed within the shadows of an arched vestibule at street level, the unmarked metal door gave no indication of what lay behind it, not that any local or tourist in their right mind would pause to wonder. The thick slab of steel was shielded by a tall iron grate. Outside the entrance, a big guard loomed like a gargoyle in a knit skullcap and black leather.

The male was Breed, as was the pair of warriors who emerged from the gloom of the alleyway. At the sound of their combat boots crunching in the snow and frozen filth of the pavement, the guard on watch lifted his head. Under a thick, bulbous nose, thin lips curled away from crooked teeth and the sharp tips of the vampire's fangs. Eyes narrowed at the uninvited newcomers, he exhaled a low snarl, his warm breath steaming from his nostrils to plume into the brittle December night air.

Hunter registered a current of tension in his patrol partner's movements as the two approached the vampire on guard. Sterling Chase had been twitchy ever since they'd left the Order's compound for tonight's mission. Now he walked at an aggressive pace, taking the lead, his fingers flexing and contracting where they rested none too subtly on the large-caliber semiautomatic pistol holstered on his weapons belt.

The guard took a step forward too, putting himself directly in their path. Large thighs spread, boots planted wide in warning on the pitted pavement as the vampire's big head lowered. The eyes that had been narrowed on them before in question now went tighter with recognition as they hit and settled on Chase. "You gotta be kidding me. What the hell do you want out here on Enforcement Agency turf, *warrior*?"

"Taggart," Chase said, more growl than greeting. "I see your career has been in no danger of improving since I quit the Agency. Reduced to playing doorman for the local sip-and-strip, eh? What's next for you—security detail at the shopping mall?"

The agent pursed his lips around a ripe curse. "Takes some kind of balls to show your face, especially around here."

Chase's answering chuckle was neither threatened nor amused. "Try looking in a mirror sometime, then let's talk about who's got balls showing his face in public."

"This place is off-limits to all but the Enforcement

Agency," the guard said, crossing beefy arms over a barrel chest. A barrel chest sporting the broad leather strap of a weapons holster, with still more hardware bristling around his waist. "The Order's got no business here."

"Yeah?" Chase grunted. "Tell that to Lucan Thorne. He's the one who will have your ass if you don't move it out of our way. Assuming the two of us standing here cooling our heels for no good reason don't decide to remove you ourselves."

Agent Taggart's mouth had clamped shut at the mention of Lucan, the Order's leader and one of the longest-lived, most formidable elders of the Breed nation. Now the wary gaze strayed from Chase to Hunter, who lingered behind his fellow warrior in measuring silence. Hunter had no quarrel with Taggart, but he had already calculated no less than five different ways to disable him—to kill him swiftly and surely, right where he stood—should the need arise.

It was what Hunter had been trained to do. Born and bred to be a weapon wielded by the merciless hand of the Order's chief adversary, he was long accustomed to viewing the world in logical, unemotional terms.

He no longer served the villain called Dragos, but his deadly skills remained at the core of who, and what, he was. Hunter was lethal—unfailingly so—and in that instantaneous connection of his gaze and Taggart's, he saw that grim understanding reflected in the other male's eyes.

Agent Taggart blinked, then took a step back, removing himself from Hunter's stare and clearing the path to the door of the club.

"I thought you might be willing to reconsider," Chase said, as he and Hunter strode to the iron grate and entered the Enforcement Agency hangout.

The door must have been soundproof. Inside the dark club, loud music thumped in time with multicolored, spinning lights that lit a central stage made of mirrored glass. The only dancers were the trio of half-naked humans gyrating together in front of an audience of leering, hot-eyed vampires seated in booths and at tables on the floor below the stage.

Hunter watched the long-haired blonde in the center wind herself around a Lucite pole that climbed up from the floor of the stage to the ceiling. Swiveling her hips, she lifted one of her enormous, unnaturally round breasts up to meet her snakelike tongue. As she toyed with the pierced nipple, the other dancers, a tattooed woman with spiked purple hair and a dark-eyed young man who barely fit inside the shiny red vinyl pouch slung around his hips, moved to opposite sides of the mirrored stage and began their own solo routines.

The club reeked of stale perfume and sweat, but the musty tang couldn't mask the trace scent of fresh human blood. Hunter followed the olfactory trail with his gaze. It led to a far corner booth, where a vampire in the standard-issue Enforcement Agency dark suit and white shirt fed judiciously from the pale throat of a naked, moaning woman sprawled across his lap. Still more Breed males drank from other human blood Hosts, while some in the vampire-run establishment seemed intent on satisfying more carnal needs.

Beside him near the door, Chase had gone as still as stone. A low, rumbling growl leaked from the back of his throat. Hunter spared the feeding and onstage spectacle little more than an assessing glance, but Chase's gaze was fixed and hungry, as openly riveted as any of the other Breed males gathered there. Perhaps more so.

Hunter was far more interested in the handful of

heads that were now turning their way within the crowd of Enforcement Agents. Their arrival had been noticed, and the simmering looks from every pair of eyes that landed on them now said the situation could get ugly very quickly.

No sooner had Hunter registered the possibility, one of the glaring vampires reclined on a nearby sofa got up to confront them. The male was large, as were his two companions who rose to join him as he cut a clean path through the crowd. All three were visibly armed beneath their finely cut, dark suits.

"Well, well. Look what the cat dragged in," drawled the agent in the lead, a trace of the South in his slowly measured words and in his refined, almost delicate, features. "How many decades of service with the Agency, yet you never would have deigned to join any of us in a place like this."

Chase's mouth curved, barely concealing his elongated fangs. "You sound disappointed, Murdock. This shit was never my speed."

"No, you always held yourself above temptation," the vampire replied, his gaze as shrewd as his answering smile. "So careful. So rigidly disciplined, even in your appetites. But things change. People change, don't they, Chase? If you see something you like in here, you need only say so. For old times' sake, if nothing else, hmm?"

"We've come for information about an Agent named Freyne," Hunter interjected when Chase's reply seemed to take longer than necessary. "As soon as we have what we need, we'll leave."

"Is that so?" Murdock considered him with a curious tilt of his head. Hunter saw the vampire's gaze drift subtly away from his face to note the *dermaglyphs* that tracked up the sides of his neck and around his nape.

It took only a moment for the male to discern that Hunter's elaborate pattern of skin markings indicated he was Gen One, a rarity among the Breed.

Hunter was nothing close to the ages of his fellow Gen One warriors, Lucan or Tegan. However, sired by one of the race's Ancients, his blood was every bit as pure. Like his Gen One brethren, his strength and power was roughly that of ten later-generation vampires. It was his rearing as one of Dragos's personal army of assassins—a secret upbringing known by the Order alone—that made him far more lethal than Murdock and these couple dozen Agents in the club combined.

Chase seemed to snap out of his distraction at last. "What can you tell us about Freyne?"

Murdock shrugged. "He's dead. But then, I expect you already know that. Freyne and his unit were all killed last week while on a mission to retrieve a kidnapped Darkhaven youth." He gave a slow shake of his head. "Quite the pity. Not only did the Agency lose several good men, but their mission objective proved less than satisfactory as well."

"Less than satisfactory," Chase scoffed. "Yeah, you could say that. From what the Order understands, the mission to rescue Kellan Archer was fucked six ways from Sunday. The boy, his father, and grandfather—hell, the entire Archer family—all of them wiped out in a single night."

Hunter said nothing, letting Chase bait the hook as he saw fit. Most of what he charged was true. The night of the rescue attempt had been a blood-soaked one that had ended with too much death, the worst of it being dealt to the members of Kellan Archer's family.

But contrary to Chase's assertion, there had been survivors. Two, to be exact. Both of them had been secreted away from the carnage of that night and were now safe in the protective custody of the Order at their private compound.

"I won't disagree that things could have ended better, for both the Agency and the civilians who lost their lives. Mistakes, although regrettable, do happen. Unfortunately, we may never be certain where to place the blame for last week's tragedy."

Chase chuckled under his breath. "Don't be so sure. I know you and Freyne went way back. Hell, I know half the men in this club traded favors with him on a regular basis. Freyne was an asshole, but he knew how to recognize opportunity when he saw it. His biggest problem was his mouth. If he was mixed up in something that can be tied back to the kidnapping of Kellan Archer or the attack that left the Archer Darkhaven in rubble—and just for argument's sake, let's say I'm goddamned sure Freyne was involved—then the odds are good he told someone about it. I'm willing to bet he bragged to at least one loser sitting in this shithole of a club."

Murdock's expression had been tightening with every second that Chase spoke, his eyes beginning to transform in fury, dark irises sparking with amber light for every decibel that Chase's voice rose into the crowd.

Now half the room had paused to stare in their direction. Several males got up from their seats, human blood Hosts and half-drugged lap dancers pushed roughly aside as a growing horde of offended Agents began to converge on Chase and Hunter.

Chase didn't wait for the mob to attack.

With a raw snarl, he leapt into the knot of vampires, nothing but a flash of swinging fists and gnashing teeth and fangs.

Hunter had no choice but to join the fray. He waded

into the violent throng, his sole focus on his partner and the intent to pull him out of this in one piece. He threw off every comer with hardly any effort, disturbed by the feral way Chase was fighting. His face was drawn taut and wild as he landed blow after blow on the crush of bodies pressing in on him from all sides. His fangs were huge, filling his mouth. His eyes burned like coals in his skull.

"Chase!" Hunter shouted, cursing as a fountain of Breed blood shot airborne—his patrol partner's or another male's, he couldn't be sure.

Nor did he have much chance to figure it out.

A blur of movement on the other side of the club caught Hunter's eye. He swung his gaze toward it and found Murdock staring back at him, a cell phone pressed to his ear.

An unmistakable panic bled into Murdock's features as their gazes locked over the brawling crowd. His guilt was obvious now, written in the whitening tension around his mouth and in the beads of perspiration that sprang up on his brow to glisten in the swirling lights of the empty stage. The Agent spoke swiftly into his phone now, his feet carrying him in an anxious rush toward the back of the place.

In the fraction of a second it took for Hunter to toss aside a charging Agent, Murdock had vanished from sight.

"Son of a bitch." Hunter vaulted past the fracas, forced to abandon Chase to pursue what he knew to be the very lead they'd been hoping to find tonight.

He broke into a run, relying on his Gen One speed to carry him into the back of the club and through a door that was still ajar, swinging onto the narrow brick corridor where Murdock had fled. There was no sign of him either left or right in the alleyway, but the sharp echo of running footsteps on an adjacent side street carried on the frigid breeze.

Hunter took off after him, rounding the corner just as a big black sedan screeched to a halt at the curb. The back door was thrown open from the inside. Murdock jumped in, slammed it tight behind him as the car's engine roared to life once more.

Hunter was already plowing toward it when the tires smoked on the ice and asphalt, then, with a leap of screaming metal and machinery, the vehicle swung into the street and sped off like a demon into the night.

Hunter wasted not so much as an instant. Leaping for the side of the nearest brick building, he grabbed hold of a rusted fire escape and all but catapulted himself up onto the roof. He ran, combat boots chewing up asphalt tiles as he hoofed it from one rooftop to another, keeping a visual track on the fleeing vehicle dodging late-night traffic on the street below.

When the car gunned it around a corner onto a dark bit of empty straightaway, Hunter launched himself into the air. He came down onto the roof of the sedan with a bone-jarring crash. The pain of impact registered, but for less than a moment. He held on, feeling only calm determination as the driver tried to shake him off with a side-to-side sawing motion of the wheels.

The car jerked and swerved, but Hunter stayed put. Splayed spread-eagle on the roof, the fingers of one hand digging into the top rim of the windshield, he swung his other hand down and freed his 9mm from its holster at the small of his back. The driver tried another round of zigzag on the street, narrowly missing a parked delivery truck in his attempt to shake off his unwanted passenger.

Semiauto gripped in his hand, Hunter heaved himself into a catlike flip off the roof and onto the hood of the speeding sedan. Lying flat, he took aim on the driver, finger coolly poised on the trigger, ready to blow away the male behind the wheel so he could get his hands on Murdock and wring the traitorous bastard of all his secrets.

The moment slowed, and there was an instant—just the barest flicker of time—when surprise took him aback.

The driver wore a thick black collar around his neck. His head was shaved bald, most of his scalp covered with a tangled network of *dermaglyphs*.

He was one of Dragos's assassins.

A Hunter, like him.

A Gen One, born and raised to kill, like him.

Hunter's surprise was swiftly eclipsed by duty. He was more than willing to eradicate the male. It had been his pledge to the Order when he joined them—his personal vow to wipe out every last one of Dragos's homegrown killing machines.

Before Dragos had the chance to unleash the full measure of his evil on the world.

The tendons in Hunter's finger contracted in the split second it took for him to realign the business end of his Beretta with the center of the assassin's forehead. He started to squeeze the trigger, then felt the car clamp up tight beneath him as the driver drove the brake pedal into the floor.

Rubber and metal smoking in protest, the sedan stopped short.

Hunter's body kept moving, sailing through the air and landing several hundred feet ahead on the cold pavement. He rolled out of the tumble and was on his feet like nothing happened, pistol raised and firing round after round into the unmoving car.

He saw Murdock slide out of the backseat and dash for his escape into a shadowed back alley, but there was no time to deal with him before the Gen One was out of the car as well, the barrel of a large-caliber pistol locked and loaded, trained squarely on Hunter. They faced off, the assassin's weapon raised to kill, eyes cold with the same emotionless determination that centered Hunter in his stance on the iced-up patch of asphalt.

Bullets exploded from the two guns at the same time.

Hunter dodged out of harm's way in what felt to him like calculated slow motion. He knew his opponent would have done the same as Hunter's round sped toward him. Another hail of gunfire erupted, a rain of bullets this time as both vampires unloaded their magazines on each other. Neither of them took anything more than a superficial hit.

They were too evenly matched, trained in the same methods. They were both hard to kill, and prepared to take the fight to their final breath.

In a blur of motion and lethal intent, the pair of them ditched their empty firearms and took their battle hand to hand.

Hunter deflected the rapid-fire upper-torso blows that the assassin led with as he roared up on him. There was a kick that might have connected with his jaw if not for a sharp tilt of his head, then another strike aimed at his groin, but diverted when Hunter grabbed the assassin's boot and twisted him into a midair spin.

The assassin regained his footing with little trouble, coming right back for more. He threw a punch and Hunter grabbed his fist, crushing bones as he tightened his grip then came around to use his body as a lever while he wrenched the outstretched arm backward at the elbow. The joint broke with a sharp *crack*, yet the assassin merely grunted, the only indication he gave of the certain pain he was feeling. The damaged arm hung useless at his side as he pivoted to throw another punch at Hunter's face. The blow connected, tearing the skin just above his right eye and hitting so hard, Hunter's vision filled with stars. He shook off the momentary daze, just in time to intercept a second assault—fist and foot coming at him in the same instant.

Back and forth it went, both males breathing hard from the exertion, both bleeding from where the other had managed to get the upper hand. Neither would ask for mercy, no matter how long or bloody their combat became.

Mercy was a concept foreign to them, the flip side of pity. Two things that had been beaten out of their lexicon from the time they were boys.

The only thing worse than mercy or pity was failure, and as Hunter took hold of his opponent's broken arm and drove the big male down to the ground with his knee planted in the middle of the assassin's spine, he saw the acknowledgment of imminent failure flicker like a dark flame in the Gen One's cold eyes.

He had lost this battle.

He knew it, just as Hunter knew it when a clear shot at the thick black collar around the assassin's neck presented itself to him in that next instant.

Hunter reached out with his free hand to grab one of the discarded pistols from its place on the pavement. He flipped it around in his hand, wielding the metal butt like a hammer, then brought it down on the collar that ringed the assassin's neck.

Again, and harder now, a blow that put a dent in the

impenetrable material that housed a diabolical device. A device crafted by Dragos and his laboratory for a single purpose: to ensure the loyalty and obedience of the deadly army he'd bred to serve him.

Hunter heard a small *hum* as the tampered casing triggered the coming detonation. Dragos's assassin reached up with his good hand—whether to ascertain the threat or to attempt to stop it, Hunter would never be sure.

He rolled away . . . just as the ultraviolet rays were released from within the collar.

There was a flash of searing light—there and gone in an instant—as the lethal beam severed the assassin's head in one clean motion.

As the street was plunged back into darkness, Hunter stared at the smoldering corpse of the male who had been like him in so many ways. A brother, though there was no kinship among any of the killers in Dragos's personal army.

He felt no remorse for the dead assassin before him, only a vague sense of satisfaction that there was one less to carry out Dragos's twisted schemes.

He would not rest until there were none.

CHAPTER
Two

As founder and leader of the Order—hell, as a Gen One Breed male with some nine hundred years of life and then some under his belt—Lucan Thorne was not accustomed to taking an earful from anyone.

Yet he listened in smoldering silence as a high-ranking Enforcement Agent by the name of Mathias Rowan filled him in on what had gone down a couple of hours ago in one of the Agency's private hangouts in Chinatown. The very club where he'd sent two of the Order's warriors, Chase and Hunter, on patrol that night. He could hardly pretend surprise to hear that things had gotten out of hand, or that there had been a shit storm of violence and Chase had ended up in the middle of it.

Or rather, at the start, middle, and end of it, according to Rowan.

Under normal circumstances, neither Lucan personally nor the Order as a whole would give a damn about ruffled feathers within the Agency. For as long as they'd existed, the Order and the Enforcement Agency had operated on their own terms, by their own brands of laws. Lucan had founded the Order based on justice and action; the Agency's credo had been mired in politics and empire building from the beginning.

That didn't mean there weren't good, trustworthy men among their ranks—Mathias Rowan being one of those notable exceptions. Sterling Chase had been another. It wasn't much more than a year ago that Chase had been part of the Enforcement Agency's elite, a well-bred, well-connected, well-mannered golden boy whose career trajectory might have known no bounds.

And now?

Lucan's mouth pressed flat in grim consideration as he paced alone in the living room of the private quarters that he and his Breedmate, Gabrielle, shared at the Order's underground headquarters. He couldn't discount that Chase had been a valuable asset to the Order since he'd traded in his starched white shirts and natty Agency suits for basic black combat fatigues and the give-no-quarter methods of a warrior. He'd come on board fully committed to the Order's goals and missions. He'd been a quick study on patrols and had covered more than one of the warriors' asses in the heat of their battles.

But Lucan also couldn't deny that in recent months Chase was skating on damned thin ice. He'd been losing his edge at times, losing his focus. Lucan's anger spiked dangerously close to off the charts as he listened to Mathias Rowan's recap of the all-out brawl that took place downtown.

"I've got reports of three Agents beaten to within an inch of their lives and another one who looks like someone sent him through a shredder," Rowan said on the other end of the call. "That doesn't count the walking wounded or the ones still unaccounted for either. To a man, they're all saying that your warriors came into the place looking for an excuse to start trouble. Chase in particular."

Lucan hissed a low curse. He'd had a bad feeling about putting Chase on the Chinatown patrol tonight. That was the reason he'd tasked Hunter to ride shotgun—the coolest head in the Order to accompany the loosest cannon. The fact that neither of them had called to report in for the last hour wasn't making him feel any better about that decision.

"Look," Rowan said, then exhaled a beleaguered sigh. "I consider Chase a friend, and have for a long time. He's the reason I agreed to assist when he first approached me about being the Order's eyes and ears within the Agency. As for what's going on with him personally, I can't say where the change is coming from, but for his own sake—perhaps for everyone's sake—he'd better start figuring it out. And far be it from me to tell you how to run things within your operation, Lucan—"

"Yes," he interrupted, clipped and to the point. "Far be it, Agent Rowan."

Silence held for more than a moment on the other end. Lucan felt a shift in the air around him and glanced up as Gabrielle walked into the room.

He put Rowan on hold with barely a word of warning simply because he wanted to watch his beautiful mate move. She carried an empty tea tray out of their library and quietly placed it in the kitchen. The tray had been set for two: Gabrielle and another female who'd arrived at the compound earlier that evening. Only one of the dainty teacups had been drained. Only one of the bone china plates had been cleaned of its tiny chocolate cake and sundry other frosted confections.

Lucan didn't have to guess which of the women had eaten. A dusting of chocolate powder rode the lush bow of his auburn-haired mate's perfect mouth. He licked his own lips as he watched Gabrielle, hungered as always for a taste of her. If not for the disturbing business at hand, to say nothing of the more minor dilemma that awaited his decision in the other room, Lucan might have dismissed all the demands on him except the one that would get him naked with his woman in the least amount of time.

The quick glance she shot him said that she knew the direction of his thoughts. Of course, the truth of it was probably written all over his face. It took only a graze of his tongue to feel the sharp edge of his emerging fangs, and the way his vision was sharpening, he guessed his eyes were more amber than gray now, his desire transforming him to his true nature in much the same way that blood thirst would.

A slow smile spread over Gabrielle's lips as she walked toward him. Her big brown eyes were deep and soft, her fingers tender and inviting as she reached up to stroke his tense cheek. Her touch soothed him as always, and his growl sounded more like a purr as she weaved her fingers into his dark hair.

With Mathias Rowan parked at the end of the silenced line, Lucan held the phone away from him as he tilted his head down toward Gabrielle's mouth. He brushed his lips across hers, his tongue sweeping lightly across the trace dusting of cocoa that flavored her kiss.

"Delicious," he whispered, seeing the hungered glow of his irises reflected in the fathomless depths of hers.

Gabrielle wrapped her arms around him, but she was

frowning as she held his gaze. She kept her voice quiet, all but mouthing the words. "Is everything okay with Hunter and Chase?"

He nodded, pressing a kiss to her brow. It felt awkward dismissing her concern. In the year and a half that he'd been blood-bonded to Gabrielle, they had shared everything. He trusted her more than he had ever trusted anyone else in all of his considerable years of life.

She was his mate, his partner, his beloved. As his most precious confidante, she deserved to know what he was feeling as a man. What he feared in his heart and soul, as the head of this compound, which had at some point begun to feel more like a household to him than the strategic nerve center of the Order's mission headquarters.

While his warriors battled daily with their own personal demons, while the Order had taken a few hits, weathering some shattering losses as well as some much-needed triumphs—while the compound's population had swelled to almost double what it had been not even two years past as several of the warriors fell in love and found their mates—one disturbing fact remained.

They hadn't yet been able to stop Dragos and his madness.

That Dragos was still breathing, still able to cause the kind of bloodshed and destruction he'd orchestrated last week with the abduction of a Darkhaven youth from a powerful Breed family and the subsequent razing of their residence that had killed all inside was a failure Lucan took very personally.

It was a reality that had struck him far too close to home.

But that was something he couldn't share with Gabrielle, not now. He couldn't bear to make her feel the same dread that haunted him. He had been shouldering as many of his burdens as possible on his own. Until he had all the answers, until his plans were in place and ready to be acted upon, the rest was his to bear.

"Don't worry, love. Everything is under control." He placed another tender kiss on her brow. "How are things going in the other room?"

Gabrielle gave a mild shrug and shook her head. "She doesn't talk much, but it's no wonder, considering all she's been through. All she wants is to go home to her family. Also understandable, of course."

Lucan grunted, in total agreement. He wanted nothing more than to send their guest on her way. Sympathetic to the woman's situation or not, the last thing he needed was another civilian underfoot at the compound for the next few days. "I don't imagine we've gotten any further word on her ride out of here, have we?"

"Nothing in the last hour. Brock said he or Jenna will call right away if the weather clears enough in Fairbanks to let them out."

Lucan cursed. "Even if the blizzard stops right now, they're easily a full day away yet. I'll have to put someone else on this instead. Maybe it's a good way to get Chase out of my hair for a while. Hell, after what I just heard tonight, it might be the only thing to keep me from killing him."

Gabrielle narrowed her gaze on his, all business now. "No way are you going to send that poor woman off to Detroit with Chase as her escort. Not happening, Lucan. I'll take her there myself before I let that happen."

He hadn't been totally serious to begin with, but he wasn't about to argue with her. Not when her chin was held at that stubborn upward angle that said she had absolutely zero intention of backing down. "Okay, forget I said it. You win." Grabbing her close with one arm, he let his hand roam down to the curve of her behind. "How come you always win?"

"Because you know I'm right." She moved in tighter, rising up on her toes until her mouth was brushing his. "And because—admit it, vampire—you wouldn't have me any other way."

With one slender brow arching, she nipped at his lower lip then slid out of his embrace before he could rise to her challenge. Not that he wasn't already rising. Gabrielle smiled, fully aware of his condition as she pivoted around and began to walk back toward the library and her waiting guest.

Lucan paused until she was out of the room, working to regroup his thoughts. Clearing his throat, he took Rowan off hold and put the phone back to his ear. He'd let the Agent hang in uncertain silence for long enough.

"Mathias," he said. "I want you to know that the Order appreciates all you've done to assist us thus far. As for what happened tonight in that club, I assure you it had not been my intent. I realize being the Agency's director for the region, this puts you in an uncomfortable position."

It was as close to an apology as he could muster. Although the long-standing, if unwritten, policy between Lucan's warriors and the Agency's members had been to refrain as best as they could from shitting in one another's yards, circumstances of late had changed.

As in changed everything, and drastically.

"I'm not worried about myself," Rowan replied. "And I don't regret my decision to help you. I want Dragos apprehended, whatever it takes. Even if that means making a few enemies of my own inside the Agency."

Lucan grunted in acknowledgment of the vow. "You're a good man, Mathias."

"After all the bastard's done, especially the terror of last week, how could I not want him stopped just as badly as you and your warriors do?" Rowan's voice was edged with a passion Lucan understood very well. "It doesn't shock me that there is corruption within the Agency, least of all that a Neanderthal like Freyne would ally himself with a twisted madman like Dragos. I only wish I'd seen that possibility before it blew up in my face the night of Kellan Archer's rescue."

"You aren't alone in that regret," Lucan replied, sober at the thought. He'd sent several warriors out on that mission as well, added insurance that the Darkhaven youth would be brought home safely from his abductors—a trio of Gen One assassins who'd taken the boy on Dragos's orders. That primary objective had been achieved, but not without a lot of collateral damage and disturbing questions rising in its wake.

"How is the boy?" Rowan asked.

"Still recovering in our infirmary." Kellan Archer's physical abuse had been severe, but it was the mental anguish he'd suffered during and after his abduction that had Lucan even more concerned for the young Breed male's long-term well-being.

"And his grandfather?"

Lucan considered the elder Archer male in grim silence for a moment. Lazaro Archer was one of the few remaining Gen Ones in the Breed population, and an aged one at that. Nearly a thousand years old, he had lived an esteemed, peaceful life, the last couple of centuries spent in New England as the head of his family Darkhaven. He had raised strong sons who had raised sons of their own—Lucan wasn't even sure how many progeny Lazaro and his lifelong Breedmate could claim.

Not that it mattered.

Not anymore.

In a single blood-soaked evening, Lazaro's mate and all their kin who made the Boston Darkhaven their home had been wiped out. One of Lazaro's sons, the boy's father, Christophe, had been murdered at close range by Freyne, the traitor who'd been part of Kellan's Enforcement Agency rescue detail. Lazaro and Kellan were all that remained of the Archer bloodline, although their survival had not yet been made public.

"Both the boy and his grandfather are doing as well as can be expected," Lucan replied. "Until I can determine why they were targeted by Dragos, they can't be safe anywhere but here, in the compound."

"Of course," Rowan answered. There was a pause on his end, then a quiet inhalation of his breath. "Knowing Chase, I'm sure he blames himself for part of what occurred during the rescue mission . . ."

Lucan felt his brows draw tight at the reminder of yet another of Chase's recent troubles while on duty. "Let me worry about my men, Mathias. You keep a close eye on your own."

"Certainly," he replied, even-toned and professional. "I'll handle any fallout from the incident at the club tonight. If anything interesting turns up in the meantime about Freyne or his connection to Dragos, rest assured I'll be in touch."

Lucan murmured his thanks. If Rowan hadn't carved such a solid career for himself within the upper ranks of the Agency, he might have made a fine warrior instead. God knew the Order could use extra hands and a few more level heads if things got any worse in their war with Dragos.

Or if things continued to go south with a certain member of their current team.

No sooner had the thought put a hard tick in Lucan's jaw, the compound's internal line rang with a call from the tech lab. He ended his conversation with Rowan, then punched the speaker button on the intercom.

"They're here," Gideon announced before Lucan had the chance to bark out a hello. "Just watched them roll through the gates of the estate. Got them on surveillance cameras as we speak. They're driving around to the fleet hangar right now."

"About fucking time," Lucan snarled.

He cut off the intercom and stalked out of his quarters. The pound of his black combat boots echoed down the lengths of snaking, white marble passageways that ran like a central nervous system through the heart of the underground compound. He rounded a corner and chewed up the distance toward the tech lab where Gideon was stationed practically 24/7 these days.

Up ahead of him, his acute hearing picked up the whispered hydraulic whine of the secure elevator as it made its descent from the garage located topside to the compound a few hundred feet belowground.

As he passed the tech lab, Gideon came out to meet him in the hallway. The British-born warrior and resident genius of the compound was letting his inner geek have its freedom tonight, dressed in slouchy gray jeans, green Chuck Taylor sneakers, and a yellow Hellboy T-shirt. His cropped blond hair was more disheveled than usual, as if he'd raked his hands over his scalp more than once during the wait for news of Hunter and Chase.

"Been a long time since I saw that murderous scowl," Gideon said, his blue gaze sharp over the pale lenses of his rimless shades. "Looks like you're about to chew these guys up and spit them out."

"Smells like someone already did that for me," Lucan growled, his nostrils tingling with the scent of freshly spilled Breed blood even before the polished steel doors of the elevator had opened to let out the pair of errant warriors.

CHAPTER
Three

Are you sure I can't get you something else to eat or drink?"

Gabrielle came back into the library, her cheeks flushed, her brown eyes seeming somehow brighter than they had been when she'd left with the tea tray a few minutes ago. Her gaze drifting for a moment, Lucan Thorne's Breedmate brought her fingertips to her lips in an absent gesture that did not quite hide the small, private smile that curved her mouth. She blinked it away an instant later and walked over to resume her seat on the sofa.

"I'm sorry to keep you waiting. Lucan and I got caught up in a small negotiation," she said, as kind and hospitable as an old friend, despite the fact that they'd been complete strangers until just a few hours earlier that evening. "Is it too cold for you in here? Look at you, you're shivering."

"It's nothing." Corinne Bishop burrowed deeper into

her pale gray wrap cardigan and shook her head, even as a further tremor rattled deep within her bones. "I'm all right, really."

Her discomfort had nothing to do with the temperature inside the Order's compound. Luxury and warmth surrounded her here, the likes of which she could hardly comprehend. She had marveled at the astonishingly expansive underground headquarters from the moment she'd arrived, and certainly the elegant library where she was seated now with Gabrielle was the most exquisite room she'd been in for quite some time.

Her home for the past many years had been little better than a tomb. From the moment of her abduction when she was just eighteen, Corinne had been kept prisoner along with a number of other young females, all of them taken captive by a madman named Dragos for the simple fact that each of the women had been born a Breedmate.

Her hands folded in her lap, Corinne glanced down and idly ran her thumb across the tiny scarlet birthmark on the back of her right hand—the same small birthmark that every Breedmate bore somewhere on her skin. It was that teardrop-and-crescent-moon stamp that made her part of an extraordinary world—the secret, eternal world of the Breed. It was the reason she'd been lifted out of certain poverty and neglect as an infant, after she'd been abandoned at the back door of a Detroit hospital just hours following her birth.

That diminutive, bloodred birthmark had been her entree into the lives of Victor and Regina Bishop, her adoptive parents. The blood-bonded couple with a Breed son of their own had opened their sumptuous Darkhaven mansion to both Corinne and her adopted younger sister, Charlotte, giving two unwanted, unclaimed girls a loving home and nothing but the best that life had to offer.

If only she'd been adult enough then to appreciate all the blessings she'd had.

If only she'd had the chance to tell her family one more time that she loved them... before a villain called Dragos had yanked her away and thrown her into what had seemed an interminable hell.

It was the small red birthmark on the back of her hand that had caused her so much pain and heartbreak. She'd been tortured and abused, kept alive against her will and made to endure things she could hardly think about, let alone speak of now that she was free of the horrors. Both she and Dragos's other captives—somewhere close to twenty of them who had managed to survive his torment and experiments long enough to be rescued by the warrior members of the Order and their incredibly courageous, resourceful Breedmates.

For the past few days since their rescue, Corinne and the other freed captives had been living in Rhode Island, at the Darkhaven of another couple whose generosity and caring had been a godsend. Trusted friends of the Order, Andreas Reichen and his mate, Claire, had provided all of the evacuees with shelter, clothing—anything they could possibly need to help reclaim some sense of normalcy as their lives began again outside of Dragos's reach.

The only thing Corinne needed was her family. She had been astonished to learn that of all the Breedmates captured and imprisoned by Dragos, she was the only one taken from a Darkhaven family. The other females had all been collected from runaway shelters or plucked from solitary existences, unaware that they were special in any way until Dragos's evil tore the blinders from their eyes.

But Corinne had known what she was. She'd had a family that had loved her, one that had surely missed her and eventually mourned her when the decades passed without her return. She was different from Dragos's other victims. Yet she'd suffered the same as them—perhaps more, as the thought of her anguished parents and siblings had made her defiant in the face of her captor.

The urgency to be back where she belonged, back among the people who could help her heal—perhaps the only people capable of helping her recover everything she'd lost during her time in captivity—was a need that consumed her, more and more as the days and hours ticked past, costing precious time.

She could only hope that they would welcome her into their fold once more. She could only pray that during the long years she'd been gone they hadn't forgotten her. She could only wish with all her heart that they might still love her.

She glanced up and met Gabrielle's concerned look. "When did Brock think he would be back in Boston?"

Gabrielle exhaled a soft sigh as she slowly shook her head. "Probably not for another day or so. It could be longer than that, if the snow doesn't let up in Fairbanks very soon."

Corinne could hardly hide her disappointment. Coming out of her captivity and discovering that her childhood bodyguard from Detroit was one of her rescuers had given her the first true taste of hope. Brock had become a member of the Order in the time since her disappearance. He had also recently fallen in love. It was that love that had taken him to Alaska a few days ago, but he'd given Corinne his word that as soon as he and his mate, Jenna, returned, they would personally see to it that she made it safely home to Detroit.

Corinne needed Brock's support. He'd always been her confidant, a true friend. As a young girl, she had always trusted him to keep her safe. She needed to know she was safe now and to be certain that no danger could touch her as she made her journey home.

Some frightened little part of her worried that she might not have the strength to knock on her family's front door without someone like Brock, someone she could trust completely, standing at her side.

"I understand from Claire and Andreas that you haven't been in touch with anyone back home," Gabrielle said gently, breaking into her thoughts. "They have no idea that you're even alive?"

"No," Corinne replied.

"Wouldn't you like to call them? I'm sure they would want to know that you're here, that you're safe and sound and coming home to them soon."

She shook her head. "It's been so long. I remember our old telephone exchange, but I wouldn't even know how to reach them..."

"That's not a problem, you know." Gabrielle gestured toward a flat white box that rested on the nearby desk in the library. "It wouldn't take more than a minute or two to find them on the computer. You could call them right now. If you'd like, you could even talk to them on video."

"Thank you, but no." The terms and concepts were all new to Corinne, almost as overwhelming as the idea of speaking to either of her parents without being there in person to touch them, to feel their arms wrapped around her once again. "It's just that I...I wouldn't know what to say to them after all this time. I wouldn't know how to tell them..."

Gabrielle gave an understanding nod. "You need to be there in person to do this."

"Yes. I just need to go home."

"Of course," Gabrielle said. "Don't worry. We'll make sure you get there as soon as possible."

They both looked up when a quiet knock sounded on the doorjamb from the corridor outside the library. A pretty blonde with pale lavender eyes opened the door from the hallway and peeked into the room.

"Am I interrupting?"

"No, Elise. Come in." Gabrielle stood up and motioned the other woman inside. "Corinne and I were just chatting while we waited for word from Brock and Jenna."

Elise stepped inside and gave Corinne a warm smile. "I thought I'd come down and sit with you both for a while until everyone comes in from patrols."

Corinne had been introduced to some of the Order's women when she'd arrived earlier that evening. Elise's mate, she recalled, was a warrior named Tegan. She'd been told that he and most of the other members of the Order were out on missions elsewhere in the city, all of them focused on the single goal of hunting down Dragos and all those loyal to him.

The thought gave her a great deal of reassurance. Surely with an extraordinary group like this determined to catch him, Dragos stood no chance of escape.

And yet he had.

Time and again, as Corinne understood it, he'd managed to stay one step ahead of the Order. They were a powerful force, but Corinne knew firsthand that Dragos was not without his own power. He had his own soldiers, his own terrible tactics.

And he was mad—dangerously so. Corinne knew this firsthand as well, and the awful memories of that knowledge swelled up on her like a wave of darkness now, before she could stop them. She staggered under the weight of her remembered torture as she rose from the sofa to stand beside Gabrielle and Elise. The anxiety came up fast this time, faster than it had a short while ago. When Gabrielle had left her alone in the library, Corinne had somehow managed to wrest herself back under control.

But not this time.

The floor-to-ceiling bookcases wobbled in her mind's eye as the walls of the library seemed to squeeze in, collapsing inward from all sides. On the wall across from her, a large tapestry, stitched to depict a glowering dark knight on a black charger, now seemed to twist and distort, the man's handsome features and his beautiful horse both mutating into something demonic and mocking.

She closed her eyes, but darkness didn't make things any better. Suddenly she was back in Dragos's prison cells. Back in the lightless pit, naked and shivering. Alone in a dank void, waiting for death. Praying for it, as her only means of escape from the horror.

Corinne sucked in a mouthful of air but felt only the smallest gasp of oxygen feed her lungs as the space around her condensed toward nothingness.

"Corinne?" Gabrielle and Elise both said her name at the same time. Both women reached out to hold her up, keep her steady.

Corinne heard herself gasp for breath. "Need out … have to get out of this cell—"

"Can you walk?" Elise asked her, her voice urgent but in control. "Hold on to us, Corinne. You're going to be okay."

She managed a nod as they helped her out to the corridor. Cool white marble spread out in both directions. The passageway was wide and endless, instantly soothing. She let the gleam of pale, pristine walls fill her vision as she took a deep breath and felt some of the constriction in her lungs begin to ease.

Yes, thank God.

Already it was better.

Gabrielle reached out to smooth some of Corinne's dark hair from her eyes. "Are you all right now?"

Corinne nodded, still breathing hard but feeling the worst of her anxiety fade away. "Sometimes I just... sometimes I feel like I'm still in there. Still locked in that awful place," she whispered. "I'm sorry. I'm so embarrassed."

"Don't be." Gabrielle's smile was sympathetic without being pitying. "You don't have to be sorry or embarrassed. Not among friends."

"Come on," Elise said. "We'll take you up to the mansion. We can have a little stroll around the grounds outside until you feel better."

As the compound's garage elevator came to a cushioned stop belowground, Hunter glanced at his wounded patrol partner in silent assessment.

Head hung low on his shoulders, matted golden-brown hair drooping over his brow, Sterling Chase leaned against the opposite wall of the car, his breath sawing through his teeth. His black fatigues were torn and blood-soaked, lacerations and swelling contusions making a battered mess of his face. His nose was surely broken, his upper lip split open and bleeding onto his chin. More than likely, his jaw had been fractured as well.

The warrior's injuries from the brawl in the city were numerous, but nothing that wouldn't heal with time and a few decent feedings.

Not that Chase seemed at all concerned about his condition.

The elevator doors whispered open and he swaggered out to the corridor ahead of Hunter, arrogance in every stride.

Lucan blocked his path just a few steps out. Put his palm in the center of Chase's chest to stop him physically when the other male appeared disinclined to pause. "Have a good time in Chinatown tonight?"

Chase grunted, his split lip tearing wider as he gave Lucan a dark smirk. "I gather Mathias Rowan has been in contact with you."

"That's right. More than I can say for either one of you," Lucan replied tersely, his furious gaze traveling briefly from Chase's battle-worn appearance to Hunter, whose fatigues were stained with their own share of spilled Enforcement Agent blood. "Rowan told me all about the shit that went down. He says he's got multiple dead and wounded and every Agent he's spoken to has put the blame for the unprovoked assault squarely on you, Chase."

He scoffed in response. "Unprovoked, my ass. Every one of the Agents in that place was looking for a reason to piss me off."

"And you couldn't wait to oblige them, that it?" At Chase's answering glower, Lucan shook his head. "What you are is reckless, my man. This shit tonight is just one more mess you've left for someone else to deal with. It's getting to be a pattern with you lately, and I don't like it. Not one fucking bit."

"You sent me out to do a job," Chase shot back darkly. "Sometimes things get messy."

Lucan's eyes narrowed, anger radiating off his body now, a palpable heat that Hunter could feel from where he stood just a few steps away with Gideon. "I'm not sure you know what your job is anymore, Chase. If you did, you wouldn't be coming back here empty-handed, reeking of spilled blood and attitude. Far as I'm concerned, you failed out there tonight. How much intel did you gather on Freyne? Are we even one fucking scintilla closer to getting a lock on Dragos or any of his possible other associates?"

"Perhaps we are," Hunter interjected.

Now Lucan swung his scowl on him. "Explain."

"An Agent named Murdock," Hunter replied. "He approached Chase and me when we arrived at the club. We had words, but he wasn't forthcoming with any useful information. Once the fight broke out, he appeared notably anxious. I saw him make a phone call to someone before he escaped amid the chaos."

"This is a lead?" Chase muttered dismissively. "Of course Murdock would run. I know this guy. He's a coward who'd rather put a knife in your back than face a fight head-on."

Hunter ignored his patrol partner's commentary as he held the keen stare of the Order's leader. "Murdock took off for the alley out back of the place. A car was already coming around to pick him up. The driver was a Gen One assassin."

"Good Christ," Gideon remarked from beside Hunter,

shoving his hand through the short blond spikes of his hair.

Lucan's face hardened, while Chase had gone utterly silent where he stood, listening as intently as the others now.

"I pursued the vehicle on foot," Hunter continued. "The assassin was neutralized."

He reached around to the back waistband of his fatigues and pulled out the detonated collar he'd removed from his kill. Gideon took the ring of charred black polymer out of his hand. "One more to add to your collection, eh? You're racking up quite a score lately. Good work."

Hunter merely blinked at the unnecessary praise.

"What about Murdock?" Lucan asked.

"Gone," Hunter replied. "He fled the scene while I was disabling the driver. By then it was a choice of either tracking him down or going back inside the club to retrieve my patrol partner."

The decision to aid his fellow warrior had given him more than a moment's pause at the time. Logic and training as one of Dragos's soldiers demanded he carry out his missions as a single entity: efficient, impersonal, and utterly independent. Murdock was a quantified target. Interrogating him would surely provide valuable intel; his capture was imperative to the success of the night's patrol. To Hunter, apprehending the escaped Agent had seemed a logical enough objective.

But the Order operated under a different tenet, one he had pledged to follow when he'd joined them, no matter how it contrasted to the world he had once known. The warriors had a code among themselves for every mission, an understanding that if a team went out together, they came back together, and no man was ever left behind.

Not even if it meant forfeiting an enemy asset.

"I know Murdock," Chase said, lifting the back of his hand to his chin to wipe away some of the blood that slicked his skin. "I know where he lives, I know the places he's likely to hang out. It won't take me long to find him—"

"You're not doing shit," Lucan interrupted. "I'm pulling you off this mission. Until I say otherwise, any and all Agency contact goes through me. Gideon can dig up everything we need on Murdock's properties and personal habits. If you feel you've got anything more useful to add, turn it over to Gideon. I'll decide how and when—and I'll decide who—is best to go after this asshole Murdock."

"Whatever." Chase's blue eyes glittered darkly under his lowered brows. He started to walk away.

Lucan's head pivoted only slightly, his voice as low as distant thunder. "I didn't say we were finished."

Chase scoffed. "Sounds to me like you've got it all under control, so what do you need me for?"

"That's something I've been asking myself all night," Lucan replied evenly. "What the fuck do I need you for?"

Chase muttered something low and surly under his breath in response. He took another step and suddenly Lucan was right in front of him, having moved so quickly it had been hard for even Hunter to track him. He shoved Chase with a hard dose of Gen One strength, a frontal blow that sent the other warrior flying into the corridor wall.

Chase righted himself with a hissed curse. Eyes flashing like bright coals, he charged forward with a fang-bearing snarl.

This time it was Hunter who moved the fastest.

Intercepting the threat to the Order's leader—*his* leader—he placed himself between the two vampires, his hand clamped around Chase's throat.

"Stand down, warrior," he advised his brother-in-arms.

It was the only warning Hunter would allow. If Chase so much as flinched with further aggression, Hunter would have little choice but to crush the fight out of him.

Teeth and fangs clamped together, lips peeled back from his gums, Chase held his stare in a thick, answering silence. Hunter felt a shift of movement in the space of the corridor behind him. He heard a feminine gasp—just the softest pull of air through parted lips.

Chase's gaze drifted in that direction and some of the taut fury left him at once. As he relaxed, Hunter let go of him and stepped back from the confrontation.

"What's going on out here, Lucan?"

Hunter turned along with the other males in the corridor and found himself facing Lucan's mate, Gabrielle, standing behind them with two other females. Hunter knew the fine-boned blonde with the pale lavender eyes. It was she—Tegan's mate, Elise—who'd gasped, her hand still lifted toward her mouth.

"I'm out of here," Chase muttered, notably subdued as he brushed past Hunter and the others and stalked off down the corridor toward his quarters.

Hunter hardly noticed the warrior's departure.

His attention was riveted on the third female who stood in the passageway now. Petite and fair-skinned behind the curtain of long ebony hair that partially hid her face from his view, she held him utterly transfixed in that moment. He couldn't look away from the large greenish blue eyes that tapered delicately at their outer corners. At a loss to categorize their specific color, he didn't try, instead attempting to determine why he found her presence so arresting.

"Is everything all right?" Gabrielle asked, moving over to Lucan in obvious concern.

"Yeah," he replied. "It's all good now."

Hunter drifted closer to the unidentified woman, hardly aware his feet were moving until he was standing directly before her. She looked up at him then, lifting the perfect oval of her face until her gaze had traveled past the blood-spattered length of him and their eyes were locked on each other.

She was a stranger to him, yet, somehow, strangely familiar too.

He cocked his head, trying to puzzle out the peculiar sense that he'd seen her somewhere before. He blurted the thought that was banging around in his brain. "Do I know you...?"

Gabrielle cleared her throat and walked over as if she meant to protect the female from him. "Corinne, this is Hunter. He's a member of the Order. Say hello, Hunter."

He grunted the greeting, still staring at her.

"I saw you the night of the rescue," she said quietly. "You were one of the warriors who brought me and the others to Claire and Andreas's Darkhaven."

So, she'd been among the captives Dragos had been holding. He supposed that made sense. He gave a vague nod, his curiosity somewhat satisfied by her reminder. But he hadn't seen her in Rhode Island, he was almost certain of it. He felt sure he'd remember that face, those luminescent eyes.

"I'm afraid we still don't have an ETA on Brock and Jenna," Gideon told the dark-haired beauty. "The weather report out of Alaska doesn't look good for another three days, minimum."

"Three more days?" Corinne's smooth forehead creased with a small frown. "I really need to get home. I need my family now."

Lucan blew out a sigh. "Understood. Since Brock is a few thousand miles and a couple of blizzards away from Boston at the moment, someone else will have to—"

"I will take her." Hunter felt Lucan's stare land on him the instant the words left his mouth. He met the other Gen One's gaze and gave a decisive nod. "I will see that she gets home safely to her family."

It seemed a simple enough task to manage, yet everyone in the immediate vicinity had fallen into a sudden, lengthy silence. The most stricken of all seemed to be Corinne herself. She stared up at him mutely, and for a second he wondered if she was going to refuse his offer.

"It will take about fourteen hours by car," Gideon said. "That's a couple of days total, since we're talking about night travel only. If you left right now, you could put in about a hundred miles before the sun starts to rise. Or I could have one of our corporate planes fueled up and ready to go at sundown. A couple hours of flight time and you're there."

Lucan stared hard at him, then gave a nod. "The quicker, the better. I'm gonna need you back on patrol tomorrow night."

"Consider it done," Hunter replied.

CHAPTER
Four

Chase sat in the dark alone, hunkered down on his haunches in a shadow-filled corner of the compound's small chapel.

He didn't know why his boots had carried him in here, to the quiet, candlelit sanctuary instead of his personal quarters farther down the corridor. He'd never been one to seek counsel or forgiveness from a higher power, and God knew he was likely too far gone for prayer anyway.

He sure as hell wasn't holding out any hope of absolution. Not from above, and not from Lucan or his other brethren of the Order either. Not even from himself.

Instead he nursed his fury. He welcomed the agony of his wounds, the fiery kiss of deep pain that made him feel alive. Just about the only thing that gave him any feeling at all. And, like a junkie, he pursued that feeling with reckless, desperate abandon.

Better than the alternative.

Pain was the dark, wicked high that kept him from craving another, more dangerous mistress.

Without pain, all he would have was hunger.

He knew where that would end, of course.

His intellect wasn't as lost as his body or his soul; reason told him that one day this ugly itch of his would kill him. There were some nights—more and more, lately—that he simply no longer cared.

"Sterling, are you in here?"

The feminine voice made his head jerk up, commanding his full attention just as it had in the corridor outside the elevator a few minutes ago. He cocked his head and listened for her movements, even as the addict in him craved the isolation of the shadows that concealed him from her sight.

He drew upon those shadows, reaching deep into the well of his personal Breed talent to gather the gloom around him. It was a struggle to summon his gift; harder still to hold it in place. He let go not even a moment later, hissing a rough curse as even the shadows abandoned him.

"Sterling?" Elise called softly into chapel.

Her footsteps were careful as she entered, as though she didn't feel entirely safe with him. Smart woman. But still, she didn't pause to back away and leave as he would have liked.

"I've just been to your quarters, so I know you didn't go there." She exhaled, her sigh sounding confused and not a little sad. "You can hide from my sight, but I feel your presence in here. Why won't you answer?"

"Because I have nothing to say to you."

Harsh words. And wholly undeserved, particularly by the female who was Tegan's Breedmate of the past year, and, long before that, the mourning widow of Chase's own brother. Quentin Chase had been blessed immeasurably when Elise chose him for her mate—and he'd had no idea that his younger brother had harbored a secret, shameful lust for the happiness Quent and Elise had known.

At least he no longer had to contend with that unwanted desire.

He'd weaned himself of his fixation. There was a tarnished nobility in him that wanted to believe he'd been able to let his want of Elise go because she had given her heart to another of his brothers—a brother-in-arms who would kill for her, die for her, just as she would for him.

Tegan and Elise's love was unbreakable, and although Chase had never lowered himself to test it, the simpler truth was, his thirst for pain had since replaced Elise as the primary object of his obsession.

Yet he still found himself holding his breath as she drifted farther into the chapel and found him hunched in its back corner, his spine wedged into the angle of the stone walls.

Silent, she walked the short distance between the two columns of wooden pews. At the one closest to where he crouched on the floor, she seated herself on the edge and merely stared at him. He didn't have to look over at her to know that her pretty face would be etched with disappointment. Probably pity as well.

"Maybe you didn't understand me," he said, little better than a snarl. "I don't want to talk to you, Elise. You should leave now."

"Why?" she asked, staying right where she sat. "So you can sulk in private? Quentin would be appalled to see you like this. He would be ashamed."

Chase grunted. "My brother is dead."

"Yes, Sterling. Killed in the line of duty for the Enforcement Agency. He died nobly, doing his best to make this world a safer place. Can you honestly say that's what you're doing?"

"I am not Quent."

"No," she said. "You're not. He was an extraordinary man, a courageous man. You could have been even better than him, Sterling. You could have been so much more than what I see before me right now. You know, I've heard how you are on missions lately. I've seen you come in like this too many times, torn up and volatile. So full of rage."

Chase stood up and stalked away from her a few paces, more than ready to be finished with the conversation. "What I do is my own business. It's none of your concern, nor am I."

"I see," she replied. She rose from the pew to approach him. She scowled, slender arms crossed over the front of her. "You'd rather everyone who cares about you simply left you to bleed alone, is that it? You want me and everyone else to just let you sit in a dark corner somewhere and feel sorry for yourself."

He scoffed and swung a hard glare on her. "Do I look like I'm feeling sorry for myself?"

"You look like an animal," she replied, her voice quiet but not so much so that he would mistake it for fear. "You're acting like an animal, Sterling. I look at you lately, and I feel like I don't even know you anymore."

He held her confused stare. "You've never known me, Elise."

"We were family once," she reminded him gently. "I thought we were friends."

"It wasn't friendship I wanted from you," he answered flatly, letting her absorb the frank admission he'd only had the balls to dance around politely until now. When she took a wary step back toward the open aisle, he chuckled, self-satisfied. "Feel free to run away now, Elise."

She didn't run.

That single backward step was all she allowed. Tegan's mate was no longer the sheltered waif who had pledged herself to Quentin Chase. She was a strong woman, had been through her own brand of hell and back, and she hadn't broken. She wasn't about to break for Chase now, no matter how forcibly he tried to push her out of his life.

As if to prove it to himself, he closed the distance between them.

He was filthy with blood and grime; even he could hardly stand the stench of himself. But despite the scant inch or two that separated him from Elise's pristine beauty, she didn't turn away. Her expression was one of sadness and expectation, even before he opened his mouth to say the words that would free him of this last fragile tether on his past.

"The only thing I ever wanted from you, Elise, was to spread your legs and—"

She slapped him hard across the face, a solid *crack* that echoed in the quiet of the chapel. Her pale purple eyes glittered in the candlelight, swimming with unshed tears.

Not a single one fell, not for him.

Probably never again, by the stricken look she held on him.

Chase withdrew, a staggered step backward, the ringing bite of her hand still hot on his skin. He brought his fingers up to touch his stinging cheek.

Then, without another word or thought for what

might lay ahead of him, he vanished from Elise's condemning stare—and fled up the chapel stairwell, into the wintry night outside—using all the speed his Breed genetics could offer him.

Corinne stood at the edge of a wide marble terrace patio that overlooked the snow-filled rear courtyard of the Order's estate on ground level. Alone for a moment while Gabrielle fetched coats for them inside the mansion, she tipped her head back on her shoulders to draw in a long breath of cold December air. The winter sky was dark and cloudless above her, a fathomless sea of midnight blue speckled with bright, glittering stars.

How long had it been since she'd smelled the crisp, faintly smoky scent of winter on the breeze?

How long since she'd felt fresh air against her cheeks?

The decades of her imprisonment had crept by slowly at first, in the days when she'd been determined to mark the time, fighting every second as though it may have been her last. After a while, she'd realized it wasn't her death her captor wanted. For his purposes, he'd needed her alive, even if barely. It was then that she'd stopped counting, ceased fighting, and her concept of time had blurred into a single, never-ending night.

And now she was free.

Tomorrow, she would be home with her family.

Tomorrow, her life would start over and she would be a new person. She had survived, but in her heart she wondered if she could ever be whole again. So much had been taken from her. Some things that could never be won back.

And others . . .

She would have time later to mourn all the things she'd lost to Dragos's evil.

Closing her eyes, she breathed in another deep, cleansing draft of the bracing night air. As she released it, the sound of a child's laughter startled her into a jolt.

At first she thought it was only a trick of her mind, one of the many cruel games that darkness had liked to play on her during her time in captivity. But then the delighted little giggle came again, carrying on the breeze from somewhere in the vast garden courtyard beyond.

It was the laughter of a young girl—a child of perhaps eight or nine years, Corinne guessed, watching as the girl raced happily through the calf-deep snow, bundled up like a pink snowman in a thick parka and matching pants.

Behind her just a few paces came a pair of grossly mismatched, unleashed dogs, tongues lolling joyfully out of the sides of their mouths as they pursued her. Corinne couldn't help but smile at the stubby brown terrier that tried so desperately to get ahead of the larger, more elegant dog. For every unhurried gait of the beautiful, wolfish gray-and-white animal, the scrappy little mutt barked and jockeyed in its wake, finally dashing right through its companion's long legs in order to be the first to reach the girl.

She squealed as the small dog raced up on her ankles and tackled her, barking merrily as the second dog loped up to them with its thick tail wagging and began to lick the child's face.

"Okay, okay!" the little girl giggled. "Luna, Harvard—okay, you win! I surrender!"

As the pair of dogs let up on her to wrestle and growl with each other instead, two women now strode across the snowy lawn from another section of the garden courtyard. One of them was clearly pregnant beneath her oversize down coat, walking at a careful pace alongside a tall, athletic-looking female who held the pair of leashes in her mittened hand.

"Play nice, Luna," she called to the larger of the two dogs. It responded at once, abandoning its canine playmate to lope over and run a happy circle around its obvious owner.

"That's Alex," Gabrielle said, strolling out to the edge of the terrace where Corinne stood. She was wearing a dark wool coat, and held another out to Corinne. It carried the faintest fragrance of cedar, and felt as comfortable as a warm blanket as Corinne slipped into it. "Alex is Kade's mate," Gabrielle continued. "She was out with him when you arrived earlier tonight, so you didn't get the chance to meet her."

"I remember her, though," Corinne replied, her thoughts spinning back to the eve of her rescue. "She and a few other women were the ones who helped bring us out of those cellar cages. They were the ones who found us."

Gabrielle nodded. "That's right. Alex and Jenna were there, along with Dylan and Renata. If Tess wasn't about to pop any day now with Dante's baby, I think she'd have been right there with them too."

Corinne glanced back out to the courtyard as the two women spotted them and each lifted a hand in greeting. The young girl fell into another round of giggles, flopping into a nearby drift with the two dogs eagerly chasing after her.

"The adorable little hellion over there is Mira," Gabrielle said, shaking her head at the child's antics. "Renata had been looking after her when the two of them lived in Montreal. When she and Nikolai fell in

love last summer, they brought Mira home to the compound with them to live together as a family." Lucan's
mate was beaming when she glanced back at Corinne. "I
don't know about you, but I love a happy ending."

"The world could use a lot more of them," Corinne
murmured, warmed by Mira's good fortune even as a
cold sort of ache opened like the tiniest fissure in the
center of her being. She pushed the emptiness away as
Alex and Tess walked together, up the wide marble steps
of the terrace patio.

Gabrielle's breath misted into the darkness. "It's not
too cold for you out here, is it, Tess?"

"It's wonderful," replied the heavily pregnant beauty
as she waddled alongside Alex. Her cheeks were flushed
a rosy pink inside the deep hood of her parka. "I swear,
if Dante tries to keep me cooped up inside the compound for one more day, he may not live to see his son's
birth." The threat was diffused completely by her dancing aqua eyes and sunny smile. She stuck out her mitten-
covered hand. "Hi, I'm Tess."

Corinne briefly clasped the handful of warm wool
and gave a small nod of greeting. "Nice to meet you."

"Alex," said the other Breedmate, offering her hand
and a welcoming smile as well. "I can't even tell you
what a relief it is to know that you and the others Dragos had taken are safe now, Corinne."

She nodded in response. "I am grateful to you all,
much more than words can ever say."

"And tomorrow night Corinne is going home,"
Gabrielle added.

"Tomorrow?" Alex glanced over in question. "Does
that mean Brock and Jenna are on their way back from
Alaska now?"

"They're still delayed by the snowstorms," Gabrielle

replied. "But Hunter has volunteered to escort Corinne to Detroit in Brock's place."

In the lengthening silence that seemed to fall over the women of the Order, Corinne relived the moment that the immense, eerily unreadable warrior had blurted his offer to take her home. She hadn't expected it from him, certainly. He hadn't seemed the charitable sort, not even on the night of her rescue, when he and a few other warriors from the Order had driven Dragos's freed captives to the Darkhaven in Rhode Island.

Hunter had been hard to miss that night. With his chiseled, forbidding features and six-and-a-half-foot frame of bulky muscle, he was the kind of male who dominated any room he entered without even trying. While the hours after the rescue had been ripe with emotion for everyone involved, Hunter had been the quiet one, the one who kept to the periphery and merely carried out his tasks in stoic efficiency.

Later that night, one of the other women had whispered that she'd overheard Andreas and Claire talking privately about Hunter. She'd said it sounded as though he had once—not long ago—been allied in some way with Dragos. Corinne could hardly pretend that she hadn't recognized the air of danger that surrounded the mysterious warrior. She couldn't deny that the thought of being near him unnerved her, then and now.

It didn't take much to picture him as he had been in the compound a short while ago, with his bloodstained combat clothing and the arsenal of terrible weapons that he wore circled around his slim waist. It took far less effort to recall the striking golden color of his eyes and the way his hawklike stare had locked on her the instant he saw her.

Why she had caught his attention so thoroughly, she

couldn't begin to guess. All she knew was she'd felt trapped by his penetrating gaze, scrutinized in a way that had made her feel both enlivened and exposed.

Even now her skin tingled with the remembered awareness of him.

She shivered with the feeling, though her body was nothing close to cold within the insulating folds of her coat. Nevertheless, she tried to rub away the sensation, running her hands up and down her arms to dispel the peculiar, heated prickle of her nerve endings.

"Hunter!" Without warning, little Mira leapt up from her game in the snow and launched into a headlong run toward the terrace patio. "Hunter, come out with us!"

Corinne pivoted her head along with the other women, following Mira's excited dash right past and up to the set of open French doors that looked out over the grounds from the mansion behind them.

Hunter stood just inside those framed glass doors.

He was no longer dressed in gore-covered head-to-toe black, but recently showered, wearing loose-fitting denim jeans and an untucked white button-down shirt that hinted at the elaborate pattern of the *dermaglyphs* that covered his chest and torso. His big feet were bare despite the time of year, and the short damp spikes of his blond hair hung limply over his brow.

And he was studying her again . . . studying her still. How long had he been standing there?

Corinne tried to look away from him, but his piercing golden eyes would not release her. His gaze didn't move from Corinne to acknowledge the approaching child until the last moment, as Mira giddily threw herself into his strong arms.

He lifted her effortlessly and held her aloft in the crook of his left elbow, listening as the little girl chattered animatedly about all of her day's adventures. Corinne could hardly hear what he said, but it was obvious that he favored the child, holding his voice to low, indulgent tones.

In the few moments that he conversed with her, something passed over his otherwise unreadable face. Something that made him go quite still. He sent one further glance in Corinne's direction—a lingering glance that seemed to bore straight through her—before slowly setting the child down on her feet. Then he walked away, back into the heart of the compound.

Even after he was gone, even after Mira had run back to play with the dogs in the snow-filled yard and the other Breedmates had resumed their own conversation, Corinne could still feel the unsettling heat of Hunter's eyes on her.

He *had* seen Corinne Bishop's face somewhere before.

Not during her rescue from Dragos's prison cells. Not at the Darkhaven in Rhode Island either, where she and the other freed captives had been brought for shelter and protection.

No, he had seen the woman months earlier than that, he was certain now.

The realization had hit him like a physical blow when he'd scooped little Mira up into his arms a few moments ago. All it had taken to remind him was a glimpse into the child's innocent face—into the young Breedmate's eyes, which held the power to reflect the future.

Although specially crafted contact lenses usually muted Mira's gift, as they did tonight, there had been a time, months ago, when Hunter had inadvertently looked into her mirrorlike eyes and saw a woman pleading for his mercy, begging him not to be the killer he'd been born.

In the vision, the woman had tried to stay his hand, asking desperately that he spare this life—just this one, just for her.

Let him go, Hunter...

Please, I'm begging you... Don't do this!

Can't you understand? I love him! He means everything to me...

Just let him go... you have to let him live!

In the vision, the woman's expression had fallen when she realized he would not be swayed, not even for her. In the vision, the woman had screamed in heartbroken anguish an instant later as Hunter pulled his arm out of her grasp and delivered the final blow.

That woman was Corinne Bishop.

CHAPTER
Five

His given name was Dragos, like his father before him, although there were few who knew him as such.

Only a handful of necessary associates, his lieutenants in this war of his own making, were privy to his true name and origins. Of course, his enemies knew him now too. Lucan Thorne and his warriors of the Order had exposed him, driven him to ground more than once. But they hadn't yet won.

Nor would they, he assured himself as he paced the walnut-lined study of his private estate.

Outside the tightly shuttered windows that blocked the scant midday light, a winter storm howled. Wind and snow gusted off the Atlantic, buffeting the glass and shaking the shingles as it whipped up over the steep rocks of his island lair. The tall alpine evergreens surrounding his large estate whistled and moaned as the gale slammed westward, heading toward the mainland, just a few miles away from the isolated crag he now called home.

Dragos relished the fury of the storm that raged outside. He felt a similar tempest churning inside him every time he thought about the Order and the strikes they'd made against his operation. He wanted them to feel the lash of his anger, to know that when he came to collect his vengeance—and he would, very soon—it would be blood-soaked and complete. He would give no quarter, grant no mercy whatsoever.

He was still ruminating over the plans he had for Lucan and his heretofore unbreachable, secret Boston compound when a polite rap sounded on the closed doors of his study.

"What is it?" he barked, his temper as short as his patience was thin.

One of his Minions opened the door. She was pretty and young, with her strawberry blond hair and dewy, peaches-and-cream face. He'd spotted her waiting tables in a podunk fishing town a couple of weeks ago and decided she might prove amusing to him back at his lair.

And so she had.

Dragos had fed upon her behind a restaurant Dumpster that reeked of fish guts and brine. She'd put up a struggle at first, scratching at his face and kicking him in the moments before his bite had fully taken hold of her delicate throat. She'd let out a short scream and tried to put her knee into his balls.

He raped her for that, brutally, repeatedly, and with pleasure. Then he'd drained her almost to the point of death and made her what she was now—his Minion, selfless, devoted, utterly enslaved to him. She no longer resisted anything he demanded of her, no matter how depraved.

The girl entered his study with a demure incline of her head. "I have this morning's mail from your box on the mainland, Master."

"Excellent," he murmured, shadowing her as she walked in with a handful of envelopes and placed them on his large desk in the center of the grand room.

When she pivoted to face him, her expression was bland but receptive, the hallmark look of a Minion awaiting its Master's next command. If he told her to drop to her knees and suck him off then and there, she'd do it without the slightest hesitation. She would respond with equal obedience if he told her to pick up the silver letter opener and slice it across her own throat.

Dragos cocked his head and studied her, wondering which of the two scenarios would amuse him more. He was about to settle on one when his eye strayed to a large white vellum envelope sitting atop the rest of his incoming mail on the desk. The Boston return address and handwritten calligraphy on the front of the invitation captured his full attention.

He dismissed the Minion with a bored flick of his wrist.

Seating himself in the thick leather cushions of his desk chair as the girl quietly exited the study, he picked up the white envelope and smiled, brushing his fingers across the carefully hand-lettered script that spelled out the alias he'd been using in human circles of late.

Dragos had assumed so many false identities over the centuries of his existence, among both his own Breed kind and humans, he hardly bothered to keep track anymore. It no longer mattered; his time of hiding who he was, and what he was capable of, had nearly reached its end. He was so close now. Never mind the recent interference of the Order. Their efforts to thwart him were insignificant, and had come too late as well.

The holiday party announcement in his hand was just another step along his path to triumph. He'd been courting the junior senator from Massachusetts for the better part of a year now, tracking the ambitious young politician's every move and ensuring that the pockets of the senator's campaign coffers remained more than amply full.

The human believed he was destined for greatness, and Dragos was doing everything he could to see that he climbed as high and as fast as possible. All the way to the White House, if he had anything to say about it.

Dragos opened the envelope and scanned the details of the invitation. It was to be an exclusive event, a high-priced dinner and charity fundraiser for the senator's power-broker pals, not to mention his most influential—and most generous—campaign contributors. He wouldn't miss this party for the world. In fact, he could hardly stand the wait.

In just a few more nights, he would tilt the table so far in his favor, no one would be able to stop him from seeing his vision through to its fruition. Certainly not the humans. They would be clueless until the very end, just as he intended.

The Order wouldn't be able to stop him either. He was making certain of that even now, having sent one of his Minion pawns out to retrieve the specialized weapons he needed to combat Lucan and his warriors in this new brand of warfare and to ensure that none in the Order would be left standing to get in his way again.

As he set the senator's invitation back down on the desk, his laptop computer chimed with an incoming email message from an untraceable free service. Right on schedule, Dragos thought, as he clicked to open the report from his Minion in the field. The message was simple and succinct, just what he'd expect from a former military serviceman.

Assets located.
Initial contact successful.
Moving forward with retrieval as planned.

There was no need to reply. The Minion knew his mission objectives, and for security purposes, the email address would already be deactivated on the other end. Dragos deleted the message from his in box and leaned back in his chair.

Outside, the winter squall continued to bluster. He settled back and closed his eyes, listening to its fury in a state of satisfied calm, content with the knowledge that all the pieces of his grand plan were at last falling into place.

His name was Dragos, and soon every man, woman, and child—Breed and human alike—would bow to him as their overlord and king.

Everything had changed.

That was the thought that had been drumming around in Corinne's head from the moment she and Hunter arrived in Detroit the next evening.

Decades of imprisonment in Dragos's laboratories had left her struggling to adapt to countless new changes and advancements in the world she once knew, from the way people talked and dressed, to how they lived and worked and traveled. From the moment of her release, Corinne had felt like she'd somehow drifted into another plane of reality, a stranger lost in a strange future world.

But nothing had struck so close to the bone as the feeling she had as she and Hunter left the airport in a car provided by the Order and made the drive into the city to her parents' Darkhaven. The vibrant downtown she remembered was no more. Along the river, land that had been open spaces was now crowded with buildings—some sleekly modern, lights glowing from high-rise offices; other structures appearing long vacant, derelict and broken. Only a handful of people strolled the streets, shuffling quickly along the main avenue, past the lightless corridors of neglect.

Even in the dark, the dichotomy of the Detroit landscape was shocking, unbelievable. Block by block, it looked as if progress had smiled on one lot of land while spitting on another.

She didn't realize how worried she was until Hunter brought the large black sedan to a stop in front of the moonlit Darkhaven estate she once called home.

"My God," she whispered from her seat beside him in the car as relief washed over her. "It's still here. I'm finally home . . ."

But even the Darkhaven looked different from what she recalled. Corinne fumbled to unclasp her confining seat belt, anxious now, and more than ready to be free of the uncomfortable restraints that Hunter had insisted she wear for the duration of the drive. She leaned forward, peering out the dark-tinted passenger window. Her breath left her on a hitching sigh as she looked past the heavy wrought-iron entry gate and perimeter fence, neither of which had been there when she was last home.

Was it merely a sign of dangerous times for all of the

city, or had her disappearance made her indomitable father feel so vulnerable that he would wall himself and the rest of his family behind a prison of their own? Whatever the cause, guilt and sadness clenched her heart to see the ugly barrier surrounding such once-peaceful grounds.

Beyond the fortresslike entrance sat the stately red brick manor whose many curtained windows glowed with soft light at the end of the long, cobblestone drive. The tall oak trees flanking the driveway had matured and thickened in her absence, their naked winter boughs reaching across to one another high over the pavement like a canopy of sheltering arms. Ahead, halfway up the wide lawn that spread out in front of the large Greek Revival house, the limestone fountain and wishing pool where she and her younger adopted sister, Charlotte, used to play in the heat of the summer as little girls had at some time been replaced with decorative boulders and a collection of burlap-shrouded topiary.

How vast the grounds had seemed when she was a child living here. How magical this private, special world had seemed to her back then.

How terribly she had taken it all for granted just a few years later, as a young headstrong woman who couldn't seem to get far enough away fast enough.

Now she wanted back inside with a need that was nothing short of desperate.

Corinne brought her fingers up to her mouth, a small sob catching in the back of her throat. "I can't believe I'm actually here. I can't believe I'm home."

Impulse had her grabbing for the door handle, ignoring the low growl of her stoic companion beside her in the driver's seat. Corinne climbed out of the vehicle and walked a few paces up the private drive toward the iron gate. A gust of cold wind blew across the snowy landscape in front of her, chilling her face and making her burrow a bit deeper into her thick wool coat.

At her back, she felt a sudden heat emanating toward her and knew that Hunter was there now. She hadn't even heard him get out of the car to follow her, he moved so stealthily. His voice behind her was low and deep. "You should remain in the car until you are safely delivered to the door."

Corinne stepped away from him and walked up to touch the tall black bars of the closed gate. "Do you know how long I've been gone?" she murmured. Hunter didn't answer, just stood in silence behind her. She closed her fingers around the cold iron, exhaling a short puff of steam on her quiet, humorless laugh. "This past summer, it would have been seventy-five years. Can you imagine? That's how much of my life was stolen from me. My family up there in that house...they all think I'm dead."

It hurt her to think of the pain her parents and siblings had gone through with her disappearance. For some time after she'd been taken, Corinne had worried how her family was coping. For so long after her abduction, she'd clung to the hope that they would search for her—that they would never stop searching until she was found, especially her father. After all, Victor Bishop was a powerful man in Breed society. Even back then, he'd been wealthy and well connected. He'd had every means at his disposal, so why hadn't he torn apart his city and every one between here and her prison until his daughter was found and brought home?

It was a question that had gnawed at her every hour of her captivity. What she hadn't known then was that her abductor had gone to sick lengths to convince her family and all who knew her that she was no longer alive. Brock, who had been her childhood bodyguard long before he'd become a warrior for the Order, had taken her aside after her rescue and explained all that he knew of her disappearance. Although he'd been gentle with the facts, there could be no softening the horrific details of what Brock had revealed to her.

"A few months after I was taken, a female's body was pulled from the river not far from here," she told Hunter quietly, repulsed by what she had learned. "She was the same age as me, the same height and build. Someone had dressed her in my clothes, the very dress I had been wearing the night I was taken. They did something more too. Her body . . ."

"The woman had been mutilated," Hunter interjected when revulsion made her own words trail off. She glanced back at him in question. He met her gaze with a matter-of-fact look. "Brock has spoken of your disappearance. I am aware of how the body had been altered in an attempt to conceal the victim's identity."

"Altered," Corinne replied. She dropped her chin, frowning over her right hand, the one that bore her distinctive Breedmate birthmark. "To convince my family the dead female was me, her killer or killers had also cut off her hands and feet. They even took her head."

Bile rose from her stomach as she considered the cruelty—the utter depravity—it would take to do something like that to another person.

Of course, the things Dragos had done to her and the other Breedmates imprisoned in his laboratories had been only fractionally less heinous. Corinne closed her eyes tight on the barrage of memories that flew at her like bats from out of the darkness: Dank concrete cells. Cold steel tables outfitted with unforgiving, inescapable, thick leather cuffs. There had been many needles and probes. Tests and procedures. Pain and fury and utter hopelessness.

The terrible, soul-wrenching howls of the mad and the dying, and those who were lost somewhere between.

And blood.

So much blood—her own, and that which was regularly forced down her throat so that she, like the other females who'd been taken, would remain youthful and viable specimens for Dragos's twisted purposes.

Corinne shuddered, wrapping her arms around the deep, cold void that seemed to blow through the center of her now. It was a hollow ache, one she had been trying to keep at bay for a very long time. It had only cracked open wider in the days since her rescue.

"It's cold," said her stoic escort from Boston. "You should return to the vehicle until I've seen you safely delivered to the house."

She nodded, but her feet remained still. Now that she was standing there—now that the moment she'd prayed for for so long to come true was actually happening— she wasn't sure she had the courage to face it. "They think I'm dead, Hunter. All this time, I haven't existed to them. What if they've forgotten me? What if they've been happier without me?" Doubt pressed down on her. "Maybe I should have tried to contact them before I left Boston. Maybe coming here like this isn't such a good idea."

She pivoted around to face him, hoping to find some sense of reassurance that her fears were ungrounded. She wanted to hear him say that her sudden attack of nerves was nothing more than that—something comforting that Brock would have said if he'd been with her now. But Hunter's expression was inscrutable. His hawklike golden eyes stared at her, unblinking. Corinne blew out a soft breath. "What would you do if it was your family up there in that house, Hunter?"

One bulky shoulder lifted slightly beneath his black leather trench coat. "I have no family."

He said it as casually as he might remark that it was dark outside at the moment. A statement of the obvious. One that didn't invite questions, yet only made her want to know more about him. It was hard to imagine him in any other way than the sober, almost grim, warrior who stood before her. Hard to picture him with the softly rounded face of a child instead of the bladed angles of his cheekbones and unforgiving, squared line of his jaw. He was impossible to imagine without the black combat attire and arsenal of blades and weaponry that glinted within the folds of his long coat.

"You must have parents," she prodded, curious now. "Someone must have raised you?"

"There is no one." He glanced past her then, a momentary flick of his gaze. His jaw went rigid, golden eyes narrowed and flinty. "We have been noticed."

No sooner had he said it, security floodlights mounted around the estate came on one after the other, illuminating the yard and driveway. The glare was blinding, inescapable. Worry seeped into Corinne's veins as half a dozen armed men poured out from somewhere behind the lights. The guards were Breed, of course, and coming at her and Hunter so fast and hard, Corinne could barely track them.

Hunter had no such problem.

He stepped in front of her in an instant, guiding her around to his back with a firm but gentle arm even as he moved into a ready combat stance. He didn't draw any of his weapons as her father's guards charged up to the gate with menace in their eyes, each of the six vampires brandishing a big black rifle, the barrels now trained on Hunter's chest.

Corinne couldn't help but notice that even without the threat of a gun in his hand, the sight of Hunter alone seemed to have taken her father's guards more than a little aback. None of their own kind would mistake him for anything but Breed, and based on their collective looks of wariness as they took in his black fatigues and lethal coolness, it hadn't taken them more than a second to figure out that he was also a member of the Order.

"Put down your arms," Hunter said, his unnerving calm having never sounded so deadly. "I have no wish to harm anyone."

"This is private property," one of the guards managed to blurt out. "No one passes the gate unannounced."

Hunter cocked his head. "Put. Down. Your. Arms."

Two of them obeyed as though on instinct. As another started to lower his rifle too, a sharp *hiss* sounded from a device clipped to his collar. A detached male voice came out of nowhere: "What the devil is going on out there, Mason? Report in at once!"

"Oh, my God," Corinne whispered. She recognized that booming baritone the instant she heard it, even when raised in uncharacteristic anger. Hope soared through her as though on wings, scattering all of her earlier fears and uncertainty. Peering from behind Hunter, she practically screamed her relief. "Daddy!"

The company of guards couldn't have looked more stunned. But when she tried to move around Hunter and step forward, one of them raised the long barrel of his gun. Hunter was up against the gate in a second—even less than that, Corinne had to guess. She watched in astonishment as the warrior placed himself in front of her like a living shield of muscle and bone and pure, deadly intent.

She couldn't tell how he'd been able to grab on to the guard's rifle so effortlessly, but one moment the black steel snout was pointed at her and the next it was bent at a severe angle, wrenched between the iron bars of the gate. Hunter sent a warning look at the rest of her father's men, none of whom seemed eager to test him.

Victor Bishop's voice came over the communication device again. "Someone tell me what the hell is going on. Who's out there with you?"

The guard named Mason was someone Corinne recognized now. He had been a part of the Bishop household for as long as she could remember, a kind-hearted but serious Breed male who'd been a friend of Brock's and used to like jazz music almost as much as she did. Back then, he'd worn his coppery-golden hair stylishly slicked back with pomade. Now it was cut shorter, a bright orange cap that made his widening eyes seem even larger.

"Miss Corinne?" he asked hesitantly, gaping at her in obvious disbelief. "But... how? I mean, good lord... is it—can it really be you?"

At her mute nod, a smile broke over his face. The guard whispered a soft curse as he grasped the communication device on his coat's lapel and brought it closer to his mouth. "Mr. Bishop, sir? This is Mason. We're down at the front gate, and, uh... well, sir, you are not going to believe this, but I am looking at a miracle out here."

CHAPTER
Six

The female was safe and his job here was done.

That's what Hunter told himself as Corinne Bishop was taken into the hands of her father's security detail. The guards immediately opened the gates to her amid repeated apologies for the inadvertently hostile way she had been met. The one named Mason had moist eyes as he stared at her, his voice cracking with barely restrained emotion as he rubbed a hand over his face and murmured his disbelief at seeing her standing before him. Waving the other guards ahead, Mason wrapped a protective arm around Corinne's petite shoulders and started to walk her up the cobbled drive.

Hunter hung back just inside the gate, watching her make her way toward the mansion ahead.

The task of seeing her safely delivered home was met, which left him free to return to the airport where the Order's private plane waited to take him back to Boston. In a moment, Corinne Bishop would be ensconced inside her family's Darkhaven, and in just a few short hours, he could resume the more urgent business of pursuing Dragos and the army of Gen One killers who served him.

Yet there was still the matter of Mira's vision...

Corinne turned around to look at him as she was led farther up the driveway by her father's guards. Her long ebony hair caught in the cold breeze, whipping dark strands across her pale cheek and brow. Her lips parted as though she meant to speak, but the words were lost, clouding as her breath caught on the wind and flew away. Her gaze lingered on him. He felt that prolonged, haunted glance reach out to him across the distance, as palpable as a touch.

As he watched Corinne Bishop being guided away from him, he saw instead the tear-stained face and wild desperation of the woman in Mira's precognitive vision. He heard her voice, wrenched with fear and anguish.

Please, I'm begging you...

I love him...

You have to let him live...

Beneath the logic that reminded him the child seer's gift had never been wrong yet, something unfamiliar tugged at Hunter from inside. The stealth tactician in him was quick to suggest that the vision was a puzzle demanding to be resolved. The assassin in him cautioned that Mira's precognition might lead him to an enemy to be discovered and destroyed.

But there was another part of him that looked at Corinne Bishop in that moment, with her tender beauty and the steely resilience that had carried her out of Dragos's dungeons with her spine held straight, and he couldn't fathom being the one to finally crush her as he had in Mira's vision.

He felt an odd respect for her, for what she might have suffered at Dragos's hands. Odder to him still, he realized that he didn't want to be the one to cause Corinne Bishop's pain and tears.

It was that illogical, far-too-human part of him that made him glance away from her and begin to pivot back toward his waiting vehicle at the end of the drive. If he left now, the chances were good that he might never cross paths with the female again.

He could go back to Boston, and the vision be damned.

As he took the first steps, the front door of the mansion was flung open on a keening feminine wail. "Corinne! I have to see her! I want to see my daughter!"

Hunter paused to look over his shoulder as an attractive brunette female raced out of the house. She hadn't stopped to grab a coat, had apparently left whatever she'd been doing and run outside in just a white satiny blouse and a narrow, dark skirt. Her high-heeled shoes clicked and skidded as she flew over the cobbled drive, sobbing as she hurried toward the guards and Corinne in the center of the long driveway.

Corinne broke away from the others and rushed to meet her. "Mother!"

The two women fell into a fierce embrace, both of them weeping and laughing, clutching each other tightly as they each spoke in a rush of whispered words punctuated by joyful tears.

Victor Bishop was only a moment behind his relieved mate. The Darkhaven's head of household came up in silence, his face pallid and slack in the moonlight, black brows lowered over unblinking dark eyes. A choked cry snagged in the Breed male's throat. "Corinne . . ."

She glanced up as he said her name, nodding as he

tentatively approached her. "It's really me, Daddy. Oh, God . . . I never thought I'd see any of you again!"

Hunter observed the continued reunion, listening as Corinne's stricken father tried to make sense of everything that was happening. "I don't understand how any of this can be," Bishop murmured. "You've been gone so long, Corinne. You were dead . . ."

"No," she assured him, stepping out of his arms to meet his stunned gaze. "I was taken away that night. You were made to believe I was dead, but I wasn't. All this time, I was kept like a prisoner. But none of that matters now. I'm just so glad to be home again. I never thought I'd be free."

Victor Bishop's head shook slowly. His brows sank lower, deepening his look of confusion. "I can hardly believe it. After all these years . . . How is it possible that you're standing here in front of us now?"

"The Order," Corinne replied. Her gaze found Hunter through the cluster of Bishop's guards. "I owe my life to the warriors and their mates. They found the place I was being held. Last week they rescued me and several other captives and brought us to a safe house in Rhode Island."

"Last week," Bishop murmured, sounding both surprised and disturbed. "And no one thought to tell us? We should have been informed that you were all right— we should have been told that you were alive, for crissake."

Corinne gently took his hands in hers. "I couldn't let you hear it from anyone but me, in person. I wanted to be able to see your faces and put my arms around you when I told you what happened to me." Her expression went solemn, almost mournful, a look that did not escape Hunter's notice. "Oh, Daddy... there's so much I need to tell you and Mother both."

While Corinne's mother hugged her tight and stifled another sob, Victor Bishop's jaw was growing increasingly taut. "And what of your abductor? Good God, please tell me the bastard who stole you from us is dead—"

"He will be," Hunter replied, his interruption drawing the eyes of everyone gathered there. "The Order pursues him as we speak. Soon the one who did this will be no more."

Bishop's narrow look scanned Hunter from head to toe. "Soon isn't good enough when it's my family at risk, warrior." He gestured to his men. "Shut that gate and arm the perimeter sensors. We shouldn't stay out here any longer. Regina, take Corinne into the house. I'll be right behind you."

Bishop's guards hurried to carry out his commands. As Corinne's mother steered her toward the house, Corinne broke away and walked back to where Hunter stood. She held out her hand to him. "Thank you for bringing me home."

He stared for a moment, torn between her strong, steady gaze and the pale, delicate hand that reached out to him, waiting for his acknowledgment.

Hunter took her slender fingers into his grasp. "You are welcome," he murmured, careful not to crush her as his large hand devoured her much smaller one.

He wasn't used to physical contact, and he'd never known any need for gratitude. Still, it was impossible not to notice how soft Corinne's skin was against his palm and fingertips. Like warm velvet against the rough scrape of his hard, weapon-callused hand.

It shouldn't have meant anything at all, but somehow

the idea of touching this female piqued all kinds of interest within him. Unwanted, unwarranted interest, a point made all the more clear as Corinne's anguished pleas from Mira's vision echoed in the back of his mind.

Let him go, Hunter...

Please, I'm begging you... Don't do this!

Can't you understand? I love him! He means everything to me...

He released her from his loose hold, but even after the contact was broken, her warmth stayed nestled in the cradle of his palm as he fisted his hand and brought it back down to his side.

Corinne quietly cleared her throat, folding her arms across herself. "Please tell everyone in the Order—Andreas Reichen and Claire too—that I will be eternally grateful for all they've done."

Hunter inclined his head. "Live a good life, Corinne Bishop."

She stared at him for a long moment, then gave him a faint nod and pivoted to rejoin her mother. As the two females started for the house together, Victor Bishop stepped into Hunter's line of vision, his head turned to watch the women walk back up the driveway. When they were well out of earshot, he exhaled a low curse.

"I never dreamed this moment would come," he murmured as he looked back at Hunter once more. "We buried that girl decades ago. Or, as it turns out, what we thought was that girl. It took a long time for Regina to give up hope that there had been some mistake and the body my men pulled out of the river months later wasn't actually her daughter."

Hunter listened in silence, watching Bishop's face twist and redden with emotion as he spoke.

"It nearly destroyed Regina, losing Corinne. She kept

hoping for a miracle. She held on to that hope for longer than I imagined could be possible. Eventually, she did let go." Bishop ran his palm over his creased brow and slowly shook his head. "And now . . . thanks to God and the Order, tonight she finally has her miracle. We all do."

Hunter did not acknowledge the praise, nor the outstretched hand of the Darkhaven vampire in front of him. He kept his eyes trained on Corinne's retreating form as she and her mother walked the remainder of the long driveway, then entered the open front door of the warmly lit house up ahead. He watched until the door was closed behind them and he was assured that his temporary ward was fully transferred to the shelter of her family's arms.

In the lengthening quiet, Victor Bishop cleared his throat as he let his hand drift back down to his side. "How can I ever repay the Order for what you've done here tonight?"

"Keep her safe," Hunter said, then he turned away from Bishop and walked to his waiting vehicle at the street.

A furious throb was drumming in Lucan's veins as he sat with several members of the Order in the compound's tech lab. His elbows planted on the edge of the long conference table, he and the others listened in disgust as Gideon reviewed his findings concerning Murdock, the Enforcement Agent who'd fled the scene last night at the private club in Boston and had yet to surface anywhere.

"In addition to the sip-and-strip clubs he tends to frequent, our boy Murdock also seems to prefer his blood Hosts on the rare side—as in very young. There's more than one blemish in his records with the Agency for solicitation of an underage human, and not just solicitation with intent to feed. Also some citations for excessive force among both Darkhaven civilian populations and humankind. Keep in mind, this is just the shit in his general file. If I dig any deeper than the surface, there's bound to be a whole other pile of nasty on this guy."

Gideon had hacked in and pulled up the vampire's records from the IID, the information database that logged nearly every known Breed individual in existence. There were exceptions, of course, namely Lucan and an untold number of other early-generation Breed born centuries before any kind of technology had been in place. Lucan glanced at the flat-panel monitor where a photograph of a prissy brown-haired male with an oily, too-smug smile filled the screen.

"What about family? Anyone we can squeeze for intel on this asshole's possible whereabouts?"

Gideon shook his head. "Never took a Breedmate, and there is no recorded kin on file anywhere. Another thing, Murdock's only been local for the past fifty-odd years. Before that, back around the time of his documented problems with kids and violence, he was part of the Agency in Atlanta. Looks like the director of that region personally recommended Murdock for transfer and promotion to his position up here."

Across the table, seated in black fatigues and patrol gear like the gathered male warriors, Nikolai's mate, Renata, scoffed. Her chin-length brunette hair swung around her jaw line as she leaned back and crossed her arms over her chest. "What easier way to get rid of a problem than packing it up and shipping it somewhere else? I saw plenty of that going on among the orphanage staffs in Montreal."

"Sounds like this scumbag Murdock needs to be put down," Rio said from the other side of Niko and Renata. His topaz eyes smoldered with contempt, making the web of combat scars that riddled the left side of his face look all the more savage.

Another of the warriors, Kade, gave a nod of his spiky-haired dark head. "Too bad Hunter and Chase didn't finish him off at the club last night. Might've done the world a favor."

"Murdock is scum," Lucan agreed, "but if there's any chance he might be connected to Dragos or his operation—even remotely connected—then we need to make sure he keeps breathing long enough to lead us there."

"What about Sterling?" It was Elise who spoke, her voice tentative as she turned to look at Lucan from her seat between him and her mate, Tegan. While the rest of the assembled group had been occupied with talk of their missions and the new priority of locating Agent Murdock, Elise had been quiet, pensive. Now she wore her worry in the flat press of her mouth and in the stormy lavender of her eyes. "He's been gone for nearly twenty-four hours. Has there been any word from him at all?"

For a moment, no one said a thing. Sterling Chase's absence was the elephant in the room, the topic on everyone's mind, if not their tongues.

"No word," Gideon answered. "His cell rings straight to voicemail and he's not returning my calls."

"Same here," Dante put in from the other side of the conference table. Of all the warriors, Tess's mate was easily Chase's tightest ally. Just a year or so ago, when Chase had come on board with the Order, he and Dante had been at each other's throats. In the time since, they'd had each other's backs as friends and brethren. But even Dante seemed doubtful about Chase now. "I tried him just before we came into this meeting but got no answer. Harvard's dodging us hardcore this time."

"That's not like him at all." Elise glanced at Tegan as he reached out to draw her hand into his. "He's too responsible to just take off like this without any explanation."

"Is he?" Tegan's question was gentle, but there was tension in his jaw—a fierce protectiveness—as he looked at his troubled Breedmate beside him. "I know you want to think the best of Chase, but you need to look at him through clear eyes now. You saw him last night, Elise. You told me how he acted with you in the chapel. Was that the Chase you think you know?"

"No," she answered quietly, her eyes downcast as she slowly shook her blond head.

Earlier that day, Elise had relayed to everyone her confrontation with Chase in the moments before he'd left the compound, how he'd lashed out at her, full of anger and crudeness. Lucan had bristled to hear about the whole thing, but no worse than Tegan. The other Gen One still vibrated with palpable malice toward Chase's actions, despite the care with which he handled his beloved mate's feelings for her former kinsman.

"I shouldn't have struck him," Elise murmured. "I knew he was upset. I should have walked away and left him alone. That's what he told me to do. I shouldn't have pushed him—"

"Hey," Tegan said, tenderly lifting her chin with his

fingertips. "You didn't push him out that door last night. He went willingly." Tegan glanced Lucan's way then. "Let's face it, Harvard's been walking a damn thin line for a while now. Maybe it's time we all start looking at him with clearer eyes. Time we stop making excuses for Chase and acknowledge what I'm sure more than one of us has been thinking about him lately."

Lucan caught the meaning in Tegan's knowing stare and in the statement that hung over the room like a funeral shroud. Hell, how could he mistake Tegan's point, considering Lucan's own recent history and the battle he'd waged not so long ago to resist falling victim to the weakness that plagued all of the Breed?

"Bloodlust," Lucan said, grim with the thought. He glanced up at the faces of his Breed brethren seated around the table, more aware than any of them—except Tegan, that is—of what it meant to become addicted to the thirst. Once a vampire stepped foot on that path, the decline was swift. Plummet too far and you never came back. "No offense, T, but I hope you're wrong."

Tegan's stare remained steady, too certain. "And if I'm not?"

When no one else filled the answering silence, Dante hissed a curse. "Either way, we need to haul Harvard's ass back into the compound and set him straight. Someone needs to tell him to pull his shit together before it's too late. I'll pound it into his thick skull personally, if that's what it takes."

Lucan wanted to agree with Dante's argument but found himself shaking his head the longer he considered it. "Chase knew what he was doing when he walked out of here. And if he didn't, then he sure as hell knows now. We've got bigger problems to deal with than cleaning up another of Harvard's messes. He's AWOL, and that's coming on the heels of a fucked-up mission that might have gone even further south if not for Hunter having been with Chase on patrol. Let's not forget it was Chase who failed to keep Lazaro and Christophe Archer safe during Kellan's rescue last week. He's been screwing up left and right. Frankly, he's becoming a liability."

"I can go after him, try to bring him around," Dante insisted. "I mean, Christ, Lucan. He's proved to be solid in combat. He's saved my ass more than once, and he's done a lot of good for the Order since he's been on board. Don't you think he deserves some benefit of doubt here?"

"Not if his behavior jeopardizes the Order's objectives," Lucan replied. "And not if his presence here endangers the security of this compound or anyone within these walls. Like Tegan said, nobody pushed Chase out of the fold. He walked out of here on his own free will."

Dante stared in grim silence, along with the others seated around the table.

This wasn't a call Lucan wanted to make, but he was leader here, and, ultimately, his word was law. None of the warriors would argue the subject any further. Not even Dante, who slumped back into his seat and muttered a low curse.

Lucan cleared his throat. "Now, let's get back to Murdock—"

Before he could finish the thought, the tech lab's glass doors hissed open and Rio's Breedmate, Dylan, rushed into the room. Her freckle-spattered face was pale against the fiery color of her hair, her eyes wide with panic.

"Tess sent me," she blurted, skidding to a sharp halt. "She's in the infirmary. She needs help quick!"

Dante shot out of his seat. "Oh, fuck. Is it the baby?"

"No." Dylan shook her head. "Nothing like that—Tess is fine. It's Kellan Archer. Something's wrong with him—really wrong. He's in a lot of pain. We can't get him to stop convulsing."

The meeting broke up in a rush of movement, Lucan and Dante leading the way. Everyone scrambled down to the infirmary at the other end of the corridor.

Dylan hadn't been exaggerating when she said the situation with young Kellan Archer was bad. The Breed youth was doubled over on his infirmary bed, clutching at his abdomen and moaning in obvious agony.

"His nausea started worsening about half an hour ago," Tess volunteered as the group crowded into the room. Kellan's grandfather, the Gen One civilian Lazaro Archer, stood at one side of the bed, Tess at the other. Her hand rested lightly on the teen's back as another deep convulsion rippled through his body.

"What's wrong with Kellan?" asked little Mira, who stood nearby with Gideon's mate, Savannah. The girl clutched an opened book to her chest, as though she'd recently been reading from it. Her eyes were wide and anxious. "Is he going to be okay?"

"Kellan's got a bad tummyache," Savannah told her, glancing to Gideon and Lucan as she guided the child away from the bed. She spoke and moved with utter calm, but her dark brown eyes were grave with concern.

The fact was, no one knew what was wrong with Kellan Archer. Instead of rebounding after he'd been abducted and tortured on Dragos's command, he seemed to be getting weaker. He needed to feed, that much was certain, but he wasn't yet in any shape to venture top-side and find a Host on his own.

Bad enough Lucan had been forced to open the Order's headquarters to Lazaro Archer and his grandson after Dragos razed their Darkhaven and obliterated their kin. If things didn't improve with Kellan damn soon, Lucan was going to have to break yet another rule of the compound and bring a human inside to feed the kid.

Renata reached out to take Mira's hand. "Come on, Mouse. Why don't you come with Savannah and me for a little while? We can come back when Kellan feels better, all right?"

Mira nodded but kept her head turned toward the youth suffering on the bed until the other two Breedmates had removed her from the room. No sooner had they gone, the young vampire doubled over into a deeper spasm, saliva dripping from his open mouth.

"Please," Lazaro Archer said. "Please, do something to help my boy. He's all I have left—"

A terrible groan ripped out of the Breed youth's throat. He gagged and wheezed, then, with a great heave of his torso, he leaned across the infirmary bed and began to vomit. A stream of liquid shot out of his mouth as he pitched forward and retched again.

Dante leapt forward and pulled Tess out of the way, sheltering her against him. Dylan and Rio rushed to grab paper towels from the cabinet nearby while Elise stepped in to comfort the youth and help clean him up.

He kept heaving, spasms racking him even after his body had expelled what little it had to give up. He tried to speak, an embarrassed moan of apology, but only managed a raw rasp of sound.

"Shh," Elise whispered, stroking his damp hair where he'd crumpled on the mattress. "It's okay now, Kellan. Don't worry about anything except feeling better."

Dylan was on her hands and knees below, mopping up the mess on the floor as Rio worked on stripping away the soiled blanket and sheet. Lucan heard Dylan's indrawn gasp and watched as she suddenly went very still next to Kellan Archer's bed.

"Um . . . you guys?" She stood up then, a wad of wet paper toweling in her hand. "I think I know what was making Kellan sick."

Lucan stared, a feeling of sickness opening up in his own gut as Dylan held out the soiled, soggy clump. In the center of it was a coin-size silver disc.

"Ah, Christ. Ah, fuck me," Gideon murmured. His face went slack as he reached out to take the object out of its wet nest of spittle and stomach acid. "I don't believe this. Son of a bitch!"

"What is it?" Tegan asked, grim as the rest of them.

"It's a GPS chip," Gideon replied. "A goddamn tracking device." He raked a hand over the top of his head and turned to face Lucan. "We've been compromised."

Lucan exhaled, the magnitude of his mistake hitting him like a freight train plowing into the center of his being.

Now it all made sense. The abduction of Kellan Archer. The too-easy rescue. The simultaneous attack on Archer's Darkhaven—an attack that was so thorough, it would have ensured the boy had no place else to go but back to the compound and into the protection of the Order.

Dragos had staged the entire thing, all for this purpose.

He knew where they lived now. He'd known for days,

ever since Lucan had made the decision to allow the civilians into the Order's home.

The only question that remained was how long it would be before Dragos or his army of homegrown killers brought this war right up to the mansion's front gates.

CHAPTER Seven

Are you hungry, darling? I've asked Tilda to prepare something nice for you, but if you'd like anything to eat before the dining room is ready, you need only ask and I'll get it for you. Anything you wish—"

"I'm fine." Corinne turned away from the window in the room she'd been brought to a short while ago, after her mother had ushered her into the house and her father had disappeared into his study to confer with Mason and the other Darkhaven guards.

The fuss and activity were making Corinne uncomfortable. Now that she was home, all she wanted was a few private moments alone with her parents. Time enough to tell them how badly she'd missed her family . . . and how desperately she needed their help.

When her mother began to wonder aloud about calling the kitchen for a tray of food to be brought up to the room, Corinne walked over and clasped hold of her hands. "I'm all right, really. Please, don't feel you have to fuss over me."

"But I can't help it. Do you know how many times I prayed for the chance to fuss over you again?" Regina Bishop's skin was moist and cool, her fingers trembling as they gripped Corinne's in an urgent hold. Tears swam in her kind eyes. "Good lord, are you really here? I'm looking at you—I feel you, alive and beautiful as ever, but I can hardly believe this is happening. We lived a nightmare after you went missing."

"I know," Corinne acknowledged softly. "I'm sorry for what all of you went through too."

"Lottie cried for weeks after you disappeared. She'll be so happy to learn that you're home again."

Corinne smiled at the thought of reuniting with her little sister. Although both were born with the Breedmate birthmark, she and Charlotte were not blood related. Nevertheless, they'd been fiercely devoted to each other—perhaps all the more so, having been born into neglect and abandonment as infants, only to become family as wards of the Bishops.

"Is she here, Mother?"

"Oh, no, darling. Charlotte has her own Darkhaven in London with her mate and their two sons. In fact, her youngest and his Breedmate just celebrated the birth of their first son a few weeks ago."

Corinne felt a bittersweet jolt in her core. Five years Corinne's junior, Lottie had been a gawky adolescent at the time of Corinne's abduction. Now she was grown up with a mate and adult children of her own. Corinne should have been happy for her sister; deep down, she was. But the news only drove the point more sharply that time had marched on while Corinne was gone.

Far more painful was the reminder of all the things

she had lost—the precious things that had been taken from her—while Dragos held her imprisoned. Now that she was here, back in her parents' home, she could put all of her energy into reclaiming the pieces of her own broken life.

"I didn't see Sebastian when we came in earlier," she said, recalling the handsome, studious Breed youth who'd been so patient with his adopted sisters. He'd been twenty the year Corinne was abducted. Now he was probably leader of his own Darkhaven, with a beautiful Breedmate and half a dozen sons of his own as well.

The long silence that met her question made Corinne draw in an anxious breath.

Regina Bishop's mouth quivered. "Of course, you wouldn't know. We lost Sebastian to Bloodlust more than forty years ago now."

Corinne closed her eyes. "Oh, God. Not our sweet Sebastian."

"I know, darling." Her mother's voice was small, still rife with grief over her son all these decades later. "Sebastian had changed in the years after you went missing. We knew he was struggling, that his thirst was consuming him, but he withdrew from us. He tried to hide his problems from us, wouldn't accept help. He'd been on a terrible killing spree in the city that night. When he came home, he was covered in blood. None of us could reach him. He was Rogue by then, too far gone to be saved. And he knew it. Sebastian was always so perceptive, so smart and sensitive. He locked himself in your father's study. We heard the gunshot not even a moment later."

"I'm so sorry." Corinne hugged her, feeling the anguish as the other woman stifled a tight sob. "It must have been awful."

"It was." Sorrowful eyes met her gaze as she withdrew from her mother's embrace. "Until you've lost a child—and until tonight, I'd thought I'd lost two—no one can imagine what it's like to feel such hollowness inside."

Corinne said nothing, unsure how to respond. She bore her own emptiness, endured her own loss, even now. It was that loss that had brought her home, even more so than her own selfish needs for comfort and the sheltering arms of her family.

"You must recognize this room, don't you?" her mother asked abruptly, wiping at the corners of her eyes.

Halfheartedly but glad for the momentary distraction, Corinne took in her surroundings. Her glance traveled over the elegant dark cherry sleigh bed and the antique chest and dresser that still looked so familiar to her, despite all these years. The linens and window treatments were different. So were the walls, no longer swathed in yards of shimmering peach silk but painted a soothing matte shade of dove gray. "This used to be my bedroom."

"It still is," Regina replied, a forced brightness in her voice. "We'll put it back exactly as it was before, if that's what you'd like. We can start tomorrow, darling. I'll take you shopping for a new wardrobe in the morning, and we can make an appointment with my decorator to refurnish the whole room, top to bottom. We'll set everything back to rights and it will seem as though you've never been gone a day. Everything can be made exactly the same as it was before, Corinne. You'll see."

Corinne was hardly aware she was shaking her head until she noticed her mother's crestfallen expression. "Nothing can ever be the same. It's all changed now."

"We'll fix it, darling." Her mother nodded as if her certainty alone would make it so. "You're home now, and that's the most important thing. None of the rest matters."

"Yes," Corinne murmured. "It does matter. Things happened to me while I was gone. Terrible things that I need to tell you about. You and Daddy both..."

She hadn't meant to blurt it out like this. Her intent had been to sit both her parents down together and gently walk them through the circumstances of her captivity as best she could. Now she knew there would be no graceful way to convey the truth, as she watched dread creep into Regina Bishop's pretty face.

The two of them could have passed as sisters in public, both of them youthful looking, the process of aging halted near thirty years old. It was the same for all Breedmates, due to their genetic anomalies and the life-giving power found in a Breed male's blood. Corinne was gone seventy-plus years, but she'd hardly aged. She'd been kept alive, deliberately kept young and viable because that's where her value had been to her captor.

Regina Bishop saw this truth now; Corinne watched the realization dawn, as though her mother hadn't really looked at her closely until that very moment. "Tell me," she whispered. "Tell me what happened to you, Corinne. Why would anyone want to hurt you?"

Corinne gave a slow shake of her head. "Why would anyone want to hurt any of the young Breedmates who were captured along with me? Insanity, maybe. Evil, certainly. That's the only way to explain the things he did. The torture and experimentation..."

"Oh, darling," Regina cried, the words lost within a choked intake of breath. "All this time? All these years, you've been made to suffer such things? To what end?"

"We were used for a very specific purpose," Corinne replied, her voice sounding wooden even to her own ears. "The one who took us—the one who locked us in a lightless prison and treated us no better than cattle—needed our bodies to help him grow his own army. We weren't his only captives. He also had another, a creature I'd only heard about in stories Sebastian used to tell Lottie and me to frighten us."

Her mother's face drained of all its color. "What are you saying?"

"There was an Ancient imprisoned in the labs too," she said, speaking past Regina Bishop's recoiled gasp. "Our captor used him for experimentations as well. And he used him for breeding, to father Gen One vampires who'd be raised in service—enslavement, more like it—to the madman who'd controlled all of us."

For a long moment, her mother simply stared, mute and pale. A tear rolled down her cheek as the understanding settled on her fully. "Oh, my dear child . . ."

Corinne cleared her throat. She'd gone this far now; she needed to speak the rest. "I fought every chance I got, but in the end they were stronger. It took a long time, but eventually—thirteen years ago, as best I've been able to guess—they got what they wanted from me." She had to draw a deep breath in order to continue. "While I was in those awful laboratory cells, I gave birth to a son. I have a child out there somewhere. He was stolen from me just hours after he was born. Now that I'm free, I intend to get him back."

Something wasn't right.

As Hunter parked the car in the Order's private hangar at the airport, he kept thinking back to Corinne's reunion with her Darkhaven family. He kept wondering why his predator's instincts were circling back around to Victor Bishop like a hound on a trail that had nearly gone cold.

Nearly, but not quite.

Something about Bishop's reaction toward Corinne's reappearance didn't ring true. The Breed male had seemed shocked, certainly, and obviously moved to see the young woman who'd been dead to all of her kin for such a long time.

As any Darkhaven leader would be, Bishop had been notably concerned about the immediate security of his home and its inhabitants. He'd been cautious and protective, all things to be expected. Yet Hunter had detected something more in Bishop, something that seemed to run deeper than his outward expression of astonishment and relief at Corinne's unexpected homecoming.

There had been a remoteness to Victor Bishop's gaze as he looked at his daughter. There had been a hesitancy to the man, a hint of distraction in his demeanor, even as he'd embraced her and told her what a relief it was to see her again. Victor Bishop was hiding something. He was holding back somehow with Corinne; Hunter was sure of it.

Then again, who was he to judge when it came to any demonstration of emotion?

He had been raised to deal in logic and facts, not feelings. His instincts were honed toward stealth and combat, toward the pursuit and destruction of any given target. In those things, he was expert. And it was those very things that awaited him in Boston—both the pursuit of the Enforcement Agent who'd fled the club in

Chinatown and the rooting out and destruction of Dragos and his untold number of homegrown assassins.

But still . . .

Suspicion nagged Hunter as he got out of the vehicle and strode toward the corporate jet inside the private hangar. Ahead of him, at the lowered steps of the Cessna, one of the pilots came out and greeted him with a polite smile.

"Mr. Smith," murmured the human. He and his co-pilot were part of a discreet charter service kept on permanent retainer by the Order. Hunter knew little about the arrangement, other than that the humans who operated the private jets exclusively for the Order were top of their class and paid a good sum to ask no questions of their typically late-night clientele. "We are cleared for taxi and takeoff as soon as you are ready, Mr. Smith."

Hunter gave a faint nod of acknowledgment, his instincts still prickling as he put his foot on the first step. It was then that the realization hit him.

Something Victor Bishop had said.

What of your abductor? he'd demanded of Corinne.

Good God, please tell me the bastard who stole you from us is dead.

Although neither Corinne nor Hunter had mentioned any details about where she'd been or who had held her, Victor Bishop spoke as if he knew the blame for her capture rested on a single individual.

An individual who had the Darkhaven leader visibly anxious. "Paranoid" was the word that sprang to Hunter's mind when he recalled the hurried orders that sent Bishop's guards in a scramble to batten down the hatches of the estate and to hustle Bishop's mate and Corinne into the mansion. Now that Hunter thought about it, Victor Bishop had been acting like a man on the verge of a coming siege.

The question was, why?

"Is anything wrong, Mr. Smith?"

Hunter didn't answer. He pivoted off the plane's staircase and stalked across the concrete floor of the airport hangar, his boots thumping hard with every long stride. He got back into the car and turned on the engine.

The black sedan roared to life, tires screaming as he punched the gas pedal and headed back to confront Victor Bishop and whatever secret he was hiding.

CHAPTER
Eight

Corinne sat with her mother at the dining room table, watching in a state of quiet distraction as Tilda brought out the last of the serving platters from the Darkhaven's kitchen. The food looked wonderful, smelled even better, but she had no appetite. Her gaze kept straying toward the adjacent foyer just outside the formal dining room, to the closed doors of her father's study.

"I'm sure he'll be finished any moment, darling." Regina smiled at her from the seat at her right. "He wouldn't want us to wait for him and let Tilda's delicious meal go cold."

At the head of the table, her father's chair sat empty. A place had been set for him, but the china and crystal were there only out of tradition; none of the Breed consumed human food or drink. Corinne made no move to begin eating. She stared at the vacant mahogany chair, trying to will Victor Bishop away from his business and out to his place as the provider—the protector—of his family.

"How about we start with some soup," Regina said, lifting the cover from the large silver tureen that sat on the table between them. Aromatic steam wafted up from the deep bowl. She dipped a ladle in, then served the soup to Corinne. "Doesn't it smell delicious? It's a very delicate beef consommé with shallots and wild mushrooms."

Corinne knew her mother was only trying to take care of her, trying to bring some sense of normalcy to a situation that was anything but normal. She watched her bone china bowl fill with savory soup and vegetables and she wanted to scream.

She couldn't eat right now. She couldn't do anything until she'd spoken with her father and heard him assure her that no one—not even a sadistic monster like Dragos—could keep her away from her child. Until she heard those words and was able to believe it was possible to find her son and bring him back, nothing else mattered.

"Maybe I should go talk to him in his study," she said, already scooting her chair out from the table and standing up.

Her mother put her spoon down, fine brows furrowing. "Darling, what's wrong—"

Corinne walked out of the dining room and across the foyer, hands fidgeting anxiously at her sides with each step.

As she neared the closed doors of Victor Bishop's private office, a sharp crash of breaking glass sounded from inside.

"Daddy?" Worry pierced her center. Corinne flattened her palm against the polished wood panels and gave a few raps on the door. They were panicky, hesitant smacks of her hand, a sudden dark fear washing over her. More sounds of struggle emanated from within—a rustle of falling papers, a muffled grunt. "Daddy, is everything okay?"

She tried the latch. Unlocked, thankfully. Her mother and a pair of her father's Darkhaven guards, Mason and another Breed male, were right behind her as she pushed open the door and stepped inside.

To her shock—to her utter confusion and disbelief—Victor Bishop had been tossed supine across the surface of his desk, now choking for breath beneath the crushing grip of the large hand clamped down like a vise on his throat. The person assaulting her father was the very last person Corinne had expected to see ever again.

"Hunter," she whispered, incredulous, terrified.

Her mother shrieked Victor's name, then broke down into a gusting sob.

Behind Corinne, Mason and the other guard shifted warily. She felt their tension, sensed the two Breed males gauging their chances of drawing their weapons and disabling this unforeseen threat. They would never succeed.

Corinne saw the truth of it in Hunter's emotionless face. The look in his golden eyes was a chilling, lethal calm. Corinne saw in an instant that taking a life was something that gave this warrior no pause whatsoever. He had only to tighten his grip, just a cool flex of his strong fingers and he would crush the life from her father in a second's time.

Corinne's worry stabbed her, and in that instant of fright and concern, she felt a current of power stir deep inside her. It was her talent rising quietly, the low hum of sonokinetic energy that would permit her to grasp any sound and manipulate it to deafening heights. It prickled in her now, standing at the ready. But she couldn't risk it. Not with her father's throat caught fast in Hunter's grip.

When Mason inched slightly forward, more willing than she to test Hunter's intent, Corinne held him back with a faint shake of her head.

She was stunned, confused. What was Hunter doing back here at the Darkhaven? She didn't need to wonder how he got inside. The heavy drapery on the French doors of the study riffled in the wintry breeze coming in from outside. He had entered stealthily, an intruder with a single purpose—a single target—in mind.

"Why?" she murmured. "Hunter, what's this about?"

"Tell her." He turned that merciless gaze back onto her father. Victor Bishop sputtered, tried to claw at the unyielding grasp at his throat, but it was useless. His muscles slumped and his head fell back onto the desk with a spittle-laced, hopeless-sounding moan. Hunter barely blinked. "Speak the truth, or I will kill you right here and now."

Corinne's pulse was ticking in her temples, fear twisting her insides. She didn't know what sparked the greater worry—the lethal threat to the Breed male who'd raised her, or the dread that was gnawing at the edges of her mind as she looked at Hunter and recognized that he was not a male to act rashly.

No, he was nothing if not deliberate. She hadn't known him very long, but Hunter carried himself with a cool, capable reserve that left no room for irrationality or mistakes.

The fact that her father was in the crosshairs of this warrior's wrath put a knot in Corinne's gut. She had the deep, instinctual awareness that her world was about to crack open in front of her. She didn't think she could bear that, not after all she'd been through. Not after all she'd survived.

"No," she said, wanting to deny the feeling that was swamping her now. She clung to that denial, even though it felt as breakable as a thread in her grasp. "Please, Hunter . . . don't do this. Please, let him go."

He cocked his head toward her slightly as she spoke. Something peculiar flashed through his gaze, a flicker of distraction. Perhaps a moment of doubt? But he made no move to release her father. Then his brows lowered into the faintest frown. "He knows what happened to you the night you disappeared. He's known all along that you'd been taken, and by whom. He knows much more than that."

"No. That's impossible." Her voice sounded so small, little more than air pushing out of her lungs. She felt the thread of denial begin to fray in her grasp. "You're wrong about this, Hunter. You're making a terrible mistake. Daddy, please . . . tell him he's wrong."

Victor Bishop seemed to deflate even more in that instant. He was sweating, quivering, reduced to a state of weak surrender under Hunter's unrelenting power. The handsome face that used to instill such comfort in Corinne as a child now sagged, ruddy and glistening with beads of perspiration. His eyes met hers then, and he sputtered something that sounded like a weak apology.

Corinne went numb, feeling all the blood drain from her head and limbs. The weight settled in her feet, nearly dragging her down to her knees. The air around Mason and the other guard went palpably tense, both males waiting for the situation to either explode or dissolve.

Beside her, Corinne felt her mother's body tremble, as off balance as she was.

"Victor, you couldn't have known any such things," Regina insisted. Her pale hand hovered near her mouth, as delicate as a bird until it fell away, drifting back down at her side. "You mourned this girl when she disappeared. You were shattered, like the rest of us. You could not have pretended those feelings. I'm blood-bonded to you as your mate—I would have known whether you'd been sincere."

"Yes," he managed to croak. Corinne watched the tendons in Hunter's large hand ease up, but only enough to permit the smallest freedom. Victor Bishop was still trapped, still wholly at the warrior's mercy. "Yes, Regina, I mourned. I was shattered that she was gone. I would have protected my family by any means. That's what I did, in fact. I was only trying to protect what was left of my family, and so I had no choice but to remain silent."

Corinne closed her eyes as the words sank in, unexpected and bitter. She couldn't speak, could only lift her lids and hold the steady golden gaze of the warrior whose face revealed neither surprise nor pity. Only a grave understanding.

"I had no choice," Victor Bishop repeated. "I had no idea he would retaliate against me the way he did. You must believe me—"

"Victor," her mother gasped. "What are you saying?"

His eyes slid away from Corinne, toward the Breedmate who'd been part of his life for the last hundred-plus years. "He said he would have my support one way or another, Regina. I thought I was smarter than him. I knew I was more connected. But you see? That's what he wanted from me—my connections. He needed my endorsement to help him rise more quickly within the Agency."

Still poised to kill at his whim, Hunter issued a low growl as Corinne's father let his ugly confession spill out.

No, she corrected internally. Victor Bishop was not her father. Not anymore. He was a stranger to her, had become so more in these last minutes than he had in the many decades she'd been gone from his home.

"There were threats when I refused to join his cause," Bishop said, despair roughening the words. "I didn't realize what he was capable of at the time. My God, how could I have known what he would be willing to do?"

"Who was it that threatened you, Victor?" his Breedmate asked, the waver fading from both her voice and her demeanor. "Who stole our daughter from us?"

"Gerard Starkn."

"Director Starkn?" Regina murmured. "He's been to this house more than a dozen times over the years. He's been here before and after Corinne went missing. Good lord, Victor, it has to be fifty years ago now, but I remember you spoke at his reception when he was elected to the Enforcement Agency's high council. Are you saying that he had something to do with this?"

Corinne frowned, confused now. The unfamiliar name bred a wild, desperate hope. Maybe there was some kind of mistake here, after all. If he didn't know that it was Dragos who'd taken her, maybe Victor Bishop's hands weren't as bloodied as she feared.

But Hunter's grim glance stripped her of even that fragile hope. He gave a vague shake of his head, as if he knew the direction of her thoughts. "Dragos has used many aliases. Including this one. Gerard Starkn and Dragos are one and the same."

Corinne looked to Victor Bishop, searching for some shred of honesty in the face she no longer knew. "Did you know that? Were you aware that the man you called Gerard Starkn was actually a monster by the name of Dragos?"

His scowl deepened, eyes blank of recognition. "I've told you everything I know."

"No," she murmured. "You haven't told me everything. You knew what had happened to me, but you didn't come after me. I waited. I prayed, every day. I told myself that you wouldn't rest until I was found. Until I was saved, and back home again. But no one ever came for me."

"I couldn't," he said. "Starkn told me that if I went against him, there would be more pain. He said that if I wavered in my support of him politically, or if I tried to expose him for what he'd done to reach his position within the Agency, the price for my defiance would be far greater than what I'd already paid. You have to understand—all of you have to understand—that I did what I did in order to protect my family, what was left of it."

Regina drew in a sharp, shaky breath. "And so you simply let him keep our daughter? Corinne was family— she *is* family, damn you. How could you have been so heartless?"

"He left me no other way," Bishop answered, those stranger's eyes sliding back to Corinne. "Starkn promised that if I attempted to find you, or if I allowed anyone to suspect that he had you, I would be mourning Sebastian next. So I kept my silence. I made sure his demands were obeyed." His voice caught for a moment. "I am sorry, Corinne. You have to believe that—"

"I can never believe anything you say again," she replied, wounded, yes, but not about to break.

She'd been through worse than this. She was battered and weary from the weight of his betrayal, but there was still a long, dark road ahead of her.

As she stood there, trying to reconcile everything she was hearing, a fresh horror began to settle over her. "The girl," she said, new pieces falling into place in the puzzle of his deception. "After I had been taken, there was a girl recovered from the river . . ."

Victor Bishop held her appalled stare. "You were gone, and Starkn made it clear that you were never coming back. As long as there were questions about your disappearance . . . as long as there was hope that you might be alive—"

The truth settled over her like lead, cold and heavy. "You were the one who wanted everyone convinced I was dead. Oh, Jesus . . . you had an innocent girl killed. You had her cut in pieces, just to cover your own sins."

"She was nothing," Bishop countered as though to justify the murder. An angry edge crept into his voice as he went on. "She was common gutter trash, selling herself down by the waterfront."

"And what about me?" Corinne asked, her own outrage rising. It spilled out of her in a furious rush. "I must have been nothing to you too. You let him take me away, keep me all this time like an animal in a cage. Worse than that. Did you never wonder what was happening to me at his hands? Did you ever stop to think that he could have been torturing me, degrading me . . . destroying everything I was, bit by bit? Did you never imagine the kind of torture a sadistic lunatic like him might be capable of in the bowels of the prison where he held me and all the other captives he'd collected?"

Regina Bishop dissolved into a wracking fit of tears. Bishop said nothing, merely stared at Corinne and his mate in unaffected silence. "Let me up," he growled to Hunter, whose fingers had gone tight once more around his throat. "I said unhand me. You must be satisfied now. You have the confession you came here to wring out of me."

Hunter leaned over him. "Now you're going to tell me everything you know about Gerard Starkn. I need to know where he is and when you last saw him. I need to know who his associates are, both inside the Agency and outside of it. You'll tell me every detail, and you will tell me now."

"I don't know anything else," Bishop sputtered sharply. "It's been more than a decade since I've even thought of the man, let alone seen him. There is nothing more for me to tell, I swear to you."

But Hunter didn't look convinced. Nor did he seem inclined to release Bishop from his killing grasp, not even if he was given the answers he sought. Corinne could see the truth of Hunter's lethal intent in the steady calm of his eyes.

Bishop realized it too. He started to squirm and struggle. He bucked on the surface of his desk, kicking his legs and sending a stack of leather-bound books toppling to the floor.

Corinne's talent, humming more intensely in her veins now, latched out to grab hold of the percussion those falling books had caused. She couldn't hold it back. The noise swelled swiftly, exploding into a prolonged roll of thunder that quaked the room and rattled everything in it.

"Corinne, stop!" her mother cried, covering her ears as the racket shook and rumbled, louder and louder now.

Under the rising din, Bishop's lips peeled back from his teeth, baring the tips of his emerging fangs. Anger and fear transformed his eyes from their normal brown to the fiery amber of the Breed. His pupils thinned and stretched, becoming catlike slits.

Hunter, however, remained cool, utterly in control. He spared Corinne's burst of kinetic power only the briefest acknowledgment before seeming to tune out the distraction completely. His eyes held their golden hue, his sharply angled face taut and lean, focused but not furious. He drew his fingers tighter around Bishop's larynx.

Corinne parted her lips, panting and spent. She willed her talent to subside and was on the verge of screaming for all this madness to cease.

But it was Regina who spoke first.

"Henry Vachon," she blurted. Victor snarled, and it was difficult to tell if his anger now was directed more at his punisher or his rattled Breedmate. Regina looked away from him, lifting her chin and speaking directly to Hunter. "I remember another Breed male, also from the Enforcement Agency. He was at Starkn's side almost constantly whenever I saw him in public. His name was Henry Vachon. He was from the South somewhere... New Orleans, as I recall. If you want to find Gerard Starkn—or whatever he calls himself now—start with Henry Vachon."

Hunter inclined his head in a vague nod of acknowledgment, but he still had his hand on Bishop's throat.

"Release him," Corinne murmured quietly. She was sickened by all she'd heard, but she had no vengeance in her heart. Not even for the father who had betrayed her so callously. "Please, Hunter...let him go."

He gave her the same odd look he had earlier, the first time she'd asked him not to harm Victor Bishop. Corinne couldn't read the strange flicker that dimmed the gold of his eyes. It was a question, a silent pause of uncertainty, or expectation.

"He's not worth it," she said. "Let him live with what he's done. He no longer exists to me."

As Hunter loosened his grasp, Bishop rolled away to the floor, coughing and sputtering. Regina's kind face was stricken, red from crying. She started sobbing again now, apologizing to Corinne, begging forgiveness for what Victor had done. She tried to pull Corinne into her arms, but the thought of being touched—by anyone now—was too much for her to bear.

Corinne backed away. She felt trapped in the room, suffocating in the confines of the Darkhaven that was no longer her home and could never be again. The walls seemed to press inward on her, the floors shifting, making her stomach churn and her head spin.

She had to get out of there.

Mason held out his hand to brace her as she took an awkward step toward the study's open doors. She dodged his reach, avoiding his comforting hand and pitying eyes.

"I need air," she whispered, panting with the effort to form words. "I can't...I need to get...out of here."

And then she was running.

Through the foyer of the big house and out to the long driveway. Somewhere nearby, she heard the bright melody of Christmas music, joyous carols spilling out into the night. A soul-deep bereavement raked Corinne from within. She sucked in the cold air, rapid breaths sawing in and out of her lungs as she ran the length of the snow-edged drive.

CHAPTER
Nine

Corinne was all the way to the closed gate at the street when Hunter left Victor Bishop to the wreckage of his sins and stepped out of the Darkhaven, onto the frozen lawn. She looked very small, fragile somehow, despite the strength she'd shown inside the house. Now that she was out here, alone in the darkness, he realized just how wounded she truly was. Her body shuddered, weathering a pain he could only guess at as she clung to the black iron of the gate, shoulders slumped, head bowed low.

She wept softly as he approached. Her breath puffed in pale clouds into the darkness. Her sobs were quiet but seemed to come from a place very deep within her. He didn't know what to say as he drew nearer to her. He didn't have any words of comfort, wouldn't have the first idea what she might want to hear.

He reached out his hand, intending to place it on her quivering shoulder the way he'd seen others do in shared moments of distress. Inexplicably, he felt an urge to acknowledge her pain. She looked so alone in that moment, he wanted to show her that he recognized she'd just lost something important to her back in that house: her trust.

She noticed his presence before he had the chance to touch her.

Sniffling, she lifted her head and looked at him over her shoulder. "Did you . . . do anything to him?"

Hunter gave a slow shake of his head. "He lives, although I don't understand why you would find his death so unacceptable."

Her fine brows bunched into a frown. "He loved me once. Until a few minutes ago, he was my father. How could he have done this to me?"

Hunter stared into her fierce eyes, understanding that she wasn't looking for answers from him. She had to know, as he did, that Victor Bishop's cowardice had proven stronger than his bond to the child he'd taken in and raised as his daughter.

Corinne glanced past him, into the darkness beyond his shoulder. "How could he have lived with himself all this time, knowing what he'd done—not only to me, but to the rest of the family through the lies he told? How could he have slept after murdering that girl and using her death as part of his deception?"

"He is not deserving of the mercy you gave him tonight," Hunter replied, no malice in the statement, only a bleak truth. "I doubt he would have given you the same consideration."

"I don't want him dead," she whispered. "I couldn't do that to my mother—to Regina. He'll have to find a way to answer to her, not me. And not you or the Order either."

Hunter grunted low in his throat, less than convinced. The chief reason Victor Bishop was still breathing was the plea from his betrayed daughter. Hunter had been taken aback when she'd asked him to spare the man. He shouldn't have been. Mira's vision had predicted it, after all.

Yet not as flawlessly as he would have guessed. The situation had seemed different. Corinne had seemed different, pleading not with the impassioned desperation he'd witnessed in Mira's vision but a defeated weariness.

And not just that, Hunter reflected. The outcome of the vision had been different than the child seer had shown him. He'd stayed his hand. The course had been altered, and that had never happened before.

It felt wrong, all of it.

Part of him was being drawn back toward the Darkhaven residence even as he stood there. He'd been trained never to leave loose ends that could unravel on him later. Hunter had witnessed a broken man, someone who'd been proven pliable and weak. Those things could be manipulated by someone stronger, as they had been by Dragos all those years ago. While tonight Victor Bishop had seemed an adversary of little consequence, despite his wealth and any remaining political connections, the experienced predator in Hunter twitched with the need to finish his job.

Knowing what he did of little Mira and her extraordinary gift, he wondered how it was even possible that he'd not defied Corinne's pleas and delivered that final, preordained blow.

He saw her tremble in front of him as a chilling gust blew through the iron of the secured gate.

"I need to get out of here," she murmured, pivoting

toward the tall bars. "I don't belong here. Not anymore."

She grabbed hold of the gate in both hands and rattled it, harder and harder, a wordless cry erupting from deep within her throat. She threw her head back and railed at the star-pierced, black sky. "Let me out, goddamn it! I need to get away from this place right now!"

Hunter moved in behind her and placed his hands on top of hers. She stilled, every muscle within her going tense and motionless. Even though she had been shivering, her body felt warm against his chest. The heat was a living thing, an almost unbearable presence that made all of his senses fire up like awakened circuitry.

Corinne must have felt it too. She pulled her hands out from under his and folded her arms in front of her. He realized now how close they were, barely an inch to separate her spine from his chest and torso, her petite body caught before him in the cage of his arms.

She was so small and delicate, yet there was a defiant energy that radiated around her. It drew him closer, enticed him to breathe her in, to let his touch return to the impossibly soft tops of her small hands, and to test the silken warmth of her long dark hair against his stubbled cheek.

He wasn't accustomed to acknowledging temptation, let alone giving in to it. And so he held himself still in that bewildering moment, ignoring the sudden quickening of his pulse and the heat that kindled in his veins.

When she withdrew and ducked away, Hunter felt a swift relief. Cold air filled the space between his arms. Corinne stood to his side as he moved in closer to the locked seam of the iron gate and wrenched it open wide enough for them to slip out.

Alarms immediately went off back at the house.

Floodlights blinked on from all over, spilling illumination along the Darkhaven's entrance and perimeter walls.

Corinne looked at him under the pale yellow wash of the security lights. "Get me out of here. I don't care where we go, just get me away from this place, Hunter."

He gave her a grim nod, then motioned for her to follow him to the car he'd left parked down the street when he'd returned to confront Bishop. They ran together, Corinne jumping into the passenger seat as Hunter went around to take the wheel.

He drove off, taking note of the fact that she didn't look back even once as they left the Darkhaven behind them in the darkness. She sat rigidly in the seat next to him, her gaze distant, staring out the windshield but focused on nothing at all.

They rode in silence for more than twenty minutes, until he had navigated to a quiet part of the city and found a place to pull over. "I must report in to the compound," he said, retrieving his cell phone from the pocket of his leather trench coat.

Corinne barely acknowledged him, her vacant eyes still fixed on the far horizon.

Hunter called in, expecting to hear Gideon's typical rote greeting of "Talk to me." Instead it was Lucan who answered. "Where are you?"

"Delayed in Detroit," Hunter replied, detecting a note of urgency—of tense impatience—in the Order's leader. "Something is wrong," he guessed aloud. "Have there been developments concerning Dragos?"

Lucan muttered a dark curse. "Yeah, you could say that. We just found out he knows the compound's location. We assume he knows, that is. A few hours ago,

Kellan Archer upchucked a tracking device. Gideon's analyzing it as we speak."

"The kidnapping was a ploy," Hunter said, putting the pieces together. It made logical sense now, the unprovoked attack on the civilians that had taken place over the course of the last week. "Dragos had to ensure the Order was sympathetic to the boy, so he killed his family and razed their Darkhaven. The youth needed to be isolated, leaving little choice but for the Order to take him into its protection."

"We walked right into it," Lucan remarked tightly. "I made the decision to break with protocol and bring the boy into the compound. Hell, I might as well have opened the goddamn door to Dragos and invited him inside."

Hunter had never heard regret from Lucan. If the Gen One elder ever had doubts, he'd not aired them to Hunter before now. That he did so only emphasized the seriousness of the situation. "I know how Dragos operates," Hunter said. "I've seen the way he thinks, how he strategizes. The Archer youth has been in the compound for more than a couple of days—"

"Seventy-two hours," Lucan interjected.

Hunter had felt Corinne's gaze on him with the mention of Dragos's name. She listened quietly now, her pretty face stricken, bathed in greenish light from the dashboard of the idling sedan. Hunter could feel her dread like a chill as he continued speaking with Lucan. "Dragos had to know the device could not go undetected for very long. He will have already begun organizing for an attack, even before he put his ruse into motion. When he attacks, he will come at the compound in a way that will ensure the greatest damage to the Order."

"He's out for blood," Lucan replied. "My blood."

"Yes." Hunter knew from his time serving the power-crazed Dragos that this battle between him and the Order had turned into something personal. Dragos would seek to annihilate the obstacle standing in the way of his goals, but his rage would compel him to do it in a way that would inflict the deepest pain on Lucan Thorne and those under his charge.

The Boston compound was safe for no one now, but there was no need for Hunter to say it. Lucan knew. His sober voice reverberated with the gravity of the situation, but his heavy silence was even more telling.

"There have been complications with my mission in Detroit," Hunter told him, a report that was answered with a deep, ripe curse. He gave Lucan a rundown of what had happened at the Darkhaven with Corinne and her family, from the suspicion he had that Victor Bishop was hiding something, to the revelation that had left Corinne's future in limbo but had netted the Order what could possibly be a lead on one of Dragos's past associates.

"Henry Vachon," Lucan said, testing the name Regina Bishop had given them. "I don't know him, but I'm sure Gideon can track the bastard down. I'm sure I don't need to tell you how important it is for us to exploit any lead on Dragos that we can."

"Of course," Hunter agreed.

"I'll have Gideon run an IID search for Vachon and get back to you with what we find. You should have intel within the hour," Lucan said. "What about Corinne? Is she still with you?"

"Yes," Hunter replied, glancing at her as he spoke. "She is with me in the car right now."

Lucan grunted. "Good. I want you to keep her close.

As long as we're in chaos here at the compound, it's not a good idea for either one of you to come back right now."

Hunter scowled, still looking at Corinne's questioning face. "You're putting the female in my custody?"

"For the time being, I can't think of anywhere safer for her to be."

Despite the bad news that had hit the Order earlier that night, Lucan hadn't called off any of the assigned patrols. If anything, the mood around the compound had been stepped up a notch.

Or twenty.

To Dante, it seemed as though the countdown clock on a time bomb had been activated in that instant Kellan Archer had coughed up Dragos's tracking device. Everyone understood what it meant, and the anticipation of trouble on the horizon—the expectation of it slamming into them at any moment—had left no one unscathed.

But dread and inaction wouldn't stop the coming storm. They had to get more aggressive, plumb every corner, turn every stone, if it meant bringing them even one inch closer to getting their hands on Dragos. He had to be located, and he had to be stopped—now more than ever.

That rationale, and the fury that followed on its heels, was the only thing that had given Dante the strength to leave Tess's side and go out on patrol with Kade that night.

His heart was back at the compound, but his head was fully in the game, looking for even the most remote leads on the escaped Agent, Murdock, the presence of Dragos's assassins in the city . . . anything at all.

And all night, part of him had been keeping an eye out for leads of another sort too.

"Hold up," he said to Kade, who'd just turned the Rover onto a seedy stretch of road down by the Mystic in Southie. "Did you see that guy over there?"

Kade slowed the black SUV and peered in the direction Dante was pointing. "I don't see anyone, other than a couple of overaged streetwalkers with a fondness for Lucite heels and Forever Twenty-One fashion. Classy."

Dante was unable to share the other warrior's humor even though he had a valid point about the hookers trawling the corner at the other end of the block.

"I think it might have been Harvard," he said, all but certain that the large shadowy figure that had disappeared around the other side of an old brick warehouse had been Breed. And by the way the male moved, the way he carried himself, even as he slunk into the gloom of the ratty industrial block, Dante was more than willing to bet it was Sterling Chase. "Stop the car."

"Even if it was Harvard, I don't think this is a good idea, man—"

"Fuck what you think," Dante snapped, concern for his AWOL friend trumping everything else. "Pull over, Kade. I'm getting out."

He didn't wait for the vehicle to cease rolling. He jumped out and started jogging toward the place he'd watched the vampire go. Kade was right behind him, cursing low under his breath, but prepared to have his back regardless.

They rounded the edge of the brick warehouse and found themselves staring at a low-rent rail yard just ahead. A line of orphaned boxcars sat on one set of tracks, the side of one rusted, graffiti-tagged car wedged open just wide enough for someone to squeeze past. A group of humans stood nearby, gathered around a metal drum that glowed and sparked from the rubbish burning deep inside it. They warmed their hands over the container, passing a small crack pipe to one another.

The stoners hardly looked up as Dante and Kade strode past them. Their faces were hollow, ghostly. They stank of narcotics, booze, and rotted clothing. Their hair was filthy, bodies ripe with the stench of the unwashed. Glazed eyes stared off unfocused, their minds decayed, lost to the seductive grasp of their addictions.

"Jesus Christ," Kade hissed, disgusted. "If Chase is slumming around down here in this shithole, he must really be fucked up."

Unable to deny the truth in that statement, Dante felt his jaw tighten to the point of pain. Chase *was* fucked up. He knew it as soon as he'd heard what happened in the chapel with Elise. The fact that he had skipped out on the Order was just another nail in a coffin of his own making.

But Dante wasn't ready to give up on him.

He had to believe that Harvard wasn't lost completely. Maybe if he could find him, talk some sense into him. Give him a wake-up call about the shit that had gone down at the compound a few hours ago and let him know that he was needed.

And if all those options failed, Dante was ready and willing to kick Harvard's self-destructive ass from now into next week.

"He went this way," Dante said. "He's got to be back here somewhere."

Kade lifted his chin, gesturing toward the open railcar. Dante nodded. It was about the only place Chase could be hiding, although Dante knew as well as anyone else in the Order that if Chase didn't want to be found, his talent for bending shadows would prove effective cover no matter where he'd gone.

Together, he and Kade approached the car. Dante walked up to the gap of darkness that spilled into the big metal box. The fetid stench of more forsaken humans wafted out at him as he hoisted himself up and took a quick look around the gloom of the place. His vision was flawless in the dark, as with all of his kind. He saw no sign of Chase among the sleeping men and women, nor with the small number that huddled under a shared blanket, staring up at him with vacant looks.

Chase wasn't there, not even in the deepest reaches of the shadows.

"Harvard," he said, trying to reach out to him anyway. Maybe if he heard a familiar voice . . .

Nothing but silence.

He waited for a moment, a part of him saddened by the wasted lives that littered the dirty interior of the railcar and the ones smoking their wits away over the barrel of burning trash. They were strangers, humans, born to live and die in the span of less than a century. But in their lost, hopeless expressions, he saw his friend Sterling Chase.

Was this what lay ahead for Harvard if no one stopped his downward spiral? He didn't want to go there, didn't want to imagine that Harvard might be waging a war with demons of his own. He didn't want to believe that Tegan and Lucan could be right—that Chase might be falling into a blood addiction. There was no worse fate for one of the Breed than succumbing to Bloodlust and turning Rogue.

And once lost, there was hardly any hope of coming back to sanity.

"Goddamn him," he ground out between gritted teeth.

He dropped down from the railcar onto the frozen ground near the tracks. As he landed, he felt the knock of his cell phone shifting in his coat pocket.

He pulled it out and hit the speed dial before he could spit out an explanation to Kade. "His cell," he said, hearing the first ring begin on the other end of the line. "If Harvard did run this way, then maybe he's got his cell on—"

The words cut short as a soft trill sounded from several dozen yards away.

Kade's silver eyes glittered under his raised black brows. "Gotcha, Harvard."

They set off at a dead run, both of them hoofing it across the rail yard toward the muffled ringing ahead.

Dante didn't want to hope, a cold edge of dread warning him that even if he did find Harvard, he might not like what waited at the other end of the bleating line. With tempered expectation, he led Kade away from the rails and between a pair of sorry-looking storage buildings. He had to disconnect abruptly, cursing when the phone went into voicemail. He speed-dialed again and the ringing sounded even closer.

Holy hell, they were practically on top of him now.

There was no one around. Not a soul, not even the humans.

He and Kade ran farther, faster, until the bleating of Chase's phone was playing in stereo against his ear and from somewhere very close by.

"Over here," Kade said, dropping into a squat near a pile of frozen tarps and cast-off plastic sheeting. He dug into the heap, tossing the shit everywhere as he burrowed toward the bottom.

When he slowed down and issued a curse, Dante knew they'd reached a dead end.

Kade held up the cell phone, his face drawn with disappointment but not surprise. "He ditched us, man. He was here, like you said. But he didn't want to be found."

"Harvard!" Dante shouted, more pissed off than anything else in that moment. Worry had his gut twisted, his heart hammering in his chest. He sent his rage in all directions around him, pivoting to scan the area, futile or not. "Chase, goddamn it, I know you're here. Say something!"

Kade clicked off the ringer and slid the phone into his pocket. "Come on, let's get out of here. Harvard's gone."

Dante nodded mutely. Last night, Sterling Chase had walked out on the Order after numerous fuck-ups and excuses. Now he'd ditched the closest friend he had among the warriors. He was turning his back on all of his brethren, and based on what happened here tonight, Dante had to admit that Chase was doing so deliberately.

The Harvard he'd known would never have done that.

Kade was right.

Harvard was gone, probably for good.

CHAPTER
Ten

Hunter hadn't spoken two words to her in the time between his phone call to the Order and his driving back to the airport outside Detroit. Not that Corinne had been looking for conversation. Her head was still reeling from what had occurred at the Darkhaven, her heart still raw, rent open like a gash in the center of her being.

She had come home looking for her family and found betrayal instead. Even more painful, her hopes of having Victor Bishop's power and resources rallied toward finding her lost little boy were now completed dashed.

Who was she supposed to trust now, when the only family she'd ever known had knowingly abandoned her to a monster?

Despair clogged her throat as she sat in the dark cabin of the vehicle, mindlessly watching the passing, moonlit scenery as Hunter navigated the maze of the airport's private access roads, heading toward a complex of domed hangars adjacent to the public terminal and runways.

Corinne couldn't stop thinking about her child, the precious infant Dragos had stolen from out of her arms just moments after she'd given birth. He would be a growing boy now—an adolescent who'd never known his mother.

Helpless as one of Dragos's prisoners, she'd had no calendars, no clocks, not even the most meager comforts. She had counted her son's years the only way she could: in nine-month increments, marking the passage of time by observing the pregnancies of other captive Breedmates. Thirteen birth cycles from the time she'd held her newborn baby boy and the day of her rescue just last week.

Despite the circumstances of his horrific conception, Corinne had loved her baby deeply from the instant she saw him. He was hers, a vital part of who she was, no matter how savagely he'd come into this world. She recalled the anguish of missing him. She felt that still, the sorrow of knowing in her bones that he was alive but uncertain where he'd been taken or what had become of him.

It gnawed at her even now. She weathered the fresh sense of mourning as Hunter parked inside an unmarked hangar where the sleek white private jet waited. He took out his cell phone and made a call. His deep, low voice seemed like nothing more than background noise—a deep, oddly comforting rumble. Just the sound of him speaking, strong and calm, a confident presence, so effortlessly in control of everything around him, somehow made the swelling tides of her memories seem more navigable.

She let it anchor her as the waves of painful memories—

of her failure to hold her baby close and keep him safe—continued to swamp her.

If her disastrous reunion tonight had given her anything to hold on to, it was the resolve that had become like iron now that she understood how brutal abandonment could feel. She would not forsake her child. She would walk through the fires of hell itself to find him. Not even Dragos and his evil would keep her from reuniting with her son. She would let nothing—and no one—stand in her way.

Hunter was ending his brief phone conversation, she noticed. He disconnected the call, then tucked the tiny device back into his coat pocket.

She glanced over and their eyes met across the dimly lit interior of the car. "Is everything all right with your friends in Boston?"

Although he hadn't confided in her about his first call to the Order's compound that night, Corinne had heard enough on his end of the conversation to know that something bad had happened while Hunter had been with her. She'd heard Dragos's name and the mention of a young Darkhaven boy whose family and home had recently been lost to Dragos's violence. From the little bit she'd gathered, and from Hunter's elusive, almost forbidding, expression right now, it seemed pretty clear that Dragos had somehow managed to gain the upper hand.

"Are they in terrible danger, Hunter?"

"We are in the midst of war," he answered, his maddeningly calm voice sounding more bleak than apathetic. "Until Dragos is dead, everyone is in terrible danger."

He wasn't speaking only about the residents of the Order's compound. Not even the warriors and the Breed nation combined. The war Hunter referred to encompassed something much larger than that. He was speaking of Dragos's threat to the world in total.

If anyone else had said such a thing, she might have chalked it up to dramatics. But this was Hunter. Exaggeration wasn't a part of his personal lexicon. He was factual and concise. He was exact with both his words and his deeds, and that only made the weight of his statement settle all the more heavily on her.

Corinne sat back, unable to hold his piercing golden stare. She swiveled her head and looked out the tinted passenger-side window of the car, watching the side of the small jet open to allow the stairs to fold out and descend to the concrete floor of the hangar.

"Are you sending me back to Boston?"

"No." Hunter turned off the car's engine. "I'm not sending you anywhere. You are to stay with me for the time being. Lucan has charged me with your temporary safekeeping."

She glanced away from the waiting aircraft and ventured another look at her remote companion. She wanted to argue that she didn't need anyone's safekeeping, not when she'd just tasted freedom, bitter as that taste had been so far. But his announcement raised a bigger question. "If we're not going to Boston, then where is that plane headed?"

"New Orleans," he replied. "Gideon has been able to substantiate Regina Bishop's recollection of Henry Vachon. He owns several properties in the New Orleans area and is presumed to reside there. As of this moment, Vachon is our most viable link to Dragos."

Corinne's heart thumped hard in her chest. Henry Vachon was the Order's best link to Dragos...which meant he was also *her* best link to Dragos. Perhaps the only link she had to finding out what had happened to her son.

As much as she wanted to reject the idea of being leashed to Hunter or to anyone else, a larger part of her understood that she had few options and even fewer resources at her disposal. If hitching her wagon to Hunter would bring her closer to Henry Vachon and any information regarding her child, she had to do it. Anything for her child.

"What will you do," she asked, "if you are able to find Vachon?"

"My mission is simple: Determine his connection to Dragos and extract any useful intelligence I can. Then neutralize the target to disable any potential future fallout."

"You mean you intend to kill him," Corinne said, not a question but a grim understanding.

Hunter's stark eyes showed no waver whatsoever. "If I determine that Vachon does in fact have an allegiance to Dragos—past or present—he must be eliminated."

She felt herself nodding faintly, but inside she was unsure what to think. She couldn't feel pity for Henry Vachon if he had anything to do with her ordeal, but another part of her wondered how Hunter's brutal occupation must impact the one who dealt so frequently in death.

"Does it ever bother you, the things you have to do?" She spoke the question before she'd had a chance to decide if it was her place to ask it or not. Before she'd had the time to worry whether or not she wanted to know the answer. "Does life truly mean so little to you?"

Hunter's harsh, handsome face didn't flinch. The angles of his high cheekbones and square-cut jaw were rigid, as unforgiving as sharp-edged steel. Only his mouth seemed soft, full lips held with neither a scowl nor a smirk, only placid, maddening neutrality.

But it was his eyes that held her the most transfixed. Beneath the crown of his close-cropped blond hair, his eyes were penetrating, probing. As sharply as they bore into her, however, they seemed even more determined to reveal nothing of themselves no matter how deeply she searched.

"I deal in death," he answered then, no apology or excuse. "It is a role I was born into, one I was trained to do very well."

"And you never doubt?" She couldn't help pressing, needing to know. Wanting to understand this formidable Breed male who seemed so solitary and alone. "You never question what you do—not ever?"

Something dark flashed across his face in that instant. There was a flicker of evasion in his eyes, she thought. Brief but impossible to miss, and shuttered a second later by the downward sweep of his lashes as he palmed the car keys and dropped them into the center console of the vehicle.

"No," he answered finally. "I don't question anything my duties require me to do. Not ever."

He opened the driver-side door and began to step out of the vehicle. "The plane is ready for us. We must go now, while the night is still on our side."

"They're on the way to New Orleans now."

Lucan glanced up as Gideon ended his call with Hunter and came back to the tech lab's conference table where Tegan and he stood, poring over a set of unrolled blueprints. "No further issues with Corinne Bishop or her kin in Detroit?"

"Hunter didn't seem to be concerned," Gideon replied. "Said he had the situation under control."

Lucan grunted, wry despite the weight of the discussion previously under way. "Where've I heard that line before? Famous last words from more than one of us over the course of the past year and a half."

"Yup." Gideon cocked a brow over the rims of his pale blue shades. "Usually followed not long afterward by a call from the field that the situation so assuredly under control has gone suddenly and totally FUBAR."

Lucan himself wasn't above blame on that score, nor was Tegan or Gideon, for that matter. Still, this was Hunter they were talking about.

Tegan seemed to pick up on his line of thinking. "If I hadn't seen that male come back bleeding on occasion from some of his nastier missions, I'd say he was made of steel and cables, not muscle and bone. He's a machine, that one. He doesn't fuck up—it's not in his DNA. There won't be any surprises from Hunter."

"There better not be," Lucan replied. "We've sure as hell got our hands full enough as it is."

With that, the three of them turned their attention back to the plans Lucan had spread out on the table. The blueprints were something he'd been working on privately for the past few months, soon after he began to realize how vulnerable the compound was becoming the longer Dragos eluded the Order's grasp.

It was the design for an all-new headquarters.

He'd already procured the land—a two-hundred-acre tract in Vermont's Green Mountains—and the plans were nearly complete for a sprawling, high-security, state-of-the-art bunker that could house a small town in its many underground chambers and specially designed facilities. It was immense, incredible, exactly the kind of place the Order needed now that Dragos knew the compound's location.

The only problem was, a facility of that size and scope was easily a year or more out of reach.

They needed something today, not down the road.

"Maybe we need to think about splitting up," Gideon suggested after a while. "None of us is without money or holdings of our own. I mean, none of our properties are as secure as this compound is—rather, as secure as it was. But we're not without options. Maybe the smartest, fastest thing would be for each of us to take our mate and move to other locations."

Tegan's green eyes glittered darkly as he slid a grave look at Lucan. There was no need to ask what the other Gen One warrior was thinking. Lucan and he, although historically not always on the best of terms, were the last of the Order's founding members. For some seven centuries—since the Order's inception—they'd fought side by side, lived through numerous personal hells and triumphs. They had killed for each other, bled for each other . . . sometimes even wept for each other. Only to arrive at this place together.

Together, not divided.

Lucan saw a raw, medieval ferocity in Tegan's gaze now. He understood it. He felt it too.

"The Order will not splinter," Lucan replied, terse with fury for what Dragos was forcing them to consider. "We are warriors. Brethren. We are kin. We will not let anyone scatter us in terror."

Gideon nodded, solemn and silent. "Yeah," he said, meeting their gazes. "Fuck me, right? Total crap idea. I don't know what the hell I was thinking."

They shared a tense chuckle, all of them acutely aware that the rest of the compound had entrusted them to decide the fate of everyone. And their choices were damned few. Dragos had them trapped like fish in a barrel now, and at any given moment he might start shooting.

"Reichen and Claire have properties in Europe," Gideon pointed out. "I mean, not that it would be ideal in terms of vacating the compound here and relocating abroad, let alone at a moment's notice."

Lucan considered the option. "What about the tech lab? We can't afford to take the heat off Dragos, even if we do clear out of here. How quickly would you be able to set up shop in another location?"

"It wouldn't be totally seamless," Gideon replied. "But anything's possible."

"What about Tess?" Tegan's question dropped on them like a hammer. "You really think she'll be up to the kind of move you're talking about? For that matter, do you think Dante is willing to take that risk?"

Tegan shook his head, and Lucan knew he was right. They couldn't ask Tess and Dante to jeopardize her health and well-being, or that of their soon-to-arrive son, on a relocation effort of that magnitude.

Not to mention the fact that Lucan had his doubts about the viability of setting up the Order's new headquarters so far away from Dragos's presumed base of operations. It would be a hell of a lot easier to keep the pressure on the bastard from close range.

As Lucan grappled with the impossibilities of the situation, he caught a movement in his periphery and noticed Lazaro Archer walking past the glass walls of the lab. The Gen One civilian paused at the doors and lifted his hand in a gesture of permission.

Lucan glanced to Gideon. "Let him in."

Gideon leaned over to his workstation and pressed a

button, releasing the tech lab's doors with a soft hydraulic *hiss*.

Lazaro Archer strode in, six foot five and formidable, his first-generation genes giving him the look of a warrior even though he'd lived his many hundred years away from combat and bloodshed.

Until Dragos set his sights on Archer's family, that is.

"How is Kellan?" Lucan asked, seeing the stress of all that had happened showing in the somber Breed elder's eyes.

"He is getting better by the hour," Archer replied. "It was the device that was making him so sick, apparently. He's a strong boy. He'll come through all of this, I have no doubt."

Lucan gave him a slow nod. "I'm glad for you both, Lazaro. I regret that your family was caught in the middle of the Order's war with Dragos. You didn't ask for it. You sure as hell didn't deserve all that you've been through."

Archer's dark eyes went a bit sharper as he walked up to the table to join the warriors. His gaze fell briefly over the unfurled blueprints before coming back up to look at Lucan. "Do you remember what I told you, that night, after my Darkhaven was reduced to ash and rubble, my only son, Christophe, gunned down beside me in the vehicle where we waited for word of Kellan's rescue? I made you a pledge."

Lucan did remember. "You told me that you wanted to help destroy Dragos. You offered your resources to us."

"That's right," Archer replied. "Whatever you need, it's yours. The Order has my utmost loyalty and respect, Lucan. All the more so now, after what happened today with Kellan. My God, when I think that all of you are in far worse jeopardy simply for having come to our aid—"

"Don't," Lucan interrupted him. "There is no blame here. Not against you or the boy. Dragos used you. He will pay for all he's done."

"I want to help," Archer said again. "I'd heard from some of the women that you were in here discussing plans to move the compound."

Lucan's glance traveled from Tegan and Gideon back to Archer. "We had hoped to be able to, but it may not be feasible at this time."

"Why not?"

Lucan gestured to the blueprints. "We have plans in the works, but they can't be implemented in time to make a real difference. Our only other option is to relocate our operations overseas, but with Dragos focusing his efforts here in New England, as far as we can determine, pulling up stakes to run a few thousand miles away isn't exactly our best choice."

"What about Maine?"

Lucan frowned. "We have a handful of acres here and there, but nothing that could work as a viable base for the entire compound, temporary or otherwise."

"You don't," Archer replied slowly. "But I, on the other hand, do have just such a place."

CHAPTER Eleven

Chase roused slowly, a sickly sweet, smoky stench drifting up his nostrils and pulling him out of the darkness of a thick, heavy sleep.

His eyes refused to open. His body was sluggish, limbs weighted down, leaden where he sprawled facedown on the cold hard surface that had apparently been his bed. He groaned on a parched throat, nothing but cotton dryness in his mouth. With effort, he managed to lift one eyelid and peer into his fetid surroundings.

He was in an old railcar. Rusted out in places, small holes had eaten through the metal and now emitted blinding white light from outside.

Daylight.

Rays shone in from above his head where the roof was little more than delicate lace, some of it haphazardly patched over with scrap wood and plastic sheeting. Not enough cover for him. One bright nimbus of sunlight was aimed directly onto the back of his bare hand. It had seared an ugly burn into his skin—part of the stench that had woken him.

"Holy fuck." Chase hoisted himself up and scrambled on his haunches into a shaded corner.

That's when he saw the other source of the railcar's foul odor. A dead human male lay nearby where he'd been sleeping. The man's army green parka had been wrested off his shoulders, his face twisted in horror, ghastly white. His throat had been punctured and torn in numerous places. "Savaged" seemed a better way to describe the grotesque evidence of Chase's frenzied feeding.

He remembered his raking thirst. He recalled slipping inside the occupied shelter of the railcar, sending the homeless addicts screaming when they saw his glowing eyes and bared fangs. As the humans fled their makeshift shelter, he'd grabbed the slowest of the bunch, culling the easiest prey from its herd.

The big man had gone down fighting, but he'd been no match at all. Nothing could have stopped the feral need that had been spiraling so dark and deep inside Chase as he'd thrown the human to the filthy floor of the railcar and fed.

He'd drained him.

Killed him.

Shame for that engulfed Chase as he looked at what he'd done. He had crossed a line here, broken an immutable tenet of Breed law. He had trashed his own sense of honor, the one thing he'd clung to so steadfastly through all his years of life.

And there was the matter of the Order. He had squandered their trust. Last night when Dante and Kade had spotted him, gone after him out of concern, he'd cowered in the shadows of the rail yard like vermin. They had known he was there, using his talent to conceal himself, deliberately ignoring their calls. If they'd had any faith left in him at all, he'd smashed it to bits by refusing to face them.

It hurt to shut them out—Dante, especially—but it would have hurt him even more to let either of his fellow warriors see him in the state he'd been in. He'd been hunting all night, had already fed once but it hadn't been enough to sate him. Thirst had driven him down into the squalor of the industrial area near the river, where whores and addicts—failures, like him—tended to cluster. His thirst had known no shame, only craving and need.

Chase craved still, despite having clearly drunk more than his fill only hours ago.

He glared at the dead human, offended by the sight and stench of it. He needed to get out of there. With a fresh, needy ache blooming in his gut, Chase stripped the corpse of its coat, then pulled off the heathered gray sweatshirt and baggy jeans. His own clothes, the black fatigues he'd worn when he left the Order's compound the night before, were blood-soaked and revolting from careless feedings. He took them off, then put on the human's clothes. The jeans and sweatshirt were on the small side for one of Chase's kind, and probably hadn't been cleaned since their former owner had picked them up at Goodwill.

Chase didn't care, so long as he didn't draw undue notice by walking around looking like he'd murdered someone. Taking his ruined fatigues in one hand, he walked to the partially ajar door of the railcar. He pushed it wider and stared out at a sight few of his kind would ever willingly witness.

Sunlight beat down from a bright blue midmorning

sky. It illuminated the ground below, glinting off the dirty snow and frozen mud of the rail yard. Despite the ugliness of his immediate surroundings, there was a beauty in that moment—that first glimpse of daylight on a crisp new dawn—that defied the squalor around him.

It defied even the urgency of his thirst, making him pause where he stood and simply look at the miraculous world he inhabited. The one he felt slipping through his fingers with every throbbing pulse through his veins.

Chase lifted his arm like a visor to shield his hypersensitive eyes from the impossible glare. He tipped his face up and let the unfamiliar, glorious heat of morning warm his face.

It started to sting.

Before long, it started to sear.

How long would it take for the sun to bake him crispy? Probably half an hour, he guessed, savoring the acid burn as his skin across his cheeks and brow grew hotter. Thirty minutes, and there would be no more hunger. No more shame. No more struggle to keep himself out of the abyss that seemed so welcoming, so blessedly dark and endless.

He considered the notion for a long, excruciating while, testing his will.

But he failed, even in that.

With the talons of his thirst sinking deeper into him, Chase stepped off the edge of the railcar and dropped to the ground below. He crossed the tracks and pitched his ruined warrior's garb into the smoldering belly of a smoking rubbish barrel.

Then he slunk off quickly to find shelter to wait for nightfall, when he could begin his hunting once more.

* * *

They had arrived in New Orleans in the dark early-morning hours and took a taxi from the airport to a hotel in what Hunter assumed was the heart of the tourist area. Street noise and music had echoed up from below their fourth-story window until long past daybreak, creating a racket that had kept his senses on full alert, anticipating the slightest hint of trouble.

Not that he'd had any intention of sleeping. He hardly needed rest; an hour or two at most each day. It was how he'd been trained, a discipline that kept his body ready for any situation, his mind prepared to engage with hair-trigger response.

Corinne, on the other hand, had slept like the dead upon their arrival.

He knew she'd been exhausted, physically drained. Her emotions had been taxed as well, although if she'd wanted to collapse in a fit of unproductive self-pity and tears, he had to give her credit there. She'd held up with remarkable strength. She'd seemed resolved since they'd left the Bishop Darkhaven. Defiant, even.

She'd been agreeable enough when he'd told her she was under his guardianship, and there had been no irrational histrionics when he'd informed her that his mission for the Order was going to take him—both of them—right into the potential enemy territory of Henry Vachon, a known ally of her captor and tormentor. Corinne had seemed almost eager at the idea, a fact that sparked a watchful curiosity in him.

Now he listened to the sounds of water moving in the tub of the adjacent bathroom. Corinne had gone in to freshen up shortly after noon, having slept all the way through the morning while he pored over maps of the city and outlying parishes in the lightless gloom of the hotel room's curtain-drawn living area.

He'd noticed she had neglected to close the door tightly, and for the past thirty-seven minutes—the full duration of her time spent reclining naked in the tub— he'd had to purposely avoid looking at the thin wedge of golden lamplight that poured into the darkness where he sat.

He rallied his focus to the spread-out maps he'd picked up from the hotel lobby on their arrival. They were abbreviated street listings, intended mostly for tourists whose main objectives were, apparently, finding the nearest restaurants, bars, and jazz clubs. Hunter would get further intelligence on Henry Vachon from Gideon shortly; until then, he felt it a beneficial use of his time to familiarize himself with the various streets and districts. Perform some virtual reconnaissance until sundown, when he could venture out and see Vachon's city for himself.

Anything to keep his gaze from straying toward that partially open door across the room.

His resolve was tested when he heard the gurgle of water draining as she pulled the stopper. Her skin squeaked against the porcelain as she moved about in there, liquid splashes indicating she had climbed out of the tub. He saw her slender arm reach out to take a thick white towel from a polished metal bar on the wall. He heard the rustle of terry cloth as she began to dry the water from her body.

He forced his eyes back to the work that covered the coffee table in front of him. With total concentration he studied the portion of the map where they were currently staying, intent on committing the multicolored grid and its corresponding street names to memory: Their hotel was in an area called the Upper French Quarter. This part of the city encompassed numerous blocks between Iberville Street to St. Anne Street and was hemmed in on one side by a street named North Rampart and, on the other, the Mississippi—

Through the wedge of softly lit open doorway, he caught a glimpse of Corinne's bare thigh. The towel traveled down, then her foot came up to rest on the closed lid of the toilet as she dried off the lean, slender length of her calf.

A heat that had been kindling in his belly now drifted lower.

Hunter wanted to look away.

He meant to.

But then she shifted again, and his gaze rooted on the small, rounded curve of her breast. The nipple crowning it was flushed dark rose, a tantalizing contrast to her creamy skin. He stared at that sweet pink bud peaking at the swell of her soft, pale flesh. He'd never seen a female's naked breast before. On film and television at the compound on occasion, of course, but none of those hard-looking, grossly inflated examples could compare to the delicate perfection he saw in Corinne's naked form.

He wanted to see more of her; it shocked him how much he wanted that. As he watched her move in and out of his scant field of vision, arousal began to coil around him and tighten. His skin felt hot and confining, drawn too tight across his chest and up along his neck. Lower still, the tightness was worsening by the second, his sex stirring, stiffening with the sudden upticking rush of blood through his veins.

He growled quietly under his breath, though whether from shock or shame, he wasn't sure. He didn't want to feel this curiosity for her, this unwelcome sexual aware-ness. He'd been trained—disciplined without compromise from the time he was a boy—to be above base needs or desires.

Yet he could not wrest his attention away from Corinne Bishop now.

Even as he shifted to alleviate the binding annoyance of his too-snug clothes, he stared, stealing another look, hoping for a longer glimpse. Wishing for a brief fumble of the large white towel so he could feast his eyes on her completely and sate the curiosity that had him leaning onto his elbow for a more advantageous field of vision.

His temples pulsed, almost as insistently as the throb that had settled in his groin. Had he not been raised so rigidly, so ruthlessly, he might have been tempted to stroke his hand over the demanding pound of his arousal, if only to relieve the ache. Instead he fought the urge. Thinly.

Everything male in him was locked on to her in that moment, and Corinne would have to be unconscious not to feel the weight of his hungry eyes on her.

Perhaps she did sense something, after all.

She pivoted around suddenly and tried to sidestep away from the gap in the narrowly opened door. As she moved, the towel he'd been willing her to drop slipped out of her grasp. It swung down on one side, baring the column of her spine and the upper curve of her heart-shaped backside.

His breath ceased, caught in a low rasp in his lungs. Not from the feminine beauty of her body but from the savagery that had evidently been wreaked upon it at some point.

A web of angry red scars tracked across the smooth canvas of her back, from shoulder to buttock. Hideous welts left from a lash—probably a length of chain as well, based on the ruination of her skin—left him stricken into a dull sort of wonder.

What had she been forced to endure?

Just how deeply had Dragos's evil cut her?

All the heat he'd felt just a moment before was eclipsed by the sight of those scars. He felt something elusive and unfamiliar wash over him in that instant, feelings that seemed to rise up at him from somewhere deep inside, an inaccessible place, long out of his reach. Regret for what had been done to her flooded through him, along with a dark, swelling wave of fury for the beast responsible.

He cursed, unable to keep the contempt inside him.

Corinne's head whipped around, wet black hair slapping against her bare shoulders as she hurried to cover herself with the towel. Her eyes clashed with his gaze through the slim gap of the open door. There was challenge in her unflinching look, a rawness that made him feel as though his knowledge of her wounds was as deep a violation as the punishment itself had been to her.

Hunter glanced away, casting his gaze back to his maps.

He kept his eyes averted out of respect—out of sympathy he didn't even realize he was capable of until now. He listened as Corinne's bare feet padded a couple of steps across the tiles of the bathroom floor.

The door creaked as she slowly closed it and latched it tight, blocking him out.

CHAPTER
Twelve

Yes, of course. I understand." Victor Bishop stood near the fireplace in his study that afternoon, speaking on the Darkhaven's private line. He'd debated making the call, but only because of the potential wrath his unwelcome news might bring down upon him.

In the end, he'd figured it was in his best interest to reaffirm his alliance, make certain that he raised a flag of the proper color lest he find himself under unprovoked enemy fire yet again.

"If I can provide any further information, rest assured, I will contact you at once." He cleared his throat, despising the fear that put a wobble of awkwardness in his voice. "And, please, ah, if you would...be sure he knows that I had nothing to do with any of this current turn of events. I have never betrayed his confidence. I am now, and I will remain, at his service."

With barely an acknowledgment, only a muttered

word of good-bye, the call abruptly disconnected on the other end.

"Damn it," Bishop snarled, taking the phone away from his ear. He pivoted around, half tempted to pitch the cordless receiver into the nearest wall. He drew up short, surprised to find he was not alone.

Regina stood behind him, silent, her red-rimmed eyes condemning.

"I thought you were still in bed," he remarked, knowingly curt as he strode past her and carefully replaced the phone on its console at his desk. "You look tired, dear. Perhaps you should go back and rest a while longer."

She had taken to her bed right after Corinne and the warrior from Boston left the Darkhaven. He hadn't tried to talk to her in the hours since; he knew that his admission last night was a breach he could never mend. Not even his shared blood bond with Regina would be enough to mend what was now broken. They were linked to each other by blood and vow, but her trust, her love, would never truly be his again.

He had to admit, part of him was relieved. The lie had been a burden for too long, far too taxing to keep the mask of bereaved, bewildered father in place when his visceral connection to Regina was always there, ready to trip him up. It felt good to have everything in the open now. Liberating despite the contempt he felt like a burning poison seeping into him.

Regina's contempt, pouring out at him through her accusing stare and the frantic thud of her pulse, which reverberated within his own veins.

"Who were you speaking to, Victor?"

"It was no one important," he replied, dismissing her with a narrowed glare.

She took a step toward him, both hands fisted down at her sides. "You're lying to me again. Or rather, still. It sickens me to think how long you've been lying to me."

Anger flared in him. "Go back to bed, dear. You're clearly overwrought, and I'd hate for you to say things you'll regret later."

"I regret everything now," she said, looking at him with a pained frown. "How could you have done the things you did, Victor? How could you live with yourself, knowing what you'd done to Corinne?"

"What you don't seem able to grasp," he growled, "is that what I did, I did for us. For our son. Starkn would have come after Sebastian next. I wasn't about to put our boy, our flesh-and-blood child, at stake—"

Regina gaped at him as though he'd struck her. "Corinne was our child too, Victor. She and Lottie were as much our children as Sebastian. We brought them into our lives, into our hearts, just the same as if they'd been born to us."

"It wasn't the same to me!" he snapped, bringing his fist down on the desk. Futile rage coursed through him when he thought about his boy, the sensitive, overly contemplative youth who should have had the world in the palm of his hand. The promising son, who might have had all that and more, if not for the web of deception Bishop had so carefully spun all around them.

Not carefully enough, he reflected now.

It was that very web that had eventually found Sebastian, strangling his goodness, his future.

"It doesn't matter," Bishop murmured to his clearly outraged Breedmate. "What's done is done. It was all for nothing, anyway. We lost Sebastian regardless of everything I did to protect him."

Regina's eyes held him too closely. She stared, too

knowingly. "He was never quite the same after Corinne went missing," she said, more to herself than to Victor. "I remember how withdrawn Basti became just a few years later, how distant he seemed from us in those last couple of weeks ... before his Bloodlust took over."

Bishop hated the reminder. He hated to recall how painful it had been to realize his only son had turned Rogue—lost to his thirst, his addiction to blood, the very thing that gave all of the Breed life and strength and power. Basti had been weak, but it had been the discovery of his father's corruption that had pushed him over the edge.

Regina would have read his guilt now, even without their blood bond. "What happened, Victor? You betrayed Sebastian too, didn't you?"

Bishop ground his molars together, furious that she would make him relive what had been the worst moment of his life. Second worst—there was little that could top the day Sebastian, drunk from a killing spree, took one of Victor's own guns to his head and pulled the trigger before anyone could stop him.

"He'd figured it out, hadn't he?" she pressed. "You fooled the rest of us, but not him. He somehow uncovered the truth."

"Shut up," Bishop growled, his mind flooding with memories.

Sebastian and his sense of organization and order. How proud he'd been of the mahogany gun cabinet he'd made with his own hands, a gift for his father. He'd wanted it to be a surprise, had begun transferring Victor's prized collection of antique weapons from the old cabinet to the beautiful new one, when he'd discovered the hidden panel at the bottom.

All of Victor's darkest secrets were in that private cache.

Sebastian had learned of the whore who'd been killed to look like Corinne. There were receipts from a dress-maker's shop for clothing hastily made to Victor's exacting specifications. A note from one of Victor's jeweler friends downtown, containing a sketch of a custom-made necklace ordered to match the one Corinne had worn the night of her disappearance.

Foolish mementos that should have been burned along with the hope of ever seeing Corinne again.

Sebastian had been horrified at his discovery, but he'd kept his silence. Victor had forbidden him to speak of the matter, threatened him, for crissake. He'd told Sebastian that to expose his lie would be to invite the deaths of all of them.

The terrible secret was a burden Sebastian could not bear.

"It was you," Regina said, her voice wooden. "You were responsible for what happened to our son. My God . . . it was you who drove him to Bloodlust, to blow his brains out in this very room."

Bishop's fury exploded out of him. "I said shut up!"

Although Regina startled at the sharpness of his voice, she didn't falter. Her hands still fisted, knuckles white in her own outrage, she approached the desk where he stood. "You destroyed Sebastian's life as surely as you destroyed Corinne's, and yet that's not enough for you. You would betray her still." She glanced at the phone now cradled in its receiver. "You have, haven't you? That call you made . . . it was to save your own neck, even if it comes at her expense. I can't live like this, not with you. You are a coward, Victor. You disgust me."

He struck her, reaching across the desk to cuff her with a closed hand, hard across the face.

She dropped to the floor from the force of the blow. He came around and glared down at her, seething with anger now, his fangs filling his mouth. She didn't cower. Lifting her head, she stared him narrowly in the eyes, not even flinching at the sight of his transformed irises, which bathed her face in an amber glow. Her tongue went to the corner of her mouth, testing the small gash that bled a scarlet trickle onto her chin.

"Do you have any idea what was done to her all these years?" she challenged him sourly. "She was raped, Victor. Beaten and tortured. Experimented upon like some kind of animal. She had a baby in that prison. That's right, Corinne has a son of her own. They took him away from her. She actually thought you might help her find him, bring him back to her. All she wanted was for us to be a family again, including her and her child."

Bishop listened, but he remained unmoved. Not even Regina's tears, now streaming down her cheeks, had any effect. He was in too deep and for much too long. Rather than wasting time feeling pity or remorse for things he couldn't change, he was already calculating ways to twist this situation so that he might curry the favor of Gerard Starkn—or Dragos, whatever the powerful male had taken to calling himself now.

Offering neither a word nor a hand, he watched Regina come up to her feet. She despised him; he could feel it seething in her blood.

"I want you to leave, Victor. Tonight, I want you gone from this Darkhaven."

It was such a ridiculous demand, he laughed out loud. "You expect me to walk away from my own home?"

"That's right," she replied, steady as he'd ever seen

her. "Because if you don't, I will expose your corruption to the entire Breed nation. You, Gerard Starkn, Henry Vachon . . . all of you."

Defiant, she turned on her heel and headed for the open doorway of the study. He didn't let her reach it.

In a second—less than that—he flashed from where he'd been standing in the center of the room to directly in front of her, blocking her path into the foyer beyond.

He grabbed her fiercely by the upper arms, then spoke through gritted teeth. "You will do no such thing. You, my dear, will mind your fucking tongue. You will mind your mate, if you know what's good for you."

Her eyes went a bit wider, and he saw her throat move as she swallowed. Before she spoke, he had mistaken it for fear. "Or what?" she asked, much too bold for his liking. "What will you do, Victor, kill me?"

Although it was rare enough to be virtually unheard of, particularly in these modern, civilized times, he wouldn't be the first Breed male to lose control of the more savage side of his nature and kill his mate.

As he looked at Regina, he realized how much easier it would be for him without her now. His sins would die with her. And if Corinne, wherever she ended up, should ever think to stand in his way, it would be nothing at all to pluck her from this world like a burr trapped under his saddle. She was nothing to him now, even less than she had been the night Gerard Starkn had stolen her away.

Bishop's grip on his Breedmate tightened, almost of its own accord. She frowned, pain pinching her pretty face. "You're hurting me," she complained, casting a nervous glance over the top of his shoulder as though searching for help.

He was sick with anger now, and cold with the realization that as much as her trust in him had been shattered, so too was his faith in her. "Threatening me was a very stupid thing to do, Regina. I might have been able to excuse your contempt of me, but as you've so helpfully pointed out, you have become a threat to my way of living. You are a risk I cannot afford—"

The sudden *click* of a gun being chambered took him aback. But no more so than the feel of cold metal coming to rest against his right temple.

"You need to take your hands off her, sir. Now."

Mason.

Without looking, he knew the low, steady voice of one of his longest-serving guards. And he had seen the male in action more than once, enough to understand that he was caught in a very unpleasant predicament. Righteous to a fault, Mason would not back down from a fight unless he was no longer breathing. All the more so when he was coming to the defense of lovely Regina, whom Bishop had long suspected secretly meant more to Mason than simply the lady of the Darkhaven. Mason would protect her to his death, Bishop had no doubt.

Which meant he was going to have to bloody his hands with the lives of both of them before this day was out.

No matter, Bishop thought, devoid of mercy.

He was ready to do whatever he must to put his life—his future—on a less complicated course.

"I said let her go." Mason pushed the cold nose of his pistol a bit more insistently against Bishop's temple.

Bishop released Regina from his hold, complying with the tightly issued order, but only long enough to let the guard believe the situation was under control. As soon as he sensed Mason's trigger finger relax, Bishop railed on him with fangs bared.

Regina screamed as he knocked the weapon out of the other male's grasp. She took off running from the study as the gun clattered out to the foyer floor.

Bishop lunged for his guard. They were an equal match, Bishop having the advantage of his fierce determination, his fury like a madness pounding in his blood and brain. With an unhinged roar, he grabbed Mason by the chest and flung him with all his might against the far wall of the study. He didn't give the guard so much as a second to react.

Leaping at him, he crushed the heel of his Italian loafer into Mason's groin. The vampire bellowed in agony, his eyes burning like coals, fangs tearing out of his gums.

Bishop chuckled. He couldn't help himself from taking some enjoyment in the pain he was causing the other male. He would kill Mason slowly before strangling Regina with his bare hands.

As the thought danced through his mind, he caught a rush of movement in the foyer.

Regina had come back, hadn't gone very far at all. She had Mason's gun in her hands.

Bishop swung a hard look on her—just in time to hear the metallic *pop* of the hammer as she squeezed the trigger. The bullet discharged, sailed toward him on a small cloud of smoke. He jerked out of its path at the very last moment. Behind him, the curtained French door exploded with a crash of breaking glass. Afternoon sunlight poured in through the hole in the thick curtains, bringing with it the chill December breeze.

Bishop snorted, about to ridicule his Breedmate's shaky hands and lousy aim.

But then she fired again. She fired at him again and again and again, and this time there was no chance to evade the hail of bullets. She fired until the gun had been emptied into him.

He staggered back on his heels, looking down at the field of scarlet that seeped out of his chest. He couldn't stop the bleeding, could only stare in baffled astonishment at the hellish damage. He felt his heart labor to keep its rhythm, each breath a raw scrape of talons in his chest. His legs grew weak beneath him.

And now Mason was on his feet, standing before him, animosity rolling off his big body like a dark thundercloud.

Bishop knew this was his end.

The bullets alone might not kill him, but they had sapped him of much-needed strength. His lungs were punctured, his heart as well. But he clung fast to his fury—the only thing he had left in this, his final moment.

With a roar that seemed to shred him from deep inside, Victor Bishop began to lunge for his Breedmate.

Mason's unyielding hands stopped him. Took hold of him and lifted him off the floor. And then he was flying, pitching backward, into the tall French doors that opened out onto the lawn of his Darkhaven estate. His body crashed through the curtains and glass, coming to rest broken and bleeding on the frozen ground outside.

He stared up into the sky above him, unable to move. Unable to save himself from the excruciatingly slow death that awaited him as he peered up in wonder at the glorious, merciless light of day.

CHAPTER
Thirteen

Dragos snapped his cell phone closed, irritation still rankling him from the news he'd received a few hours ago from his lieutenant in New Orleans.

Henry Vachon, a longtime ally from his time in the Enforcement Agency, was gravely concerned that he was soon to get a visit from one of the members of the Order. Dragos didn't doubt it for a moment. Based on the information Vachon had received from a very anxious Victor Bishop in Detroit, Dragos was guessing that retaliation from the Order would be more a matter of when than if.

To soothe Vachon and ensure that the operation didn't lose yet another asset to Lucan's warriors, Dragos had called in heavy reinforcements and given them orders to kill. As for Victor Bishop, he had served his purpose long ago. Now he was nothing but a liability, no matter how he'd apparently groveled when he'd called to alert Vachon to the trouble. If Bishop was ever fool enough to show his face, Dragos would take great pleasure in tearing it off.

His foul mood of the past few hours wasn't helped at all by the hellish jostle of his limousine as his driver barreled along a godforsaken stretch of twilit, rural dirt road in northern Maine.

"Must you hit every goddamn pothole?" he barked at the Minion. He ignored the simpering apology that followed, instead glaring out the window at mile after mile of dark, encroaching forest and frozen marshland. "I've been getting tossed around back here for more than four hours since we arrived on the mainland. How much farther is it?"

"Not far at all, Master. According to the GPS, we're nearly there."

Dragos grunted, his gaze still following the bleakness of the passing landscape. They'd left the last town behind them a hundred miles ago—if the rundown cluster of fifty-year-old mobile homes and junked automobiles could actually be called a town. Human civilization hadn't seemed to stretch this far north, not in any great numbers. Or if it had, it had been beaten back down toward the cities by the rugged land and lack of industry.

Only the most intrepid souls would choose to carve their living out of this backwoods frontier. Or those with damned good reason to live off grid, as far as they could get from the human establishment they so despised.

Men like the ones Dragos was on his way to meet now.

The human government called them terrorists, disgruntled citizens looking to blame their malcontent and personal failures on anyone but themselves. Others would call them sociopathic time bombs just waiting for the next political or financial crisis to justify their violence. To most on either side of the argument, men like these were deemed insane, anomalies within the norm of human society.

Among themselves, no doubt they called one another heroes, patriots. Any one of the three awaiting him would likely go so far as to be a willing martyr, emulating the celebrity handful of their ilk who had staked and spent their lives on the altars of their righteous moral indignation. It was that fervent belief in their personal causes, that dangerous dedication and the eagerness to act on it, that had first brought these men to Dragos's attention.

The fact that the entire group of them had spent time on the U.S. government's watch list over the past decade only made the prospect of recruiting them that much sweeter.

From the backseat of the limo, Dragos glanced out the windshield as his driver slowed, then turned onto an even more narrow tract of unpaved road. This was less road than path, a sheet of hard-packed snow and ice that led into a thick stand of forested acreage.

The headlight beams bounced as the long sedan rocked and pitched along the trail. Except for the faint track of a pickup truck's chained snow tires—left by his other Minion, the one who'd arranged the meeting for him the day before—it didn't appear that anyone had been back on this chunk of godforsaken land for months.

That Minion, a former Army intelligence officer, was

waiting outside a ramshackle barn at the end of the road.

He walked up to the passenger-side door of the limousine as it jounced to a stop.

"Master," he greeted, bowing his head as Dragos climbed out. "They await you inside."

"Tell my driver to kill the engine and the headlights and wait for me here," Dragos murmured. "This shouldn't take long."

"Of course, Master."

Dragos stepped carefully onto the icy path that meandered toward the dim light glowing from inside the old barn. He couldn't help pausing to look at the dilapidated, sagging wooden structure with its rotting boards and aged, wafting livestock stench. Nor could he help the smile that curved his mouth as he thought about the victory that would soon be his.

How ironic that within this inauspicious wreck of a building—in the hands of a radical few local losers—lay the perfect means of ensuring the total, irrevocable demise of mighty Lucan Thorne and his damnable Order.

Corinne sat on one of the two double beds in the New Orleans hotel room, clicking from channel to channel on the television remote control. The activity had kept her mind occupied for a little while, kept her from prowling the confines of her small quarters like a caged cat. But the novelty of so much chatter and noise, all the vivid images flashing by onscreen with just a push of a button, had long since worn off.

She glanced at Hunter, who'd seemed to grow more

distant, more silently aloof, with every passing minute since the sun had set. He had spoken to Gideon on his cell phone about an hour ago, discussing Hunter's intended plan for locating and infiltrating Henry Vachon's known properties in the area. When he found Vachon, he would remove him to an isolated location and interrogate him for information on Dragos. He only needed to uncover Vachon's current whereabouts and break in without getting caught or killed in the process.

It all sounded very bold, extremely dangerous.

She turned off the television, leaving the remote on the bed as she got up to look at the marked-up map that was spread out on the sofa table across the room. Hunter had since discarded the paper map in favor of the electronic one on his cell phone.

She studied the circled areas where the Order believed Vachon's properties were situated. During the flight from Detroit and the time she'd spent sequestered in the hotel room awaiting nightfall with Hunter, Corinne had been puzzling out a way to find Henry Vachon on her own and plead her case to him about getting back her son.

If she let Hunter find him first, Vachon was as good as dead. But if she could somehow intercept that meeting, bargain for Vachon's mercy with whatever meager means she had left, perhaps there was a chance she might find her child. It worried her, the thought of putting herself back within the reach of one of Dragos's loyal followers. But then, if Henry Vachon had indeed been present the night she was abducted, then she had already seen his worst. She had faced his depraved cruelty once and survived; she would face him and Dragos both all over again if it might lead her to her son.

It was a desperate plan. A foolish one, which could be tantamount to suicide.

But she *was* desperate. And she was willing to risk everything she had on the hope of reuniting with her boy.

She glanced at Hunter, standing near the glass sliding doors, his big body silhouetted by the moonlight and the glow of streetlamps on the boulevard below. Music hummed in the air outside the hotel, the soft wail of a saxophone, someone playing the blues. She drifted toward the glass too, drawn as always to the soothing sounds of poetry conveyed in notes and chords. She listened for a while, watching the old man on the opposite corner of the street play his battered brass horn with all the passion of someone less than half his age.

"When will you leave to begin looking for Vachon?"

Hunter lifted his head and met her glance. "As soon as possible. Gideon is searching for records on Vachon's properties, old building plans, security schematics, things that will assist with my reconnaissance. If he is able to turn up any useful data within the hour, he will call me with it."

"And if he doesn't find anything to help you?"

"Then I will proceed without it."

Corinne nodded, unsurprised by his frank reply. He didn't seem like someone who would let obstacles stand in his way, even if it meant stealing into an enemy's camp with nothing more than his wits and whatever weapons he happened to have on his body. "Do you think Vachon will tell you where Dragos is?"

Hunter's face was grimly confident. "If he knows, he will tell me."

She didn't want to guess how he would go about making sure of that. Nor could she hold his piercing gaze for longer than a moment when he was standing just a couple of feet away from her.

Being this close to him, feeling the palpable weight of his golden stare, only reminded her of how startled she'd been to find him watching her while she'd bathed that afternoon. She'd been more than startled. She had been astonished—utterly shocked by the heat that had smoldered in his otherwise inscrutable stare. A rush of warmth raced through her when she relived it now, all the worse when there was no door to close between them.

She should have been affronted that he'd seen her, if not afraid. Then, like now, Hunter's gaze unsettled her. Not from the fear she expected she should feel but from her own sense of awareness. The stoic warrior hadn't looked at her as some object he needed to protect or pity, but as a woman.

At least, until he'd seen her scars.

The outward evidence of what she'd endured was ugly enough, but the more terrible wounds she bore inside. There was still a raw and wounded part of her that hadn't come out of Dragos's nightmarish prison, a part of her that might never make it out to the daylight. She'd left so much of herself behind in those dank laboratory cells, she wasn't sure she'd ever be whole again.

It was that part of her that had seized up at the idea of being shut in such a small space as the hotel room's tiny bathroom. She'd left only the smallest gap in the door, just enough to reassure herself that she could see beyond the small enclosure, that she had the power to walk out at any time. That she wasn't locked in or helpless, waiting for her next round of torture by the one who held the key.

Even now, just thinking about confined spaces and

barred doors seemed to make the four walls contract inward on her. Pulse quickening, throat clenching up in the rising swell of her anxiety, Corinne turned to face the wide sliding door that looked out over the city from the small balcony. She put her hands out, palms pressed against the cool glass as she simply focused on breathing and tried to will her heart to calm.

It wasn't enough.

"What's wrong?" Hunter asked, frowning as she sucked in a couple of quick, hitching breaths. "Are you ill?"

"Air," she gasped. "I need ... air—"

She fumbled with the mechanism on the glass door, finally yanking it open and all but stumbling out to the balcony. Hunter was right beside her as she clung to the wrought-iron railing and drew in gulp after gulp of the cleansing, open night air. She felt his presence like a wall of heat at her side, the large shape of him looming close, watching her in silent concern.

"I'm okay," she murmured, everything still spinning around her, lungs still caught in a vise. "It's nothing ... I'm all right."

He reached out and took her chin gently in his hand, turning her face toward him in the dark. His scowl was deeper now, those probing golden eyes searching beneath the furrowed line of his brow. "You are not well."

"I'm fine. I needed some fresh air, that's all." She drew back slightly and he let his hand fall away. The warmth of his touch lingered. She could feel the broad lines of his fingers ghosted on her skin as she exhaled a shaky breath.

He stared at her, watching her tremble even though it was barely cold in the sultry New Orleans night.

"You're not well," he said again. His voice was softer this time, but no less firm. "Your body needs more rest. You need nourishment."

His gaze went to her mouth as he spoke. It lingered there, putting a new kind of clamor in her veins.

"When was the last time you had a meal, Corinne?"

God, she didn't even know. Probably more than twenty-four hours by now, since the last thing she'd eaten was at the compound in Boston before they'd left for Detroit. She gave him a vague shrug. She'd long become accustomed to the empty feeling of hunger during her time in captivity. Dragos had fed her and the others only frequently enough to keep them alive. Sometimes, when her rebellion had landed her in solitary confinement, she'd been allowed to eat even less than that.

"I'm okay," she said, uncomfortable with Hunter's probing scrutiny and concern. "I just needed to be outside for a little while. All I need is a bit of air."

Looking none too convinced, he cast a measuring glance over the balcony to the street below. Sounds drifted up on the pleasant night breeze: people talking and laughing as they strolled by, vehicles rumbling over cobblestones on the adjacent avenue, the musician on the nearby corner segueing from one soulful tune to another. The aromas of roasting meats and spicy sauces put a traitorous growl in Corinne's stomach.

Hunter looked back at her then, his head cocked in question.

"Okay," she said. "I could eat something, I suppose."

"Then come with me," he replied, already stalking back toward the room.

Corinne followed, part of her simply eager to be down on the vibrant street outside, back among the living. A more cautious part of her understood that if she was to put her plan in motion tonight—seeking a way to contact Henry Vachon on her own—then she had better fill her stomach and gird herself for the desperate mission that lay ahead of her.

CHAPTER
Fourteen

They ended up at a small restaurant a few blocks from the hotel and away from most of the tourist traffic.

It didn't look like much to Hunter. A dark cave of a place with no more than twenty tables corraled on the opposite side of a modest, rough-hewn stage and postage stamp-size dance floor. The trio onstage was playing something slow and sultry, the female singer pausing to nod appreciatively at the man on the piano and another who blew a string of mournful notes from a short brass trumpet.

The air was clouded with the mingled odors of greasy food and strange spices, grill smoke and perfume, and far too many human bodies for his liking. But Corinne seemed more than pleased to be there. As soon as she'd heard the music pouring out into the street, she had homed in like a missile and insisted it was where she wanted to eat.

Hunter had no stake in the matter. As it was her body

that required sustenance, he'd been more than willing to let her decide where they would go.

As for his own needs, it had been a few days since he'd fed. He'd gone longer, but it was unwise to push his Gen One metabolism much closer to a week without sating its thirst. He felt the twinges of that thirst quirking in his veins as he sat at the corner table with Corinne, his back to the nearby wall, his gaze perusing the crowd of humans who filled the cavernous old establishment.

He wasn't the only Breed male visually sifting the throng of *Homo sapiens*. He'd spotted the pair of vampires as soon as he and Corinne had walked in. They posed no threat at all, just a couple of Darkhaven civilians idly evaluating potential Hosts the same way he was. As soon as they noticed him watching them from across the way, they retreated into the hazy shadows like a couple of minnows that had just gotten a whiff of a shark in their pool.

After the young males disappeared, he glanced across the little table at Corinne.

"Is your meal sufficient?" he asked.

"Incredible." She set down her drink—some kind of clear, alcohol-based concoction that had been poured over ice cubes and a fat wedge of lime. "Everything is or, rather, *was* delicious."

He'd hardly needed to ask, based on how quickly— and enthusiastically—she'd attacked the plate of almond-crusted fish and steamed vegetables. And that had been after she'd already had a bowl of spicy soup and two crusty rolls from the basket perched at the edge of the table.

Even though she clearly enjoyed the food, she seemed to grow quiet, pensive, the longer they sat there. He watched her run her fingertip along the rim of the short cocktail glass. When her gaze met his across the candlelit table, he found himself snared in her exotic dark eyes. The glow of the small flame played with their color, darkening their usual greenish blue to deep forest green. There was a hauntedness to Corinne Bishop's eyes, her most painful secrets walled behind an impenetrable thicket of changeable green.

He didn't think she would tell him her thoughts. And as much as he found himself curious, he didn't think it his place to ask. Instead he sat in silence as she closed her eyes and swayed with the music coming from the stage. Above the din of voices and serving clatter, he heard Corinne humming softly along with the singer's sorrow-filled words.

After a long moment, her lids lifted and she found him looking at her. "This is an old Bessie Smith song," she said, regarding him expectantly, as though he should know the name. "It's one of her best."

He listened, trying to understand what Corinne enjoyed about it. The sound was pleasant enough, a lazy stroll of a song, but the lyrics seemed mundane, almost nonsensical. He shrugged. "Humans write songs about strange things. This singer seems overly affectionate toward her new kitchen appliance."

Corinne had her glass to her lips, in the midst of finishing the last swallow of her drink. She stared at him for a long moment before a smile broke over her lips. "She's not singing about a kitchen appliance."

"She is," he countered, certain he hadn't misheard the lines. He studied the singer now, then gave Corinne an affirming nod when the lyric came around again. "Right there. She says after her man left her, she went out and bought the best coffee grinder she could find. She says it more than once, in fact." He scowled, unable to find logic in any of the words. "Now she's moved on to some apparent affection for a deep-sea diver."

Corinne's smile widened, then she laughed out loud. "I know what the lyrics say, but that's not what they mean. Not at all." Her eyes still dancing with amusement, she cocked her head at him in question. Studying him now. "What kind of music do you like, Hunter?"

He wasn't sure how to answer. He'd heard some of the stuff the other warriors played at the compound, but he had no particular affinity toward any of it. He'd never thought about music one way or the other, never paused to consider if any of it appealed to him. What would be the point in that?

Now he looked at lovely Corinne Bishop, sitting just an arm's length across from him, bathed in candlelight and holding him in her beautiful, smiling gaze. He swallowed hard, struck by just how exquisite she truly was.

"I like . . . this," he replied, unable to drag his gaze away from her.

She was the first to break eye contact, looking down as she took the crisp white napkin from her lap and dabbed at the corners of her mouth. "It's been so long since I've had a wonderful meal like this. And blues music, of course. I used to listen to this kind of music all the time . . . before."

"Before you were taken," he said, seeing her expression grow reflective, haunted. He knew she'd been very young when Dragos had abducted her. He'd heard she had been full of life, always laughing and ready for adventure. He could see traces of that in her now, as she unconsciously swayed with the more lively tune that was coming from the stage, her foot tapping out a quiet beat beneath the table. "Brock has mentioned to me that he used to accompany you out to dance clubs when he knew you in Detroit."

"Accompany me?" When Corinne's head came up, she wore a wry half-smile. "If that's what he told you, he was just being polite. I was an insufferable pest when Brock bodyguarded for me. I used to drag him out to every jazz club in a fifty-mile radius of the city. He didn't approve, but I think he knew that if he refused to take me, I'd find a way to go on my own. I'm sure there were many times he must have hated having to watch over me."

Hunter shook his head. "He cared for you. He still does."

Her answering smile was soft, reassured. "I was very glad to see that he is happy. I'm glad he's found a mate in Jenna. Brock deserves all the good in life."

She went quiet as the waitress came by to clear the dishes and remove the empty cocktail glass. "Bring ya 'nother vodka gimlet, shugah?"

Corinne gave a dismissing wave of her hand. "I'd better not. This one already seems to be going straight to my head."

Hunter declined as well, his glass of beer sitting untouched, ordered only for appearances' sake when they'd first arrived. After the server left them alone, Corinne glanced across at him in the wobbling glow of the candlelight. Her pupils were dark pools, mesmerizing and endless. When she spoke, her voice was husky and soft, tentative somehow. "What about you, Hunter? What were you like growing up? Somehow, I don't think you were the wild, impulsive type."

"I was neither of those things," he agreed, recalling his grim beginnings. He was serious and disciplined for as long as he could remember. He had to be; failure in any area of his upbringing would have meant his death.

She was still looking at him, still trying to puzzle him out. "I know you said you don't have family, but have you always lived in Boston?"

"No," he replied. "I came there when I joined the Order this past summer."

"Oh." She appeared surprised by that, and not entirely pleased. "You've only been with them for a short while." She glanced back down at the table and brushed at some errant bread crumbs. "How long were you in service to Dragos?"

Now he was the one caught by surprise.

"That first night, at Claire and Andreas's Darkhaven," she explained. "Someone heard them talking about you. About the fact that you used to be allied with Dragos." She watched him closely, carefully. "Is it true?"

"Yes." Simple. Honest. A fact she apparently already knew. So, why did he feel the sudden want to bite the word back? Why did he have the impulse to reassure her that though he might have served Dragos, he posed no threat to her?

He couldn't tell her that. Because in the pit of his gut, he wondered if it was true.

Did he pose no threat to her?

Mira's precognition seemed to indicate otherwise. Since leaving the Detroit Darkhaven, he'd been trying to dismiss the vision as having already played out—albeit altered, the prophesied outcome thwarted—during his confrontation with Victor Bishop.

But something wasn't right about that.

Nothing had ever altered the child seer's visions before. He would be a fool to think it should happen now, just because he was finding himself intrigued with darkly beautiful, damaged Corinne.

He heard her quick but subtle exhalation as she absorbed his frank admission. Instead of leaning forward on the small table, he noticed she was now gradually inching away, physically retreating until her spine came up against the back of her chair. For a long moment, she remained silent, staring through the dim light and thin haze that hung in the room.

"How long did you serve him?" she asked, guarded now.

"For as long as I can remember."

"But not anymore," she said, studying his face as she spoke. Searching, he guessed, for some sign in his expression that she could trust him.

He kept his features schooled, deliberately neutral, as he tried to decide if it was she who had something to conceal from him. "Now I do for the Order what I used to do for Dragos."

Her eyes held his, bleak with understanding. "Death," she said.

Hunter tilted his chin in acknowledgment. "I want him and all who serve him destroyed. If I have to hunt him and every last one of his followers down, one by one, I will see it done."

He was only stating fact, but Corinne looked at him with a strange softness in her wary expression. There was a question in her gaze, too tender for his liking. "What did he do to you, Hunter? How did Dragos hurt you?"

To his own astonishment, Hunter found he could not speak the words. He'd never been reluctant to admit the isolation and discipline of his upbringing. He had never cared enough about himself or anyone else to feel any inkling of humiliation for having been raised no better than an animal—worse than that.

He'd never been ashamed of his Gen One origins before—sired by an Ancient, the last surviving otherworlder who, along with his alien brethren, had fathered the entire Breed race on Earth. Dragos had secretly kept the powerful vampire drugged and incarcerated inside his laboratory for some long decades. That same savage creature had been unleashed by Dragos on countless captive Breedmates, like Corinne and the other recently freed females.

Like the unknown Breedmate who had given birth to Hunter while imprisoned in those fetid cells.

He had no idea what might have happened to her, had no memory of her whatsoever. But seeing Corinne Bishop, having seen the evidence on her delicate back of the many tortures she had endured, Hunter knew a sudden, deep shame that made him want to deny any link to Dragos or the horrors of his labs.

A tendon twitching in his jaw, he replied, "You don't need to concern yourself with what happened to me. None of it was any worse than what Dragos did to you."

Her frown deepened with disapproval. Even in the dark, he could see color rising into her cheeks. No doubt, she knew he was referring to her scars. Scars he wouldn't have seen if he hadn't been spying on her in her bath.

He waited for her to get angry at the reminder; she had the right, he supposed. He wouldn't have denied that he'd looked. He probably wouldn't have denied that he'd admired what he saw. All night, he'd been trying to forget the thought of her naked in the hotel room bath. The memory came back vividly now, insistent, despite his effort to banish it from his mind.

As for the scars, they'd been shocking, but they hadn't dimmed her beauty. Not in his eyes.

It stunned him how tempted he was to tell her that, whether or not she'd want to hear it.

Corinne stared at him for too long, then she scooted her chair back and started to rise. "I'm going to find the restroom," she murmured.

He stood up with her, his eyes scanning the crowd. "I will go with you."

"To the ladies' room?" She gave him a dismissing look. "Wait here. I'll be right back."

Short of tailing her across the restaurant, she gave him little choice but to cool his heels at the table. He watched her retreat toward the lighted sign marked *"Femmes,"* then she disappeared through the dark, swinging door.

Corinne spent only a minute or two in the restroom, standing with her back resting against the wall opposite the nicked-up porcelain sink and chipped mirror. Just long enough to catch her breath, to collect her thoughts as best she could. Her one cocktail with dinner really had gone straight to her head. Why else would she have been sitting at the table with Hunter, talking about music and reminiscing about her past, when she should have been quizzing him about whatever information he and the Order had gathered on Henry Vachon?

If Hunter hadn't brought up her scars, or the none-too-subtle reminder that he'd seen them and a lot more back at the hotel, she might still be sitting there, losing herself in the simple pleasures of good food and drink and the music she'd loved so much as a girl. She had even been enjoying Hunter's stiff company, which only emphasized how badly the little bit of alcohol had affected her.

She stepped out of the restroom, back into the smoke-wreathed cavern of the restaurant. Standing up, without the restroom wall to keep her steady, her head was light, her legs loose as she drifted toward the three-piece band that was serenading a dance floor crowded with slowly swaying couples.

Corinne stood at the edge of the small square of worn wood flooring and watched the people move among the candlelight and shadows. Bodies pressed close together, arms wrapped around one another as the music enveloped the entire club. She smiled wistfully, unable to keep the smile from her lips as she recognized the sultry but defiant lyrics.

Another Bessie Smith song. Another pull toward the past, back to a time when she was innocent, unaware of just how cruel and ugly evil could be.

She closed her eyes and felt the familiar old music wash over her, tempting her toward its safe harbor. It was only illusion; she knew that. She couldn't run away from where she stood now, no matter how much she longed to erase everything she'd been through. She couldn't ignore where she'd been, what she'd lost . . . what she still needed to do.

She knew all of this, but with the singer's voice lulling her into a gentle sway at the edge of the dance floor, she couldn't resist the sweeping pull. It was only for a minute, a brief indulgence that she savored, eyes closed, senses adrift, floating on a tranquil tide.

When she lifted her lids a moment later, Hunter was standing right in front of her.

He didn't say anything, just towered over her, a looming wall of muscle and dark energy, the heat of his presence making the scant few inches that separated them seem like nothing at all. His harshly sculpted, handsome face was inscrutable as ever. But his eyes glowed with the embers of a banked, but slow, smoldering fire.

It was the same look she'd seen in his eyes back at the hotel, only now there was no door to close between them. There was no place for her to hide from the heated gaze of this dangerous, deadly man. But it wasn't fear that flooded her veins as Hunter looked at her now. It wasn't anything like that at all.

Something electric, something unbidden and powerful, passed between them in that instant. It was the only way she could explain how her hands reached out to him, her palms coming to rest on his broad shoulders. The only way she could fathom the impulse that made her rest her cheek on his strong chest and whisper, "Dance with me, Hunter. Just for a moment?"

Holding on to him, she rocked slowly to Bessie's lyrics, her ear pressed against the heavy thump of Hunter's heart. He wasn't dancing, but she didn't mind. His heat surrounded her, made her feel safe even though he was likely the most dangerous person in the room.

His arms went around her after a long moment, his big hands resting lightly, tentatively at the base of her spine. He was stiff, almost awkwardly so. She couldn't hear him breathing anymore, only the rising drum of his heartbeat, so heavy and intense it nearly drowned out all other sound.

She lifted her head and glanced up at him, her hands still braced on his thick shoulders. His golden eyes were throwing off amber sparks, his pupils narrowing toward catlike slits. Desire rolled off him, unmistakable and hot. She moved back a hesitant step, putting fractional space between them, even though her own pulse was clattering with a sudden, intense awareness.

And need.

It startled her, how deeply it pierced her. Desire was something foreign to her after all she'd been through. After what she'd endured, she thought she would never crave a male's touch. But she did now. Unbelievably, perhaps stupidly, she craved this stony, lethal warrior's touch more than anything else in that moment.

She forced herself to take another hitching step backward. "Thank you for the dance," she murmured, confusion clashing with the warmth that was spiraling through her. "Thank you for this. For bringing me here tonight. I thought I'd forgotten what it was like to feel . . . normal." She glanced down, away from the searing heat of his eyes. "I didn't think it was possible for me to feel . . . anything anymore."

His answering touch was light but firm beneath her chin. He lifted her face on the edge of his fingertips, until their gazes were locked once more. He lowered his head toward hers.

And then he was kissing her.

Gently, unhurried, he brushed his lips across hers. His kiss was almost tentative, as though he didn't know how to take more than what she was willing to give him. As intoxicating as his mouth felt against hers, it was also sweet, the first time she'd ever been touched so carefully, so full of tenderness. That a formidable male like Hunter could possess such patience and restraint astonished her.

It wasn't easy for him. She saw that truth a moment later, as their lips parted and she glanced up into golden eyes transformed into twin fires that seared her with their amber heat. His head bowed toward hers, only a breath between their mouths in the hazy gloom that surrounded them. The tips of his fangs gleamed bright white behind his upper lip. Color flushed the *dermaglyphs* that tracked in graceful arcs and flourishes along the sides of his neck and around to his nape.

He wanted her.

The thought should have terrified her, not drawn her closer. She gazed up at him, yearning against all reason for another taste of his sensual mouth. His hands trembled against the small of her back where he still held her from their brief dance. When he brought one up to stroke her cheek, his touch was feather light, as gentle as his kiss, despite the callused roughness of his weapon-hardened fingers.

Corinne exhaled shallowly as he caressed the pad of his thumb across her lower lip. Her chin lifted on the edge of his fist, he bent his head down toward hers once more . . .

And then he froze.

Tension swept him in an instant—a new tension, this one cold and battle-wary. His eyes flicked up to take in the crowded club. "We have trouble," he said, snapping back into warrior mode. "It's not safe now. I need to take you out of here."

"What is it, Hunter?" She tried to follow the direction of his focus, but he was more than head and shoulders taller than she. "What do you see?"

"Vampires," he said, his voice low, discreet. "A group of them just came in from the front of the restaurant. There's a Gen One among them. One of Dragos's assassins."

Corinne's heart slammed hard against her rib cage. "Are you sure?"

"There can be no doubt."

His reply was so grave, she had to struggle to catch her breath. "Do you still see them? What are they doing?"

"Searching the crowd." His hand found hers and wrapped around it tightly. "My guess is they're looking for us."

He pulled her deeper into the crowd on the dance floor, weaving through the oblivious couples, his gaze never leaving the presumed area of the incoming threat.

"Why would they be looking for us?" she asked as she hurried along at his side, panic fluttering on dark wings in her breast. "How would Dragos know we were in New Orleans?"

"Because someone told him where to look," Hunter answered tersely. "Someone I should have killed when I had the chance."

Victor Bishop.

Oh, God. He had betrayed her once again.

What a stupid mistake to think he wouldn't. Even worse, she had made it possible by persuading Hunter to spare him. Now she could only hope it wouldn't cost either one of them their lives.

Sick with the thought, furious with regret, Corinne held tightly to Hunter's hand as he hauled her through the crowd toward the darkened rear of the establishment.

CHAPTER
Fifteen

They burst out the back door of the place, Hunter's sole objective to get Corinne Bishop to safety. As the steel door swung open onto the rear alleyway, a pair of Breed males wearing Enforcement Agency suits scrambled to attention at their post outside.

Too late.

Hunter had them sized up and dismissed as insignificant obstacles even before the first one had a chance to reach for the firearm holstered at his side. Releasing Corinne's hand, Hunter grabbed the head of the male in front and gave it a violent twist. The spinal column cracked like muffled gunfire as the body dropped lifelessly to the ground.

The second guard went down just as swiftly.

Hunter glanced back at Corinne, who stood behind him, stricken into silence. "Come," he said. "We don't have much time."

Hunter pulled his cell phone from his pants pocket as

they raced along a maze of narrow back alleys. He called Boston and relayed to Gideon what was happening.

"Shit," the warrior muttered on the other end. "If Dragos is worried enough to send assassins down to New Orleans, I guess it's safe to assume that the connection between Dragos and Vachon is a valid one."

"Which means the connection between Bishop and Dragos remains as well," Hunter replied as he navigated past a voodoo shop selling chicken's feet and other animal parts down one particularly strange alley. "That's an issue I will take up with Bishop later."

Gideon blew out a sharp exhalation. "No need, my man. Victor Bishop was killed this afternoon in his Darkhaven. The report filed with the Agency in Detroit stated that he'd attacked his Breedmate and might have done much worse if he hadn't been stopped by one of his security staff at the estate."

"Who killed him?"

"Guy named Mason, according to the reports."

Hunter grunted in acknowledgment, recalling the protective manner of the Darkhaven guard who'd been at the gates when he and Corinne arrived. He glanced at her now and saw the look of understanding creep over her pale features as she struggled to keep up with his long strides. At least Victor Bishop had wounded her for the last time. Some irrational part of him wished it had been his hands that ended the duplicitous bastard for all he'd done to her. "We need someplace to go," he told Gideon.

"You're not at the hotel?"

"No. The maps and my weapons were left in the room."

"Well, consider them gone. You can't go back there now, my man. Too damned risky."

An obvious conclusion, Hunter thought. If Dragos's men had been sweeping the city for some sign of them, he had to assume they would also be checking area hotels.

"Listen," Gideon said. "You just lost the advantage of surprise with Vachon. Lucan's here with me now and he agrees. Taking this mission on solo right now is too risky. Plus, you've got the female to think about. Lucan says it's time to abort. Head back to the plane. I'm gonna see about getting you the hell out of there right now."

Hunter felt an argument rising to the tip of his tongue. It tasted odd to him, he, who'd been raised to follow commands, to never question his orders. But part of him wanted to see this out—wanted to see Henry Vachon and Dragos both punished for what had been done to Corinne and the others. It grated to think this lead would go cold simply because he'd forfeited one tactical advantage.

Before he could make that point to his brethren in Boston, Gideon came back on the line. "I just spoke to the pilots. They'll be gassed up and waiting for you to arrive. How far are you from the airport?"

Hunter navigated out of their current alleyway and found a street he recognized that would lead to one of the main thoroughfares through the French Quarter. "We're on foot now, but twenty minutes at the most by vehicle."

"Get there," Gideon said. "Call in once you're airborne. Then we'll find someplace for you both to lay low until the shit settles down up here. We can't afford to take any more hits to our ranks. Bad enough we're down one man already."

"Down one?" The remark caught him unaware. Something cold and tight clutched in his belly at the thought of losing one of his fellow warriors. "Has there been a death in the field?"

"Shit, you haven't heard. It's Harvard. He's gone—walked out the night before you left for Detroit and hasn't been seen or heard from since. Dante and Kade found his cell phone down by the river in Southie. Hate to say it, but it looks like Chase stepped off the ledge and has no intention of coming back." Gideon went quiet, contemplative for a moment. "You asked if there's been a death in the Order? I'll tell you what, that's exactly how it feels around here right now. About the only thing that'll feel worse is when, somewhere down the line, someone reports in from patrol that they've smoked a Rogue and it turns out to be Harvard."

"I hope that night will not come," Hunter said, struck by how deeply he meant it.

"You and all the rest of us back at the ranch," Gideon replied. "In the meantime, let's hope nothing else goes to hell, right? So, get your asses to the airport ASAP. Report back once you and the female are safe."

"Consider it done," Hunter answered grimly.

He slid the phone back into his pocket and ran with Corinne to search for a means of transportation out of the city.

He didn't notice the humans until they were nearly upon him.

Head down, Chase had his mouth fastened to the neck of a blood Host he'd followed out of a crack house in the bowels of the city a short while ago. Now he grunted in irritation as the approaching vehicle's headlight beams bounced off the brick walls of the narrow side street where he crouched with his prey.

The police cruiser prowled slowly between the old apartment buildings, the side-mounted spotlight flicking on as it neared the halfway mark.

Chase hunkered down, pulling his limp Host deeper into the shadows of the boxy Dumpster that would shield him only until the cops were right in front of it. The straw-haired blonde moaned, whether from the lull of his suckling at her carotid or the buzz of the cocaine that tainted her blood with its sickly sweet tang, he wasn't sure. She tried to move, but he held her down, not quite sated even though he knew he had taken more than his fill already.

The police car crept farther along, edging ever nearer to where he greedily fed.

Some shred of sanity warned him to reach for the shadows. He grabbed at them with his mind, tried to bend them to his will, to gather the gloom around him in order to hide from the threat of the human law enforcement that was mere seconds away from turning their obnoxious light in his direction.

Chase scrabbled to bend the shadows, but his talent was too hard to hold. It wobbled weakly—there and gone, there and gone—lasting no more than mere seconds at a time.

He snarled, frustrated by the loss of control.

How much longer before his ability slipped from his grasp completely? He'd seen the effects of Bloodlust on others. He knew its destructive power. The addiction would eat away his Breed-born talent, then his sanity, his humanity . . . and eventually his soul.

The thought seeped through the haze of his avaricious feeding, as bitter as the drug-laced blood that coursed down his throat. With a growl, he tore his mouth from the wound and licked it sealed, repulsed by himself and the human he might have drained dry if not for the interruption of the approaching police.

He dragged her barely conscious body farther behind the large trash container. She would recover in a short while, recalling nothing of the past few minutes. She'd shake off her strange lethargy and get up, free to return to the addiction that had brought her to this squalid street in the first place.

As for him?

Chase grunted, his head still buzzing as he wiped the blood from his chin where he squatted in the filth of the alleyway. The slow creep of the police cruiser kept him cowered at the edge of the Dumpster for much longer than he liked. He waited, watched, wary as the car came to a halt in front of where he crouched, brakes squeaking. The vehicle's siren gave a short *whoop* before the blue strobes lit up, bathing the alleyway in pulsating light. One of the doors opened, then closed with a soft *thump*.

"Someone back theh?" A firm voice, all business in the heavy Boston accent. Hard-soled boots crunched on the frozen pavement. A sharp *hiss* of static came from the cop's radio as he moved in closer. "No loiterin' allowed out here, 'specially you degenerate crackheads and junkies." Another step closer. Two more and the human would be right in front of him. "Ya gonna hafta gitcha stoner ass gone, unless you'd rather we bring you down to the sta—"

Chase sprang out of his hiding spot like something out of a bad dream.

In one great leap, he launched himself up and over the head of the confounded cop. He came down onto the hood of the parked cruiser as light as a cat, then kicked off just as neatly and tore away on foot before either of Boston's finest had a chance to register what they'd just witnessed.

Chase ran with all the speed he possessed through his Breed genetics. He still had that, still had the strength and stamina of his wilder nature. If anything, the over-fill of blood he'd consumed amplified the beast in him. It drove him on, sent him deeper and deeper into the night, farther and farther out of the bright lights and bustling holiday traffic of the main thoroughfares.

He didn't know how long he'd been running.

He wasn't sure where he was when he finally slowed enough to notice that he was far out of the city. No longer tearing through streets, parking lots, or neighborhoods but plunging through snow-covered open fields and thick copses of suburban woodland. Ahead of him, not far in the distance, a broad granite hill bristling with pines swelled from out of the surrounding country-side. It registered dimly, one of the humans' sprawling forest preserves. One of the few remaining patches of natural terrain held sacrosanct from the threat of urban sprawl that choked it from all sides.

The location pricked something buried in a dark corner of his mind, a fleeting thought that he should know this place. He'd been here once, years ago. Chase shook off the mental distraction as he entered the wooded preserve, no longer caring where he was, only that he was moving, putting the glare of the city miles behind him.

He dropped down onto his haunches in a stretch of thick-forested land, resting his back against the trunk of a soaring oak tree. Naked branches trembled above his head, the moon struggling to peek through the dense, nighttime cloud cover. For a long while, the only sound he heard was his own harsh breathing, the pounding beat of his pulse throbbing in his heaving chest.

He sat there, unsure where his thirst would take him next.

In truth, he could hardly be bothered to give a damn.

Lips curled back from his teeth and fangs, he sucked in the wintry air, shuddering from the cold and the clenching of his poisoned gut. Even though his insides twisted, gorged on too much blood taken too often, he couldn't keep himself from wondering where to find his next fix. He stared up at the midnight sky and tried to guess how long he had yet to feed before dawn would drive him back into hiding to await the night once more.

Oh, yeah, he thought, chuckling to himself in half-mad amusement. All he needed was to give in to the taloned beast that had its hooks stuck hard in him already.

Yet it was that beast that whispered to him as the woods went eerily quiet all around him. He went still, the predator roused to sharp, utter attention.

Some untold distance from where he rested, a twig snapped in the darkness. Then another.

Chase went motionless, silent. Waiting.

Someone approached from deep within the thicket.

He saw him an instant later—a boy, thin, denim-clad legs pumping, booted feet racing as he tossed an anxious glance behind him toward the blackness of the woods at his back. He wore a winter jacket, but beneath the open zipper, his shirt was torn, splashed with dark stains.

It was such an abrupt, bizarre intrusion, it didn't seem

real. He thought the boy a hallucination at first. Some strange trick of a wasting mind.

Until the pungent scent of fear filled his nostrils. Bone-shredding, abject fear.

And blood.

The boy was bleeding from a small wound in his neck, twin rivulets that did not escape Chase's acute notice. The scent of fresh red cells slammed into his senses like a freight train. He rolled into a crouch on his hands and knees as the child ran closer to where he hid.

And then, suddenly, the boy was not alone.

A woman emerged from out of the darkness several yards behind him. Then another child, this one older, a teenager with rounded, terrified eyes. A man crashed out of the distant bracken a moment later. Followed by another woman, limping and sobbing. She too was spattered with blood, bleeding from a bite mark on her forearm. They careened off in separate directions, fleeing like a spooked herd of deer.

Like the sporting game they were, Chase realized, the truth of what he'd stumbled into dawning on him with cold understanding.

Blood club.

That was the niggling familiarity of this place. He had been here once before, more than a decade ago, he and Quentin and a squad of raiding Enforcement Agents, responding to rumors of an illegal hunting party organizing a night of sport at Boston's suburban Blue Hills Park.

He didn't have to hear the animal howl of one of the vampires in pursuit of these doomed humans to know he was standing in the midst of a game for the most depraved of his kind. Banned by Breed law for centuries, clubs that arranged the pursuit of humans as sport—and anything else a vampire could desire—had been condemned but not completely abolished. There were still those who defied the laws. There were still those closed social circles with their very exclusive memberships, catering to the Breed's perverted elite.

Chase searched for the contempt that he should have felt for something so reprehensible. He felt the flicker of outrage, his old Agency ethics tingling with the impulse to intervene, but it wasn't enough to keep his fangs from ripping farther from his gums as the coppery fragrance of spilling blood permeated the thicket. Hunger coiled inside him, making his pulse run hot and wild through his veins.

As the humans neared the unplanned blind where he crouched, he got to his feet.

His amber gaze burning his vision, he stepped out of his hiding place and directly into their path.

CHAPTER
Sixteen

They arrived at the airport in a low-riding purple El Camino that Hunter had commandeered off the street in New Orleans.

The man who'd left the vehicle idling at the curb had been involved in a heated argument with a couple of scantily clad young women on the corner—women he seemed to think owed him money. While he'd jumped out of the car to shout and curse at them, Hunter had put Corinne in the passenger side, then smoothly slid behind the wheel and sped off before the man had the chance to notice they were gone.

The Order's jet awaited them in the private hangar as they drove the stolen vehicle into the cavernous space. Corinne glanced at Hunter, still trying to reconcile the tender touch that had held her in the jazz club with the lethally efficient violence that had taken two lives in the alley outside it. "Those guards back in the city," she murmured as he put the car into park and cut the engine. "You snapped their necks like they were nothing more than twigs."

His expression was unreadable, completely neutral. "We have to go now, Corinne. Gideon has already called ahead to alert the pilots. They'll be waiting for us inside."

She swallowed past the lump of ice that had been lodged in her throat since they fled the club. "You murdered those men, Hunter. In cold blood."

"Yes," he said levelly. "Before they had the opportunity to do likewise to us."

I deal in death.

That's what he'd told her, just last night. Born into the role of assassin and trained very well to do unthinkable things. Before now, it was only words. Only the threat of danger. Now she was seated beside him, about to follow him out of their stolen car and onto the plane that would take her with him God-only-knew-where next.

And yet, when he got out from behind the wheel then walked around to open her door and hold out his hand to her, she took it.

She walked with him, across the concrete floor of the hangar toward the lowered staircase that led up to the cabin of the private jet. Hunter climbed the steps ahead of her, then gestured her toward the spacious cabin.

"The pilots must be in the cockpit," he said as she walked past him to head toward one of the dozen large, leather reclining seats inside. "I will tell them we're here."

Corinne swiveled her head to nod in acknowledgment.

But as her attention swept back toward Hunter, everything seemed to go terribly silent around them. His eyes sparked with warning. He reached for her.

"Corinne, get out. Get out of here right n—"

Before she had the chance to react, something huge—a Breed male, easily as large as Hunter and garbed in head-to-toe black form-fitted clothing—exploded out from the closed cockpit area behind him.

Hunter pivoted with lightning speed, meeting his attacker and grabbing hold of the hand that gripped a nasty-looking black pistol. Shots rang out—one bullet lodging into the ceiling above Hunter's head, two more blasting into the interior sides of the cabin. A window popped, its tempered glass spiderwebbing around the large hole the round left in its wake.

Corinne crouched behind the tall back of a leather seat, watching in a mix of terror and astonishment as Hunter chopped into his assailant's wrist with the edge of his hand. The gun dropped to the floor of the cabin, kicked away by Hunter's boot as he landed another series of similar bare-handed, cutting blows to the other male's neck and jaw.

This one didn't break like the pair of guards outside the jazz club. He was a match for Hunter in size, and as Corinne stared in frantic horror, she realized that he was also equally matched in deadly skill.

The other male grabbed Hunter by his neck and slammed him into the nearby wall. He battered Hunter with blindingly swift punches to his face and skull. Hunter managed to twist out of the punishing hold. With one hand clamped down on his attacker's wrist, he wrenched the other male's arm until Corinne heard the bones crunch under the strain.

Yet Hunter's attacker uttered nothing more than a grunt as he pivoted around to face him, working to get the advantage once more. Hunter didn't seem willing to let him have it. He smashed his boot heel into the side of the other male's kneecap, then delivered another hard blow to his midsection, then the side of the black-clad skull. The assailant went down to the floor, the knit head covering slipping off with the impact, baring his face.

Corinne inhaled a startled gasp.

While Hunter's thick hair was cropped close to his skull, this vampire's head was shaved totally bald. An intricate pattern of Gen One *dermaglyphs* tracked up around his ears and across the top of his domed head. Their color was muted, showing none of the fury and pain that would have made another Breed male's skin markings livid with deep, turbulent colors. Beneath the dark slashes of the intruder's brows, fierce gray eyes were as flat and cold as steel.

He was as calm and cool as Hunter. And every bit as lethal.

Although the two of them looked different from each other, they were also the same.

Both of them born assassins.

Both of them trained to kill on Dragos's command.

In the instant it took for her to realize that, Hunter had his foot aimed to come down on the other male's face. As his thigh muscles flexed and the boot heel started its hard descent, the other male rolled out of the way and launched himself toward the jet's small galley between the cabin and the wrecked cockpit door.

With his surely broken arm dangling useless at his side, the intruder reached out and pulled down a cabinet full of glassware. He whirled on Hunter, brandishing a long, glittering shard of crystal like a blade. He made a swipe, a strike evaded only narrowly as Hunter dodged aside then plowed his fist into his attacker's lower abdomen. The blow staggered him, the glass blade shattering under their feet as the struggle pushed farther into the galley.

Corinne could have run out. She should have, probably. But the thought of leaving Hunter to contend with this seemingly unstoppable killer was out of the question. She crept out from behind the cabin seat, looking for some means to help him. Her talent was useless to her here. Without the aid of a steady sound wave, her ability to warp the volume of audio energy could not be summoned.

But if she could get her hands on the gun that lay only a few yards between her and the combat zone . . .

She saw it too late.

Hunter's attacker was already jockeying toward it himself, fending Hunter off while he grappled with his foot to bring the weapon within reach.

They pivoted and strained, alternating blows that would have knocked lesser males unconscious. And then, in a moment that passed so quickly Corinne could hardly register the motion, Hunter's assailant made a grab for the gun and came up with it aimed squarely at his face.

"No!" Corinne's feet were moving even before she could take a breath and shout once more. She raced up behind the other male and flung herself onto his back. Holding on with one hand, she raked the fingernails of the other into the soft flesh of his face and eyes. She gouged as hard as she could, animalistic in her need to prevent one of Dragos's beasts from harming someone she cared about.

The trained assassin didn't so much as gasp at her attack. His elbow came back hard against the side of her face, crushing her lips against her teeth. She tasted blood in her mouth. Felt it trickle down her chin as her lip split open.

And then she was flying backward, tossed off his broad back like she was nothing at all.

Failed or not, her attempt to distract had given Hunter just enough opportunity to knock the gun off its aim as the intruder squeezed off another round. Hunter bowed his head and rammed into the other male with the full force of his body, thick shoulder plowing the other male backward on his heels.

Hunter shoved him toward the open door at the top of the lowered staircase. They both tumbled out of the plane together. Corinne got up and ran to the opening, watching as the two landed hard on the concrete below.

Hunter sent a quick glance up at her—just enough to ascertain that she was all right. She felt the heat of his golden eyes as they lit on her face, on the thin trail of blood that she now wiped from her chin.

She heard his low growl, the first sound he'd uttered during the entire length of his punishing struggle. When he turned back to the semiconscious assassin who lay pinned beneath him on the ground, Hunter's movements were precise and unflinching. He took the gun from the slackened hand of his attacker and rose to his feet. Straddling the large, black-clad body, Hunter aimed the nose of the weapon at the hairless, *glyph*-covered head.

No, that wasn't quite right, Corinne noticed now.

He wasn't aiming at the assassin's head exactly, but rather at the peculiar ring of hard black material that circled his neck like some kind of collar.

Even from the top of the stairs, she could see the assassin's eyes go wide with understanding as Hunter leveled the gun on that ring of thick, dull black. Now she saw fear in the other male. Now, finally, she saw his acknowledgment of defeat.

Hunter fired.

A flash of light answered the *crack* of gunfire, so piercingly bright Corinne had to shield her eyes from its sudden blast. When it cleared an instant later, thin smoke rose up from the place where the assassin lay, his large body lifeless on the concrete, his head cleanly severed.

"Oh, my God," she whispered, unsure what she'd just witnessed.

Hunter came out from behind the lowered staircase as she reached the bottom step. "Are you all right?"

She nodded her head, then shook it weakly, trying to understand what had happened here. "How did you... What did you do to him?"

Stoic once more, except for the amber sparks that glittered darkly as his gaze dropped to her split lip, Hunter steered her away from the carnage on the ground. He walked over and retrieved the thick black ring from the charred neck of the assassin. "The pilots were dead before we arrived. Dragos must have eyes all over the city now. He may send more like this one after us. We have to go now."

She stole an incredulous glance over her shoulder as he guided her away from the body. "Are you just going to leave him there?"

Hunter gave a grim nod. "The hangar doors are open. Come morning, the sun will destroy what's left of him."

"And if it doesn't?" she pressed. "What if Dragos or his men get here first and they realize what you've done? What if they come after you?"

"Then they will know what awaits them if they try."

He put his hand out to her, palm up, waiting for her to take it. "Let's get out of here, Corinne."

She hesitated, uncertainty gnawing at the edges of her conscience. But then she slipped her hand into his and let him lead her away from the carnage.

CHAPTER
Seventeen

The human female screamed when she saw Chase emerge from behind the cover of the large oak. Her face bathed in the amber light of his transformed gaze, she sent up another blood-curdling shriek and veered sharply in an attempt to avoid him.

He could have felled her easily.

He might have, but in that next instant the woods erupted with the oncoming rush of the blood club in pursuit of their fleeing game. From out of the darkness at the humans' heels, a vampire descended from a great, airborne leap to tackle one of the running men. As he sank his fangs into his prey's throat, three more Breed males emerged from the shadows at great speed, all of them converging on the terrified humans like a pack of slavering wolves.

That's when Chase spotted a face he recognized.

Murdock.

The son of a bitch.

Chase had heard rumors of the male's perverse interests during his time in the Enforcement Agency, so he supposed it should come as no surprise to see Murdock bounding out of the gloom to grab hold of the little boy in the bloodied shirt.

But it did surprise Chase. It diverted his attention from his own blood thirst more effectively than a good hard dose of midday sun. It enraged him to see Murdock after the altercation a couple of nights ago in Chinatown—time that seemed a hundred years past to him now.

And it repulsed him to watch Murdock seize a hank of the child's hair in his fist as he threw him to the ground, prepared to wrench the delicate neck into a better angle for him to feed.

Chase flew at the vampire with a savage roar.

He knocked Murdock off the struggling, weeping boy. As the young human made a frantic escape, Chase tumbled with Murdock into the snow and bramble. He drove his fist into the vampire's jaw, reveling in the vicious *crack* of shattering bone beneath his knuckles.

One of Murdock's blood club pals noticed the intrusion. He dropped the human he had caught and leapt onto Chase's back. Chase bucked him off. The vampire crashed hard into a nearby tree.

Murdock started struggling, about to get away. Before he could get the chance, Chase grabbed a fallen branch of jagged oak and smashed it into Murdock's kneecap. He howled in agony, rolling away to cradle the shattered limb while Chase turned his attention to the other vampire, who was coming right back at him, hissing through bared, bloodied fangs.

Chase pivoted up from the ground with the hard

length of oak gripped tightly in his hand just as Murdock's companion was charging up on him. Chase thrust the jagged branch out in one swift, furious motion—staking the bastard through flesh and sternum, right into the heart.

The remaining two blood club participants seemed to lose interest in their sport when they saw one of their own fall deadweight to the ground, blood gushing from the gaping wound in his chest, and another writhing in anguish in the frozen bracken nearby. They froze where they were, slackened grasps letting their horrified prey loose to escape.

Chase swung toward them, his eyes shooting feral amber beams into the dark woods, his gore-slickened weapon clutched in his hand, ready to do more damage.

Without a single word, the pair of law-breaking Agents bolted in opposite directions, disappearing into the night.

The woods fell silent once again, except for Murdock's pained groans.

Chase drew in a cleansing breath. Intellect and reason slowly filtered in through the dark fog of his fury and the nagging thirst that still rode him. The situation he now found himself in was hardly ideal. One dead Agent bled out on the ground. Two more on the loose, certain to identify him as having attacked them unprovoked. Given his reputation lately, there would be few who'd believe him if he said he'd stumbled upon an illegal blood hunt and only did what he had to in order to break it up.

And then there was the problem of the escaped humans, the runners. He knew as well as any of his kind how dangerous it was to allow humans back into the general population without first scrubbing their memories of all knowledge of the Breed. Centuries of careful coexistence could be wiped out in an instant if enough hysterical humans were to scream the word "vampire."

Chase snarled, torn between responsibility for his race and the deeper, more personal need to wring Murdock for any information on Dragos.

Chase knew the right thing to do. He took a step away from Murdock, ready to fall in behind the escaped humans and contain the situation.

The wail of distant sirens, growing louder by the second, gave him pause. He could be too late already.

He glared down at Murdock.

With a muttered curse, he hefted the injured vampire up onto his shoulder, then bounded off into the thicket with him.

There was enough gas in the tank of the pimp's purple El Camino to carry them a good distance out of the city. This far from New Orleans's revived central hub, the homes were small and sparse, many still in disrepair or derelict from the ravages of the hurricane that had blown through years prior.

As Hunter drove, he kept a calculating eye on the eastern horizon where day was soon to break. Already the deep blue quiet on the other side of midnight was giving way to the pastel shades of morning. He glanced at Corinne, who sat silent in the passenger seat. Her split lip was swollen and bruised. Her eyes were trained on the empty road ahead. She seemed weary, her delicate shoulders trembling from either shock or chill; he wasn't sure which.

"We will stop soon," he said. "You need to rest, and dawn is coming."

Her nod was vague, little more than a tremor of acknowledgment. She inhaled a shaky breath. Blew it out slowly. "Did you know him?"

Hunter didn't have to ask who she was referring to. "I'd never seen him before tonight."

"But you and he..." She swallowed, then ventured a sidelong look at him. "You fought the same way. Neither one of you would have stopped until the other was dead. You were both so vicious, so relentless. So unemotional as you went about it."

"We were both trained to kill, yes."

"At Dragos's command." He felt her stare fixed on him as she spoke, saw her stricken expression in his peripheral vision. "How many are there?"

Hunter shrugged, uncertain. "I could only guess at our numbers. We were never told about each other. Dragos kept us isolated, with only a Minion handler to look after our basic needs. When we were called into service, our work was always done alone."

"Have you killed many people?"

"Enough," he replied, then scowled and shook his head. "No, it won't be enough until I see Dragos dead and gone. Even if I have to take down every one of the others like me in order to get to him. Then it will be enough."

She turned her gaze back to the road, quiet and contemplative. "What was the thing you used to kill the assassin back at the airport? He was wearing some kind of collar. You took it when we left, and I saw that you were aiming for it when you shot him. The explosion from it was blinding."

Hunter could still see the piercing blast of light in his mind. There were times when he could still feel the confining bite of his own collar, the one he'd shed the night he joined the Order. "It's an obedience device of Dragos's design. Inside, the collar houses concentrated ultraviolet light. It cannot be tampered with or removed without triggering the detonator. Only Dragos can deactivate the sensor."

"Oh, my God," she whispered. "You mean it's a shackle. A lethal one."

"Effective, certainly."

"What about you?" Corinne asked. "You don't wear a collar like that."

"Not anymore."

She watched him carefully, her eyes rooted on him as he turned off the main road and followed a side street toward what looked to be an abandoned row of houses. "If you used to wear that awful device too, how did you manage to get free?"

"Dragos had little choice but to release me. He'd assembled a meeting of his allies last summer at a private location outside Montreal. The Order discovered what he was up to and moved in to attack. Dragos commanded me to provide the sole cover while he and his men fled out the back."

He felt Corinne's grave understanding in the quiet way she listened. "He was sending you out alone against how many of the Order? He meant for you to die."

Hunter shrugged. "It only showed me the measure of his desperation, and his contempt for me. He and I both knew that if I didn't charge out to confront the warriors in those next few moments, he and his associates stood no chance of escaping. I told him I would go, but only if he released me from my bond."

It had been a long while since he'd thought about that night in the forests outside Montreal. In truth, his journey toward freedom had begun even earlier that summer—the night he'd stolen into the private lodge of a Gen One vampire named Sergei Yakut on orders to kill from Dragos and found himself staring into the mesmerizing, mirrorlike eyes of an innocent little girl.

"It was Mira who gave me the courage to demand my freedom," he said, a warmth opening in the center of his chest at just the thought of the child. "She is a seer. She has the gift of precognition. It was in her eyes that I saw myself released from Dragos's control. If not for her, I might never have known it was possible to live any other way."

"She saved your life," Corinne murmured. "No wonder you care for her like you do."

"I would lay down my life for her," he answered, as automatic as breathing.

And it was true. The observation jolted him on some level, but he couldn't deny the fondness he had for the little girl. He had become fiercely protective of her, just as he was coming to feel protective of the beautiful woman seated beside him now.

But where his affection for Mira was a soft warmth, his regard for Corinne Bishop was something altogether different. It went deeper, burned with an intensity that only seemed to grow stronger every moment they were together. He desired her; that much had become evident when they'd kissed earlier. He wanted to kiss her again, and that was a problem.

As for the other feelings she stirred in him, he didn't know what to make of that. Nor did he want to know. His duty was to the Order, and there was no room for distractions. No matter how tempting they might be.

It took Corinne a long while before she responded. "Every child deserves to have someone willing to do whatever it takes to keep them safe, to ensure their happiness. That's what family is supposed to be, isn't it?" When she looked at him now, her expression seemed troubled, haunted somehow. "Don't you think that's true, Hunter?"

"I would not know." He slowed in front of a dark little shotgun house with boarded windows and a sagging front porch. It looked abandoned, as did the rest of the meager homes that still stood after the waters had receded years earlier. Cracked, weed-choked cement foundations marked the places where other houses had been. "This one should suffice," he told Corinne as he put the vehicle in park.

She was still staring at him oddly from across the wide bench seat of the El Camino. "You never had anyone at all—not even when you were a child? Not even your mother?"

He killed the engine and took out the key. "There was no one. I was taken away from the Breedmate who bore me in Dragos's laboratory when I was still an infant. I have no memory of her. The Minion handler assigned to me by Dragos was responsible for my rearing. Such as it was."

Her face had gone pale and slack. "You were born in the lab? You were ... taken away from your mother?"

"We all were," he replied. "Dragos engineered our lives from the instant we were conceived. He controlled everything, to ensure we became his perfect killing machines loyal only to him. We were born to be his assassins. His Hunters, and nothing more."

"Hunters." The word sounded wooden on her

tongue. "I thought Hunter was your name. Is it your name?"

He could see her confusion. Her frown furrowed deeper as she quietly processed all that she was hearing. "Hunter is the only thing I've been called from the day I was born. It is what I am. What I will always be."

"Oh, my God." Her soft exhalation trembled a bit. Something else flickered across her face in that moment, something he could not place. It looked like sorrow. It looked like fresh, dawning horror. "All the infants born in Dragos's labs were taken away. They've all been raised like you were? All those innocent baby boys. That's what became of them all..."

It wasn't asked as a question, but he answered her with a frank, solemn nod.

Corinne closed her eyes, saying nothing more. She turned her head away from him, toward the dark glass of the passenger window.

In the suddenly awkward and lengthening silence, Hunter reached down and opened the driver-side door. "Wait here. I'll go check the house and make sure it's suitable shelter."

She didn't answer. She didn't even look at him, her face now tucked into her right shoulder. As he walked away, he thought he noticed tears sliding down her cheek.

Corinne all but vaulted out of the vehicle as soon as Hunter had gone into the house. The prolonged drive in the confining space would have been enough to spike her anxiety, all the more so considering what she'd witnessed at the airport tonight. But it was something far worse that sent her fleeing the car for the dank, predawn outdoors.

Fear and horror gripped her, threatening to turn her stomach inside out as she stumbled toward a concrete slab in the derelict yard next door. She sank down onto the damp foundation and buried her face in her hands.

In all of her many nightmares over what might have become of her son, never had she imagined the brutal fate Hunter had just described to her.

Hunter.

Good lord, it wasn't even a true name. Just a label for an object, no different from one that might be used to refer to a blade or a pistol, or any other tool manufactured for the sole purpose of destruction.

Insignificant.

Expendable.

Inhuman.

She wiped at the tears that had begun falling even before Hunter had left the vehicle. Her heart ached for his past suffering, but it tore apart in her breast at the realization that her baby boy—the beautiful, innocent child she'd loved instantly on sight—was still trapped inside the ugly world of Dragos's making.

A sob rose in her throat as she remembered the sweet face of the squalling infant she'd delivered some thirteen years ago. She could still picture his tiny fists flailing as the Minion nurse carried him across the labor room to wash him and wrap him in a plain white blanket. She could still see his eyes—almond shaped and bluish green, like her own, his *dermaglyph*-covered scalp crowned with a smattering of silky black hair, the same color as hers.

Her son would have her sonokinetic ability too, inherited genetically from her the same way he would inherit his Gen One strength and power from the creature who'd sired him. The talent Corinne gave her son was something Dragos could never take away from him. That ability would forever stamp him as hers, no matter what Dragos had done to him in the years he'd had to bend him to his twisted missions and ideals.

Her son had a name as well. Corinne had whispered it to him in that first moment their eyes had met and locked in the delivery room. He'd heard her, even at a scant few minutes out of her womb, she was sure of it. And he'd heard her cry for him as the Minion nurse carried him away an instant later, never to be seen again.

God, how many days and weeks and months—how many years—had she mourned his absence from her life? And now, to think what he'd been born into. It made her sick with anguish to imagine what he might have become in the thirteen years Dragos had controlled him.

Hope churned desperately within her. Maybe he wasn't living that awful existence, after all. Maybe he'd been taken away from her for some other purpose, not shackled to Dragos's whims by a deadly ultraviolet collar. Not forced to exist as a killing machine without knowing who he truly was, without anyone to hold him or nurture him or love him.

And if he was one of the many Gen One boys Dragos bred as assassins in his labs? Maybe he'd somehow escaped his horrific enslavement as Hunter had. Maybe her son wasn't living at all anymore. For one shameful second, she wished him dead, if only to spare him the bleak existence Hunter had described.

But he was alive. She knew it the same way every parent must know, regardless of how much time or distance separates them from their child. Deep in her marrow, she was certain her little boy was still breathing.

Somewhere...

The hopelessness of finding him when she didn't even know where to begin looking pressed down on her as she sat alone on the concrete slab, staring out at the vast, empty wasteland of what had probably once been a pleasant neighborhood on the outskirts of New Orleans. Now there was next to nothing left of it. Displaced families, homes in neglect and ruin, countless lives rent apart by a force they had been powerless to stop.

She had weathered her own storm in the decades Dragos had imprisoned her. He hadn't beaten her yet. He hadn't won. Nor would he, so long as she had breath in her body.

She could only pray that her son was equally resilient.

Hunter had managed to get away and start a new life, after all. But then, Hunter'd had the Order there to help pull him out of his previous existence. He'd had Mira to instill that much-needed glimpse of hope that he might have a chance, a way out.

What did her son have?

He didn't know there was someone who loved him and wanted him to be free. He couldn't know there was hope, slim as it was, that someone longed to find him and give him the life he deserved.

As for Corinne, she didn't know where her son was, let alone if he could be salvaged. And then there was Hunter and the Order. To them, her son was just another of Dragos's deadly assets. One they were all pledged to destroy—most of all Hunter, who knew better than anyone how dangerous the others like him were. The Order had declared war on Dragos and all who served him, and for good reason. They would view her child as an enemy.

Although she didn't want to think it, there was a terrified part of her that worried they might be right.

Corinne wiped the back of her hand across her damp cheek as Hunter came out of the house next door. He saw her sitting there and strode over through the ragged, mud-choked grass. He was darkness against the dim shadows of the approaching dawn, his big black combat boots chewing up the turf as his long, muscular legs carried him nearer. His coat flapped behind him like a black leather sail with each rolling stride.

He scowled as he drew close. "Why did you leave the vehicle?"

She dashed away the last of her tears. "I don't like tight spaces. Besides that, it's been a long night, and I'm tired."

He paused in front of her, staring down at her in question. "You are crying."

"No." The lie was likely too brisk to be convincing, but to her relief, Hunter didn't press the issue. His gaze was rooted on her mouth, his brows furrowing deeper.

"Your lip is bleeding again."

Instinctively, she darted her tongue out to find the small cut she'd sustained earlier that night. She tasted blood—only a faint trace, no cause for alarm. But Hunter's eyes were fixed on her still. His pupils narrowed. Amber glinted in the gold of his irises.

"Dawn is coming," he said, his voice a low, raspy growl. "Come with me. The house has been vacant for some time. It will provide us adequate shelter."

She got up and followed him. The abandoned residence smelled of mildew and the sour tinge of brine and dried mud. Hunter walked ahead of her, pulling together the stiffened drapes that still hung over the broken window in the living room. Above their heads, a ceiling fan drooped like an upside-down tulip, its wooden blades warped from the floodwater that had risen to engulf them for God knew how many days before it had finally receded.

Only a few items of furniture remained in the place amid the smashed mementos, peeled wallpaper, and dust-covered debris that littered the floor. Hunter stepped over it, navigating the best path for her. At an adjacent, open doorway down the hall, he paused to motion her forward.

"I've cleared a spot in here where you can rest a while."

Corinne walked to him and glanced inside. Most of the floor space was empty, swept clean of the filth that plagued the other areas of the house. A thin, mud-stained mattress had been shoved upright on its side against the far wall, held in place by a substantial but storm-wrecked chest of drawers.

Hunter took off his long leather coat and spread it out in the center of the cleared floor. "For you to sleep on," he said, when she turned a questioning look at him.

"What about you?"

"I will report in to the Order, then stand guard in the other room while you rest." He pivoted to move past her, back into the hallway.

"Wait. Hunter..." She wrapped her arms around herself, already feeling too much alone in the confines of the dreary little room. "Will you stay with me here... just until I'm asleep?"

He stared, unspeaking, for almost longer than she could bear. She knew he was probably the last person she should look to for comfort, especially after what she'd seen him do tonight. After all she'd heard of his upbringing and his personal mission for the Order, she knew this deadly male was potentially the worst ally she could have in her need to find—and save—her child.

Yet when she looked at Hunter in the soft shadows of the storm-ravaged house, she didn't see ruthlessness or savagery. She saw the same restraint and tenderness that he'd shown her at the jazz club in the city, in the moments before he'd kissed her so unexpectedly on the dance floor. His golden eyes simmered with that same heat now, the warmth of his gaze drifting slowly to her mouth.

Now Corinne had gone speechless, motionless, unsure what disturbed her more: the thought of kissing him again, or the thought that he might simply turn away and leave her standing there by herself.

"Lie down," he murmured, his voice thick and rough-edged. The points of his fangs gleamed behind his lush upper lip as he spoke.

Corinne backed away from him and eased herself down onto his splayed coat. He moved toward her in a slow, predatory prowl, then sank down beside her as she stretched out tentatively on her side atop the buttery soft black leather. His body was a long wall of heat along her spine and curved backside, his thighs firm and solid against hers. Even though they were fully clothed, her every nerve ending came alive with awareness. Need unfurled deep within her, a slow stretching of feather-light wings, putting a flutter in her already erratic heartbeat, stealing her already shaky, shallow breath.

Hunter's arm came around her, a band of heavy bone and muscle caging her gently against him. Power radiated from every inch of his body, but instead of fear or anxiety at the sensation of being hemmed in, Corinne felt protected.

She felt safe, something she hadn't known for a very long time.

Safe in the arms of the most lethal man she'd ever known.

CHAPTER
Eighteen

Midmorning at the Order's Boston headquarters normally meant lights out, shut-eye time for Lucan and the rest of the compound's residents.

Not today.

And although no one had said as much, as the head of this expanding household Lucan knew that the tension gripping them all was nearing the breaking point. Even Mira seemed subdued, the perceptive child seer quietly eating the last few bites of her pancakes and sausage beside Renata at the large dining table instead of chattering at her usual mile-a-minute speed.

The impromptu breakfast gathering had been Gabrielle's idea. The fact that the Order's female residents had been dining in the compound alongside their warrior mates instead of up in the mansion at street level had been at Lucan's insistence. Although it felt odd having everyone crowded into Gabrielle and his quarters, nineteen people gathered around the long table Gabrielle had special-ordered months ago from a local Dark-haven craftsman, it was far more palatable than the thought of having anyone out of his sight in the daylight hours when he could do nothing to protect them.

Protect them? Shit.

What a goddamn joke that had become.

Lucan scoffed to himself, well aware that the Order had never been more vulnerable. The once-certain security of the compound had been reduced to a flimsy veneer of safety now that Dragos had access to their precise location.

Not only that, but Dragos was apparently going on the offensive elsewhere too—case in point, the status call Hunter had made to headquarters a couple hours ago. The attack at the airport hangar by one of Dragos's Gen One assassins had left the two charter pilots dead and Hunter stranded in New Orleans with the civilian female Corinne Bishop. They were currently holed up in a post-Katrina ruin awaiting sundown and Lucan's further instructions.

Then there was the lingering matter of Sterling Chase's absence. Lucan had declared the warrior cut loose from the fold since he'd gone AWOL, but the fact was, it bothered him to have lost Harvard. It bothered everyone, and his absence from the table—and the missions—was felt by the whole of the Order. But wanting him back wasn't bringing him back, and since it was Chase's decision to walk out, it was going to have to be his decision to walk back in.

The only good thing to happen around the compound recently was the safe return of Brock and Jenna from Alaska late last night. The massive Breed male from Detroit and his pretty human mate sat at the other end of the table from Lucan, Brock's long, dark fingers woven through Jenna's slender, paler ones as the couple conversed with Kade and Alex. The fact that Jenna wasn't a Breedmate didn't seem to make her bond with Brock any less intense. Then again, calling Jenna Darrow human wasn't quite accurate anymore, considering the rice-size bit of alien DNA and biotech material the woman had been carrying in her spinal cord for the past couple of weeks.

She'd only been gone for a few days, but in that time the small *dermaglyph* that had so spontaneously appeared on the nape of her neck before she'd left had begun to creep around toward her shoulders. It was the damnedest thing, seeing a Breed skin-marking on the flesh of a human—a female human, besides. Add to that the fact that Jenna's body seemed to heal from injuries at a rate similar to that of Lucan's kind, combined with her newfound superhuman strength and agility, and the former trooper from Alaska was shaping up to be one hell of an addition to the Order's personnel arsenal.

Just how far Jenna's genetic transformation would eventually go was still anyone's guess.

Jesus, what a strange fucking trip it had been, Lucan thought to himself as he scanned the circle of faces assembled around the table. Most of those faces had been unknown to him just a year and a half ago, and now they were as familiar to him as blood kin.

Even Lazaro Archer and his grandson, Kellan, seemed less like strangers than members of the compound's family in the handful of days they'd been under the Order's watch. Lazaro had proven himself a strong, honorable male. As for Lucan, he remained humbled by the other Gen One's offer of his stronghold in Maine as the Order's temporary headquarters. It was a lifeline they needed, and one he meant to take advantage of as soon as possible.

"I want to thank you again for your offer, Lazaro," he said, glancing to the left side of the table where Archer sat, smiling idly as he listened to the spirited debate taking place between his teenage grandson and young Mira over a book they'd both recently read.

Lazaro Archer's dark blue eyes were solemn as he met Lucan's gaze. "Please, no need to thank me. I owe you and the Order more than I can ever possibly repay. You saved Kellan's life, and you saved mine. I will always be in your debt. Besides," he added with a shrug of his broad shoulder, "the place up north has been sitting idle practically since I had it built in the 1950s. Eleanor thought the whole concept ridiculous—she laughed, said I was crazy when I told her I wanted to build a secured bunker and bomb shelter under the house, like so many humans were doing during the period of their so-called Cold War. She said in the event of a nuclear disaster, she'd rather go up in a cloud of dust like the rest of the population than cook like a bunch of canned sardines underneath our house. Never was able to convince her to spend so much as one night up there. As headstrong as she was beautiful, my Ellie."

Lucan watched the Breed elder's expression turn wistful as he spoke of his Breedmate. It was one of the first times he'd mentioned her name since the attack on their Darkhaven had killed her and the rest of Archer's household. Eleanor Archer and everyone else in the private residence had been reduced to ash and rubble at Dragos's command. All those lives lost so that Dragos could catch a firmer grasp around the Order's throat.

Lazaro Archer exhaled and shook his head. "I haven't thought of the place—or Ellie's dislike of it—in a very long time. As I told you earlier, if you find the property suitable for the Order, consider it yours."

Lucan nodded in acknowledgment. "We'll make that decision tonight, when we head up to have a look at the place."

From a few seats down the other side of the table, Gideon caught Lucan's eye and piped in with more details. "I've got a laptop loaded with CAD software and communications that we'll bring with us to the site. We can import photos of the place, inside and out, then the software will convert them to blueprints and schematics on the fly. I've also got satellite receivers ready to roll so we can get some comms hooked up as soon as we get there and run the tests I'll need in order to prep for the relocation."

Lucan could barely suppress his grin at hearing Gideon slide into full geek mode. "The technical hocus-pocus is all yours while we're up there."

He noticed that Savannah had grown quiet beside Gideon as they talked about the night's planned trip north. Gideon hadn't missed his mate's reaction either. He gave her hand a gentle squeeze where it rested on the table. "Don't worry, love. It's just a field trip, not a mission. No guns or explosives involved. More's the pity," he added, cracking a cockeyed smile.

Even from where Lucan sat, he could see that Savannah's soft brown eyes were sober. More than sober, they were bleak with flat-out terror. Her voice was tender, more wounded than Lucan had ever heard it. "I can't make jokes about this, Gideon. Not anymore. This shit is getting too goddamn real for me."

Abruptly, she got up from the table and started clearing her empty plate and silverware. Like some unstated demonstration of feminine solidarity, Gabrielle, Elise, and Dylan quickly followed Savannah's lead, picking up what they could, then disappearing right behind her through the swinging door that led into the adjacent kitchen.

Gideon cleared his throat. "Apparently I'll be doing some feather-smoothing before we head out tonight."

Lucan grunted. "Maybe a little groveling too."

"She worries about you," Tess said to Gideon, her hand resting over the large curve of her pregnant belly. "She'll never let on how much, because she knows you need her to be strong. But it's there with her always." At Gideon's acknowledging nod, Tess turned a tender look on her own mate, Dante, beside her. "The worry is there with all of us, every time one of you goes out on a mission. Every time you leave the compound, you're carrying our hearts with you."

"Precious cargo," Dante said, lifting her hand from atop the round swell of their unborn child and pressing his lips to her palm.

Tess's answering smile twisted into a pained grimace. She sucked in air, then blew it out in a slow hiss. "Your son is getting restless again already this morning. I think I'd better . . . head back to our quarters and . . . lie down . . . for a little while."

Dante sprang into action, gingerly helping her up with Renata, Jenna, and Alex acting as spotters on either side of them. Lucan was on his feet before he realized it, as were the rest of the mated Breed males in the room, all of them standing there in wary silence, probably looking as useless as they felt.

"I'm okay," Tess blurted, too breathless for Lucan's liking. She walked slowly, carefully, one arm cradling the underside of her belly, the other clutched tight to Dante as he gently steered her away from the table.

Technically she wasn't due for another couple of weeks, and although Lucan was no expert on such things, he had to guess that the Order's pending delivery would be arriving sooner than later.

"Can you make it to the sofa in the other room, babe?" Dante asked, tense and concerned, the devoted, doting father-to-be.

Tess dismissed the question with a curt wave. "I want to walk . . . it's better if I move a bit. Once I lie down, I'll be there for a while."

"Okay," Dante said. "We'll take it nice and slow, all right? That's it, babe. Slow steps. You're doing great."

The couple said some quick good-byes, then began an unhurried trek back to their quarters in the compound. Gabrielle came back to the dining room with Savannah and the others, just in time to see that Tess and Dante were gone. After a few moments of awkward silence, Mira turned a concerned look on Renata.

"Is Tess's baby ready to be born?"

Renata's sober glance traveled the anxious faces in the room before lighting back on Mira with a nurturing, patient smile. "Yes, I think so, Mouse. It's not going to be long at all before the baby arrives."

Mira frowned. "Hunter better hurry up and come home, or he won't get to meet the baby when it gets here. Where is he, anyway?"

"Still on a mission," Niko replied, smoothly stepping in like the father figure he'd become to the little girl. "Hunter's got some important things to do down in New Orleans, but he'll be coming back as soon as he can."

"Well, that's good," Mira declared. "Because he needs to be here before Christmas for sure. Do you know he's never had Christmas before? I promised I would make him a decoration for his room."

At the girl's mention of the impending holidays, a further pall fell over the dining room. Lucan felt the weight of so many gazes deliberately avoiding him, everyone waiting for him to go all grinch and announce to an innocent child that there would be no Christmas at the compound.

Hell, he wasn't even sure there would be a compound by Christmas, which was—damn, less than two weeks away.

Renata dropped down into a crouch next to Mira's chair at the table. "I've got an idea, Mouse. Why don't you come with me and show me what you're making for Hunter?"

"Okay," she answered, then turned to Kellan with a bright grin. "You wanna see too?"

"Sure." The teen shrugged as though he couldn't care less, but he was out of his seat as soon as the word left his lips. He loped along sullenly behind Renata and Mira, a loose shuffle of gangly arms and legs.

"Renata's right about the baby, you know." Savannah addressed everyone in the room. "I've got a lot of good Southern midwives in my mama's line, and I've attended enough births myself to know that we're probably looking at a matter of days before Tess goes into labor. The way she's carrying, we could be down to a matter of hours."

Lucan felt a scowl pressing into his brow. "Days or hours? We need a few more weeks."

Lazaro Archer met him with a sage look. "Nature doesn't give a damn for convenience, and never has."

Lucan grunted, well aware of that ironic truth. He also knew they could buy valuable time if they could drop a hammer on Dragos somehow, get the bastard on the run again. It was time that they needed to assess a possible relocation of the compound, and time that Tess and Dante deserved in order to deliver their baby under some semblance of normal, peaceful conditions.

He looked over at Gideon. "Best-case estimate, how soon can you be up and running if we determine the move to Archer's holding is viable?"

"Have laptop, will travel. Assuming we can establish satellite access up there without any issues, I can get our basic systems limping along in a few hours. The whole enchilada—networks, telecom, security cams, heat and motion sensors, et cetera—is going to take a couple of weeks, minimum."

Lucan expelled a curse along with his low sigh. "All right. Not great news, but we'll have to make it work. What about leads on Dragos?" he asked the assembled group. "Anything turn up on Murdock's possible whereabouts?"

"Nothing firm," Tegan replied from the other end of the table. "I've questioned a few of his known associates, but they came up empty. No one I've found has seen or heard from him since the incident the other night in Chinatown. Meanwhile, Rowan's putting out feelers on Murdock from within the Agency. One way or another, we'll find the son of a bitch."

Lucan nodded grimly. "Let's make it soon, yeah? Right now, he's our best shot at getting the drop on Dragos from this end. While we're working that angle, Hunter's going to run recon tonight on Henry Vachon in New Orleans. Based on the attack Dragos ordered last night, it appears the connection between Vachon and him is more than valid."

A few grave glances met his from the group, silent acknowledgment of the close call Hunter and his civilian companion had survived with one of Dragos's assassins. Brock's expression was the most concerned. Understandable, considering the history he'd had with Corinne Bishop back when he had served as a bodyguard for her family's Darkhaven in Detroit. The warrior had been nearly unrestrainable when he'd been brought up to speed on the details of Corinne's ill-fated reunion with Victor Bishop and the revelations that had resulted from her trip back home to Detroit. He was still visibly outraged over the news.

"Henry Vachon is obviously scum, with or without a fresh connection to Dragos," he said, his deep voice rumbling with fury. "I'd personally like to see the bastard drawn and quartered, but I hate the idea that Hunter has to leave Corinne unguarded for so much as a minute while he collects the intel we need."

"It concerns me too," Lucan replied. "Hunter's comfortable that they're in a safe place for the time being, but they need to find better shelter. Unfortunately, we can't risk area hotels, nor can we be sure of any of the local Darkhavens. We have to assume anyone in the civilian population down there could have secret ties to either Henry Vachon or Dragos himself."

"What about someone in the human population?" Savannah's question had all heads turning in her direction. "I know someplace they'd be safe for a while. It's not far from the city, but it's about as off-the-beaten-path as you can get."

"Savannah," Gideon interjected slowly. "We can't ask her—"

"Who is the human in question?" Lucan asked.

Savannah met his gaze. "My sister Amelie. She's been living on the Atchafalaya Swamp for more than seventy years. And she's trustworthy. The fact that Gideon and I are alive today, standing here in front of you all, is testimony to that."

Gideon nodded, albeit reluctantly. "Savannah and I owe Amelie Dupree our lives. She's solid, Lucan. I'd stake my life on that. I have, actually."

"Amelie knows what Gideon is," Savannah added. "She's known about him since the night he showed up on her doorstep looking for me some thirty years ago, and she's kept our secret all this time."

The newsflash that a human down in the Louisiana swamps was privy to the Breed's existence didn't exactly warm Lucan's cockles. Still, he knew he'd be a fool not to consider the option Savannah and Gideon had just handed him. Human alliances were hardly his first choice—in fact, they ranked about dead last as far as he was concerned—but the situation was desperate and time was definitely not on the Order's side at the moment. "How long do you think it might take to contact your sister?"

"I can call her right now," Savannah said. "I know she'll be willing to help us. All I need to tell her is when she should expect her company to arrive."

"Tell her they'll be there as soon as night falls," Lucan replied.

CHAPTER
Nineteen

Corinne had slept without waking until well into the afternoon. Even though Hunter now crouched on his haunches across the small bedroom from her, he could still feel the soft curves of her body pressed against him. He could still smell the fragrance of her hair and skin from the hours he'd spent wrapped around her while she'd dozed.

Now he watched her breathe in and out, anticipating each slow inhalation, mesmerized by the beat of her pulse, which had kicked into a faster tempo beneath the fine alabaster skin at the base of her elegant throat.

His hunger for her hadn't lessened despite the physical distance he'd been glad to put between them. He wanted her in a way that startled him, one that surpassed even the most primal Breed thirst. His desire for her had disturbed him before, but now, after the torment of having held her against him for most of the day, she had invaded all of his senses. Worse than that, she had invaded his logic, making him fixate on her comfort when he should be planning his recon mission for later that night.

He tried to wrestle his focus back to the call he'd received from the Order a few hours ago. They'd found a safe house for Corinne and him about an hour's drive west of the city. Come sundown, he would take her to the assigned shelter then set off on his own to investigate Henry Vachon's known locations and hopefully collect solid intel on where the bastard could be found. The anticipation of closing in on one of Dragos's likely lieutenants made the predator in him itch for nightfall.

Corinne let out a moan on the makeshift pallet on the floor. Hunter sprang to his feet, thoughts of Dragos and his colleagues thrust aside the instant she began to stir. Her legs scissored as though she were struggling to break free from some invisible restraints. Her mouth twisted into a grimace as she sucked in air, rapid, distressed-sounding gulps.

Hunter eased down behind her on his leather coat and gathered her to him. He didn't know what to say to calm her. He had no experience to draw from, so he simply wrapped his arms around her loosely as she thrashed and shifted in his embrace. She was panting now, whispering indiscernibly, panic seeming to rise to a head with each passing second.

He felt the frantic tick of her pulse as a scream ripped from her lips. It was a single word, a gasped exclamation that startled her awake, her face now less than an inch away from his. Her eyelids flipped wide open.

"You are safe," he told her, the only words he had as he stared into the terrified green-blue pools of her gaze. He brought his hand up slowly and swept a tendril of dark hair off her damp brow. "You're safe with me, Corinne."

She gave him a faint nod. "I had a nightmare. I thought I was back there ... in that awful place."

"Never again," he told her. It was a promise, one he realized just then that he was prepared to die for. She didn't flinch away as he continued to stroke the delicate slope of her cheek and jaw line. Her eyes, however, remained fixed on him, studying him.

"How long did you stay with me while I slept?"

"A while."

She gave a small shake of her head, not stopping him from letting his fingers stray into the silky warmth of her unbound hair. "You stayed for a long time. You held me, so that I could sleep."

"You asked me to," he replied.

"No," she countered gently. "I only asked you to stay until I fell asleep. What you did was ... very kind." Her eyes were locked on him with such open gratitude, it humbled him. When she spoke again, her voice had grown quiet, as though the words were difficult to summon. "I'm not used to being held. I can hardly remember what it's like to be touched with any amount of care or tenderness. I don't know how I'm supposed to feel anymore."

"If I am causing you discomfort—"

"No," she answered quickly, reaching out to press her palm lightly against his chest. It remained there, a slender patch of heat resting over the heavy thud of his heartbeat. "No, you don't cause me any discomfort, Hunter. Not at all."

He frowned, watching his big hand caress the impossibly delicate contours of her face. His fingertips were callused from handling weapons and dealing in violence. His skin rasped against the velvety perfection of hers. "You are the finest thing I've ever touched. I want to be careful with you. I worry that you'll break under my rough hands."

She smiled at that, a deep curve of her lips that had him burning to kiss her. "Your hands are very gentle. And I like the way you're touching me now."

Her whispered praise went through his body like a jolt of lightning. His pulse hammered in his ears, blood rushing through his veins and arteries like a sudden, swelling flood of lava. The tips of his fangs stretched, responding as obviously as another part of his anatomy. He fought the severed response of his body, certain he could rein it in as he traced the edge of her jaw, then trailed the pad of his thumb over the supple curve of her lower lip. God, she was soft. So beautiful.

She exhaled a small, pleasured-sounding sigh as he continued to study her with his hands and eyes. "Are you always so careful and tender with your women?"

He shrugged, stopping short of admitting that there had been no other women—not even once. He was raised as a machine, denied all physical contact save discipline. Until the past couple of days he'd been with Corinne, he hadn't known to crave anything more.

"Intimacy had no place in my upbringing," he told her. "This is not the kind of contact I was trained for."

"Well, you're doing just fine, if you ask me."

Again she smiled, and again his body responded with a kick of hot, coiling need. He knew she had to feel the vibration that seemed to thrum through every cell in his being. She had to feel the hard jut of his arousal, where it pressed insistently against her thigh, which had somehow wedged itself between his legs as they lay there, not even a bare inch separating them.

He wanted to kiss her. He wanted to ease some of the ache that was opening up inside him as he curved his hand around the tender arch of her nape and drew her closer. She didn't resist, not even for an instant.

Hunter moved toward her and slanted his mouth across hers. The kiss they'd shared the night before had been unexpected, sweet and tentative. This kiss was something else entirely.

Their lips melded together, faces pressed close, hands reaching out, holding tight. This kiss was starved and urgent, greedy with mutual need. Hunter cupped his palm around the back of Corinne's head to drag her deeper into his embrace. Every beat of his heart sent fire shooting through his veins. His fangs throbbed, erupting out of his gums to their full length and filling his mouth. His cock pulsed against the delicious softness of her body, igniting something primal in him, something animal and not entirely within his control.

He didn't think his desire could ratchet any higher, but then he felt the slick prodding of Corinne's tongue as it skated maddeningly along his upper lip. He groaned something unintelligible, incapable of words when his body was on the verge of snapping its tethers. He parted his lips on a rasped breath and nearly lost his mind when the tip of Corinne's tongue darted inside.

They kissed for a long few moments, his entire body tense and rock-hard while Corinne seemed to go even more pliable in his arms, melting into his embrace. He felt the soft crush of her breasts against his chest, and curious, he reached down to rub his palm over the thin fabric of her sweater. He cupped one of the small mounds, marveling at how erotic it felt to caress her and hear her tremulous gasps of pleasure in response.

He couldn't get close enough now. He needed more of this ... more of her.

Pulse raging, desire roaring through him with an intensity that nearly overwhelmed him, Hunter rolled her onto her back beneath him. He covered her with his body, his mouth fastened to hers in a demanding kiss, the pounding force of his arousal making his hips grind against her pelvis.

Although he'd never tasted sexual release, the need for it now drove into him with razor-sharp talons. He felt Corinne writhe beneath him, heard her moan as he slid his hands up the length of her arms. The need to possess her, to claim her, slammed into him with every throbbing beat of his pulse.

It took him a moment to realize Corinne was still moaning, not with the same fierce hunger that throbbed in him but with something that sounded disturbingly like fear.

He had her hands pinned above her head, his fingers clamped around her delicate wrists like shackles. She was writhing beneath him still, and through the dull haze of his selfish need, he suddenly understood that she was struggling, squirming to get free from the unyielding press of his body.

Her moan broke like a whimper, then a breathless sob.

Appalled at himself, Hunter rolled away from her at once. "I'm sorry," he blurted, feeling worse than stupid as she scrambled up from the floor, her arms crossed over herself like a shield. "Corinne, I didn't mean to ... I'm sorry."

She slid him a withered glance. "You don't have to apologize. I shouldn't have let you. I should have known I couldn't do this," she said, sucking in a hitching breath. "I'm not ready for this, Hunter. Maybe I'm crazy to think I ever could be."

When she turned away from him, he struggled to drag himself back to his senses. "Is it because of Nathan?"

Her head snapped back to him. Her expression was aghast, eyes wide with alarm. Her voice was hardly audible. "What did you say?"

"Nathan," he replied. "That's the name you called out in your sleep, just before you woke from your nightmare. Is he the reason you're not ready? Is it because your heart belongs to another male?"

She wasn't breathing. She stared at him unmoving for what seemed like forever. "You don't know what you're talking about," she answered at last, the words clipped with finality. "I didn't call out anyone's name in my sleep. You must have imagined it."

He hadn't, but he refrained from pushing her any further. Their moment together was shattered, over in that very instant. Although his pulse was still thrumming, his sex still rampant and aching for release, he could see that she wanted nothing to do with him now. Her silence lengthened, her face shuttering as she backed away from him, wary now. The look in her eyes seemed to accuse him somehow, as though she'd suddenly remembered he was a stranger to her . . . maybe even an enemy.

He felt awkward, embarrassed, confused. Things that were foreign to him until now, because of this woman. Because of his care for her, and the cornered look that she gave him as she put even more space between them.

Mira's vision came back to him like a slap across the face. Corinne's pleading. Her tears. Her begging for him to spare the life of the male she couldn't bear to lose.

And now Hunter was sure he knew that male's name. Nathan.

He didn't know why the knowledge should set his teeth on edge, but it did. He clamped his jaws together so hard his molars ached.

"Hunter," Corinne began, breaking off to inhale a shaky breath. "What happened between us just now—"

"It will not happen again," he finished for her.

When lust and pride bit into him with twin spurs, he mentally tamped the useless emotions down. He grasped for the rigid discipline that had always served him so well—a discipline that seemed intent on eluding him when he met the look of wounded confusion that swam in Corinne Bishop's lovely eyes.

"The sun will be setting soon," he told her. "We'll leave as soon as it does."

She flinched, worry edging her expression now. "Where to?"

"A safe house has been arranged. You'll stay there while I resume my mission for the Order."

He turned, and left her standing behind him in the room alone.

"Mr. Masters, I certainly do appreciate the generosity you've shown my campaign in recent months. This check—" The senator arched a well-groomed brow as he glanced once more at the sizable corporate donation. "Well, sir, quite frankly, a contribution of this magnitude is humbling. It's unprecedented, really."

Dragos steepled his fingers under his chin and smiled from his plush guest chair on the other side of the upwardly mobile politician's desk. "God bless democracy, and the United States Supreme Court."

"Indeed." The senator chuckled somewhat uncomfortably, his Adam's apple straining against the starched white collar of his tuxedo shirt and crisp black bowtie. His flawlessly styled golden blond hair was combed back loosely from his handsome face, the dusting of gray on either side of his temples giving the thirty-something senator an air of wisdom and distinction.

Dragos wondered if he'd earned those distinguished-looking stripes at a pricey salon, then decided he didn't care. It was the senator's politics—and his elite Ivy League connections—that interested Dragos the most.

"I'm honored that you and TerraGlobal have demonstrated such faith in my campaign's objectives," he said, adopting an earnest look that probably scored Boston's charming, most-eligible bachelor everything he'd ever asked for in his privileged young life. "You have my personal assurance that all the money you've contributed will be put to prudent, good use."

"I have no doubt, Senator Clarence."

"Please," he said, sliding the check into the top drawer of his desk and locking it. "You must call me Robert. Ah, hell, call me Bobby—all my friends do."

Dragos returned the polished smile. "Bobby it is."

"I want you to know, Mr. Masters, that I share your commitment to the real issues that are impacting our great nation. I've promised to do my part in Washington to help bring us back to where we deserve to be—where we *need* to be, as the greatest country in the world. And I want you to know that my fight is only beginning now that I have the honor of holding this office at such a crucial time in our history. I'm here because I mean to make a difference."

"Of course," Dragos intoned, patiently sitting through the red-white-and-blue highlights of a stump speech he'd heard more than once while Bobby Clarence was on the campaign trail. "You and I share many of the same interests. Not the least of which being your dedication to anti-terror initiatives. I admire your zero-tolerance stance on those who would engage in such deplorable activity. I commend you on being willing to draw a hard line when it comes to matters of national security."

Bobby Clarence leaned forward across his desk, eyes narrowed with practiced intensity. "Between you and me, Drake—if I may?" Dragos gestured for him to continue, smiling to himself as he granted permission for the human to address him by one of his many aliases. "Between you and me and these four walls, I wouldn't be opposed to bringing back public executions when it comes to any and all terrorist scumbags, especially the ones sprouting up like weeds from our own American soil. Hang the bastards by their balls and turn a pack of starving dogs on their entrails, I say. Unfortunately, my handlers would probably tell me that doesn't make a great campaign slogan."

He broke into a gregarious laugh, humor that Dragos shared, though not for precisely the same reasons. Dragos's chuckle was one of private amusement and the almost giddy anticipation of the moment he would pull the strings that would result in his ultimate triumph over the Order.

The speakerphone on the senator's desk buzzed with an incoming call. He politely excused himself, then lifted the receiver to his ear and pressed the button. "Yes, Tavia? Mm-hmm. All right, that's fine. Ah, damn. Is it that time already? Please phone the chairman's office and apologize for me, will you? Tell him I'm in my last meeting of the day and he'll have to go on ahead of us to the benefit. We'll join up with him and the others as soon as possible. Yes, I know how he hates last-minute changes of plans, but I'm afraid he's just going to have to deal with it." Bobby Clarence sent a good-old-boy wink in Dragos's direction. "Tell him I'm delayed on account of a Homeland Security matter. That ought to give him something to chew on until we get there."

The senator wrapped up the call from his aide and offered Dragos an apologetic shrug. "No one told me that getting elected would be the easy part of this whole gig. Staying on top of my schedule is something else, especially around this time of the year. I tell you, I've spent more time in a damned tuxedo the past month than I have in the trenches where I belong."

"You're a man in demand," Dragos replied, sensing that the exasperation over fat-cat parties and frou-frou social functions was just part of the golden boy's public facade. It had certainly played well in the elections, and that was all that mattered to Dragos, since he was betting a good deal of cash on the fact that the shiny bright star from Cambridge would get him face-to-face with humankind's true power brokers.

"You have appointments to keep, and I shouldn't delay you any longer," Dragos announced, rising from the guest chair despite the senator's rush to assure him he had all the time in the world to talk with him. "Thank you for agreeing to see me on short notice and so late in the day, besides."

Senator Clarence came around the desk and helped Dragos shrug back into his cashmere coat. He reached out and took Dragos's hand in a friendly clasp. "It's been my pleasure talking with you today, Drake. I welcome the opportunity to do it again, anytime."

He walked with Dragos to the door and opened it for him. Standing on the other side, her hand raised before her as though she was only a second away from knocking, was a very tall, very attractive young woman dressed in a charcoal gray business pantsuit and high-collared, ivory blouse. Her thick, caramel-brown hair was fastened in a long ponytail at her nape, not a single strand out of place. All combined, it was a look that might have been offputting on a less beautiful woman, but not here.

"Ah! Tavia," Bobby Clarence blurted as Dragos came to a halt right in front of her, struck by the sight of the young woman mere inches from his face. She took an abrupt step back, her intelligent gaze snapping from Dragos's intrigued smile to her employer's smooth grin. The senator placed his hand on Dragos's shoulder. "Drake, have you met my personal aide, Tavia Fairchild?"

"A pleasure," he purred, dipping his head in greeting.

"Mr. Masters," she replied, accepting his offered hand and giving it a brief but firmly professional shake. "We haven't had the opportunity to meet, but I recognize your name from various correspondence of the senator's."

"Tavia's memory for names and faces is uncanny," boasted her proud boss. "She's my secret weapon, always keeping me on time and in the know. Or at least, trying to."

"I have no doubt," Dragos replied, hardly able to take his eyes off the woman.

Dark lashes shuttered her spring-leaf green gaze almost anxiously in the instant before her attention flicked away from him, leaving him to wonder if on some instinctual level the female sensed he was more than he appeared beneath his conservative suit and cashmere coat. Dragos remained fascinated by her, enthralled really, as she turned to the senator and handed him a small gift-wrapped box festooned with a red ribbon and a cheery sprig of fresh holly. "For the chairman's wife. It's an antique brooch I found at a shop on Newbury Street last weekend. I figured since she collects cameos—"

"What'd I tell you, Drake?" Bobby Clarence said, jerking his perfectly square chin in her direction as he took the gift and gave it a little rattle. "Secret weapon. She's always making me look better than I really am."

Tavia Fairchild seemed to take the praise in stride, remaining unflappably on task. "Shall I call down to the garage and ask them to bring the car around for you, Senator Clarence?"

"Yeah, that'd be great, Tavia. Thanks." The senator clapped Dragos companionably on the shoulder again as his pretty aide pivoted back toward her desk and picked up her phone to summon his driver. "Can I persuade you to come along, Drake? We could talk some more, and I'd be happy to introduce you to some of the good folks at tonight's First Responders benefit. I think you'd find a lot of like-minded individuals who'd enjoy sharing their thoughts with you on some of the things we've been discussing."

Dragos allowed an indulgent smile. "I'm afraid I couldn't possibly." His sights were set a bit higher than the union yokels of the city's firefighters and police departments. "Thank you for the offer. However, I really should go now."

"You sure?" the senator pressed with a winning grin. "The food alone will be worth it. Those guys love to eat. You would too, especially at five hundred bucks a plate, prepared by the best Italian chef in the North End."

"Alas," Dragos demurred, "I maintain a very strict diet. Italian food does not agree with me."

"Ah, I'm sorry to hear it." Bobby Clarence chuckled

as he strode over to a nearby closet and shrugged into an expensive-looking silk-lined coat. "You will be at the holiday party tomorrow night at my place, won't you?"

Dragos gave him a nod. "I wouldn't miss it for the world."

"Excellent. Tavia really knocked herself out, putting the whole shindig together for me—right down to the hand-inscribed invitations."

"Is that so?" Dragos turned another appraising look on the young female, who had since retrieved her own coat and handbag and was in the process of shutting down her computer and putting the office phones on voicemail.

"I'm not supposed to announce this publicly," Senator Clarence added, "but we've confirmed a surprise guest of honor tomorrow evening. A good friend and mentor of mine from my Cambridge days. Someone I'm certain you'll be interested to meet, Drake."

Although the young politician was playing at subtlety, Dragos needed no further hint to guess that the VIP and good friend of Bobby Clarence was none other than his favored college professor who had hitched his savvy wagon to another rising star and landed in the second-highest seat of power in the country. It was that very connection that had made Bobby Clarence so valuable to Dragos.

By tomorrow night, Dragos would own the minds—and souls—of both men.

"Until then," he said, reaching out to the senator and giving the unsuspecting human's hand an enthusiastic pump. He glanced at Bobby Clarence's pretty assistant and offered a courtly bow of his head. "Miss Fairchild, a pleasure to finally meet you."

With her shrewd gaze following him, and the senator's optimistic good-bye echoing into the adjacent hall-way, Dragos exited the office and headed for the eleva-tor. By the time he reached the street level and climbed into his own waiting limousine, his cheeks burned from the wide spread of his contented, unabashedly eager, smile.

CHAPTER
Twenty

It took about an hour to make the drive to the safe house the Order had arranged for them. They were several miles off the highway, traveling along an unpaved road that led them deeper into an area of low-lying marshlands and clusters of eerie, moss-strewn cypress.

As Hunter made a turn into an unmarked driveway—Corinne assumed it was a driveway—the car's headlights illuminated several pairs of glowing yellow eyes hovering at ground level up ahead. The dense scrub brush shook as the swamp creatures hiding within it scurried back into the gloom of their wild domain.

"Are you sure this is the right place?" Corinne asked as Hunter drove deeper into the darkness. "It doesn't look like anywhere someone would put a house."

"There is no mistake," he replied. "This is where Amelie Dupree resides."

It was the first thing he'd said to her the whole trip. The impassive soldier was back in full effect now, not that she should be surprised at his all-business tone. They hadn't exactly left things on the best terms earlier.

Although she'd wanted to talk about what had happened—explain her panicked reaction to what had been so pleasant, so incredibly pleasurable at first— embarrassment had kept her tongue pressed to the roof of her mouth. That, and the stunning, abject alarm at having heard Hunter voice her son's name out loud.

She hadn't been prepared for that. Still wasn't, in fact. The instinct to protect her child, to deny his existence if it might mean keeping him safe from discovery, safe from harm, had risen up in her in much the same way as she would yank her hand away from an open flame. The lie had been a reflex, and now it lay between Hunter and her like a chasm.

She glanced away from his unreadable face as the car slowed and the beams lit up the weathered gray wood shingles of a rustic old house nestled deep among the ghostly, moss-draped trees. An elderly black woman in a floral housedress stood beneath the shelter of the covered porch, watching them approach. Her arms had been crossed under her ample bosom, but as the car neared and came to a stop, she lifted her hand in a slow wave of greeting.

Hunter turned off the engine and pocketed the keys in his leather coat. "Wait here until I tell you it's safe."

As he stepped out of the vehicle and walked around to meet the old woman, Corinne wondered what kind of threat he expected might wait for them with her. But she could see from the way he carried himself, the hard line of his shoulders and the loose gait of his long legs, that it was his training in control of his actions now.

Having spent so many hours in close company with him, it was easy to forget how massive he was, how purely lethal he could be. He radiated danger, even without the skills that had made him one of Dragos's deadliest foot soldiers. Having felt his mouth move so tenderly on hers, it was easy to forget how unforgiving his hands could be if he sensed an enemy threat or had cause for suspicion. He was taking no chances here, no matter how minute they might seem. Corinne wanted to dismiss his caution, but if he was overprotective, she realized with no small amount of humility that it was because he meant to keep her safe.

He moved with pantherlike grace and military precision, and as he strode up to their smiling, grandmotherly hostess, for a moment Corinne worried the poor old woman might shriek with fright and run the other way. She didn't. Corinne heard a molasses-smooth voice through the glass of the passenger-side window, welcoming Hunter and her and bidding them to come inside.

Hunter swiveled his head and met Corinne's gaze. He gave a vague nod, then came over and opened her door before she had the chance to climb out on her own. He walked back with her toward the elderly woman and placed Corinne's hand in the outstretched palm that waited to greet her.

Clouded, milky eyes darted back and forth sightlessly as Amelie Dupree clasped Corinne's hand in a warm hold. Her smile was broad and radiant, filled with a kindness that seemed to radiate from deep within her. And when she spoke, her aging voice was a sweet, musical rasp. "Hello, child."

Hunter made quick introductions while Amelie's blind gaze searched them out in the dark. She gave Corinne's hand a motherly pat. "You come on in now, child. I got a kettle about to whistle on the stove and a pot of gumbo been simmerin' all afternoon."

"Sounds delicious," Corinne said, left with no choice but to follow along as Amelie Dupree led her up the creaky steps of the porch. She glanced back at Hunter, noting he'd stayed behind, his cell phone already pressed to his ear, no doubt checking in with the Order to let them know they'd arrived without incident.

The house didn't look like much from outside, but inside the furnishings were new and well kept, the painted walls bathed in warm earth tones and adorned with art and several decades' worth of framed photographs. One particular picture caught Corinne's eye at once as she walked along behind Amelie Dupree, marveling at the old woman's ability to navigate the room without assistance or hesitation.

Corinne paused to look closer at the photograph that drew her attention. It wasn't current—it had to be many years old, based on the odd clothing and yellowed tinge under the glass. But the face of the vibrant young woman with the round halo of ebony curls was unmistakable. Corinne had met her at the Order's Boston compound.

"My beautiful baby sister, Savannah," Amelie Dupree confirmed, having come back to stand next to Corinne. "Half-sister, actually. We had the same mama, God rest her sweet, tormented soul."

"I didn't realize," Corinne said, resuming her trek behind the gray-haired woman into the cheery yellow kitchen at the back of the house.

The tea kettle had just begun to whistle on the stove. Amelie felt for the knobs, unerringly cutting off the gas to the kettle while the covered pot of gumbo bubbled on the next burner. She opened the cupboard and took out a pair of earthenware mugs.

"Do you know my sister?" she asked, her splayed fingers traveling the surface of the counter now and landing on a tin canister.

"I've met her only briefly," Corinne replied, unsure how much she should divulge to someone outside the Order's compound, even if there was a blood relation. "Savannah seems very nice."

"They don't come any better, I can promise you that," Amelie confirmed, a smile in her lilting voice. "We don't get to talk but a few times a year, but we pick up right where we left off, like she's never been gone."

Corinne watched the old woman place teabags into the mugs then reach for a potholder that hung on a small hook suction-cupped to the front of the stove. She was tempted to offer help, but Amelie Dupree was remarkably capable on her own. Using the index finger of one hand to mark the rim of the mug, she poured the hot water without scalding herself or spilling a single drop. Corinne herself would have been hard-pressed to be so exacting.

"And how is that fine man of hers?" Amelie casually asked as she walked the two steaming cups over to the table. "If you met my sister, I know you must've met Gideon too. The pair of them have been joined at the hip for going on—my lawd, it must be at least thirty years now."

The elderly woman sat down, motioning Corinne toward the chair beside her. Since Hunter seemed to be taking his time outside, she sat down and blew gently across the top of her mug.

"Mm-mm," Amelie intoned contemplatively, her

sightless gaze seeming lost in thought. "Hard to believe it's been so long since all that trouble took place."

"Trouble?" Corinne asked as she sipped carefully at the hot tea. She couldn't deny that she was curious to know more, not only about the woman who'd opened her house to Hunter and her but also about the couple who seemed such an integral part of the Order.

"I don't like to dredge up bad memories, child, and this one's about the worst." She reached out to cover Corinne's hand with her own, giving it a little pat. "Too much blood was shed that night. Two lives nearly lost right outside on my front lawn. I knew Gideon was different the first moment I laid eyes on him—this being years before old age started stealing my sight, a' course. I never would've guessed what he truly was, if I hadn't seen it with my own eyes. The gunshot wound should've killed him. The one that hit Savannah should've killed her too—would have, if he hadn't done what he did to save her. If he hadn't bitten into his own wrist and given her his blood."

Corinne realized she was holding her breath, listening in rapt fascination. "You saw him feed her . . . you know what he is, Amelie?"

"Breed." The old woman nodded. "Yes, I know. They told me everything that night. They entrusted me with their lives, and it's a truth I mean to take to my grave when my time eventually comes." Amelie took a sip of her tea. "That man outside . . . he's also one of Gideon's kind. Even a blind old woman like me can see that. He has a dark power about him. I felt it vibrating off him before he even got out of the car."

Corinne stared down into her mug. "Hunter is a bit . . . intimidating, but I've seen the good in him. He's honorable and courageous, like you and Savannah know Gideon to be."

Amelie gave a low grunt. She was still holding Corinne's right hand, her thumb rubbing idly over the teardrop-and-crescent-moon birthmark. As she continued to trace the outline of the small mark, Corinne realized she was studying it. "It's just like hers," she murmured, her smooth brow creasing. "Savannah has this very same birthmark, except hers is on her left shoulder blade. Mama used to say it was the place where the fairies kissed her before placing her in Mama's womb. Then again, Mama was a bit touched herself."

Corinne smiled. "Every Breedmate is born with this mark somewhere on her body."

"Hmm," the old woman mused. "I guess that makes you and Savannah sisters of another kind, then, doesn't it?"

"Yes, I suppose it does," Corinne agreed, warmed from both the tea and her hostess's kind acceptance. "Have you lived here for a long time, Amelie?"

She gave a bob of her grayed head. "Seventy-two years I've been in this very spot. Born right in that other room, matter of fact. Same as Savannah, though by the time she came along, I was already grown and old enough to help deliver her. I've got twenty-four years on my baby sister."

Seventy-two years old, Corinne thought, studying the aged face and silvery gray hair. If not for the Ancient's blood that had been forced upon her all the time she'd been in Dragos's laboratory prison, her body would be roughly twenty years more weathered than Amelie Dupree's. It seemed ironic to her now that the very thing she despised—the life-giving nutrients from a creature not of this earth—had allowed her to survive Dragos's torture. It had kept her strong when all she'd wanted was to lie down and die. It was because of that alien blood that she had a son out there somewhere, a piece of her heart that she worried was slipping farther and farther out of her reach.

"Do you have other family?" she asked Amelie when the ache in her chest started to be more than she could bear.

The elderly woman beamed. "Oh, my, yes. Two daughters and a son. I've got eight grandbabies too. My kin is all spread out now. The kids, they never did love the swamp the way I do. It's not in their blood, in their bones, the way it is with me and my late husband. They took off to the cities as soon as they were able. Oh, they come to see me every week or so, make sure I'm getting on all right and help take care of things around the house, but it's never enough. 'Specially the older I get. Age makes you want to hold everyone you love close as you can."

Corinne smiled and gave the warm, age-lined hand a gentle squeeze. She was glad for the elderly woman's blindness in that moment, grateful that the tear leaking from the corner of her eye would go undetected. "I don't think you need to be old to feel that way, Amelie."

The kindly woman's face tilted slightly, a thoughtful expression coming over her features. "Has it been a long time since you've seen yours, child?"

Corinne stilled, suddenly wondering if the cloudy eyes saw more than she assumed. Feeling ridiculous, she lifted her free hand and waved it briefly in front of Amelie's gaze. No reaction whatsoever. Had the old woman somehow peered into her mind? She glanced over her shoulder, making sure Hunter was nowhere that he might overhear. "How could you possibly know—"

"Oh, I'm not psychic, if that's what you think," Amelie said around a soft chuckle. "Savannah's the only one in our family line with any kind of true gift. According to Mama, the girl was more gypsy than Cajun, but who's to say? Savannah's daddy was little more than a rumor in our family. Mama never seemed eager to speak of him. As for me, I've just midwived enough years to recognize a woman who's given birth. Something changes in a woman after she's brought a life into the world. If you're sensitive to such things, you can feel it—like an intuition, I guess."

Corinne didn't try to deny it. "I haven't seen my son since he was an infant. He was taken away from me soon after he was born. I don't even know where he is."

"Oh, child," Amelie gasped. "I'm so sorry for you. I'm sorry for him too, because I can feel the love you have for him in your heart. You need to find him. You must not give up hope."

"He's all that matters to me," Corinne replied quietly.

But even as she said it, she knew that wasn't entirely true. Someone else was coming to matter to her as well. Someone she wanted to trust with the truth. Someone she felt sick at having pushed away and lied to, when he'd shown her nothing but tenderness.

She hated the wall he was erecting between them. She wanted to tear it down before it got any higher, and that meant opening herself up to him completely. She wanted to trust him, and that meant giving him the power to prove her right ... or wrong, if she turned out to be the fool.

All she knew was she had to give him that chance.

"Will you excuse me for just a moment, Amelie? I want to see what's keeping Hunter."

At the old woman's nod of agreement, Corinne got up from the table and walked back through the front of the house. Before she even got out to the porch, she saw that Hunter and the purple car were gone.

He had left for his mission without even saying a word.

Murdock came back to consciousness on a choked scream.

Chase watched the vampire flail and struggle on the chain that held him suspended by his ankles from the central beam of an old, empty grain silo somewhere deep in podunk. Blood ran from the hours-old lacerations and contusions that riddled the Agent's naked body. The air inside the silo was bitter cold, added torture for the son of a bitch who'd stubbornly refused to tell Chase what he needed to know.

For most of the daylight hours they'd spent within the rat-infested shelter, Chase had tried beating the intel out of Murdock. When that didn't work, and when Chase's thin patience had started to snap with the setting of the sun outside and the pricking of his thirst, he'd picked up Murdock's own blade and tried slicing the truth from him.

At some point, the vampire had passed out. Chase hadn't noticed until his own hand was bathed in the other male's blood, the big body drooping limply, unresponsive to any amount of inflicted pain.

And so Chase had put down the blade and waited.

He watched Murdock struggle back to alertness, chains jangling in the enclosed shelter. The male coughed and spit blood onto the floor some six feet beneath his head. A large stain already lay on the filthy concrete, the congealing pool of blood and piss soaking into the moldy remnants of long-forgotten livestock feed and scattered, ice-encrusted vermin droppings. The glossy puddle of fresh red cells drew his eye like a beacon, making him yearn to forget this business that needed to get done and instead head out to hunt.

Murdock bucked and thrashed, hissing when his bleary eyes met Chase's unblinking stare from across the floor of the silo. "Bastard!" he roared. "You don't know who you're fucking with!"

Chase wrapped his fist a bit tighter into the end of another long chain—this one slip-knotted around Murdock's neck—and gave it a good, hard yank. "Does that mean you're ready to tell me?" He stood up, slowly looping the chain's slack around and around his fist as he approached. When there was only a couple of feet of space remaining, he paused. "What's your connection to Dragos? And fair warning—if you continue to tell me the name means nothing to you, I'm going to pound your fucking face into a mashy pulp until you figure it out."

Murdock let out a growl, his narrowed, blood-crusted eyes flaring with amber rage. "He'll kill me if I talk to you."

Chase shrugged. "And I'm going to kill you if you don't. This here is what you'd call your classic rock and a hard place. Since I'm the one holding the chain and the blade that's going to start cutting you up into bite-size pieces, I suggest you try not to piss me off any more than you already have."

Murdock glared. His jaw was held tight, but there was a note of fear in his coal-bright eyes. "There are others who are closer to Dragos's operation than me. Whatever it is you're looking for, I'm not the one you want to talk to."

"Unfortunately, you're the only one I've got hanging around at the moment. So stop testing my patience and start talking." To drive home his point, Chase wound another bit of chain around his fist.

Christ, he hated being so close to the male. Not only because of the strong urge to smash his brains out for his participation in the blood club, among his other repulsive sins, but also because of all the goddamned blood. Although Breed blood offered no nourishment to their own kind, the sight and scent of so much fresh, spilling hemoglobin made the feral part of Chase coil like a viper in the pit of his stomach.

Murdock would hardly be able to miss the fact that Chase's fangs were filling his mouth. His own gaze mirrored the same amber fire that seared him from between the battered slits of Murdock's eyes, though not from pain or fear or fury, but from the taloned grip of the hunger that had somehow begun to ride him nearly every waking moment.

That savage part of him snarled as he forced himself to get right up in Murdock's face. "Tell me where to find Dragos."

When the answer didn't come fast enough, Chase hauled his arm back and swung the chain-wrapped hammer of his fist into the side of Murdock's skull. The vampire howled, a tooth shooting out of his mouth in a stream of dark red blood.

Chase's gut clenched, a hideous, wild thrill soaring through his veins as he watched Murdock spew a scarlet river onto the concrete below. A sick, rabid glee urged him to throw another punch, to tear the wailing piece of shit apart like he so richly deserved.

It took him aback, how powerful the darkness inside him was becoming. How demanding the savagery, how deep-seated the madness felt now that it had him in its grasp.

In truth, it terrified him.

He pushed it down—as far down as he could force it to go—and reached out to grab Murdock by his chin. It was a struggle to find his voice amid the churning roar of the battle taking place inside him. When he finally spoke, his voice was gravel, scraping in the back of his throat. His lips peeled away from his teeth and fangs on a snarl. "Where. Is. Dragos?"

"I don't know," Murdock gasped. Chase raised the ball of chain to strike again. "I don't know! I don't know—I swear to you! All I can tell you is he wants to see the Order destroyed—"

"No shit," Chase interjected tightly. "Now tell me something I don't know, before I end you right here and now."

Murdock sucked in a few quick breaths. "Okay, okay...he has a plan. He wants to get rid of all of you—the entire Order. He says he has to, if he stands any chance of seeing his grand scheme through to its fruition."

"Grand scheme," Chase repeated, feeling like maybe he was finally getting somewhere. "What the fuck is Dragos up to?"

"I'm not sure. I'm not part of the inner circle. I reported to a lieutenant of his who came up to Boston from Atlanta. Freyne reported to him too."

"What's this lieutenant's name?" Chase demanded. "Tell me where I can find him."

"Don't bother," Murdock replied. "No one's heard from him since last week, so odds are he pissed Dragos off and got himself killed. Dragos doesn't give anyone the chance to fuck up twice."

Chase growled a low curse. "Okay, then tell me some more about his inner circle. Who else is in it?"

Murdock shook his head, scattering raindrops of blood onto Chase's boots. "No one knows who's got that kind of access to him. He's very careful like that."

"How does he plan to take out the Order?"

"I don't know. Something big. Something he's been working toward for a while, from what I've heard. He's been trying to find out where the compound is. Before Freyne was killed, he mentioned something about a decoy. Some kind of Trojan horse—"

"Ah, fuck," Chase muttered.

A sick suspicion snaked through him when he considered how Dragos might go about doing something like Murdock just described. Through the haze of his gnawing hunger, he thought about the night of Kellan Archer's rescue. The annihilation of Lazaro Archer's Darkhaven—an attack that had left the Order with little choice but to bring the two surviving members of that family into the compound for protection.

Had the whole thing played out the way Dragos had intended it to? Could the son of a bitch have used the incident to somehow expose the Order's headquarters? And to what end? The possibilities were numerous, every one of them driving into his gut like an iron stake.

Chase mentally jerked his focus back to the interrogation. "What else do you know about his plans?"

"That's it. That's all I know."

Chase narrowed a look on the vampire, anger flaring along with suspicion. He shook his head. "I don't believe you. Maybe you need something to help jog your memory."

He smashed his fist into Murdock's head again. A gash ripped open on the vampire's cheek, and Chase could not contain the animal growl that erupted from him at the sight and scent of still more blood.

"Speak, goddamn you," he hissed, the bare thread of his humanity being devoured by the beast that was snapping at its bit. "I won't ask you again."

Murdock seemed convinced now. He coughed, a wet, broken sound. "He's using humans in law enforcement to be his eyes and ears. He's been making Minions, lots of them. I heard he's been talking about a politician recently—that new senator that just got elected."

It had been a long time since Chase gave a shit about human politics, but even he wasn't so far removed that he wasn't aware of the promising young Ivy Leaguer who had come fresh out of Cambridge and seemed destined for a fast rise to the national stage. "What's any of this got to do with him?" Chase demanded.

"You'll have to ask Dragos," Murdock sputtered through a split lip and swelling jaw. "Whatever his plans are, there's a good chance they involve this Clarence guy in some way."

Chase considered it for a moment, staring at the Agent in contempt. "You sure that's all you can tell me? I'm not going to find out something more interesting if I knock a hole in the other side of your fucked-up skull?"

"I've told you everything now. I don't know anything more, I give you my word."

"Your word," Chase muttered low under his breath. "You expect me to take the word of a pedophile blood clubber who would sell out his own kind to a twisted piece of shit like Dragos?"

Murdock's eyes took on a cautious, worried gleam. His southern drawl seemed thicker for the blood that was leaking from the side of his mouth. "You said you wanted information, and I gave it to you. Fair's fair, Chase. Cut me loose. Let me go."

Chase smiled, genuinely amused. "Let you go? Oh, I don't think so. It ends for you right here. The world will be a hell of a lot better place without the likes of you in it."

Murdock's answering giggle had a maniacal edge to it, as though he understood he had no hope of walking away from the situation and meant to go out swinging. "Oh, that is rich, Sterling Chase. Your self-righteousness knows no bounds, does it? The world will be a better place without me in it. Have you looked in a mirror lately, my boy? I may be all the things you called me, but you're no prize either."

"Shut the fuck up," Chase growled.

"Don't think I didn't notice the fact that your eyes have been throwing off amber like a furnace this whole time. How long has it been since your fangs weren't filling your mouth?"

"I said shut up, Murdock."

But he didn't. Damn him, he wouldn't. "How desperate would an addict like you have to be not to be tempted to get down on your hands and knees and lap up the blood that's spilling out of me onto that shitty floor below? Wouldn't your holier-than-thou buddies back at the Order love to see you like this—like the fucked-up Rogue you truly are? Do the world a favor and take yourself out of it."

Chase couldn't tolerate any more. He couldn't stand to hear the truth, especially coming from scum like Murdock. He swung his chain-reinforced fist into the vampire's face, sending him swinging by the length of chain at his ankles. Chase yanked Murdock back and hammered him again, blow after punishing blow. He pounded until there was little left to hit.

Until Murdock's body hung lifeless, the awful truth silenced at last.

Chase dropped the chain from around his throbbing fist. Then he released the one holding Murdock aloft. The body hit the floor of the old silo in a heavy *thump* of flesh and bone, the chain rattling down behind it.

Chase turned around and walked out, leaving the door open for the other predators of the night to feed on the carcass and tomorrow's sun to take whatever remained.

CHAPTER
Twenty-one

For once, it seems luck is on our side, Lucan."

Gideon stood in the center of the cavernous bomb shelter hidden beneath Lazaro Archer's Cold War–era Darkhaven a couple hours north of Augusta, Maine. As Archer had warned, the place wasn't anywhere close to the size and complexity of the Order's compound, but Lucan had to agree with Gideon: It seemed to be the best option—the only immediate option—they had at the moment.

Nestled on a remote, two-hundred-acre plot of virgin forest that had likely seen more moose and black bear than humans in the past couple of centuries, the property was nothing if not private. The residence itself was a sprawling ten-bedroom, eight-thousand-square-foot fortress of stone and thick timber. Rugged, compared to the elegant mansion back in Boston or the sophisticated brownstone where Lazaro Archer and his family had lived before Dragos's act of mass destruction. The land surrounding it was impenetrable and forbidding, a natural perimeter wall made of soaring pines and thorn-spangled bracken.

"I wish I had more to offer you," Archer said from beside Lucan. His rugged face was limned in pale light from the fluorescent security lamp that hung overhead in the concrete tunnel leading back up to the house. "I cannot fully express how deeply I regret my family's role in Dragos's plans. That he used Kellan as an unwitting pawn—"

"Forget it," Lucan replied. "None of us would be in this situation if it weren't for Dragos. As for this holding, like Gideon says, it's an advantage we sure as hell need right now."

Archer nodded as the three of them resumed their walk up the long, underground tunnel. "Although the house has been unoccupied all these years, a local property management company has been responsible for the maintenance and upkeep—"

"Let them know their services are no longer required," Lucan replied. "If the contract needs to be paid out, let me know and arrangements will be made to take care of any expenses or incidentals."

"Very well," Archer said. "How soon do you expect to begin the relocation?"

Lucan slanted a look at Gideon. "Can you be ready to roll out the first wave of equipment by tomorrow night?"

Gideon's eyes were sharp and determined over the rims of his light blue shades. "Layout is tight but workable. May have to go with a combo of hardwire and coax instead of wireless based on the material and thickness of the walls down here, but yeah...I can make it happen as soon as tomorrow night."

Lucan nodded. "Sounds like we're in business."

Gideon stepped over to walk on the other side of Archer. "Before we go, I'd like to take another look at the security system you have in place, Lazaro."

"Yes, of course."

Lucan's cell phone vibrated in his coat pocket as Gideon and Archer continued discussing the property's finer points. "Yeah, babe?" Lucan said as he connected to Gabrielle's call. "Is everything good back home?"

"Ah, yes and no," she answered. Even if her hesitant voice hadn't given her away, he would have known something was up. Through the blood bond he shared with his Breedmate, Lucan felt the mix of excitement and anxiety spiking in her veins like it was his own.

"What's going on?"

"It's Tess," she said. "Lucan, she's having contractions. The baby's on the way."

Hunter ditched the stolen El Camino in the swamp several miles away from Amelie Dupree's house and made the rest of the trek into New Orleans on foot. He'd found no activity at the first of Henry Vachon's residences and had gone on to stake out the other Darkhaven address Gideon had given him.

For more than an hour, his reconnaissance had netted him nothing except the knowledge that Henry Vachon enjoyed a princely lifestyle in a mansion big enough for a dozen people but inhabited by just himself and a small cadre of rank-and-file Breed guards. Hunter reduced that number by three as he stole up to the back of the house and efficiently slit the throats of the men posted at the door.

He crept inside what appeared to be an old servants'

quarters, then swiftly, soundlessly, took the stairs leading up to the second floor of the estate.

A Gen One assassin waited for him at the top of the stairwell. Hunter still had the blade in his hand. He threw it, but the other male's reflexes knew the assault was coming, and quick, well-trained hands batted the dagger away. Hunter braced his hands on either side of the stairwell wall and lifted himself into a kick as his opponent launched himself toward him.

They connected in midflight, coming down hard on the steps and rolling for a few before Hunter managed to get the upper hand. He had another blade sheathed on his weapons belt. He drew it and sliced in an instant, one swipe of his hand cutting cleanly across the Gen One's throat, the return sweep ripping through black nylon combat clothing, skin, muscle, and bone. The assassin went limp, bleeding out on the stairs while Hunter got back to his feet and climbed the rest of the way to the living quarters on the floor above.

He heard movement behind a closed door down the hallway. He stalked toward it and kicked the thing in, smashing it off its hinges. As the splintering wood showered down onto the richly hued rug of a sumptuous bedroom, he caught a glimpse of a retreating figure disappearing into an adjacent bathroom. Hunter followed, flashing there in less than an instant.

Henry Vachon cowered on the marble floor between the gold-trimmed toilet and a deep, sunken tub. He had a cell phone in his hand, fingers typing madly over the tiny keypad. Hunter let the bloodied blade in his fist fly, taking off one of Vachon's fingers in the process.

The vampire hissed in pain, eyes wild with surprise and fear. The cell phone slipped from his hand, smashing into pieces against the unforgiving polished stone floor.

"What the hell are you doing here?" Vachon demanded, his voice shrill and grating. "What do you want from me?"

Hunter cocked his head. "I'm sure you know. I want information."

"You're a fool if you think I'll give anything to you," he shot back, cradling his ruined hand. Blood bloomed like an opening flower against his chest, staining the front of his white silk shirt and tailored gray trousers. "My loyalty won't be broken by the likes of you. I'll take it to my grave."

Hunter took a step forward, unfazed by the challenge. "I know more than a hundred ways to inflict maximum pain on a body short of killing it. A hundred more will make you wish for death. One of them is sure to loosen your tongue."

Vachon clumsily rose to his feet in the corner, his socks sponging up blood, sliding on the glasslike surface of the floor. "Is the Order worth the price you will pay for crossing Dragos? You're putting a very large target on your back by betraying the one who created you, assassin."

Hunter shook his head. "Dragos is no creator. He is a destroyer. He is a coward and a madman, one who murders innocents and tortures helpless women and children. Dragos and all those loyal to him will soon be dead. As for you, Henry Vachon, I will take more than a little satisfaction in personally ending your worthless life."

The male's expression faltered a bit, a crease pressing into the center of his brow. "Me? What have I done to you?"

"Not to me but to her," Hunter replied, finding it strangely difficult to keep the anger from his voice.

"The Bishop chit?" Vachon seemed genuinely taken aback, but only for a moment. His smile was perverted, a profane twist of his mouth. "Ah, yes. Been sniffing around her skirts, have you? A male would have to be blind and dumb not to crave a sample of that. Even a male like you, raised to be more machine than flesh."

Hunter felt a hot flare shoot into his bloodstream but he refused to be baited. Let Vachon think what he would about him; his opinion, like his very existence, was meaningless. "Dragos is intending a strike against the Order. You will tell me when and where and how this attack is to be carried out."

Vachon only stared at him, a disturbing glint in his dark eyes. "Have you fucked her, assassin? Or do you merely long to?"

"There was a beacon forced into the stomach of a civilian," Hunter went on, ignoring the jabs even though the idea of this offal speaking about Corinne so crudely set his jaw on edge. "If Dragos means to use this beacon to lead him to the Order's headquarters, does he intend to invade the compound or execute some manner of destruction?"

"She's a fine piece of ass, that one," Vachon purred. "Believe me, I can understand how a female like that might scramble a male's head, make him forget who— and what—he truly is. How much discipline would it take to resist crawling inside something so hot and tight and—"

"Do not speak of her," Hunter snapped, astonished by the surge of rage that was arrowing up his spine. His eyes were hot in his skull, his vision burning with amber fury. He tried to speak and was surprised to feel the full presence of his fangs, the tips like razors against his tongue. He glared with murderous rage at Henry Vachon. "You are far beneath her. Too far to even mention her name, you disgusting son of a bitch."

"Beneath her?" Hunter didn't like the amused chuckle that spilled from between Henry Vachon's thin lips. "I've been on top of her and behind her. More than once. Dragos and I both took our turns the night we grabbed her out of that club in Detroit. Spirited little hellion. She fought like a demon. Fought as hard as she could for years after he locked her up with the others, for all the good it did her."

The ugly words—the hideous truth of what he was hearing—snapped the fragile, last thread of Hunter's control. He leapt on Henry Vachon, knocking the male against the wall and cracking the polished marble with the force of their impact. He didn't realize how blind with hatred he was in that moment.

He didn't realize how lost he was to the explosion of his rage until he tasted blood on his tongue and saw that he had Vachon's neck caught between his teeth and fangs.

With a raw cry, Hunter sank his jaws deeper around the vulnerable flesh and tendons. He shook his head, tearing out the vampire's throat and silencing his offending words for good.

Blood was everywhere—in his eyes, in his hair. Running down his chin. He tasted it like bitter poison sliding down his esophagus.

He stared down at the desecration, at the savaged horror of Vachon's twitching, dying body, still held upright in his bloodied hands. His head went a bit hazy for a second. Images flashed into his mind.

Vachon, with his hand caught tight and fisted in

Corinne's long dark hair, holding her down as he raped her. It was so vivid, so goddamned real.

Fury roared up on Hunter. He tipped his head back on his shoulders and bellowed as a fresh round of images crowded into his vision: Vachon and Dragos, observing the Ancient who was restrained and drugged on a long laboratory table. Not far away, there was a cage of roughly two dozen women, all of the imprisoned Breedmates screaming and weeping as one of them was dragged out by a Minion and walked toward the table like a sacrifice heading for the altar.

Hunter groaned, sick with the realization of what he was witnessing.

But how was it possible?

Another image slammed into his mind. This time it was Vachon supervising the removal of heavy lab equipment into the back of several large freight carriers under the cover of deep night. Crate after crate loaded into the waiting trucks, with Dragos giving his sober approval from where he stood nearby.

Holy hell.

These were Vachon's memories.

Memories carried on his blood.

Hunter could still taste the awful tang of it on his tongue. He felt his talent stir to life inside him, making itself known to him for the very first time. The blood—Breed blood—gave him the power to look inside another's memories.

Jesus Christ.

This was the gift that had eluded him all his life? He felt sick with the knowledge.

He wanted to spit the bitter taste of Vachon's blood from his mouth. Instead he latched on to the vampire's shredded throat and drank some more.

CHAPTER
Twenty-two

Chase punched the number into the city payphone's keypad for the third time. Then, for the third time, he blew out a curse and slammed the receiver back onto its cradle before the line had a chance to ring on the other end.

"Fuck," he muttered, raking his fingers over the top of his head where a migraine had been pounding for most of the night.

He knew the source of the headache. The same piercing pain was boring into his stomach, urging him to forget the phone call he seemed incapable of making and turn his sights toward something more productive.

His body shook with the need to feed. He tried to ignore the cold jangle of his veins, the knocking deep inside him that had his nerves on edge, restless and twitchy. At least his fangs had receded. His gaze wasn't casting amber light on the filth of the dark inner-city corner where he stood, nor reflecting back at him like slitted cat's eyes in the chipped chrome trim of the pay-phone box.

He wasn't totally lost, at least. Racked with searing, unabating hunger or not, he hadn't fallen to Bloodlust. He wasn't Rogue, not yet.

Still, he was in a bad way and he knew it.

Not so far gone that he wasn't revisiting everything Murdock confessed and chilled with the ramifications of what it could mean to the Order.

He picked up the receiver again and pounded out the number he knew would somehow route him to the secured line Gideon had set up at the compound. He held his breath as the call connected and started to ring. Halfway through the second tone, the line was picked up.

"Yeah."

Chase frowned, caught off guard by the deep voice that didn't carry Gideon's familiar tinge of a British accent. He started to reply, but the word came out all rusty, his throat parched and burning from the thirst he needed to ignore. He swallowed past the sawdust feeling and tried again. "Tegan . . . that you?"

"Harvard" came the Gen One warrior's flat reply. It wasn't a greeting. Not even playing at friendly. "What the hell do you want?"

The attitude wasn't undeserved, but it stung neverthe-less. Chase drew in a breath and let it out slowly. "Sur-prised to hear you on dispatch duty, Tegan," he said, hoping to break some of the ice on the other end of the line. "Gideon usually doesn't like anyone playing with his toys down there in the tech lab."

"I'll say it again, Harvard. What do you want?"

So, the ice wasn't going anywhere. He should have figured that, he supposed. After all, he was the one who walked out on the Order. Nothing said they had to take him back or, hell, even acknowledge that he existed. Chase cleared his dry throat. "I need to talk to Lucan. It's important."

Tegan grunted. "Too bad. I'm all you got right now. So, start talking or stop wasting my time."

"I found Murdock," he blurted.

"Where?"

"Doesn't matter now. He's dead." A few yards up the street, a late-night hooker stepped up onto the curb and started rambling toward Chase on spiked red stilettos. Her short winter jacket was unzipped, baring a whole lot of leg and cleavage and too much bare throat for his shaky state of mind. Chase tore his gaze away from the potential meal on heels and dropped his forehead against the cool metal of the payphone box. "Murdock gave me some information that Lucan's going to want to hear. It's not good, Tegan."

The warrior exhaled a ripe curse. "Didn't think it would be. Tell me what you know."

"Dragos is stepping up his game. He's made Minions inside local law enforcement agencies, according to Murdock. Apparently he's also got a hard-on for some local politicians. Murdock mentioned something about that new senator who just got elected."

"Christ," Tegan said. "I don't like the sound of any of this."

"Right," Chase agreed. "But that's not the worst of what I learned. Murdock told me Dragos has his sights set on taking out the Order. He said Dragos talked about using some kind of Trojan horse. I've got a bad feeling it has something to do with the Archers coming into the compound last week."

"You don't say," Tegan remarked, sounding bored

now. "News flash for you, Harvard. After you pulled your disappearing act a few nights ago, the kid coughed up a tracking device. He has no recollection of where it came from or how it got inside him. Since his abductors beat him unconscious soon after they took him, it was probably force-fed to the kid while he was out cold."

"Shit," Chase hissed. "So Murdock was right. And now Dragos knows the location of the compound."

"So it would appear," Tegan replied.

"What's the plan, then? How does Lucan want to handle the situation over there? You can't just sit back and wait for Dragos to make his move..."

Chase realized there was a lot of silence on the other end of the line. Tegan was listening, but his lack of response seemed too deliberate to be misconstrued. "What we do about it is Order business, my man."

There was no animosity in the statement, but the warrior's point was clear enough. Order business. And Chase had no place in the discussion anymore.

"Unless you're calling because you want to come back in," Tegan continued. "If you do, fair warning: You'll probably have to put those fancy Harvard lawyering skills to work if you want to talk Lucan into it. Same with Dante—he's more pissed off at you than anyone else over here."

Eyes closed at the well-deserved rebuke, Chase hung his head and exhaled a long sigh. The last thing Dante needed was to be dealing with this bullshit when his mate was just a few weeks away from delivering their son. "How are he and Tess doing?" Chase murmured. "They settle on a name for that baby yet?"

Tegan was quiet for a long moment. "Why don't you come back to headquarters and ask them yourself?"

"Nah," Chase replied, his mouth on automatic pilot

as he lifted his head and glanced out at the drug addicts and prostitutes—losers, all—who loitered around the rundown street in the armpit of Boston's low-rent district. "I'm not even in the city right now. Not sure when I'll be heading back—"

Tegan cut him off with a low curse. "Listen to me, Harvard. You're fucked up. We both know what's going on, so word of advice, don't try to bullshit me. You've got a serious problem. Maybe you're in deeper than you know how to get out, but the fact that you're talking to me right now—the fact that you're standing there, debating whether you're still sane or past the brink of caring, tells me that you've still got a chance to turn your shit around. You can come back in, but you've got to do it before it's too late to set things right."

"I don't know," Chase murmured. Part of him wanted to grab the offered olive branch with both hands and not let go. But there was another part of him that balked at the need for kinship or forgiveness. That part of him couldn't stop looking at the young, all-too-willing woman who had now parked her miniskirted ass against the red brick wall of the building next to him. She'd been watching him too, no doubt experienced enough to read the note of interest in his hooded eyes.

"Chase," Tegan said, voicing his name like a demand as the seconds ticked by without further response. "You've got a serious choice to make, my man. What do you want me to tell Lucan?"

The hooker gave him a nod and started slinking her way over. Chase felt a growl curl up the back of his throat as she drew nearer. The hunger that lurked so close to the surface of his consciousness came alive despite his best effort to tamp it down. His gums throbbed with the emergence of his fangs.

"Goddamn it, Chase." He was already pulling the receiver away from his ear when Tegan's deep voice vibrated through the plastic. "You're digging your own fucking grave."

Chase put the phone back in its cradle, then stepped around to take the young woman into the shadows with him.

Hunter sped through New Orleans on foot, his head still buzzing with the barrage of memories he'd drawn from Henry Vachon's blood. He'd seen unbelievably foul things. Horrible acts carried out on Dragos's approval and through Vachon's own sick will as well.

It took all of Hunter's learned discipline to keep from reliving the worst of those memories—the ones involving innocent young Corinne, the violation and torment she'd suffered at the hands of both Breed males on the night she'd been abducted. Hunter trained his focus instead on a different memory siphoned from Henry Vachon in the final moments of the vampire's life.

As he'd breathed his last, a moment Hunter had made sure was spent in supreme agony, Vachon gave up the location of a storage facility in neighboring Metairie—the facility where, within the past few months, Vachon had delivered some of the contents of Dragos's hastily disassembled lab.

The white brick building sat on a flat corner lot near the freeway and the railroad, a block of two-story condominiums across the street and a vacant corporate headquarters next door. Hunter moved silently over the moonlit, cracked concrete of the storage facility's adjacent fenced-in parking lot, past the handful of rental trucks and stored RVs sharing the thin yellow light of a single pole-mounted security lamp. The place was closed for the night, glass doors at the front shuttered from the inside by a metal curtain.

Hunter circled around to the side, flashing past the closed-circuit camera that watched from the upper corner of the building. Halfway around the building, a metal door marked "No Entry" gave him simple enough access to the facility. Hunter grasped the handle and bent it until the lock mechanism broke loose. He slipped in, and headed for the unit number Vachon's blood memories had provided.

It was located at the far end of the facility's interior hallway. Hunter made quick work of the industrial-strength padlock, breaking it free with a firm yank. He opened the corrugated metal door and stepped inside the ten-by-fifteen-foot box. As he crossed the threshold, he felt a faint vibration in his inner ear and glanced down to see that his foot had tripped a motion sensor's silent alarm. He wouldn't have much time before someone responded to the alert.

Fortunately, there wasn't much to see inside the unit. A fireproof safe sat just past the entrance. Toward the back stood a pair of squatty, round stainless-steel drums capped with a hydraulic vacuum seal that looked like a polished metal steering wheel. He recognized the containers from the memories he'd gathered from Henry Vachon, but he would have known their purpose even without the help of his talent.

Cryogenic storage containers.

They were plugged into a large portable power supply, their internal temperature gauges reading negative 150 degrees Celsius. Hunter unscrewed the seal of the container nearest him and lifted the heavy lid. Icy clouds of liquid nitrogen frothed out of the open top. Hunter waved it away and looked inside at the countless vials stored within the deep freeze. He didn't have to pull any of them up to understand they would contain cell and tissue samples, all of them originating in Dragos's secret laboratory.

The physical results of experiments and likely genetic testing, things Hunter could only guess at as he stared at the numerous vials nested several layers down into the container.

As astonished as he was repulsed, Hunter turned his attention to the safe. He broke open the small panel door and found a stack of paper files and photographs, along with a handful of portable computer storage disks.

He had to get this material—everything in Vachon's storage unit—into the Order's hands.

With that goal in mind, he went to the adjacent parking lot and hotwired one of the box trucks sitting in the dark lot outside. He drove it around to the side entrance and left it idling as he ran back up to the unit to collect the contents.

He had loaded the safe and one of the cryo containers into the truck and was about to turn around and get the last one when he realized he wasn't alone. The silent alarm had apparently gone straight to Dragos, if the Gen One assassin crouched in battle stance outside the open trailer of the truck was any indication.

The big male vaulted off the balls of his feet and sprang forward, a blur of head-to-toe black against the night outside. He crashed into Hunter, driving them both farther into the truck. They knocked against the cryo container, stainless steel ringing out like a bell with the force of the impact.

Hunter came up hard and plowed into the assassin's

stomach with his shoulder. The male went down onto his back, but stayed there for only an instant before he was up on his feet once more, coming at Hunter with a dagger gripped tight in his hand.

A vicious fight ensued. Hunter saw a window of opportunity as the assassin swung to dodge one of his blows and left his head and neck an open target. Hunter drove the edge of his hand into the other male's larynx, a dead-on hit that crushed the vampire's windpipe. The assassin wheezed and staggered for an instant, then leveled a murderous look at Hunter and charged forward again with his blade.

Hunter blocked it with a deflective swipe of his arm. He pivoted his elbow, wrapping his hand around the assassin's wrist. The move brought the assassin's forearm down with a hard *crack* across the front of Hunter's thigh, snapping the limb and rendering it useless. As the blade clattered to the floor of the truck and the assassin lurched forward, Hunter grabbed hold of the black UV collar and swung the Gen One's head down against the edge of the cryogenic storage container.

Blood spurted from the punishing strike. But the assassin wasn't ready to give in just yet. He threw a punch at the front of Hunter's kneecap, a blow that might have taken him down if Hunter hadn't seen it coming. He kicked the assassin back, reaching around to give the lid on the container of liquid nitrogen a hard crank. It unscrewed and Hunter threw it open. Before the assassin could regain his footing yet again, Hunter hauled him up off the floor. He shoved him headfirst into the frothing subzero container, then brought the lid down and held the male pinned beneath it.

It took a few minutes before the vampire stopped struggling.

The body went limp, arms and legs unmoving in the mist of frigid air that continued to pour out onto the floor in a rolling cloud of white.

After another long moment, Hunter lifted the lid. The assassin's head was frozen solid, slack-jawed, the blue lips and dull, unseeing eyes encrusted with ice crystals. Hunter pushed the corpse aside. It fell with a hard thud at his feet, the thick black collar circling his neck crackling as it broke into several pieces and fell away.

The interruption in his current task handled, Hunter went back to grab the last cryo container and load it into the truck.

CHAPTER
Twenty-three

Corinne heard a noise in the guest bedroom as she toweled off from her bath at the safe house. "Amelie?" she called from behind the partially open door. It had to be after midnight, but Corinne was too anxious for sleep. "Just a second. I'll be right out."

She unfolded the robe her hostess had given her and slipped it on, her hands quickly working the sash belt of the thick pink chenille garment that felt like velvet and smelled like sun-warmed, line-dried cotton. Certain her scarred body was covered, she drew the bathroom door open a bit wider and stepped out to the bedroom.

It wasn't Amelie.

It was Hunter, covered in blood. Bruises rode his sharp cheekbones. His hands were fisted at his sides, knuckles scraped and contused. She'd never seen him look so raw, so steeped in the violence of his profession.

"My God," she whispered, moving toward him in shock and concern. "Hunter . . . are you all right?"

"Never mind the blood. It isn't mine," he said, unaffected, his deep voice calm as ever.

When he started to take off his gore-stained leather coat, Corinne hurried over to help him. "The boots too," she said, eyeing the blood that covered them as well.

While he bent to unlace one of them, she hunkered down to loosen the other. She felt him watching her in an odd silence—odder than his usual man-of-few-words way. He seemed to study her now, his hooded, dark gold gaze still enigmatic, but edged with a softness she hadn't seen in him before.

"I'll take those," she said, picking up his large black combat boots in one hand, the long leather coat in the other. "Come with me."

She turned to carry everything back into the bathroom, Hunter following behind her. She set the coat and boots in the tub, then reached for one of the clean washcloths that was folded on the back of the commode. She ran it under the faucet in the tub, wringing out the warm water as Hunter stood over the sink near the door.

She'd been upset with him all night, angry that he'd left without telling her. Worried that he'd gone off to do his dangerous work for the Order and might have gotten himself killed. Now she could only stare at him, relieved that he'd come back in one piece, even if he did look like he'd strode through a war zone to get there.

She sat on the edge of the tub and watched as he ran cold water into the basin and scrubbed his face. When he was done, he cupped several handfuls into his mouth, swished it around and spat it out. Over and over, like there was a taste he couldn't get rid of no matter how hard he tried. Water dripped off his chin as he looked over at her, the hard angles of his face seeming even more severe in the vanity's bright globe lights above his head.

"Your shirt is ruined," she said, noting still more blood soaked into the black knit fabric of his combat gear. She walked to him and set the damp washcloth down on the rim of the sink. He said nothing as she took the hem of his sticky, gore-soaked shirt and lifted it up, baring his *glyph*-covered torso and broad, muscular chest. He stood back as she filled the basin with cold water and put the shirt into it. While she did this, he picked up the washcloth and scrubbed himself clean. He dropped the soiled cloth into the sink with his shirt.

"You found Henry Vachon." It wasn't a question, because the evidence seemed clear enough as the water turned red in the basin. She glanced at Hunter and met his sober nod. "You killed him?"

She expected a flat confirmation, an emotionless statement of fact that was the warrior's usual mode of response. Instead, Hunter reached out and gently took her face in his hands. He bent his head to hers and kissed her with a care that stole her breath away. When his mouth eventually left hers, he looked into her eyes with quiet but fierce intensity. "Henry Vachon will never harm you again."

Corinne couldn't help the way her body melted into Hunter's tender kiss. Her heart melted a bit too, warmed by the careful way he touched her now and by the way his entrancing golden eyes held her gaze so warmly. She wanted to linger in the pleasure of both, but a knot of dread was forming in the pit of her stomach.

Vachon was dead. The fact that one of the monsters from her life's worst nightmares breathed no more should have been welcome news to her. It was, but with Henry Vachon's death, his connection to Dragos—the only link Corinne had toward finding her son—was severed now too.

Reluctantly, she drew out of Hunter's tender hands. "Were you able to get any information out of him on Dragos or his operation?"

Hunter nodded gravely. "After I left Vachon's estate, I found a storage facility in another part of the city. There was laboratory equipment inside, as well as a safe containing computer records and paper files with photographs and notes from the lab."

Hope kindled dimly at the thought. "What kind of files? What kind of equipment? Where is this storage facility? We need to go there. We need to look at everything we can. Some of what you found might lead straight to Dragos."

Hunter was nodding as she spoke. "I took everything out of the unit. It's in a box truck I've hidden near the swamp behind this house. But you're right. There are bound to be useful clues that could lead the Order to Dragos. I intend to take the contents to Boston as soon as possible."

More than anything, Corinne wanted to race outside to find the truck Hunter mentioned and rip through everything he found. She felt certain that the key to locating her son was contained somewhere in those lab records and files. It had to be, or she stood precious little chance of ever knowing where her child might be.

She looked up at Hunter, knowing she'd deceived him by withholding the truth about her son. She stared into his earnest, intense gaze and felt the same twinge of guilt she had felt earlier that day. He kissed her again, and the guilt she bore was made worse, more distasteful for the fact that Hunter was standing there being so tender and kind with her.

Corinne glanced down at the floor, shamed and frightened. "There's something you need to know," she said softly. "Something I should have told you before now. I should have told you what happened to me while I was in Dragos's prison, but I was scared. I needed to be sure that I could trust you—"

"I know what they did." His deep voice vibrated in her bones. He guided her chin up until she was looking in his eyes once more. "I know what Dragos and Vachon did to you the night you were taken. I know how they violated you."

This wasn't the truth she meant to divulge to him, but all the same, Corinne's breath burned in her lungs. She was confused, horrified. Sickened to think Hunter was aware of her deepest humiliation. She'd wanted to die that night; part of her *had* died then, her innocence robbed in one horrific moment. Her voice trembled a little. "H-how could you know...?"

"Vachon. He boasted about it, just before I killed him." Amber sparks smoldered in Hunter's golden eyes as he spoke. "I ripped out his throat with my teeth and fangs. I couldn't control my rage when I realized what that sadistic son of a bitch had done to you—that he had enjoyed it."

Corinne listened to his account of what he did, momentarily distracted from the confession she still hadn't made to him. She could hardly believe that the rigid, flawlessly disciplined warrior was admitting to having lost control.

Over something that had been done to her.

"I made sure his death was agony," Hunter went on. "I wanted him to suffer. I wanted him to bleed."

And he had, Corinne thought, less appalled than astonished by the depth of violence Hunter had inflicted on the other male. He'd practically bathed in Vachon's blood, from the way he'd looked just a few minutes ago.

"It was his blood that showed me what he'd done, Corinne. I saw all of Henry Vachon's guilt, all his secrets. His blood showed me everything."

She frowned, uncertain what he was telling her. "I don't understand."

"Neither did I, not until tonight," Hunter said. "When I sank my teeth into Vachon's neck, I swallowed some of his blood. That's never happened before, that I've ingested Breed blood. As soon as it slid down my throat, his memories opened up to me."

"You're a blood reader," she replied. "You never knew what your ability was?"

He shook his head. "Dragos made sure all of his assassins knew as little as possible about their heritage or the things that might make them unique. I didn't know my talent until Vachon's foul blood awakened it."

And now he knew her degradation. Good lord, could he possibly have seen all the beatings and violations? Did he see how she'd been stripped and broken, forced to endure unspeakable torture along with the other captives trapped in Dragos's prison cells?

Corinne turned away from Hunter, feeling exposed. She felt dirty and ashamed, embarrassed that he had this awful, ugly knowledge of her ordeal that even she wasn't quite prepared to confront. She drifted into the bedroom, needing space to catch her breath, collect her thoughts.

She didn't realize Hunter had followed her until she felt the warmth of his hands come to rest lightly on her shoulders from behind her. He turned her around to face him. He offered no words, simply wrapped her in his arms and held her against the heat and strength of his body.

Corinne clung to him, too needful of the solid protection of his arms to deny herself the comfort of feeling him holding her close. Hunter bent his head, brought her mouth up to his. He kissed her, a slow melding of his lips on hers. His bare chest was warm and velvet-soft under her palms. She felt the faint, raised pattern of his *dermaglyphs*, felt the quickening of his heartbeat pounding beneath her roaming fingertips.

She drew back from his kiss and met his hooded gaze. His golden irises were hot with amber, their pupils thinning rapidly as the air quickened with the heat of desire.

She knew where this was heading. To her astonishment, the thought didn't terrify her as she expected it would. But she couldn't pretend that she was prepared, or that she knew how to touch him—how to be with him—the way another woman might.

He kissed her again, and she felt the gentle graze of his fangs against her lip. Beneath her hands, his *glyphs* were pulsing and alive, his breath sawing swiftly in and out of his lungs.

"Hunter, wait..." She could hardly find the words, but she needed him to understand what being with him meant to her. "I haven't done this before. You know what happened while I was..." She couldn't say it. Couldn't speak the words that would allow Dragos and his sick deeds into this moment that belonged to her and Hunter alone. "You need to understand that I haven't ever...made love."

He stared at her, something dark and possessive in his hooded, amber-gold gaze. "Neither have I." He gave a slow shake of his head as he tenderly stroked her cheek. "There has been no one, not ever."

Corinne swallowed, struck mute for an instant. "Never?"

His touch traveled along the tilt of her chin, then skated softly across her lips. "Intimacy was forbidden. It was a weakness to want physical contact. It was a flaw to desire anything, especially pleasure." He kissed her again, and a low growl rumbled deep in his chest. "I never knew what it was to crave a woman's touch. Or to hunger for a woman's kiss."

"And now you do?" she asked hesitantly.

"Since I met you, Corinne Bishop, I've been thinking of little else."

She couldn't hold back her smile at that confession, despite that he said it with more than a little bemusement. Perhaps even a trace of annoyance. She reached up and twined her fingers around his nape. He took the cue and bent his head to catch her in another deep kiss. This time, it was searing. She felt his passion in the hungry way he covered her mouth with his and in the erotic demand of his tongue as it swept along the seam of her lips, pushing inside as soon as she parted them to draw a shallow breath.

She moved with him, letting him draw her toward the bed. He peeled away the robe as he guided her down onto the mattress, then spread out next to her. Lips still locked together, hands still exploring each other with avid interest, Corinne felt his fingers trace one of the scars that riddled her torso. Most had healed with the forced ingestion of the Ancient's blood, but there were others, wounds that had been inflicted with the intent that they'd be permanent. Wounds meant to break the spirited young woman who'd fought her subjugation for longer than had been wise.

"Don't," she whispered, her voice choked and anxious. "Please, Hunter...don't look at them. I don't want you to see everything that's ugly about me. Not tonight."

She hoped to feel his touch move away from the hideous marks, but instead it lingered. He drew up onto his elbow and slowly took her in from head to toe. His hot gaze took its time studying the scars left behind from frequent electrical torture and the various punishments that had often gone on for weeks without end.

She knew how terrible she must look to him, but Hunter was gazing at her with open admiration, as though she were the most beautiful thing he'd ever seen.

"Nothing about you is unattractive to me," he murmured. "The scars are just scars. Your body is soft and strong, perfect to me. I could never tire of looking at you. I know I could never tire of touching you like this."

As though to emphasize his point, he brought his head down to her torso and kissed the worst of her flawed skin. Slowly, he worked his way up to her mouth and pressed another achingly possessive, dizzyingly hot kiss to her lips.

His *glyphs* were surging with dark color now, the elegant tangling of his Gen One patterns alive with indigo, gold, and wine—all the lush colors of Breed desire. Corinne touched the beautiful swirls and arcs, tracing her fingers down across his abdomen, where the otherworldly skin markings disappeared beneath the waistband of his fatigues.

She ran her fingertip along the edge of the loose black pants. Heat permeated into her palm as she tentatively moved her touch a bit lower. Beside her ear, Hunter let out a low groan. His big hand came down over hers, his long fingers engulfing her, pressing her caress toward the hard ridge of his erection.

She knew no apprehension or uncertainty as she touched him over the straining zipper. His sex felt enormous, hard as stone. To her amazement, the thought gave her a dark, sensual thrill, not the jolt of panic she feared would ruin everything.

Hunter buried his mouth in the crook of her neck, driving her mad with his tongue as she took her time exploring the breadth and feel of him through the thin barrier of his clothing. She felt his hand drift tentatively down between her legs, felt him cup her with his palm, kneading her gently. Pleasure unfurled deep inside her, spreading a delicious heat all the way to the tips of her fingers and toes. All too soon, he moved on, and then his hand was guiding hers over him, helping her to unfasten his fatigues, pushing the rest of his clothing away.

Both naked now, they lay side by side, indulging in long, unrushed moments of kissing and touching, caressing and stroking as they learned each other's bodies. Corinne could feel the steely jut of his sex against her hip. It stoked a heated curiosity in her, a need to be closer . . . to take him deep into her body.

She hooked her leg over his, bringing their hips together even tighter than before. Hunter was gritting his teeth, his jaw clamped so tight she thought it a wonder he didn't crack his molars. When she stroked her fingers over his bulky shoulder, delighting in the rush of color that flooded his *glyphs* in the wake of her touch, she noticed he was shaking.

He was holding himself back, letting her set their pace.

She leaned forward and kissed him, using her tongue to show him that she was ready. That she knew what was going to happen between them now and she welcomed it. Hunter groaned and dragged her flush against him. The thick length of his arousal kicked hard between her thighs.

"Come inside me," she whispered against his mouth. She reached down and guided him there. "Make love to me, Hunter."

The broad head of his sex nudged at her core, hot and unyielding. She shifted to meet him, then sighed with pure, unabashed pleasure as he cleaved into her in one long unhurried stroke, filling her completely. Tears sprang behind her closed eyelids at the intensity of their joining. Sensation flooded her, every fiber in her being responding to his glorious invasion. His entire body felt as rigid as stone beneath her hands. He shook with immense restraint, moving within her gingerly, so carefully, so reverently, she wanted to weep.

Rocking into her, pushing her toward a bliss she'd never known let alone imagined was possible, he caught her moan in a sensual kiss. And then she was shattering, a sweet detonation of pleasure and emotion that broke loose inside her as the wave of her first orgasm carried her senses heavenward on a choked cry of release.

Hunter lost himself in the sweet sounds—the stunning power—of Corinne's passion. She felt so good wrapped around him, her petite body shuddering and quaking, one tiny tremor after another stroking the hard length of his shaft as he pumped his hips against her.

Never had he felt anything so glorious.

Never had he imagined pleasure like this could be possible. It ruled him in that moment, demanding that he give it full rein even when he wanted to take his time, make this moment last so he could savor every second of it.

He wanted to take care with Corinne. He wanted to be gentle with her after all the abuse she'd known from other males. And so he held himself to a controlled pace, even as she was coming apart beneath him, every sweet convulsion of her sex a hairbreadth from undoing him. He kissed her and caressed her, holding her close against his body, thrusting and withdrawing with utmost restraint until her climax reached its crest and began to ebb.

Her breath trembled near his ear. Then it hitched softly and he felt a warm moisture against his cheek. She shuddered in his arms again, and through the dizzying haze of his pleasure, he realized she was crying.

"Corinne," he gasped, drawing back to look at her in concern. He froze, unable to move in the face of her tears. "Ah, God. I'm hurting you—"

"No," she whispered around a quiet little sob. "No, this doesn't hurt at all. It feels so good. You're making me feel something I've never known before, Hunter. I didn't know it could be like this. It's overwhelming how good you feel to me right now. I don't want it to end."

Relieved that she was all right, he kissed her and settled back into his rhythm. That she was weeping with pleasure because of their joined bodies made him want to pound his chest with his fists and roar his pride to the rafters. It was a strange impulse, animalistic and possessive and raw, but he felt all those things and more when he gazed down at Corinne's tear-streaked, beautiful face, her breath puffing softly from between her parted lips as he rocked into her with long, indulgent strokes.

She moaned as he found a stronger tempo, her short fingernails digging into his shoulders as she clung to him. Her thighs circled his hips, pulling him into a tighter hold against her body. Her wet heat gloved him so firmly, wringing him inside out as a furious wave began to build and swell at the base of his cock.

He tried to hold it back. He growled with the force of his will, but it wasn't enough. Corinne's body continued to milk him, driving him toward a fevered pace that only made him hunger all the more. He thrust deeper with each hard stroke, faster, until the coiled pressure snapped its leash and roared through him like fire in his veins.

He bit back the shout that would have rattled the house, burying his face in the curve of Corinne's delicate neck as his whole body jerked and convulsed and the first true orgasm of his life jetted out of him in a scalding stream of release.

He murmured something unintelligible as his cock spasmed with delicious intensity against the tight, warm sheath of her sex. He couldn't hold back the ragged curse, no more than he could hold back the instant reanimation taking place inside her. He was hard again, every nerve ending enlivened and ready to start all over.

Corinne's fingers trailed lazily across his back as she moved subtly beneath him, a wordless invitation he wasn't about to refuse. "You don't need a moment to catch your breath?" she asked, a sensual smile in her eyes when he glanced down at her.

"All I need right now is more of this," he growled. "More of you."

"I need that too." Her arms looped around the back of his neck and she drew him toward her for a slow, heady kiss. Her tongue teased the seam of his lips and he was lost.

Hunter thrust deep, inch by inch, filling her up. There was no staving off his desire for her now. No amount of discipline strong enough to hold him in check now that he'd had a taste of true pleasure with Corinne. Cupping her breast in his palm, he returned her fevered kiss, their tongues tangling as their bodies undulated in a shared rhythm, giving and taking with equal measure.

She broke first, panting and moaning, her graceful spine arching up beneath him as her sex clenched his in a rippling fist of sensation. His own release was right behind hers. He shuddered hard, driving home with a need so fierce it owned him.

As he gathered her close and felt the hot rush of his seed erupting deep within her, Hunter knew a bliss that eclipsed everything else. He entertained—just for a split second—the notion of living a normal existence, without the dark past that had shaped him. He wondered—pointlessly, his logic warned him—what it might be like to have a female at his side, to experience what some of the other warriors had with their mates.

It was a dangerous indulgence, dreaming. But no more dangerous than the sudden rush of protectiveness, of primal possessiveness, he felt when he thought about Corinne. He'd killed for her tonight, and he would do so again without hesitation, if he thought she might come to harm.

And in the back of his mind, as he sated himself in her body and took his comfort in her tender arms, he wondered if he might be the biggest threat to her happiness of all.

CHAPTER
Twenty-four

Dante paced the corridor outside the compound's infirmary, trying not to think about the fact that his beautiful, courageous Tess was in utter agony on the other side of the door. She'd been in labor all night and now, well into the morning. The contractions had only been worsening, growing more and more frequent with every passing hour.

Tess was handling the whole thing like a champ.

As for him, every time he heard her groan with the onslaught of another labor pain, he thought for sure he was going to pass out cold.

Which is why he'd finally removed himself to the hallway a short time ago. Probably the dead last thing Tess needed was to watch him become white as a sheet at her bedside, his knees turning into jelly beneath him.

Through the blood bond they shared, he felt Tess's pain as his own. He wished like hell he could shoulder it all himself. Pain? He could handle that, no problem; it was the idea that the female he loved was suffering that made him want to either punch something or vomit in the corner. But he felt Tess's strength too, and he marveled at the tenacity—the purely miraculous feminine strength—that gave his mate the stamina to continue fighting through the exhaustion and the prolonged agony that was required to bring their child into the world.

He took a quick glance through the small window of her infirmary room. Gabrielle and Elise stood on either side of the bed. They'd come in a few hours ago and had been taking turns holding Tess's hands, mopping her forehead with a damp cloth, and feeding her ice cubes as the process dragged on seemingly without end. Gideon was monitoring her vitals—under his solemn oath to Dante that he would do so with his eyes closed, lest he see any more of Tess than Dante was comfortable sharing.

The best part of the whole setup, though, was Savannah. She was handling the delivery, her long family background in such things giving Dante the reassurance he needed that everything was going to be fine in the end. At least, he hoped to God everything was going to be okay.

Meanwhile, he felt pretty damn useless himself.

He took another back-and-forth stroll of the hallway, wondering where the hell Harvard was when he needed him.

If he'd been there now to see Dante hanging in the corridor like a green-gilled ghost, Chase would have busted his balls from now to next week. He'd have shamed Dante for being a straight-up wuss, would have dropkicked him back into the infirmary if that's what it took.

Shit. Dante truly missed the smart-ass warrior who'd

been his tightest friend in the Order for the past year and some change.

Ex-warrior and *former* friend, he mentally amended, still pissed as hell over the whole fucked-up situation. It didn't soften his opinion any that Chase had phoned in last night to let them know he'd gone against Lucan's direct orders and hunted down Murdock on his own.

And for what? Aside from a vague mention of Dragos's possible interest in a local politician, the most solid piece of intel Chase had managed to squeeze out of the bastard was the day-late/dollar-short fact that Dragos was looking to get a bead on the compound's location. News the Order was all too well aware of already.

From what Tegan had relayed to everyone about his brief conversation with Chase, it didn't sound like they should be counting on hearing from him again anytime soon—if ever. Tegan was of the opinion that Chase was on a serious downward slide. He'd mentioned the word "Rogue," something neither Dante nor any of the other warriors were eager to accept but found themselves hard-pressed to contradict.

Dante paced another hard track in the hallway, raking his hand through his dark hair and grinding out a muttered curse. It was past time he started getting used to the idea that Harvard was no longer a part of the Order. He was no longer a part of their lives.

Dante felt like kicking himself over the conversation he'd had with Tess recently about naming Chase as godfather to their son. He'd had to work pretty hard to persuade her that Chase could be relied upon for something that important, and now the son of a bitch had gone and made him look like a jackass for even suggesting him.

In the end, Tess's instincts in that area had proven a lot better. Gideon had been stunned by their request, and both he and Savannah had accepted the responsibility with grace and conviction. If anything should happen to Dante and Tess, they couldn't hope for better guardians for their son.

With this reassurance fresh in his mind, Dante glanced up to find Elise poking her blond head out the infirmary room door. "It's time," she said, soft light shining in her pale purple eyes. "The baby's almost here now, Dante."

He scrambled inside, his heart leaping into his throat. He moved in close beside his Breedmate, taking her hand to his lips and pressing an adoring kiss into her damp palm. "Tess," he whispered, his tongue thick, joy and worry crawling up the back of his throat. "How're you doing, angel?"

She started to answer, but then her face scrunched tight and her grasp on his hand became a vise. Savannah told her calmly to bear down, that they were almost there. Tess pulled herself up off the infirmary bed. A shredding howl tore out of her mouth, and Dante felt his legs go a bit wobbly beneath him. He held it together, though. Bad enough he'd spent the last hour propping up the corridor walls, he wasn't about to let Tess go another second without him at her side.

The pain dragged out for an excruciatingly long couple of minutes before Savannah instructed Tess to lie back again and relax. She was panting as she looked up at Dante, sweat beading her forehead. He mopped it away with the cloth Gabrielle handed him, then pressed a tender kiss to his beautiful mate's brow.

"Do you have any idea how much I love you?" he murmured, holding her aqua gaze. "You're amazing, Tess. You're gorgeous, so incredibly brave. You're going to be a great mother to our—"

Her lips peeled back from her teeth as a fresh bellow exploded from her throat and drowned him out. Dante felt the rush of hot pain as it roared through Tess's delicate body. It was beyond intense, a shredding anguish that made him want to swear off ever so much as thinking about another baby if it meant putting Tess through this kind of ordeal.

"Okay, folks," Savannah said, her voice as soothing as a balm. "Here we go now. One more push, Tess. He's almost here."

Dante bent his head down beside her face and whispered private words of encouragement, things meant only for Tess. Praise for what she was giving him tonight, and pledges of devotion for her that he couldn't adequately express in feeble words.

He held her hand as the final contraction twisted through her. He shouted with joy as his son finally appeared, a tiny, pink, squirming little bundle held aloft and squalling in Savannah's expert hands. And he wept without shame as he met Tess's beautiful, elated gaze in that next moment, loving her with every particle of his being.

He leaned over and kissed his amazing Breedmate, pulling her into his embrace and sharing the euphoria of this precious moment of their lives together, particularly knowing how it had come in the midst of so much upheaval and strife.

After a few minutes, Savannah came over with the impossibly small bundle that was their newborn son. "I know you must be eager to hold him," she said, placing the baby in Tess's waiting arms. "He's beautiful, you guys. Perfect in every way."

Tess started weeping again, tenderly touching the infant's tiny cheeks and the rosebud mouth. Dante marveled at the sight of his child. He marveled at the woman who gave him such a miracle, something equally as precious to him as the incredible gift of her love. He stroked a tendril of damp blond hair away from her face. "Thank you," he told her softly. "Thank you for making my life so complete."

"I love you," she replied, bringing his hand to her lips and kissing the heart of his broad palm. "Would you like to say hello to your son?"

"Our son," he said.

Tess nodded, so proud and lovely as he took the little bundle into his arms. His hands dwarfed the tiny infant. He felt clumsy with him, awkward as he tried to find a comfortable cradle for the newborn in his too-big arms. Finally, he learned the way to hold him, taking the utmost care to get everything right. Tess smiled up at him, her joy pouring through his veins along with his own happiness.

God, his heart was so full, it felt near to exploding.

Dante stared down into the pink, squalling face of their child. "Welcome to the world, Xander Raphael."

Corinne stood next to the bed that next morning, watching Hunter sleep. He lay naked on his stomach, an immense, masculine sprawl of beautiful, *glyph*-covered skin and bulky muscle. He snored lightly, resting as deeply as the dead.

Their night together had been incredible, and she had never felt more content than she had resting in his arms after they'd made love. But the night had been over for a while, and except for the few hours she'd been able to close her eyes and sleep, her thoughts had centered on one thing: the urgency to find her son.

It was that need that had made her rise before daybreak, slip out from Hunter's comforting warmth, and head out back to the swamp to look for the truck he'd left there on his return from Henry Vachon's. She had gotten lucky, and found the white box truck unlocked behind Amelie's house on the river. Corinne had crawled inside and spent the better part of an hour poring through the reams of paper files and photographs she'd found stuffed inside the broken safe.

Dragos's laboratory files. Decades' worth of records.

She'd thumbed through every one, searching for anything that might bring her closer to learning the fate of her son or the other infants born inside the lab. She'd found medical charts and experiment results—thousands of pages of codes and jargon that meant nothing to her. To make matters worse, none of the files contained the names of their subjects. Like some kind of callous inventory of assets, Dragos's records contained only case numbers, control groups, and cold statistics.

Everyone he'd touched—every life he'd ruined inside the hellish madness of his laboratory—meant nothing to him.

Less than nothing.

Corinne had dug through the remaining stacks of papers in a fit of impotent outrage. She'd wanted to tear all the offending records into tiny pieces. And then, nearly to the bottom of the safe's contents, her fingers brushed across the smooth leather of a large file pouch. She'd pulled it out and dumped the files into her lap, sifting through them for even the smallest shred of hope.

The hand-recorded entries were more of the same impersonal inventories that were in the other files. Except there was something different about these dates and notations. Something that had made the fine hairs at the back of Corinne's neck prickle with suspicion...with a certain, dreadful knowing.

She held the leather file pouch in her hands now, as she moved closer to the bed where Hunter was just starting to rouse. He must have sensed her in the shuttered quiet of the room. His head came up off the pillow, eyelids blinking open over the piercing gold of his gaze.

He saw that she was dressed, that she was still breathing hard from her run back to Amelie's house, and he frowned. "What's wrong? Have you been somewhere?"

She couldn't keep the truth from him any longer. Not after what they'd shared last night. She owed him that much. She owed him her trust.

"I had to know," she said quietly. "I couldn't sleep. I couldn't sit still, lying in the comfort of your arms, knowing some of Dragos's secrets were nearby."

"You left the safe house without telling me?" Hunter sat up, moved to the edge of the bed, and swung his big bare feet to the floor. His frown had turned darker, more of a scowl. "You can't go anywhere without me there to protect you, Corinne. It's not safe for you now, not even during the day—"

"I had to know," she repeated. "I had to see if there was anything that might help me find him..."

Something dark flickered across Hunter's hard, handsome face. It looked like dread to her, like grim expectation. His scowl still creasing his proud brow, he glanced to the large pouch she held in her hands.

When he didn't speak right away, she swallowed hard and forced the words from her dry throat. "I had to know if any of the records you took from Henry Vachon contained information that might lead me to my child. The child I gave birth to in Dragos's lab."

Hunter stared, then glanced away from her. His low

curse was vivid as he ran a hand over the top of his head. "You have a son."

Even though his voice was level, devoid of anger or any other emotion, it still sounded like an accusation to her.

"Yes," she said. He wouldn't look at her now. An odd distance began to spread between them, growing colder by the moment. "I wanted to tell you, Hunter. I meant to before now, but I was scared. I didn't know who I could turn to, nor who I could trust."

The emotional distance apparently wasn't enough for him. He got up off the bed and prowled, naked and immodest, to the other side of the room, adding physical space between them.

"This child," he said, throwing a dark look at her. "He is Gen One, like me? Bred off the Ancient that Dragos kept alive for his sick experimentations?"

Corinne nodded, her throat tight. "After everything they did to me while I was kept there, the worst was when they took my baby away from me. I saw him only for a few moments, right after he was born, and then he was gone. The thought of him was all that kept me alive through the things that were done to me. I never dreamed I'd actually be freed. When I took my first breath of fresh air after the rescue, I promised myself I'd spend every breath that followed—even down to my last—working to reunite with my son."

"That's a promise you can't truly keep, Corinne. Your son is gone. He was gone the instant Dragos took him out of your arms."

She didn't want to hear this. She wouldn't accept it. "I would know if he was dead. A mother's heart beats with her child's for nine months, day in and day out. In my bones—to my very soul—I still feel my son's heart beating."

Hunter exhaled a sharp curse, not even looking at her now.

She forged on, determined to plead her case. "I tried to keep track of the years, but it was difficult to know for sure. My son will be around thirteen now, by my closest estimate. Just a little boy—"

"He will be a killer now, Corinne." Hunter's deep voice shook, startling her with an anger she neither expected nor knew what to make of. His face was taut, skin drawn tight over his sharp cheekbones and rigid jaw. "We were never boys, none of us. Do you understand? If your son lives, he will be a Hunter, like me. By thirteen, I was fully trained, already experienced in dealing death. You cannot expect that it will be any different for him."

The harsh words dug a sharp ache in the center of her. "It has to be. I have to believe that if he's out there—and I know in my heart he is—that I will find him. I will protect him, the way I wasn't able to the day he was born."

Hunter was silent as he turned away from her, slowly shaking his head in denial. Corinne set down the leather file pouch and walked over to him. She laid her hand on his shoulder. The *dermaglyphs* beneath her palm pulsed hot with his anger, but she couldn't help noticing how the stormy colors muted at her touch, his body responding to her even if he seemed intent on shutting her out.

"I need to find my child, Hunter. I need to see him and touch him, make sure he knows that I love him. Now that I'm free, I have to find him. I have to try to give him a better life." She moved around in front of him, forcing him to meet her gaze. "Hunter, I need to remember everything about the day my son was born. Something might have been said or done by Dragos or his Minions that could lead me to my child. Something that may be tucked away in my memories. I need you to help me remember everything about that day."

Hunter's face went even tighter as he absorbed what she was proposing. He grabbed her hand and pulled it away from him on a growled curse. "You want my help? Do you know what that would mean?"

"Yes," she admitted. "And I know it's asking too much of you. But I'm asking because you're the best hope I have right now. You are very likely the only hope I have of finding my child."

He stared, disbelieving or disgusted, she couldn't tell. Heat flared in his eyes, but she wouldn't back down. She couldn't. Not when she felt closer than ever to the answers she so desperately needed.

"Hunter, please," she whispered. "I want you to drink from me."

CHAPTER
Twenty-five

Staring into Corinne's earnest, pleading face, Hunter felt as if he'd taken the full force of a cannon blast to his gut.

He couldn't believe what she was proposing. More than that, he realized he was furious that all this time, she'd been withholding the existence of her son—a Hunter, like him, for fuck's sake. She stood there, asking him to help her find her child, but Hunter knew all that waited for her at the end of that journey was disappointment and heartbreak.

Heartbreak he likely would be forced to deliver personally, if the teenage boy proved to be the same kind of killer Hunter himself had been at the same age. There was little hope of anything different. Hunter knew too well the kind of discipline and training—the rigid conditioning—that would have already taken place in the child's short life.

Mira's vision roared up on him in that moment. Now he understood. Now he realized with grave certainty whose life Corinne had begged him to spare in that prophesied future event. And he knew at once that the name she'd cried out in the throes of her nightmare a couple nights ago was not that of a lover but of the child she'd lost to Dragos's evil.

"Help me find my baby, Hunter," she said, the soft touch of her hand against his face an entreaty he feared he wouldn't have the strength to deny. "Help me find Nathan."

He thought about the tears she would shed if he allowed Mira's vision to come true. He considered the hatred she would surely harbor for him if she actually found her son, only to have him torn away from her again—permanently—if Hunter was forced to deal that predicted fatal blow. He could not be the one to hasten that pain for her.

And there remained the fact that if he drank her blood, he would be activating a bond to her that nothing, short of death, could break. Not even her hatred would keep him away from her if he allowed himself to taste her Breedmate blood.

"Corinne," he said gently, drawing her hand away and holding it in his own. "I cannot do what you ask. Even if my ability to read blood memories extends beyond my own kind, what you're asking would have far-reaching consequences."

"I know what it means," she insisted. "Won't you even try?"

"It doesn't work on mortal humans," he pointed out, hoping to dissuade her. "I've fed from them all my life, with no psychic effect whatsoever. There is a good chance my talent is confined to Breed memories alone. If I drink from you now, where will that leave us? You are a Breedmate. Our blood bond would be inextricable. It would be forever."

Her expression muted, eyelashes shuttering her gaze. "You must think me the worst kind of low, to press you into giving me something you have every right to save for a female who will be worthy of you, more suitable as your mate."

"God, no," he murmured, hating that she'd misunderstood. "That's not it at all. Any male would be privileged to have you. Don't you realize that? I am the one who's unworthy." He lifted her chin, imploring her to see that he meant every word. "If I drink your blood and my talent works as you hope it will, I don't want to be the one to disappoint you."

"How could you?" she asked, her brow knit in confusion.

"If my talent works and we find your son, I don't want you to despise me if it turns out the boy is beyond our help."

She gave a small shake of her head. "Despise you? Do you think I could possibly hold you responsible for what's happened to Nathan? I wouldn't, Hunter. Not ever . . ."

"Not even if I was forced to raise my hand against him in combat?"

Her expression turned fearful now, wary. "You wouldn't do that."

"If it comes down to a matter of protecting you, I would have no choice," he answered grimly. "If I agreed to help you find him, Corinne, I can make no promises that the outcome will be what you hope for."

She considered it for a long moment, time during which Hunter grappled with whether or not to divulge the vision that had been haunting him nearly from the moment he'd first laid eyes on beautiful Corinne Bishop. Some foolish part of him hoped for an out—that his talent would fail to read her blood memories or that somehow, in defiance of Mira's unerring gift of precognition, he could thwart the eventuality of Corinne's tears and futile pleas for his mercy.

In the time it took for him to run through the mental torture, Corinne drew a deep breath and met his gaze once more. There was no hesitation in her eyes, only bold, unwavering resolve. "Do this, Hunter. If you care even a little bit for me, then please, do this. I accept any risk, and I will trust you to do what you must."

He felt sick with dread at the bravery in her words. The knowledge of what likely lay ahead of them made his stomach twist with bitter bile.

But then Corinne moved closer to him. She gathered her long dark hair and swept it aside, baring her neck to him. She tilted her head, an offering he knew he would be too weak to deny. "Please," she whispered. "Please ... do this for me."

His hot gaze rooted on the small pulse that ticked beneath her delicate skin. Saliva surged into his mouth. His fangs ripped out of his gums, a fierce reminder of just how long it had been since he'd fed. Henry Vachon's rank lifeblood had been more poison than nourishment, a foulness he longed to blot out with the taste of something sweet and intoxicating, like the nectar that flowed through Corinne's tempting veins.

"Please," she murmured again, an enticement he could not resist.

Hunter put his mouth onto her neck and carefully bit down, penetrating the soft flesh with the razor-sharp points of his fangs. She gasped at the invasion, her body tensing through the momentary pain he'd inflicted. And then she was melting against him, her muscles going lax and pliant as he drew the first sip of her blood into his mouth.

Ah, God . . . she was so much more than he could ever have imagined.

Her warm blood coursed over his tongue like a balm. He felt it absorbing into his body, into his cells. Into every particle of his being.

She was sweet and warm against his tongue, her blood scent filling his nostrils with the delicate fragrance of dark bergamot and tender violets. He breathed her in, drenching his senses with the delicious taste of her, a taste that would be stamped into every fiber of his being for as long as he was alive to draw breath.

Although this was an act of compassion, of necessity, not a true blood-bonding between himself and his mate, everything Breed in him—everything hot-blooded and male—responded to the warm, sweet taste of Corinne as though she belonged to him in every way.

Arousal roared up on him swiftly, a desire that pounded through his veins and into his hardening cock like wildfire. He clutched her close as he drank still more. He felt a heat ignite deep within him and knew instinctively that the bond was taking shape regardless of intention, lashing her to him inexorably. She was his now, and the logic that had shaped him all his empty life seemed to abandon him as he tried to tell himself that allowing this visceral link—for any reason—had been a mistake.

All he knew was the heat of her blood as it filled him, the pleasure of holding her in his arms . . . the need that made him groan with desire as he lifted her and carried her with him to the bed.

He laid her down, his mouth still fixed to the pulse that beat like a tiny drum against his tongue. He wanted to make love to her all over again, wanted to strip her naked and bury himself as deep as possible within the comfort of her body.

His senses were flooded with need, his body on fire, electric and rigid with the force of his passion for her.

At first, he didn't notice the sudden flickers of darkness that jolted his mind. He tried to push them away, lost to the pleasure of everything that was Corinne. But the abrupt images kept coming, kept battering at the back of his consciousness.

Flashes of a dark prison cell.

Minions dressed in white lab uniforms, coming in to wheel Corinne away.

The screams of a female in agony . . . followed by the blustering wail of a newborn infant.

Hunter drew back from Corinne's neck, stunned, stricken.

"What is it?" she asked him, her eyes wide, fearful. "Are you okay?"

"Fuck," he gasped, amazed that his talent was responding, yet horrified for what she'd been through. More images slammed into his brain, sounds of torture and madness. The hopelessness of what had surrounded her all those years. "Corinne . . . my God. What they did to you, and for so long. I'm seeing it all . . . everything you were forced to endure."

She reached up and cupped her hand around his nape. Pain glittered in her eyes, though not as fiercely as the determination written on her lovely face. "Don't stop. Not until we find him."

He couldn't deny her, even if he'd wanted to. If Corinne had survived the awfulness in reality, then he could sift through it psychically and retrieve whatever she thought might lead them closer to her child.

Hunter drank some more, letting the terrible anguish and torture wash over him like an oily tide. He waited for something irrefutable, some solid clue that would anchor him, provide some bearings in the wasteland of agony that had been Corinne's existence in Dragos's laboratory prison.

But there was no line to grab hold of. Nothing but a brackish riptide that Corinne had somehow managed to weather on her own.

Because of the love of her child, she'd said. All because of him.

Because of the hope she held that she would reunite with her son one day.

Nathan had become her lifeline.

How would she survive if the time came—as Mira's vision had predicted—when Hunter would deny Corinne's pleas for mercy and deliver the blow that would finally take her hope away from her forever?

It was an eventuality that ate at him like poison, all the worse when he was feeding at Corinne's open vein, bonding himself to her inextricably, despite the knowledge that he was destined to break her heart.

The thought shamed him. With a self-loathing growl, he ceased drinking and gently lapped at the punctures he'd made in her throat, knowing he should seal them and release her. This hadn't been about pleasure or bonding; she'd come to him for help and he'd gleaned all he could from her memories. There was no need to continue, no matter how pleasurable it felt to be holding this female.

His female.

The declaration came from somewhere deep inside him, somewhere out of his control. He reasoned that it was only the bond speaking. His body, his senses, everything Breed within him, was attuned to Corinne now that her blood had fed him. It was merely a biological response, his primal nature staking a claim he had no right to hold.

And yet there was another part of him that recognized his feelings for Corinne were intensifying, and had been even before he'd taken the first drop from her vein. He cared for her. He wanted her to be safe, to be happy. He wanted her suffering to finally be at an end.

All things he could not promise her, so long as Mira's vision lurked like a specter in the back of his mind.

He drew away from Corinne's delicate throat and started to sweep his tongue across the punctures his fangs had left in her skin. Before he could seal the tiny wounds closed, Corinne moaned a soft protest. Her body arched into him more fevered now, hot and arousing, her slender limbs clinging to him and preventing his retreat.

He'd heard the other warriors talk about the blood bond before, but nothing had prepared him for the swamping rush of sensation—of erotic awareness—that engulfed him now. Through his talent, Corinne's blood had given him brutal glimpses of her memories, but it was a deeper connection that spoke to him now. He felt her desire. He felt her aching need, her arousal amplified by the bite that had awakened this unbreakable bond.

He pressed his mouth to her throat once more, taking another small taste of her sweetly exotic blood. He could feel it racing through his body, nourishing him, enlivening him. Her pulse beat in his own ears and in his veins as well, a shared tempo that was as strong as a war drum, driving him on.

"Ah, God . . . Corinne," he murmured against her velvety skin. Despite that the decent thing to do, the honorable thing, would be to set her away from him, he found it impossible to let her go. She writhed against him, clutching him closer. Her breath raced out of her in rapid pants as he drew slowly at her vein.

"Make love to me, Hunter," she whispered, and all of his will deserted him in an instant.

She didn't care how desperate she sounded—*couldn't* care. Not when her senses were filled with the erotic pleasure of Hunter feeding at her neck.

Corinne closed her eyes and arched against him as the pressure of his mouth at her throat—the tender graze of his fangs—made the slow melt of her body begin to boil with heightened need.

This wasn't supposed to be about pleasure. She had asked Hunter to drink from her as a necessity, very likely the only means she had of finding clues about her son. She had gone into this with the expectation that it would be unpleasant, perhaps even painful, if her past experience had taught her anything.

She should have known it would be different with Hunter. As gentle as he had been when he'd made love to her the night before, he was equally tender with her now. His hands held her carefully. His immense body, so powerful—lethal when needed—was wrapped around her protectively, his arms a comforting shelter that made her feel both safe and cherished.

She was no virgin, not her body or her blood, both having been stolen from her in Dragos's lab, but with Hunter she felt new. She felt clean.

Despite that he had agreed to drink from her, willingly bonding himself when there was no promise between them, for one reckless, utterly selfish moment, Corinne allowed herself to pretend it was real. Heaven help her, but it was easy to forget it wasn't, when he made her feel so incredibly good.

"Make love to me, Hunter," she whispered again, desperate to feel him inside her.

He gave a low, strangled moan as he swept his tongue across the twin punctures in her neck and sealed them closed. He undressed her in mere moments, his strong hands caressing her body as she floated on the intoxicating wave of pleasure induced by his bite.

When she was naked, he stood at the edge of the bed and gazed down at her, his amber-hot eyes glowing both from his feeding and from desire. The fangs that had penetrated her throat a moment ago gleamed as white as pearls, sharp points filling his mouth. His thick, jutting sex stood fully erect, as glorious as the rest of him. He looked predatory and powerful, and she had never seen anything as magnificent as this beautiful Breed male.

Corinne lay back and drank in the sight of him, marveling that he looked even more formidable unclothed than he did when fully dressed and armed for combat. Every inch of him was flawless muscle and smooth golden skin. His *dermaglyphs* tracked from nape to ankle, an intricate webwork of elaborate twists and swirls, arcs, and tapers. The Gen One skin markings pulsed like living tattoos, flooded with the rich, variegating hues of his desire.

He prowled back onto the bed, gliding his hands up the length of her legs and spreading her thighs open to receive him as he covered her body with his own. She was wet and ready for him, eager to feel him filling her. He did not disappoint. The blunt head of his penis found her core and drove home in one long, breath-stealing thrust.

"Oh," she sighed, her blood quickening as her body welcomed his sensual invasion. She gasped his name as he moved within her, not the sweet, restrained pairing of the night before but an impassioned, animal mating that had her speeding toward a swift climax.

Hunter must have known the urgency of her need. He seemed to share it. With his amber-bright eyes fixed on hers, he held himself above her and surged in and out with a passion that left her panting and boneless beneath him. Higher and higher he pushed her senses, each masterful stroke sending her reeling. She watched him through the haze of her oncoming climax, their gazes locked as he drove on, deep and hard and strong.

"Oh, God," she whispered, more breathless pant than words. And then she had no breath or words at all.

Her orgasm flooded through her. The hot wave of bliss was made all the more intense for the fierce look of pure male satisfaction that spread over Hunter's handsome face as he rocked above her. She gasped his name, her body clinging to him, her senses lost in pleasure.

He kept going, even as her climax broke and left her spiraling weightless, tingling from deep within. Hunter curled his lip back from his teeth and fangs, letting loose a throaty growl that vibrated into her marrow. His eyes searing her, his hot amber gaze possessing her, he crushed her to him and thrust with relentless vigor,

pushing her to reach for another delicious wave of release . . . and still another.

He didn't stop, not until they were both drenched and
sated, exhausted and breathless in each other's arms.

And then, when their desire reawakened to take hold
of them once more, they started all over again.

CHAPTER
Twenty-six

Amelie, let me help you with that."

It was dark by 5 P.M., a couple of hours after Corinne and Hunter had finally come out of their shared bedroom at the safe house. If Amelie had noticed their absence for most of the day, she had been too polite to mention it.

Now, as Corinne finished setting the kitchen table, she turned to assist at the stove, where Amelie was pulling on oven mitts, about to reach in and retrieve their dinner from the broiler. "Here," Corinne said. "Let me get that for you."

Amelie gave her a dismissive little cluck of her tongue. "Don't you worry about it, child. I know my way around this old kitchen like the back of my hand."

It seemed unnecessary to point out to Amelie that she didn't have the benefit of sight to guide her. As she had the day before, the gray-haired woman navigated her living space as though she knew every square inch of it by instinct alone. Corinne stood back as Amelie served up two beautifully browned slabs of buttery white fish crusted with a fragrant smattering of peppers and spices. The aroma wafted up from the broiler, making Corinne's stomach growl in anticipation.

Amelie took off her gloves, humming to one of the soft jazz songs that played on the stereo in the adjacent living room. Rounded hips swaying in time with the music, she reached for a spatula in the squatty earthenware jug next to the stove.

"I hope you like catfish," she said, pivoting to place the filets onto the pair of plates that waited on the countertop at her right elbow. Still humming and swaying to the high-pitched male voice pleading for someone to tell it like it is, she found her marks on the plates with hardly a falter. "I'll let you serve up some of that dirty rice and steamed vegetables, if you like. You can put the hot corn bread in that basket right over there."

"Of course," Corinne replied. She put some of each onto their plates, then carried both plates and the corn bread to the table and took her seat across from Amelie.

"Did any of those clothes I set out work for your man?" she asked.

Corinne started to correct her about Hunter being her *anything,* but the words took too long arriving on her tongue. Besides, after everything that had happened between them under Amelie's roof in the past roughly twenty-four hours, it would feel even more awkward for her to attempt to deny that there was something between them. "Yes, they did," she said, simply answering the question. "Thank you for letting Hunter have them."

Amelie nodded as she cut into her fish. "My son's always leaving his things here in his old room when he visits. He's a big boy, rather like your man in there. I'm glad something fit him."

"Well, we appreciate it very much," Corinne said.

She and Hunter had been able to wash out most of the bloodstains from the fatigues he'd worn to Henry Vachon's, but while the clothes were tumbling in Amelie's dryer, Hunter had been forced to borrow a sweatshirt and snap-sided track pants. To say that any of the clothes fit him was a stretch, Corinne thought, smiling to herself when she pictured him in the brightly colored sports-team shirt and shiny nylon slacks.

While she and Amelie enjoyed their dinner and the pleasant music drifting in from the other room, Hunter was in the guest bedroom talking with Gideon and using Amelie's son's computer. He'd gone back to the box truck a short while ago and brought in more of Dragos's laboratory records from the metal safe Vachon had been keeping in storage. Some of those records had been computer files, encrypted data, kept on several finger-size portable devices that Hunter was currently transferring to the Order's headquarters in Boston.

Corinne prayed there would be something useful in the records. As incredible as her time alone with Hunter had been, a heaviness lurked in her heart. She'd hoped desperately that her blood would have surrendered even a small clue about her son and where she might find him. But Hunter's talent had given them nothing to go on. Nothing except his awareness of all the degradation and defilement she'd been subjected to at her captor's hands.

Although he knew it all now, he didn't coddle her or make her feel somehow less a woman for the way she'd been treated while trapped inside Dragos's prison lab. She'd felt dirty, ashamed of the things they'd done to her. She'd felt herself powerless, a coward for having let them take her child away.

Once she had been freed, she'd felt immense guilt that she'd survived when so many others imprisoned and tortured alongside her had not. They'd had sons stolen from them too. Children they would have loved, if not for Dragos's evil. Right now, among the Breedmates taken in by Andreas and Claire Reichen back in New England, there were mothers who were mourning lost sons, nursing the same festering emotional wounds that she was.

As Corinne quietly ate her dinner, she felt a pang of selfishness for the need that spurred her to seek her own child above the rest. Slim as her hope of finding him seemed, even if she failed completely, perhaps her personal quest would also open the chance for other newly freed captives to search for their own stolen sons.

Even as she thought it, Hunter's words of warning came back to her, dark and ominous:

We were never boys, none of us . . .

If your son lives, he will be a Hunter, like me . . . fully trained . . . experienced in dealing death.

Your son is gone. He was gone the instant Dragos took him out of your arms.

No, she told herself. There was still hope.

Hunter himself was proof of that. He had managed to break from the brutal doctrine Dragos imposed on him. He was given a chance to be something more, something better. That's all she wanted for her son. That's all any of the other Breedmates would want for their sons. Perhaps if they could save Nathan, there might be hope for more stolen lives too.

Corinne held on to that hope as she finished eating the wonderful meal that Amelie had prepared.

"Everything was very good," she said, her taste buds still tingling from the peppers and spices and fresh, savory flavors. "I've never had catfish or dirty rice before. I've never had corn bread either. It's all delicious."

"Ohh, child." Amelie gave a slow shake of her head, her tone implying both shock and sympathy. "You truly have not lived, have you?"

"Maybe not." Because the woman was blind, she didn't see Corinne's wistful smile as she answered. She was glad for the privacy of her thoughts as she gathered some of the empty plates from the table. When Amelie got up to help, Corinne gently placed her hand on the woman's shoulder. "Please, sit. Let me take care of cleaning up, at least."

With a sigh that seemed equal parts resignation and contentment, Amelie sat back down in her chair at the table while Corinne cleared the rest of the dishes and flatware and started a basin full of hot, soapy water at the sink.

As she set the dishes into the suds, Corinne couldn't help feeling that the food had tasted more flavorful, the soft jazz music in the other room sounded more soothing—everything around her seemed brighter, more vivid and potent—after the pleasurable hours she'd spent in Hunter's arms. She wondered what it might be like to feel this way all the time. Was this what it was like for mated pairs within the Breed?

Was the intense warmth blooming in the center of her being simply a reaction to the physical comfort Hunter had given her, or something more?

She didn't want to let him into her heart. God help her, but for a very long time, she hadn't considered there could ever be room for anyone except the child she'd been forced to surrender. But when she thought about

Hunter's kindness toward her, when she considered all that they'd been through together in the past few days, she could not deny that he meant something to her. Something much more than the warrior she'd initially distrusted—even feared—and now looked to as her closest ally.

Her unexpected friend and, now, her lover.

The formidable Breed male who had bonded himself to her inexorably, if for no other reason than she'd begged him to.

It was a sacred gift, and he'd given it to her for use as a tool in her personal quest. He'd given her the most priceless, intimate thing he had, with hardly the slightest hesitation.

She felt Hunter's presence stir the air behind her now, yet the low rumble of his voice still made her pulse kick when he spoke. "All the memory card data has been sent to Gideon. I've also scanned the relevant paper files, in case any of it proves useful."

Corinne dried her hands on a towel, then pivoted to face him. "What did he think?" she asked, not at all reassured by his grim tone. He was holding back somehow, his face neutral. Unreadable. When she'd first met him, that schooled look had unnerved her, made her curious; now it simply worried her. "Did any of it mean anything to Gideon?"

"He will let us know." Hunter crossed his bulky arms across the large SAINTS lettering emblazoned on the tight black-and-gold sweatshirt. The sleeves barely reached halfway down his forearms, and now the fabric stretched even tighter across his broad shoulders. "The situation at the compound is not ideal at the moment. But Gideon has said he'll get back to us as soon as possible if his analysis yields anything promising."

"Okay," Corinne replied, telling herself it was a start. She had little left to lose when it came right down to it.

Nathan was still out of her reach, despite the blood memories Hunter had read for her. The lab records they'd found in Henry Vachon's storage unit were all they had to go on now—those, and Gideon's considerable technological skills. She had placed her trust in Hunter, and he in turn had placed his own in the Order. Corinne had to believe that if there was a solution, she would find it so long as she had Hunter on her side.

The hard part now would be the waiting.

She blew out a small sigh. "Okay," she said again, giving a resolute nod as though to convince herself it was all going to work out in the end.

As she turned back to the sink to finish washing the dishes, Amelie piped up from her seat at the table. "Everything all right back up in Boston with my sister and her man?"

"Yes, ma'am," Hunter replied. "Savannah and Gideon are both well."

"That's good," she said. "Those two deserve their happiness more than most anyone I know. I suspect you and Corinne do too."

Mortified at the turn in the conversation, Corinne kept her head down, scrubbing at a stubborn bit of dried rice that clung to one of the plates. She tried to concentrate on the music playing quietly over the stereo—a tune she immediately recognized—casting about for anything to focus on but the gaping silence that seemed to emanate from Hunter's direction. She rinsed the suds off the plate and set it into the wire drainer on the counter, feeling her skin prickle with a current of awareness that rippled in the air behind her. It drew closer, and when she glanced to her right, she found Hunter standing beside her, a red-and-white checkered dish towel in his large hands.

Corinne couldn't take his silence, or the meaningful look he fixed on her as he stood there, letting Amelie's assumption hang between them like a question.

"It's not like that for us," she blurted. "Hunter and I, we're not..."

Amelie's answering chuckle was as warm and rich as butter. "Oh, I wouldn't be so sure about that, child. I wouldn't be so sure about that at all."

"We're not," Corinne said, infinitely quieter this time, surprised she was able to speak at all for the way Hunter watched her, standing so close she could feel the heat of his body reaching out to her as surely as she did his gaze. His golden eyes rooted on her, hot and unflinching, sweeping her back in an instant to the hours of passion they'd shared just down the hallway from this very spot.

"I know this music," he murmured, his head cocked toward the jazz song that floated in from the living room speakers but his gaze still holding her in its heated grasp.

"Ah, yes," Amelie interjected. "That's the one and only Bessie Smith."

Not that Hunter or Corinne needed the confirmation. It was the same song that had played in the jazz club that first night they'd arrived in New Orleans. Just looking at Hunter now made that moment come back to vivid life in Corinne's mind. She felt his hard body against hers as she'd danced with him, remembered so well the tender instant when he'd kissed her that first time.

"You like Bessie too?" Amelie asked, humming softly to the lyrics.

"She's my favorite," Hunter said, his voice low, mouth quirked into a sensual curve that made Corinne's pulse thump hard in her veins. He moved closer, coming around the front of her and caging her between his arms. He bent his head toward her ear and whispered for her alone, "And this song has nothing to do with coffee grinders."

Corinne's face flamed, but it was a heat coiling lower on her anatomy that made her shudder against him as he let his mouth travel from beneath her earlobe to the sensitive hollow of her collarbone. She was vaguely aware of Amelie rising from her chair at the table. Hunter drew back only then, and Corinne took the chance to wrangle back her breath.

"Amelie, where are you going?"

"I'm old, child, and life here is simple. After dinner, I like to watch my game shows and take a nap." Her cloudy eyes wandered very close to where Corinne and Hunter stood. "Besides, you two don't need me hanging around eavesdropping when you'd rather be alone. I may be blind, but I ain't *blind*."

Before Corinne could protest, Amelie gave them a little wave and shuffled out of the kitchen toward the hallway. "Don't pay me any mind at all," she called, her singsong voice full of amusement. "I'll be watching my programs with the volume up so loud, I wouldn't hear a hurricane."

Corinne's smile broke into a soft laugh. "Good night, Amelie."

From down the hall, the sound of a door closing echoed up into the kitchen. Hunter took Corinne's hands into his, drying one then the other with the dish towel. He set it down on the counter, then wrapped his fingers around hers and led her to the center of the little kitchen.

While Bessie Smith crooned about bad love and good

sex, they held each other close and swayed together slowly. The moment felt utterly pure, unrushed, and peaceful . . . perfect. So much so, it put an ache in Corinne's heart.

And although neither of them had to say it, she saw her own thoughts reflected in Hunter's hooded, haunted golden eyes.

How long could a perfect moment—a happiness as innocent as this simple slice of time they'd found together, right here and now—truly be expected to last?

CHAPTER
Twenty-seven

Hunter stood with his back to the wall of the bedroom he shared with Corinne in Amelie's house, watching the moonlight play over her naked body from the open window. The sounds of swamp animals echoed in the distance, deadly night predators like him, called by the darkness and primed to search out fresh prey. They would hunt, and, if successful, they would kill. Tomorrow evening, the cycle would begin again.

It was simply what they did, what they'd been born to do: destroy without mercy or regret, without questioning if there was something more for them in another place. No basis from which to crave anything but what they already knew.

Hunter knew that world.

He'd navigated it without flaw for as long as he could remember.

And he damn well knew better than to permit himself to imagine pointless scenarios, especially those where he was tempted to paint himself a hero. A white knight of some improbable legend, pledged to ride to the salvation of the beautiful damsel in need, like the ones he'd read about ages ago...before his Minion handler had removed all the books from his meager quarters at the Vermont farmhouse and forced him to watch them burn.

He was no one's hero, no matter how much this time alone with Corinne was making him wish he could be.

Part of that longing was his blood bond to her. She was inside him now, her cells nourishing his, weaving a visceral connection that would likely amplify all of his feelings toward her. At least, that's what his reason insisted it was.

Better a physiological explanation than the more disturbing one that had been battering around in his head—and in the center of his chest—since the few private moments he'd spent holding Corinne in his arms, dancing with her on the worn yellow linoleum of Amelie Dupree's tiny kitchen.

If he could have stretched that moment out forever, he would have. Without hesitation, he would have been content simply to hold Corinne in his arms for as long as she'd have let him. He yearned to, even now, after they'd finished straightening the kitchen together then gone to bed and made love slowly.

The banging in his chest only intensified at the thought, all the worse when he could smell her on his skin and taste her on his tongue. He wanted to wake her and show her more pleasure. He wanted to hear her gasp his name as she wept with sexual release and clung to him as though he were the only male she ever wanted in her bed.

Madly, yet with a ferocity he could hardly reconcile,

he wanted to hear her promise him he was the only male she might ever love.

Which was why he'd denied himself the comfort of lying next to her on the bed while she slept. He had already taken more than he had a right to where she was concerned. He needed to remind himself of who he was. More to the point, who he could never be.

Their safe house hostess had been right about one thing. Corinne deserved to be happy. Now that her blood memories had shown him the horrors of her ordeal, he could only marvel that she survived, let alone managed to come out of that prison with her humanity intact. Her heart was still pure, still open and vulnerable, in spite of her heinous treatment.

The way he saw it, she had endured far worse than he. Dragos had deliberately stripped Corinne of her spirit and soul, where Hunter was simply denied his from the beginning.

When he'd first met her, Hunter had felt a curiosity about the petite female who had come out of Dragos's laboratory cells with a fire still burning in her eyes. That curiosity had evolved into a strange kinship for him—an unexpected sympathy—as he'd watched her struggle to get her bearings in a world whose foundation had shifted beneath her the first time she tried to step back onto it. Unsure where she belonged, uncertain whom she could trust, even a battle-tested warrior might have had his moments of doubt.

But Corinne hadn't crumbled. Not under the cruelty of Dragos or the depravity of Henry Vachon. Not even afterward, in the face of Victor Bishop's unconscionable betrayal. She was a stout-hearted warrior in a petite, five-foot-four frame.

All for love of her child.

Now that Hunter knew the source of her determination and courage, it only made him respect her more. He truly did want to see her happy. He hoped against all logic and reason that she could reunite with her son without the tears and anguish Hunter dreaded was waiting for her.

Delivered by his own hand.

He expelled a curse, low under his breath.

As if his knowledge of Mira's vision wasn't enough to haunt him, in drinking Corinne's blood, Hunter had added another weight to his shoulders. He'd told her that her blood had yielded nothing useful to them in searching for her son, but there had been . . . something. It had been only a small fact, but a potentially crucial one. Precisely what it was, he wasn't yet certain.

Locked in her memory of the day she gave birth to her son was a partial sequence of numbers, recited by one of the attending Minions in the delivery room. It had been a casual recitation of digits, and an incomplete one at that, cut off from Corinne's consciousness when she was administered a strong sedative soon after her baby had been born and removed from the room.

What the numbers signified, Hunter didn't know. It could be anything; it could be nothing at all. But he'd given them to Gideon along with the encrypted data files and scanned lab records, instructing the warrior to report back if the sequence returned a match of any kind.

Hunter wasn't sure what outcome he hoped for more: a confirmation for Corinne that they'd finally located her son, or no success connecting the sequence to anything useful. Nevertheless, he should have told Corinne what he'd found, whether or not it created false hope for her. He wanted to spare her that if he could.

If he could, he'd like to spare her every pain for the rest of her life.

He ran a hand over his head and let himself slide down into a crouch in the corner of the room. As he lowered to his haunches, he noticed a dark rectangular object lying on the floor just under the foot of the bed.

The leather file pouch Corinne had retrieved from the box truck earlier that morning.

Amid the all-too-pleasant distraction of their love-making, he had managed to overlook this piece when he'd gotten in touch with the compound regarding the rest of Dragos's lab records. Now he reached for the pouch and pulled out its contents.

Yellowed paper files and handwritten notes comprised the bulk of it, but it was the weathered, book-size black ledger that caught his eye and wouldn't let go. He set the pouch and paper files down on the floor beside him, then opened the cover of the ledger. A jagged scrawl crept across the top of the first page.

Subject No. 862108102484

Hunter stared at the string of numbers. It wasn't familiar to him. Not any part of the sequence he'd given Gideon, nor anything he'd ever seen before.

And yet his blood seemed to cease flowing in his veins, his limbs going cold.

He turned to the next page.

Date of Record: 08 August 1956. 04:24 AM
Result: Successful live birth of Gen One subject, first
*   to gestate full term*
Status: Hunter Program—Initiated

Hunter stared at the page until the letters blurred together and a din started up in his head. He flipped farther into the ledger, scanning the later entries, his mind absorbing facts and data even as his conscience struggled to blot the details out.

Holy hell . . .

He was looking at the birth record and developmental progress of the very first Hunter successfully created in Dragos's labs.

Him.

Corinne woke up and stretched her arm across the bed, searching for Hunter's warmth.

He wasn't there.

"Hunter?" She sat up in the dark of the bedroom, nothing but the chatter of the surrounding swamps filtering in from the window. "Hunter, where are you?"

When no answer came from anywhere, she climbed off the bed and slipped back into her clothes. Her shoes were on the floor near the foot of the bed . . . and not far from where they lay was the leather file pouch from Dragos's laboratory records.

Its contents were spilled onto the floor, papers scattered in careless disarray.

The sight of that dumped file put a strange knot in her throat. That, and the fact that Hunter was gone without a word.

She stepped into her shoes and padded quietly out of the bedroom. Amelie's television still chattered from behind her closed door at the end of the hallway, but the rest of the house was silent, empty.

"Hunter?" she whispered, knowing if he was there, his keen Breed hearing would pick up even the smallest sound as she trailed through the house toward the back screen door of the kitchen.

Where had he gone?

She guessed she probably knew. Stepping outside to the back stoop, she peered into the shadows of the swamp, which concealed the white box truck parked several dozen yards into the thicket. The grass was crisp underfoot, the night air damp and briny in her nose. She trudged through it, rubbing off the chill that was soaking through her skin and into her bones.

When she reached the truck, she found the back latch open. The double doors gapped at the center, nothing but darkness behind their battered white panels with the faded moving company signage spattered with swamp muck and dried blood from the night before. "Hunter, are you in here?"

She pulled the panels wider and peered inside. A light bulb mounted to the interior ceiling clicked on by itself. Then she saw Hunter, seated at the far back of the trailer, barefoot and shirtless, his borrowed nylon track pants riding halfway up his *glyph*-marked calves. His elbows rested on his updrawn knees, hands and head hanging loosely.

He glanced up at her, and the empty look in his golden eyes made her heart give a lurching heave behind her rib cage. "What's wrong?"

She climbed up into the truck and approached where he sat. A black soft-bound journal of some sort lay between his parted feet. "What are you doing out here?" she asked him, seating herself across from him and folding her knees beneath her. "Did you find something else in Dragos's files?"

He picked up the journal and handed it to her. When he spoke, there was no inflection in his voice whatsoever. "It was among the papers contained in the leather pouch back in the house."

Corinne frowned, lifting the cover and glancing at the handwriting scrawled across the first page. "Is it a record from the labs?" When Hunter didn't answer, she paged forward, then rapidly fanned through dozens of entries, page after page of handwritten notations. "It's a birth record. My God, this is a ledger of events. It's a detailed documentation from one of Dragos's assassin programs."

"The very first," Hunter replied.

The truth hit her even before she glanced up at him and saw the bleakness in his handsome face. This wasn't merely any aged lab record recovered from the beginnings of Dragos's twisted breeding operation . . . it was Hunter's own.

Her breath caught, uncertain what to expect, Corinne flipped farther into the ledger. Not quite a quarter in, she randomly settled on one of the many entries.

Subject: Year 4
Report: Performs at top levels of education and physical training; tests in excess of 50 points above other 5 Hunters currently in program

It came as no surprise to her that Hunter would excel in whatever he did, even at so young an age. Some of the air she'd been holding in her lungs eased out now, and she turned to another entry farther in the ledger.

Subject: Year 5
Report: Initial conditioning completed; subject removed from lab to individual cell off-site; habita-

> *tion and discipline to be monitored by assigned*
> *Minion handler*

She flipped some more pages.

> *Subject: Year 8*
> *Report: Physical and mental fitness exceeds testing*
> *expectations; concepts and practice of various*
> *stealth execution techniques mastered; handler*
> *recommends advancing subject to live target*
> *training*

A number of later entries, recorded in apparent close sequence to the one that had Corinne's blood running cold in her veins:

> *Subject: Year 8*
> *Report: First kill; training tested in field situation*
> *against human quarry (no contest)*
>
> *Report: Successful kill of civilian Breed adolescent;*
> *methods employed: hand-to-hand and short*
> *blades (subject and quarry equally armed)*
>
> *Report: Successful kill of civilian Breed adult; method*
> *employed: hand-to-hand, short/long blades (sub-*
> *ject unarmed; pursuit and capture techniques*
> *outstanding, efficient use of environment and*
> *training in execution of quarry)*

The coldness she'd felt a moment ago was ice now, a sickness rising within her when she considered the evil that would bend a child into becoming the kind of soulless monster Dragos seemed determined to have at his command. She glanced up at the stoic Gen One male—the hard-trained assassin who had somehow become her friend and lover—and she found no fear or disdain for what he had been forced to become.

She cared about him, deeply.

She didn't have to search very far inside her heart to realize that she loved him.

With emotion stinging her eyes and the back of her throat, she turned a few more dreaded pages.

Subject: Year 9
Report: Handler notes alarming rise in subject inquis-
    itiveness; frequent questions about purpose in
    life, personal origin

Report: Subject found hoarding books in cell; random
    volumes of fiction, biography, philosophy, poetry
    stolen from handler quarters

This particular entry had a further notation beneath it, scribbled by a furious hand.

Determination: Restrict access to reading material
    other than program-approved manuals, technical
    and training books
Action: Handler instructed to remove contraband
    from cell and order subject to destroy it
Consider: Rebellion to be anticipated as limiting fac-
    tor as program continues. Subjects are highly in-
    telligent, natural-born predators and conquerors.
    Discipline alone may not be enough to keep them
    submissive.
Process Improvement: Task technology staff with

*providing means of ensuring subject obedience
and loyalty within the Hunter program*

Corinne closed the ledger and moved up next to Hunter.

She was speechless, overcome with sorrow for the boy who'd never been given the chance to be a child and humbled by the man who had come through such a lonely, lightless hell and still had the capacity for gentleness and honor.

She took his face in her hands and tenderly turned him to look at her. "You are a good man, Hunter. You are so much more than what Dragos meant for you to be. You are better than the sum of your past. You must know that, don't you?"

He drew out of her grasp, scowling, shaking his head. "I killed her."

The words were spoken quietly, a simple, horrific statement of fact. "What are you talking about?"

"It's all in there," he said, gesturing to the awful ledger in her lap.

Although she hated to see what other ugliness she'd find in Hunter's early years, he had obviously read the entire thing from front to back. She picked it up again and flipped past the first page. This time, she went slower, reading through the details of his birth and the weeks and months afterward, when he—unlike her own son—had been allowed to feed from his mother's vein and not from the strangers who had ostensibly nourished Nathan when she was denied even that small gift.

And then . . . she saw it.

*Report: Subject exhibits obvious separation anxiety
when removed from presence of mother; weakness noted; behavioral flaw to be corrected*

Action: Interaction with mother eliminated; feedings switched to human and/or Minion sources

Corinne turned a few more pages, foreboding putting a tremble in her fingers as she found the entry that made all the rest of them pale by comparison:

Subject: Year 2
Report: Subject experienced chance sighting of mother in lab; subject emotional, inconsolable when refused contact by Minion handlers; incident resulted in damage to lab equipment, further defiance exhibited in subject
Determination: For benefit of subject training, potential future distraction must be eliminated
Action: Mother terminated; effective immediately, program process modified to prohibit interaction between future subjects and mothers; subjects to be provided for solely by Minion handlers

Corinne's eyes were too wet to read any more. She set the record of Dragos's madness away from her, giving it a hard, hate-filled shove.

Hunter's voice was wooden beside her. "I killed my mother, Corinne." The words were flat and emotionless, even while a couple of tears strayed, wholly ignored by him, down his rigid face.

"You didn't do any such thing." As tenderly as she dared, Corinne reached out and swept her thumb through the tracks of moisture dripping toward his tightly held jaw. She caressed his flushed cheek, her heart cracked wide open, raw and aching for this man. "Dragos did this terrible thing, not you."

"My mother is dead because of me, Corinne. Because I loved her."

There was such a depth of regret in his eyes, she could hardly find the words to offer him comfort. Nothing she said could take away the hurt he must be feeling. Loss left pain in its wake, no matter how distant the void.

Corinne knew firsthand how soulless Dragos was, so it should have come as no surprise to learn that he'd considered an innocent child's natural bond to his mother to be a weakness. A flaw in his sadistic program that could be corrected with a single, final action.

That Hunter was left holding the pieces now, after all this time, certain that he was to blame, made her want to rip out Dragos's black, diseased heart with her fingernails and crush it in her fist.

Instead she gathered Hunter into her embrace and nestled his big body against her. She kissed the top of his head and petted him gently, she the unlikely protector, her arms the shelter that held this powerful male as he fell into a still and heavy silence in the cradle of her lap.

"You did nothing wrong," she assured him. "Loving someone is never wrong."

CHAPTER
Twenty-eight

It had started snowing in Boston that evening just after dark. Dime-size flakes carried on the cold December breeze, melting against Chases's cheeks and dampening the top of his head. He stared through the dripping strands of hair that hung into his eyes, watching the bustle of incoming and outgoing service vans making final deliveries to the pricey North Shore estate of Senator Robert Clarence.

He didn't know precisely how he'd ended up lurking in the shadows across the street from the young politician's house. Like the Bloodlust that was nipping at his heels, Chase's innate curiosity would not leave him alone, despite the fact that he had no real reason to give a shit about the swanky party evidently taking place later that night.

Apparently, it was the social event of the season, based on the parade of caterers and linen rentals alone. A twelve-piece string and horn ensemble had been unloading their equipment through the back of the house when Chase arrived. The twenty-plus uniformed cops and grim-faced Secret Service detail on post at strategic locations all over the grounds had taken everything up a notch.

Chase eyed the men in their brush-cuts and black suits. Bobby Clarence was a political star on the rise, but the government-issued protection wasn't there because of him. They were too numerous and too obvious to be assigned to anything less than a top D.C. official. Chase's memory prickled with a bit of worthless campaign trivia he'd been unable to avoid hearing more than once during the human's run for his seat in the Senate. He'd been endorsed by none other than the vice president, who'd waxed rhapsodic about the brilliant university student who had impressed his toughest professor with a combination of integrity and good old Yankee sensibility.

And now that Chase was thinking about it, a grave suspicion began to settle over him.

Dragos hadn't hidden the fact from his followers that he had some interest in Senator Clarence, but what if he had his eye on someone already in a position of even greater power?

"Jesus Christ," Chase muttered, low under his breath. What if some of those cops shuffling around the grounds of the estate were Minions that belonged to Dragos? What was to stop Dragos from using this kind of gathering to further his own schemes?

Chase's old instincts fired up with a warning he couldn't ignore. Something bad was going down at this party tonight; he could feel it in his bones. The senator or his VIP guest—good God, maybe both of them—

were in danger here. Chase would bet his life on it, not that it was worth much these days.

With dread raking him even deeper than his blood thirst, Chase called on his Breed genetics to carry him onto the grounds and past the cops and Secret Service detail posted outside. He was just a cold breeze, an eddy of snowflakes dancing in his wake, as he slipped inside the house through the back door to the kitchen.

No sooner had he gone inside than two more black suits came around the corner.

Chase ducked into the walk-in pantry, going utterly silent, utterly still, as the pair of Secret Service men walked right past the very spot where he would have been standing. One of them gave the all-clear for the second floor over his Bluetooth comm device, then launched into a discussion with his companion about last night's college football game. Chase let out his breath as the armed men exited the house to join up with the detail in the yard.

He started to head for the pantry door but stopped abruptly when it swung inward, almost crashing into him.

"Did you check for the red wine in here, Joe?" A young woman entered the pantry, her head turned over her shoulder as she spoke to someone outside the large pantry. She wore a long-sleeved, high-collared gown of crushed burgundy velvet that clung like a lover to her tall, athletic frame. A mane of wavy, caramel-brown hair swished about her shoulders as she pivoted around and stepped inside. "Ah! Here it is—two more cases of Pinot Noir, just where I thought they'd be."

Chase struggled to keep the shadows gathered around him as the striking female walked right up in front of him and motioned for a swarthy man in penguin tails and a bowtie to bring his wheeled hand truck into the room.

It seemed to take forever for the human to hump it over and load up the boxes of expensive French red wine. Not that Chase minded completely. Hard as it was to maintain the illusion his talent generated, he didn't think he'd tire very quickly of looking at the self-assured, all-business woman in the oh-baby dress.

Finally, the last case hit the hand truck, bottles clanking inside. "Will there be anything else, Ms. Fairchild?"

She checked her watch. "I'll let you know, Joe. Thank you," she replied crisply. She followed behind him as he wheeled his load out the door, her shapely backside looking much too hot to belong to someone who threw off that much chill. "If any of the other servers need me, I'll be reviewing the music selection one last time with the orchestra. Tell everyone to look sharp. The senator's guests will be arriving in precisely one hour."

"Yes, Ms. Fairchild," murmured Joe the hand truck driver as the pantry door swung closed on her tall heels.

Chase released the shadows from around him as soon as he was alone. His breath rushed rapidly in and out of his lungs, his body feeling as though he'd just made a coast-to-coast sprint. His hands were shaking, his veins cramping with the need for more fuel. Damn. He was practically spent, and the party hadn't even started yet.

He pushed the door open a crack and peered outside. When he was certain there'd be no more surprises, he ducked out and used the last of his current reserves to speed up the stairs. He found an empty bedroom on the security-cleared second floor, where he intended to wait until the senator's holiday guests arrived.

*   *   *

Gideon's email had been waiting for them when they'd returned to the house a short time later. Hunter had made the call back to Boston with Corinne seated next to him at the computer and had listened with a mix of dread and grim acceptance when Gideon had informed him that the partial numerical sequence from Corinne's blood memories had come back with interesting results.

There had been two solid hits in the encrypted data files recovered from the memory cards Hunter had uploaded to the compound. The bad news was, one of them was attached to a record with zero activity recorded on it for more than five years. The good news? The second hit was from an active file.

After a bit of hacking, Gideon had discovered what appeared to be some manner of coordinates associated to the record. Using satellite confirmation, he'd triangulated a GPS signal receiving from a small town in west-central Georgia, about sixty miles outside of Atlanta. Gideon's mouth had been processing as fast as his mind when he'd relayed the intel to Hunter about an hour ago. He seemed to think that with a few more hours of exploration, the data recovered from Henry Vachon's storage unit could yield something even bigger.

As intriguing as the prospect of a future blow against Dragos's operation was, Hunter's mind was on more immediate matters.

Corinne had been quiet, contemplative, since they'd said their quick good-byes to Amelie Dupree and set out together in the box truck for the long drive ahead. They had been on the road for several hours now, heading through Alabama toward Interstate 85. Hunter guessed he could get them as far as the North Carolina border before sunrise would force him to seek shelter away from the wheel and the broad plate of glass that spanned the width of the truck's cab.

Add another sixteen hours, and he'd have Corinne safe and sound back at Reichen's Darkhaven in Rhode Island.

Of course, she didn't know that.

He'd left out that particular detail of his plans, thinking it would be better to talk to her privately, once they were on the road and alone together. Now, however, he was finding it difficult to muster the words.

Knowing he would disappoint her, likely wound her with the truth, seemed even harder after the compassion she'd shown him earlier that evening. His head was still reeling from the discovery of the laboratory ledger and all that it contained. He'd felt off balance, then and now, knocked from his axis.

That is, until he remembered the centering feel of Corinne's arms wrapped around him.

As though sensing his inner struggle now, she lifted her head from the printed Google maps in her lap and glanced over at him. "Is everything all right?"

His confirming nod felt weak to him, transparent. "You've hardly spoken since we left New Orleans. If there is anything you need—"

"No," she said, shaking her head. "If I'm not very talkative, it's just that I'm nervous. I'm scared, I guess. I can't believe we're actually on our way to find him. At last, I am on my way to find Nathan."

She spoke her son's name with reverence and so much hope it tore at him. Hunter was learning to feel many things where Corinne was concerned, but the acid burn of guilt at his deceiving her was a pain almost too much to bear. He cleared his throat and forced himself to spit out the truth. "We can't be sure how good the chances are that your son is actually at the cell Gideon located outside Atlanta. But you and I are heading farther north than that, Corinne. I'm taking you back to Rhode Island, to Andreas and Claire's Darkhaven."

"What are you talking about?" He saw her mouth go slack in his periphery. "What do you mean, we're not going to Atlanta?"

"It would not be a safe situation for you, so once you're secured with Andreas and Claire, I will return alone to investigate. It will be better this way, for everyone concerned."

His veins, courtesy of his blood connection to her now, prickled with the sudden spike of her outrage. "When were you planning to tell me this—before or after you dropped me on the Darkhaven's doorstep?"

"I'm sorry," he said, meaning it completely. "I realize this is not your choice, but aside from ensuring your safety, I also want to spare you any worry or disappointment."

"It's him at that location, Hunter," she implored. "I can feel it in my bones. Nathan is there."

Hunter glanced from the highway stretching out before him, to the beautiful, protective mother who likely would throw herself in front of a hail of wild gunfire, if she thought it would save her son. The thought made him pause, stricken to consider it. "The facts we have to go on are few, Corinne. Logically, for all we know, this intel may lead to another one of Dragos's assassins. Not to your son."

She pivoted on the long bench seat, turning the full force of her anger on him. "By the same logic, for all we know, it *is* my son."

"All the more reason I don't want you there,

Corinne." He blew a low sigh at the glass of the windshield. "If it is him, then it cannot end well."

"How do you know that?" she charged hotly. "You can't possibly be sure of that—"

Another look at her, realizing what he was about to say might destroy everything they'd shared in their short time together. "I do know, Corinne. I have seen how your reunion with your son will play out. The little girl, back at the Order's headquarters—"

"Mira?" She seemed stunned, confused. A frown settled between her fine black brows. "What does she have to do with anything?"

"There was a vision," he replied. "A vision concerning you and the boy . . . and me."

"What?" Corinne stared at him as if he'd just punched her in the stomach. Although she was clearly taken aback, there was an edge of grim understanding in her soft, level voice. "Tell me what's going on, Hunter. Did Mira see something since we've been gone from the compound?"

"No. It was months ago," he admitted. "Long before I met you."

When he glanced at her now, she looked ill to him. A paleness came over her face in the dim light of the truck's dashboard. The accusation in her eyes sliced at him like a blade. "What are you saying? What do you know about Nathan? Do you know whether or not we'll find him? Did Mira predict how this will end tonight?"

Hunter's answering silence seemed more than she could bear. "Stop this vehicle," she demanded. "Stop it right now."

He eased off the northbound, three-lane highway, gravel crunching under the tires as he slowed on the shoulder of the straightaway. He put the truck into park and turned to face Corinne beside him. She wouldn't look at him. He didn't need to see her eyes to know that they would be filled with hurt—with disbelief and confusion.

"You've had knowledge of my son all this time—even before you took me home to Detroit?"

"I didn't know the vision concerned your child, Corinne. When I first saw the premonition in Mira's eyes, I didn't even know who you were. None of it had any meaning to me at the time."

Corinne stared at him now, her eyes bleak. "What exactly did you see, Hunter?"

"You," he said. "I saw you, weeping, pleading with me to spare a life that meant everything to you. You begged me to stay my hand."

She swallowed hard, her throat clicking softly as the buzz of speeding vehicles rushed past on the road beside them. "And what did you do ... in this vision?"

The words came slowly, bitterly. As awful on his tongue as their truth would feel in his hands. "I did what had to be done. You had asked the impossible."

She sucked in a sharp breath and scrambled for the door handle. Hunter could have stopped her. He could have frozen the locks with a thought and kept her trapped inside with him. But her sorrow raked him. He leapt out after her, right behind her as she staggered out onto the moonlit, grassy shoulder.

"Corinne, please try to understand."

She was furious and wounded, shaking all over. "You lied to me!" The roar of the passing traffic grew as she railed at him, her talent gathering the sound waves and stirring them like a tempest. "You knew this ... all this time we've spent together, and you withheld this from me? How could you?"

"I didn't know who you were trying to protect. I didn't know when the prophesied events were supposed to occur. It could have been years in the future. It could have meant anything. Before I said anything to you, I needed to understand what I saw."

A semi barreled through in the fast lane, and the sound of it shook the ground as Corinne listened to him try to explain something that felt indefensible to him now.

"The pieces didn't fall into place until you told me about your son."

She closed her eyes for a moment, glancing up at the stars before turning a wet gaze on him. "And then, after all that occurred between us—after we made love, after you drank from me—you still didn't tell me what you knew?"

"Then," he said, "I cared too much to hurt you with the truth."

She shook her head slowly, then with more vigor. "I trusted you! You were the only one I felt I could trust. To think I was actually foolish enough to let myself fall in love with you!"

More violent noise rose with the force of her heightened outrage. Over their heads, a tall streetlamp popped, showering sparks from high above them. Hunter swept her out of the path of the falling embers, holding her against him despite her tears and struggles. He pressed a kiss to her brow. Forced her to look at him, into his eyes and see another truth he'd been holding from her. "I love you too, Corinne."

"No," she whispered. "I don't think you possibly can."

He caught her chin and lifted her face back up toward his. He kissed her parted, protesting lips. "I love you.

Believe me when I say you are the only woman I want to love. I want your happiness. It means everything to me."

"Then you can't push me aside if there's a chance my child is only a few hours away from where we're standing now."

Hunter frowned, knowing he was losing this battle. Perhaps the first contest he'd ever surrendered.

As gently as he could, he reminded her, "Mira's visions are never wrong. If you come with me, and we do find your son, will you be able to forgive me?"

"If you truly love me, as I love you, then that should be strong enough to change the vision." She was calming now, and with her calm came the quieting of her talent. The busy road resumed its background whoosh and hum. Behind them on the shoulder, the box truck's engine idled with a rapid tick. She reached out to him tentatively, placing her palm over the center of his chest where his heart thudded heavily. "Maybe our love can break the vision."

"Maybe," he said, wishing he could believe it.

What he did believe was the fact that if he sent her away now, she would hate him regardless of what he found at the end of the GPS signal in Georgia. To send her away now would be to crush her hope and betray her trust once more.

Hunter took her hand in his. Together they walked back to the truck and whatever awaited them at the end of the road tonight.

CHAPTER
Twenty-nine

The senator's holiday house party had been in full swing for two and a half hours and Chase was getting bored.

From his perch in the gloom of the second-floor gallery balcony, he watched the crowd of humans enjoying themselves in the grand ballroom below. Elegantly dressed people strolled and mingled, laughing and air-kissing as they attempted to juggle drinks and hors d'oeuvres and a hundred pointless topics of conversation. In the background, the twelve-piece musical ensemble played an alternating selection of secular holiday tunes and upper-crusty classical pieces.

Chase couldn't help but notice the burgundy-draped beauty who circled the fringes of the gathering like a mother hen looking after her chicks. Ms. Fairchild made a point of searching out the most hopeless of the wall-flowers, engaging them with a smile and a few minutes of what appeared to be genuinely attentive conversation. She made introductions, dragging her socially inept charges into larger groups and standing by until they had found their footing before she moved on to the next one.

He'd guessed based on her businesslike demeanor that she worked for Senator Clarence, but looking at the attractive young woman, Chase found himself wondering if the job description for the bachelor politician had extended beyond party planning and social direction. Maybe the chin-high collar and brusque attitude were just a front. She didn't seem all that chilly now. Maybe she was as hot as her form-fitting gown.

Yeah, and maybe he was losing it, sitting up here in the belfry like Quasimodo when he had more interesting things to do back in the city.

The cold knot of hunger in his gut agreed.

Chase stared down impatiently, spotting the golden boy senator making the rounds with his guests. He was smooth. A consummate professional, pumping hands, kissing wrinkled old-lady cheeks, posing for photographs along the way. It wasn't hard to imagine his charm and polish sweeping him quickly into a higher office. No doubt Dragos had noticed the same thing about him, though Chase shuddered to think what it might mean if the Order's chief adversary started turning his sights on human government figures.

Down below the gallery, there was a sudden hubbub of activity. Two Secret Service agents entered the house through the grand front foyer. Three more opened the dark cherry double doors and held them wide for the party's VIP guest to come inside, another pair of agents bringing up the rear.

Chase had already guessed who the new arrival

would be, but it still made his pulse kick with a sharp pang of dread—of dark expectation—as Senator Clarence moved into position to greet the arriving vice president. Applause went up from the other guests as the two men grinned and did the one-armed man hug before moving on to begin the requisite meet-and-greet with the rest of the avid crowd.

Chase noticed he had company coming upstairs, extra security precaution, now that the country's second highest in command was in the building. The armed agent took his position on the other end of the gallery and reported his readiness into the mic clipped to the lapel of his black suit. Chase drew back from the edge of the balcony and melted into the gloom of the hall.

As he inched away, he thought he caught a glimpse of a face he recognized all too well. A face that most certainly did not belong among a gathering of humans.

The Secret Service agent was parked right out in the open at the other end of the gallery, his big head taking in the surroundings, shrewd eyes trained to spot anything out of line. But he didn't sense the danger that Chase did. He couldn't know that one of the men standing among the other partygoers was no man at all.

Chase bent the shadows around him, gathering them close as he crept toward the railing to steal another glance.

Goddamn, he thought, confirming the worst scenario.

It *was* Dragos down there.

Like a bee in the midst of a buzzing hive, the vice president made his way with the senator through the excited crowd. All too soon, they paused in front of Dragos. The three of them spoke for a moment, trading chuckles and clasping hands before they began to head off to-

gether toward a private room adjacent to the full-to-
bursting ballroom.

Fuck.

Oh, no.

No, no, no.

Chase knew he couldn't let Dragos go anywhere alone
with either one of these important men. He could not let
that happen.

Indecision raked him as he struggled to hold his talent
in place, his gaze fixed on Dragos's slightest move. Every
Breed cell in his body urged him to leap over the balcony
and attack—kill the bastard in cold blood, before he
even knew what hit him. But to do that would be to expose himself publicly as something other than human. If
it were only he that he had to be concerned with, he
wouldn't care. But the ramifications of showing himself as part of the Breed were irreversible, and too far-
reaching.

Maybe he could create a distraction, something to
cause momentary panic. Something to make the vice
president's guards rush him away from the party and
from whatever plot Dragos was hatching as he grinned
alongside him.

Chase felt his talent slip as he grappled with what
course of action to take.

The shadows fell away, like mist through his fingers,
leaving him standing there unconcealed.

In that very instant, Ms. Fairchild looked up and
spotted him. She motioned one of the men in black over
and pointed up toward Chase. The agent spoke into his
comm device and several others poured in from all directions.

Ah, Christ.

Meanwhile, Dragos was almost out of sight with the senator and the vice president.

Chase flashed across the distance to the Secret Service man positioned on the gallery balcony. In less than a second, he'd knocked him out cold and grabbed the pistol from his side holster. Chase fired a single shot into the air. Plaster dust rained down as the bullet sank into the vaulted ceiling. In the ballroom below, chaos erupted.

People screamed and scattered, everyone running for cover.

Everyone except Ms. Fairchild. She stood stock-still in the center of all that madness, looking right at him, her eyes locked on to him like bright green lasers.

Chase quickly turned his attention on Dragos. He met the furious glower with equal hatred and fired the agent's pistol before Dragos had a chance to dodge out of the way. The shot hit him dead-on, knocking the vampire off his feet.

Gunfire returned on Chase, exploding around him from every direction.

On the ballroom floor below, Dragos went down bleeding. Dead or dying, Chase hoped to hell, but he couldn't be sure.

He ran to the nearest window, then dived through it in a soaring leap. As he sailed into the darkness outside, he felt a shredding blast of pain tear into his thigh and shoulder. He shook it off, dropping down to the snow-covered lawn below.

He heard the pound of footsteps rumbling through the house and over the grounds of the estate. The jangle of weapons, all of them ready to blow the dangerous intruder to kingdom come.

Chase vaulted to his feet and took off running.

* * *

Dragos fumed where he lay, bleeding from his gut on Senator Bobby Clarence's ballroom floor. Moments after the gunshot wound that had knocked him flat, screams and chaos still filled the air of the estate. Terrified human party guests scattered like little birds while Secret Service agents swooped en masse to whisk the senator and the vice president out of the room to safety.

Damn the Order.

How had they found him? How could they possibly have known to look for him here, of all places?

Dragos held his hands to his stomach as the hysteria continued to swell around him. Although his wound was bad, he had no doubt that he'd survive. The bullet had passed through his body. Already the bleeding was lessening, his Breed genetics well on the way to repairing the damage to his skin and organs.

A pair of black suits and several police officers pushed through the fleeing crowd to reach him. One of the government men spoke low and urgently into the comm device hooked around his ear. The other knelt down beside Dragos, joined by a couple of anxious-looking uniformed cops.

Dragos attempted to sit up, but the Secret Service agent stuck out his splayed palm to discourage him. "Sir, just try to remain calm now, all right? Everything's under control here. We've got help coming for you in just a few minutes."

He didn't wait for compliance. Confident he'd be obeyed, he went back to join his companion, leaving the two local cops to sit on watch. A few straggling party guests shuffled past, hands pressed to their mouths as they glimpsed the spilled blood on their rush to get out of the ballroom.

Dragos grunted, resenting all of these panicked humans almost as much as he despised the bastard from the Order who'd managed to derail months of work with a single gunshot. It was pride more than pain that drew his mouth into a tight line, fury more than fear that had him gritting his teeth so hard behind his lips it was a wonder his jaw didn't shatter. His fangs throbbed, already ripping out of his gums and filling his mouth. His sight, always preternaturally sharp, was growing even more acute now, the edges of his vision filling with amber light.

He had to get out of there, and fast.

Before his rage betrayed him publicly for what he truly was.

Dragos glanced over at one of the attending cops—the younger of the pair. The one who belonged to him. Crouched beside Dragos, the Minion awaited his command like an eager hound.

"Tell my driver to bring the car around back," he murmured, his voice hardly more than a whisper. The Minion leaned close, absorbing every word. "And do something to clear this goddamn room of all these prying eyes."

"Yes, Master."

The Minion rose. When he pivoted to carry out the order, he nearly ran headlong into Tavia Fairchild. She stood there, unmoving, her shrewd gaze flicking from the cop who'd almost run her down to Dragos, who looked up at her in rapt but cautious interest. Although she could only have been there for an instant, it had been long enough. She'd heard the Minion address Dragos as his master. He could tell by the slight tilt of her head, the faint narrowing of her eyes, that she was trying to process information that even her keen mind didn't have the basis to comprehend.

"Pardon me, ma'am," the Minion mumbled, stepping out of her way with an awkward bow of his head. He glanced back at Dragos and cleared his throat. "Mr. Masters, I'll be right back."

Dragos nodded, his gaze trained fully on Tavia Fairchild as he lifted himself to a sitting position on the floor. The Minion's effort to cover his slip seemed to satisfy the senator's pretty assistant. As the officer walked away, her look of confusion muted into one of concern as she turned back to Dragos.

"Paramedics have been called and an ambulance is on the way . . ." Her voice trailed off. She looked ill, the color in her cheeks draining away as she drew nearer to him and gaped at all the blood soaking his white silk tuxedo shirt and the ballroom floor underneath him. Her balance seemed a little off as she wrapped her arms around her middle. She met his eyes if only to avoid looking at his injury, and gave a small shake of her head. "I'm sorry. I'm just a little woozy. I don't do well in these types of situations. I've been known to faint at the sight of a skinned knee."

Dragos permitted a small curve of his lips. "You can hardly expect to be perfect at everything, Miss Fairchild."

She frowned, visibly embarrassed. At least her queasiness seemed to help her forget about his Minion's careless slip of the tongue. She squared her shoulders, snapping herself back into the role of the consummate professional. "I've just left Senator Clarence and the vice president, Mr. Masters. They're both unharmed and in

Secret Service custody as we speak. Their main concern was for your well-being, of course."

"There is no need," Dragos assured her. "I'm certain the wound appears much worse than it truly is." To demonstrate, he started to get up on his feet.

"Oh, I don't think you should—" She rushed forward to assist him, but it was her body that wobbled more than his, her face going pale again, cheeks sallow.

"I will be fine," Dragos told her. As he spoke, the Minion police officer came back into the ballroom and took Tavia's place at his side, gently removing her as he informed Dragos that his car was waiting out back as requested.

"Don't you think you should wait for the EMTs?" she asked, incredulous. "You've been shot, Mr. Masters. You've lost an awful lot of blood."

He gave a mild shake of his head as his Minion helped him take a few steps. "It will take more than this to stop me, I promise you."

She looked less than convinced. "You belong in the Emergency Room."

"My personal physicians are best equipped to look after me," he replied, unfazed as he was smoothly escorted away by his Minion and another officer who'd come over to lend a hand. "Besides, you have other, more pressing things to take care of, Miss Fairchild."

He gestured toward the open front entrance of the house, where outside, the yard was beginning to crowd with arriving news vans and bright camera lights. Tavia Fairchild straightened her burgundy gown and lifted her head, visibly girding herself for the onslaught of reporters already pushing their way into the house. In the distance, the siren from the arriving ambulance screamed.

As he was being led away, Dragos heard the young woman's low, whispered curse, but when he glanced back at her, Tavia Fairchild was marching out to meet the throng of vultures like the very picture of poised calm.

"Is it true the gunman had been lurking in the senator's house?" someone shouted at her.

"Where are the vice president and the senator now?" another reporter demanded.

And still more panicked questions, one after the other: "Was the shooting an attempt on Senator Clarence, or is there reason to believe the vice president was the intended target?" "Could this have been a possible terrorist act? Did anyone see the shooter?" "Is it true there was only one man responsible for the attack?" "Do the police or Secret Service know anything about who might have done this, or why?"

Dragos smiled to himself as he exited out the back of the house. Perhaps tonight's unexpected chaos would prove useful to him. Perhaps all the frenzied questions and worry were just what he needed to drive the final nail in the Order's coffin.

The bullet he'd taken tonight had been a shot fired over his prow—one he was damned good and ready to return.

As he climbed into his waiting limousine, Dragos retrieved his blood-splattered cell phone from the pocket of his tuxedo jacket. No more waiting for the opportune moment to strike against the Order. It was time to shut them down hard. Permanently, if he had anything to say about it.

With his call to a backwoods landline in northern Maine ringing on the other end, Dragos watched through the limo's dark-tinted windows as Tavia Fairchild stood under the lights of a dozen news cameras, calmly addressing the agitated crowd.

While she assured them all that everything was under control, Dragos gave the go-ahead on a mission that would soon send the entire city into a state of total hysteria.

CHAPTER
Thirty

It was after four in the morning when they arrived at the location Gideon had directed them to in rural west-central Georgia. Corinne was exhausted, fatigued from the long drive and the emotionally charged confrontation she'd had with Hunter several hours ago.

But more than either of those things, it was the thought of actually being there—a few hundred yards from the old, riverside log cabin where Nathan might be living—that had all of her nerve endings hyperalert and jangling.

If she'd been nervous before, anxious for the moment she hoped she'd soon be looking at her son and promising him the life she wanted so badly to give him, now she dreaded it just as equally. Mira's vision had changed everything. Hunter's self-described role in that vision had left her doubting everything she'd been so certain of before.

Everything, except Hunter's love for her.

It was the only thing she could cling to, perhaps foolishly, as he turned off the truck's ignition and they sat in the darkened vehicle, watching the dimly lit cabin through the five acres of woods that surrounded it.

"You swear you're coming right back?" she asked him. He'd brought her with him to the location, but he'd adamantly drawn the line at allowing her to accompany him inside the house itself. "Please, be careful."

He nodded, even as he strapped on a pair of blades to the holster that rode his thigh over the top of his black fatigues. The long-sleeved shirt she'd washed and dried at Amelie's for him completed his transformation back to the warrior who'd escorted her from Boston to Detroit not so very long ago.

But now Hunter was anything but stoic or unreadable. His golden eyes caressed her with tenderness at the same time his strong hand reached out to draw her close for his kiss. "I love you," he told her fiercely. "I do not want you to worry."

She nodded once. "I love you too."

"Stay in the truck. Keep yourself out of sight until I return." He kissed her again, harder this time. "I won't be long."

He didn't give her any time to argue or stall him. He slipped out of the cab and vanished into the surrounding darkness.

Corinne sat there, waiting and alone, instantly regretting that she'd let him talk her into remaining behind. What if he ran into problems? What if he was discovered before he was able to determine if Nathan was living in the house at all? How long should she be expected to wait before—

A *crack* of gunfire rent the silence of the night.

Corinne jolted. The sudden explosion of bright orange went up near the front of the cabin as the noise ricocheted off the trees like a thunderclap.

"Oh, my God. Hunter . . ."

Before she could stop herself, she was climbing out of the truck, running toward the cabin up ahead. She had no plan once she got there, except to search for some reassurance that Hunter was unharmed. Invincible as he seemed, he held her heart in his hands, and there was nothing that could have stopped her from going after him now.

She smelled the tang of spent gunpowder as she neared the front porch of the cabin. A dead man sprawled there, a long rifle smoking from its barrel where it lay across his chest. His face was frozen in a rictus of startled alarm, his neck snapped efficiently to the side.

Hunter.

He'd been through here.

He was somewhere inside the cabin.

Corinne crept inside carefully. Immediately, she heard the sounds of a struggle taking place beneath her. The basement. She found the stairwell door leading toward the disturbance below, and in the instant she debated the idiocy of going down there, the painted wood panel appeared to spontaneously explode from within.

The force of it knocked her back against the wall behind her. When she opened her eyes after the shock, she found herself staring into a gaze that matched her own—greenish blue irises ringed by dark lashes and catlike, almond-shaped lids. The eyes looked back at her from out of the face of a boy. A lean, muscular boy about five foot seven, his lovely face still round at the jaw with the last traces of childhood.

But he was no boy, she realized. He was dressed in

gray drawstring sweatpants and a white tank top, despite the night's chill. His head was shaved bald, his skin covered in *dermaglyphs*. A terrible-looking, thick black collar circled his neck.

"Nathan," she gasped.

The instant turned into a moment as he cocked his head at her, no expression on his face.

No recognition at all.

And the brief hesitation cost him, because now Hunter was in the room with them as well. He'd moved faster than Corinne could follow, seeming to materialize out of thin air as he came up behind Nathan.

The boy's senses were as quick as his reflexes. He faced off against Hunter. Then, moving with the same impossible speed as the larger male, Nathan put his hand out and Corinne saw that he'd removed a long, thin iron from the set of fireplace tools near the pot-bellied stove several feet away.

Instead of using the iron as a weapon, the boy cracked it into the metal exhaust pipe of the stove.

The answering *clang* reverberated through the whole cabin. Then it began to rise, to expand. She felt Nathan's power—her own power, passed down to her child through his birth—as he warped the sound waves with his mind and sent them higher, coaxing them toward a deafening racket.

She'd had no doubt this boy was hers, but now, the rush of relief and rejoice poured over her. This *was* her son. This was her Nathan.

And this boy—this dangerous young Breed male—was gathering his psychic power, pushing the full force of it on Hunter now, attempting to drive his opponent to his knees. Hunter's jaw was held tight, tendons standing out like cables in his neck and cheeks as the aural on-slaught intensified.

"Nathan, stop!" Corinne shouted, but her voice was lost under the piercing shriek of her son's talent. She tried to douse it with her own ability, but his command of the gift was too powerful. She couldn't silence it.

Amid the cacophony he'd created, he launched himself at Hunter, murder gleaming darkly in his merciless eyes. He swung the fireplace iron at him in a rapid series of blows, any one of which might have cracked open Hunter's skull had he not moved to deflect it.

And that's all he was doing, Corinne realized. Hunter delivered no strikes of his own, though he could have taken down the smaller male in an instant. Could have killed him at any moment, if that had been his intent.

But Hunter only defended, like a seasoned alpha lion patiently batting away the scrappy cub who sought to test his mettle. This was far more dangerous than play; Corinne knew better than to think it anything less. Hunter knew it too, and yet despite the aggression being dealt to him, he made no move to inflict harm.

In that moment, Corinne had never loved him more.

Nathan kept coming at him, relentless and calculating, just as his training had conditioned him to be. Corinne reached once more for a grasp on the din he'd conjured. She gathered her mind around it, tried to bunch the noise into a kinetic tool of her own.

She caught a glimpse of Nathan landing a blow of the long iron against Hunter's shoulder. Oh, God. She would die if either one of them failed to walk away from this.

Focus.

She willed herself to concentrate on the noise she was

shaping, pulling it slowly away from Nathan's control while his efforts were trained on killing Hunter.

Corinne drew the din into a power of her own.

She gathered and shaped it . . . then heaved its psychic bulk at her son.

His head came up sharply. He threw a glower on her, confusion and surprise flickering behind the grim purpose in his gaze. She could read the question in his teenage eyes.

Who are you?

But he didn't care.

He shoved back at her even harder, blasting her with the full force of his power. Corinne cried out and gripped the splitting sides of her head. Her eardrums were screaming, feeling as though they were shredding. She went down on her knees, driven to the floor by the intensity of the pain.

At the same moment, she heard Hunter's roar. Saw his face twist in fury as she dropped. Glimpsed a flash of movement as Hunter drew his fist back, then sent it flying in Nathan's direction.

No, her heart cried. *No!*

"No!" she shouted, and realized the agonizing racket had abruptly ceased.

Hunter was at her side. "Are you hurt? Corinne, please, speak to me."

"Where's Nathan?" she murmured. She blinked up at Hunter, terrified of what she might see in his face. But there was only warmth there, concern focused wholly on her.

"He will be all right." Hunter moved aside so she could peer around him to where her son lay on the floor as though sleeping. "I struck him, but he's unconscious, that's all. Come with me now. I will take him out of here."

"Mira, don't wander too far with the dogs. Stay where Niko and I can see you."

"Okay, Rennie!" Mira called back through the darkness of the courtyard gardens behind the Order's mansion. Her boots crunching in the snow as she walked, she glanced over at Kellan Archer and rolled her eyes. "They think I'm still a kid."

His olive-colored parka swished as he shrugged his shoulders. "You *are* a kid."

She stopped walking and put her mittened hands on her hips, frowning up at him. "In case you didn't know, Kellan Archer, I'm eight and a half years old."

His mouth lifted up at the corner, as if she'd said something funny. It was about the closest thing she'd seen to a smile from him, so even though she didn't get the joke, she fell in alongside him as he kept walking. They followed the trail the dogs had left in the snowy yard when they'd run off after the stick Kellan had thrown to them. Mira hurried to keep up with him, feeling a bit like the little terrier, Harvard, trailing after the larger wolf dog, Luna. It was hard for Mira's short legs to keep up with Kellan's long strides, but she took two steps to every one of his, refusing to let herself fall behind.

"How old are you, anyway?" she asked him, her breath puffing out in little clouds.

He gave her another one of his shrugs. "Fourteen."

"Oh." Mira counted off the difference in her head. "You're pretty old, then, huh?"

"Not old enough," he said, and from where she

walked alongside him, his face seemed very serious. "Today I asked Lucan if I could join the Order. He told me I had to wait until I was at least twenty before I even thought about asking him again."

Mira gaped at him. "You want to be a warrior?"

His mouth took on a hard look, his eyes narrowing on some unseen point in the distance. "I want to avenge my family. I need to win back my honor after Dragos stole it from me." He blew out a sharp laugh that didn't sound like laughter at all. "Lucan and my grandfather say those aren't the right reasons to join a war. If they're not, then I don't know what is."

Mira studied Kellan's face, her heart hurting for the sadness she saw in him. In the few days she'd spent with him since he'd arrived at the compound, Kellan hadn't said much about his family or his feelings about missing them. She had seen him crying a couple of times alone in his quarters, but he didn't know that.

He also didn't know that she'd taken it upon herself to be his friend whether he liked it or not. Every night she said a little prayer for him, a ritual she'd started the moment she first heard the boy had been kidnapped from his Darkhaven. She'd kept on praying for him, even after his rescue, because it seemed to her that he'd needed the extra help in getting better. Now it had become a habit for her, one she figured she would stop once she was able to look at Kellan and not see so much private sorrow in his eyes.

"Hey," she said, trudging alongside him deeper into the gardens as they continued on after the dogs. "Maybe I'll ask Lucan if I can join the Order someday too."

Kellan laughed—actually turned a surprised look on her and laughed out loud. He had a nice laugh, she realized, the first she'd ever heard it. He had dimples too, one in each lean cheek. They appeared as he chuckled and shook his head at her. "You can't join the Order."

"Why not?" she asked, more than a little stung.

"Because you're a girl, for one thing."

"Renata's a girl," she pointed out.

"Renata's ... different," he replied. "I've seen what she can do with those blades of hers. She's fast, and she's got killer aim. She's wicked tough."

"I'm tough too," Mira said, wishing her voice didn't sound so wounded. "Watch, I'll show you."

She veered off their path to hunt for something to throw. Searching for a good stick or a rock—anything she could use to impress Kellan with her abilities—Mira weaved through the covered flower beds, around the burlap-wrapped shrubs, and into the maze of statuary and evergreens that spread out across the long backyard of the estate.

"Just a second," she called to him from within the cover of the gardens. "I'll be right ... back ..."

At first, she wasn't sure what she was looking at. Up ahead of her on the moonlit ground, shadowed by the surrounding pines and shrubbery, was a large, dark form. Luna and Harvard stood near it, alternately pacing and pausing to sniff at the motionless shape. The little terrier whined as Mira drifted closer.

"Come here, guys," she ordered the dogs, waiting as they both loped over. Her heart was hammering in her chest, beating a hundred miles an hour. Something was wrong here, really wrong. She glanced down as the dogs circled nervously at her feet. Their paws left dark stains in the snow around her boots.

Blood.

Mira screamed.

CHAPTER
Thirty-one

$\mathbf{H}$unter brought the young assassin into the back of the box truck and laid his motionless body on the floor. Corinne was beside him, holding her son's hand, tears streaming down her cheeks.

"His hands are so strong," she murmured. "My God... I can't believe it's really him."

Hunter said nothing to spoil her moment, but he knew very well that the boy was far from safe yet. It had been a risk simply to remove him from the house. The UV collar around his neck would be programmed to allow only a certain distance from the assassin's cell without Dragos's permission. With the Minion dead on the front porch, the risk of the collar detonating was doubled.

As though the boy himself sensed the tenuousness of his situation, he began to rouse back to consciousness. He started struggling, his eyelids lifting wide. Corinne drew in her breath, her tension and worry spiking Hunter's pulse through their bond.

Hunter held the boy by the collar, his fingers wrapped around the thick black polymer. He gave a warning shake of his head. "You must be still. There is nowhere for you to go."

"Nathan, don't be frightened," Corinne soothed, her voice gentle and warm. "We're not here to hurt you."

The boy's gaze flicked between the two of them. Hunter suspected it was knowledge of the collar's purpose that kept the teenage assassin from risking escape, more so than the compassion Corinne offered. Nathan's nostrils flared as he panted under Hunter's hold, his face as untrusting as that of a trapped wild animal.

"We have to get rid of the collar if the boy stands any chance of leaving this place," he told Corinne. "Dragos may already be aware that his handler is dead. He could have sensors and communication devices planted all over the grounds."

"How can we remove the collar?" she asked, meeting his gaze with a stricken look. "I know what happens if it's tampered with. We can't possibly take a chance that it..."

When she didn't seem able to finish the thought, Hunter told her gently, "We have to try something. If we don't, it could be only a matter of seconds before the collar detonates in my hand."

She glanced away from Hunter then, looking back down at her son. He was listening to every word they said, silent but absorbing all of his surroundings. Calculating his means and odds of escape, just the same as Hunter would be doing if he was the one trapped by a pair of strangers.

"We are here because we want to help you," Corinne

told him. Her smile was sad, hopeful. "You may not remember me, but you are my son. I named you Nathan. It means 'gift of God.' That's what you were to me, from the moment I first laid eyes on you."

He stared at her for a long moment, blinking quickly, studying her face. Then his struggles began again, a careful twisting and bucking, testing Hunter's hold on the collar.

"I once wore one of these too," Hunter said, catching the wild gaze and holding it steady. "I am a Hunter, like you. But I found my freedom. It can be yours too. But you have to trust us."

The boy went wild now, and Hunter had to wonder if it was his words that had terrified him so much—the mention of freedom, a concept both foreign and dangerous to their kind—even more than the threat of the collar.

In Nathan's struggles, the thick black ring of polymer and high technology knocked hard against the floor of the truck. As it did, a small red LED blinked on.

"What's that light mean?" Corinne asked, panic edging her voice. "Oh, God, Hunter...we can't do this to him. You have to let him go...before he hurts himself. Please, I'm begging you, let him go, Hunter."

A sudden flash of Mira's vision shot through his mind at Corinne's terrified words. He pushed it away and focused on the task at hand. "If we let him go, he is dead for certain. The detonator is active now. He can't run without setting it off."

And now that the LED was blinking, time was even more fleeting. He glanced around him, searching for a tool to use in removing the collar, even while he understood too well that tampering with the device would only hasten its explosion.

Then he remembered the cryogenic containers.

The liquid nitrogen.

"Stand up," he told Nathan. "Do it carefully."

Corinne gaped at him. "What are you doing? Hunter, tell me what you're thinking."

There was no time to explain. He walked the boy over to the tanks, his hand still wrapped around the lethal ring at his neck.

"Hunter, please don't hurt him," Corinne begged, a further confirmation that Mira's precognition could not be thwarted. "Can't you understand? I love him! He means everything to me!"

Hunter held fast to his conviction that he was doing the right thing—the only viable thing—to possibly save her child. With his free hand, he reached for the hose that connected the cryo container to the tank of liquid nitrogen that fed it. He yanked it loose. White fumes spewed from the severed hose.

"On your knees," he told the boy, firmly guiding him to the floor. "Take off your shirt. I want you to place it over your head like a hood, tucked between your skin and the collar."

"Hunter," Corinne cried, weeping now. "Please, just let him go. Do it for me . . ."

Her fear clawed at him, but he couldn't stop now. "This is the only way. It's his only chance, Corinne."

Nathan obeyed, silent, uncertain. When the tank top was in place, Hunter told him, "Lie down on your stomach."

Slowly, the boy got into position on the floor. Hunter wound the tail of the cotton shirt around his hand then took a firmer hold of the collar, the liquid nitro hose in the other. He exhaled a low curse, then brought the hose toward the back of Nathan's head and held the plume of freezing chemicals directly onto the collar.

Clouds of white steam frothed up into the air. Even through the layers of fabric protecting his hand, his skin burned from the intense cold blasting the impenetrable casing and circuitry of Dragos's cruel invention.

Beneath him, Corinne's son was utterly still. He panted quickly, quietly, just a terrified kid who was giving all he had to hold himself together in what could very well be the final seconds of his life.

All too soon, the liquid nitrogen began to thin and sputter from the hose. Hunter would have liked to freeze the damned collar for a lot longer, but the tank was petering out. He'd have to take his shot right now and hope for the best.

"What's happening?" Corinne asked. "Is it working?"

"We're going to have to find out."

He threw down the hose and reached for one of the daggers sheathed on his thigh. He took it out and turned the hilt around in his hand, ready to bring the butt down on the frozen collar.

Corinne's hands took hold of his arm. "Wait." She shook her head, her face stricken with fear. "Don't do this. Please, you will kill him."

He might end up killing the boy and himself, if his gamble failed and the device went off in that next moment. With Corinne weeping, pleading futilely for him to stop—the vision playing out just as Mira had predicted—Hunter pulled his arm out of her grasp.

Then he brought his fist down on the collar.

It shattered.

The pieces broke away, crumbling down around Nathan's shirt-covered head as the device disintegrated.

Hunter got up and stood back from the boy. Corinne threw her arms around him.

"Oh, my God," she breathed, clinging to Hunter, sobbing and laughing at once. "Oh, my God...I can't believe it. Hunter, it really worked!"

Nathan was motionless for a moment, still lying prone on the floor. Then he reached up and pulled the tank top from around his head. He stood, turning to face them. His fingers shook a bit as they climbed up to trace the bare skin of his neck.

Nothing but a white-tinged ring where the chemicals had burned him. The skin would heal in a short time. The miracle was, he was free.

"Wh-what have you done to me?" he asked, the first words he'd uttered to them. His voice was deep but carried the rough scrape of fading adolescence.

"You are free," Hunter told him. "No one can control you anymore. Thanks to your mother's love, her determination to find you, you are finally free to live as you choose."

Corinne stepped away from Hunter's side and held her hands out to her son in welcome. "I want to bring you home with me, Nathan. We can be a family now."

He swung a look on her as she approached him. Guarded, mistrusting, he frowned and gave a faint shake of his shaved head.

Before Hunter could register the change in the boy, from caution to cornered, Nathan was moving. In a flash of Breed motion, he had grabbed one of the broken shards of his collar and held it tight against Corinne's throat. She gasped, totally unprepared for the assault.

Hunter growled, his eyes trained on the jagged, makeshift blade that was poised at his Breedmate's carotid.

Whether this boy was her flesh and blood or not, he had just declared himself an enemy.

And Hunter would not hesitate to kill him if the threat escalated even so much as a fraction.

Even as Nathan backed her with him toward the open doors of the truck, Corinne's eyes pleaded with Hunter for mercy. "Nathan," she said, trying once more to reach her son's humanity. "You don't have to be afraid. Let us be your friends now. Let us be your family. Just give me a chance to be the mother I should have been for you."

He moved closer to the doors, saying nothing. That damnable bit of sharp material still riding near her vein.

"Nathan," Corinne said. "Please, just let me love you—"

He shoved her forward, a violent rejection of all she'd said and all she'd done for him.

Then he bolted out of the truck, escaping into the woods as the first light of dawn was already beginning to glow on the horizon.

CHAPTER
Thirty-two

Chase hadn't actually expected to wake up. His last conscious memory had been running in a blind tear through the city, losing too much blood from the gunshot wound in the artery of his right leg and the lesser hit to his shoulder. He'd taken worse injuries in combat before, but that was then. This was now, when his body was shuddering and weak, his nearly indestructible Breed genetics hobbled by the disease that roused him awake on a pained groan.

He tried to sit up but didn't get very far. Metal restraints clamped his wrists and ankles to an infirmary bed. Another wide band of steel and leather lashed him around his middle. He cursed through his gritted teeth and gave the manacles a good hard rattle.

As his vision slowly came into better focus, he saw a dark head peering in from the hallway at him through the small window in the door.

It took Dante a minute before he finally strode inside.

As the door closed shut behind him, he stared at Chase from across the room and shook his head. "You're a fucking idiot, you know that, Harvard?"

Chase scoffed. "Thanks for the concern. I hope you didn't come all the way down here just to tell me that."

"No, I didn't," Dante replied, not rising to his bait at all. "I've been next door, sitting with Tess while she's recovering."

"Tess is in the infirmary?" Recalling the Breedmate's delicate last few weeks of pregnancy, Chase immediately felt like a first-class asshole. "Ah, Christ, man. I didn't know."

"How could you know? You weren't here."

Chase exhaled a short sigh and nodded in acknowledgment. He couldn't say he didn't deserve this cold reception. After all, he'd done just about everything he could lately to make sure he was *persona non grata* with the Order. Especially where Dante was concerned. "So, how is she doing? Everything all right with her?"

"Yeah. Tess is fine." Dante gave a faint incline of his head. "So is the baby. He's resting next door with her."

Tess gave birth already? The news flash hit Chase with double barrels. He couldn't hold back his surprise, or the regret that slapped him to realize he'd been absent for the event Dante and Tess had been looking forward to for many long months. Hell, he'd been pretty damned eager about the whole thing himself. He'd even wondered on more than one occasion if Dante had been thinking about asking him to be godfather to his son, an honor Chase was hardly worthy of, but one he would have accepted with humbled pride at one time.

A million years ago.

And now a million miles out of his reach.

That's what it all felt like to him, looking at the other

warrior's grave, disappointed expression as he approached the bed where Chase was shackled. "Well, congratulations, Dante. To you and Tess both," he said. "When did the baby come?"

"Yesterday morning, a few minutes before noon."

Chase guessed, "So, what is that, December tenth?"

"Seventeenth," Dante replied, his look going even more grim than before. "Shit, Harvard. How bad is it for you now? I mean seriously. Don't bullshit me."

"Bad," Chase admitted. His throat was parched, voice little better than a rough growl. "But I can handle it. I'd handle it a lot better if I wasn't strapped down to this damned bed like a criminal." He lifted his fisted hands as far as the steel manacles would allow. Which wasn't much at all.

"Not gonna happen," Dante said soberly.

Chase grunted. "Doctor's orders?"

"Lucan's orders. It took some convincing for him to even let Niko and Renata bring you inside after Mira found you. Didn't help matters that your face has been plastered all over the news as some kind of goddamn nutjob domestic terrorist." Dante exhaled a curse. "What'd you do, pose for pictures before you lost your mind and started shooting up the senator's Christmas party last night?"

"What are you talking about?"

"They've ID'd you, man. There was an eyewitness who provided your description to law enforcement and the freaking Secret Service. Whoever saw you nailed your face down to the last pore and whisker. They've been running the artist's sketch on every network and cable channel ever since."

"Shit," Chase muttered, remembering the laser-intense stare of the senator's attractive assistant when she'd spotted him up in the gallery of the ballroom. "It couldn't be helped, Dante. And it doesn't matter that I've been made. Dragos was there. He was trying to get close to the senator and the vice president. He's targeted both of them."

Dante went quiet, studying him as if he wasn't sure Chase could be believed. "You saw Dragos at the senator's party? You're sure of this?"

"Goddamn right, I'm sure. I watched the senator introduce him to the vice president in the middle of a ballroom full of humans. When I saw them walking off to a private meeting, I saw my shot and I took it."

Dante raked his hand through his dark hair. "You saw Dragos, and you didn't call it in to us? The Order should have been the ones to handle the situation. What the hell were you thinking?"

"One thing I wasn't thinking about was stopping to make a phone call," Chase argued. "I didn't know Dragos was going to be there. I didn't know I was going to be just a few yards away from him—close enough to put a bullet in the son of a bitch and take him down. All I had was a hunch, and I acted on it."

"Jesus, Harvard. This is not good news."

"Are you listening to me?" Chase shouted, anger spiking, adding fuel to the flame of his already tightening blood hunger. "I'm telling you I shot Dragos last night. I saw a bullet hit him dead-on and take him to the floor. For fuck's sake, maybe you should be thanking me instead of crucifying me for not following protocol. I'm telling you there's a damn good chance I killed the bastard."

"Dragos isn't dead," Dante replied soberly. "No one was killed last night. There were reports of a few injuries, but none of them was deemed life-threatening. If

Dragos was there, if you shot him like you say you did, then he was able to get up and walk away."

Chase listened, his temples banging with rising fury. "I need to get out of here. I found him once, I can find him again. I can fix this—"

"No, Harvard, you can't. And you're not going anywhere. There's too much at stake for us right now. Lucan wants your ass planted right where it is until he says otherwise."

Chase couldn't bite back his snarl. He was pissed that Dragos had escaped and pissed that Lucan, Dante, or anyone else thought they could hold him against his will. He was getting the message loud and clear that he was no longer part of the Order, and he'd be damned if that meant they could keep him from going after Dragos on his own. He wanted Dragos taken out as much as any of the warriors.

And he had another, equally pressing reason to want to be let loose from his captivity in the compound.

"I need to feed," he murmured low under his breath. "The gunshot wound in my thigh isn't going to heal very fast if I don't get some fresh red cells in my body. I need to be free to hunt, Dante."

The warrior's gaze bore into his own like a probing searchlight, leaving no shadows for Chase's deception to hide in. "You said it yourself; your leg is in bad shape. You're in no condition to hunt, even if Lucan didn't feel it would be a mistake to turn you loose topside right now."

The thirst that had been clawing at him began to rake its talons even deeper, shredding him from the inside out. He was sweating, an icy sheen that made him shudder as his stomach twisted into a tighter knot. "Can you risk leaving me in here?" he said, his voice rough as gravel, almost unearthly. "I might end up hunting inside the compound, seeing how there's a human living here now."

Dante's face blanched a bit before his eyes fired up with sparks of bright amber. "Because you're hurting, I'm gonna pretend you didn't say that. And I'm going to do you the one-time favor of not telling Brock either, because I promise you, that male would kill you with his bare hands if you so much as breathed on Jenna, human or not. Hell, keep pushing and I might save him the effort."

The coil of agony in his gut made Chase sneer up at Dante in response. "If I wanted to break out of these restraints, I could. You know that."

"Yeah, I know." Dante edged in closer, moving so quickly Chase's sluggish senses couldn't track him. He was startled to feel the cold kiss of sharp metal pressed up hard against his throat. Dante's curved twin blades bit into his flesh, one on each side of his neck, a hairbreadth from breaking the skin. "You could try to break out of the restraints, Harvard, but now you've got two good reasons why you won't."

Chase bristled at the threat, one he knew from experience that he'd better respect. "That's some tough love, especially coming from a friend."

"My friend is gone. He's been gone for longer than I want to admit," Dante said, his voice tight and controlled. Lethal, when it lacked the warrior's usual bravado. "Right now, I'm talking to the blood addict glaring up at me with bared fangs and amber-soaked eyes. He's the one who'll be eating these titanium blades if he thinks I'm wrong about him walking the thin line toward Bloodlust."

He didn't ease off with the nasty curved daggers, not

even when Chase slowly retreated, letting his spine settle back onto the mattress of the infirmary bed. The sharp edges followed him down, dangerously close, testing Chase's nerve.

He didn't dare escalate the situation.

Although he wasn't yet Rogue, Dante was right. Chase could feel Bloodlust nipping at his heels. And he couldn't be sure that the titanium wouldn't act like poison to his blood. He glowered up at Dante but made no move to try him.

"That's the first smart move you've made in a long time, Harvard."

Chase said nothing, waiting to breathe until the razor-sharp claws fell away from his throat and the warrior who had recently been his tightest companion left him alone once more in the room.

CHAPTER
Thirty-three

The long hours of daylight dragged by in excruciating slowness. Corinne felt each minute pass as though every one carved away a small piece of her heart along with it.

Nathan was gone.

After the years of hoping for the chance to see him again, after the endless prayers for a miracle that might—somehow—grant her the ability to escape her imprisonment to reunite with her child and be the family she dreamed they could be . . . he was gone.

Slipped through her fingers, not due to any prophesied end but by his own choice.

The fact that he was alive and missing hurt only slightly less than the idea that she might have lost him to the vision Hunter had described. Nathan was gone, and in the wake of that fact, Corinne was bereft.

She sat with Hunter in the back of the box truck, both of them waiting for sundown and another chance for Hunter to search for Nathan. He'd gone after him in the minutes after Nathan had fled, but Hunter's search of the area had been fruitless, dawn driving him back to the truck empty-handed.

In the time since, they had moved several miles from the log cabin homestead that had served as Nathan's cell. Hunter felt the risk of discovery by Dragos's operatives was too great to remain there any longer than they had. Corinne had reluctantly agreed.

Now all she could do was wonder where her son had run off to and pray his conditioning as one of Dragos's unquestioning soldiers didn't make him return to the very evil Corinne had wanted to deliver him from. That is, if the sun that blazed outside the truck didn't take him first.

"If you were him," she said to Hunter, "where would you go?"

Hunter reached over and took her hand in a gentle grasp, tracing the pad of his thumb over her Breedmate mark. "He is a survivor, Corinne. That's what his training has taught him to be. He is highly intelligent, and he is, I am sure, extremely familiar with his surroundings. I found a number of caves in the area when I searched for him. By now he could be hiding in any one of them." He considered for a moment, then added, "Without the collar to restrict his movement to the area immediately surrounding the cabin, there's also a chance he could be anywhere."

She nodded, appreciating that Hunter didn't feel the need to cushion her from the truth. There would be no more secrets between them anymore, no matter how small. It was something they'd promised each other as they'd made the journey to the isolated cabin in the Georgia woodlands last night, after Hunter's disclosure of Mira's vision had nearly rent them apart.

Corinne exhaled a shaky sigh. "At least we were able to change the outcome of the vision. If nothing else, at least we know now that not everything Mira sees must come true."

Hunter shook his head. "There was no altering of what I saw in Mira's eyes. The vision she showed me played out exactly as she predicted. It was my interpretation that was wrong."

"What do you mean?"

"Everything you said in those last few moments was part of it, Corinne. You asked me to spare him. You pleaded for me to let him go. All your words, just as you said them, were part of Mira's precognition." He brought her fingers up to his mouth and pressed a gentle kiss to them. "When I raised my hand and prepared to bring it down on him, you physically tried to stop me. And I let my hand drop anyway. I had to—it was the only way."

"I don't understand," she murmured. "You didn't kill Nathan. The vision was wrong."

"No," he said. "The blow I delivered should have killed him—it *would* have, if his collar had not been disabled. That was the thing I didn't know, the thing the vision had not revealed to me. I didn't realize until the moment it was happening that the strike I made against your son was meant to save his life, not take it away."

"Thank God," Corinne whispered, curling herself into the shelter of his embrace. "But Nathan is gone anyway. I've lost him, just the same."

"We will find him," Hunter said, his deep voice rumbling from all around her, low and soothing, as strong as his protective arms. "I give you my vow on this, Corinne. No matter how long it takes, or how far I must go to see it through. I will do this...I do it for you. Everything for you."

She turned her head to gaze up at him, moved by his promise.

"I love you," he told her. "My life now and for the rest of my years is committed to your happiness."

"Oh, Hunter," she sighed, emotion catching in her throat. "I love you so much. You've already shown me happiness I didn't think possible for a very long time."

He bent and dropped a kiss on her brow. "And I have never known any of the things you've made me feel in our brief time together. You have made me want to experience everything in life. I want to experience it all with you at my side...as my mate, if you deem me worthy."

"I don't want to live a day without you either," she confessed. "You are a part of me now."

"I want that," he said, catching her lips in a sensual, passionate joining of their mouths. When he drew back a moment later, his eyes were glowing bright as coals. His fangs gleamed, the sharp points extending even farther as he gazed at her. "I can't help but desire you. I want to taste you again. This feeling I have for you is more than intense," he said roughly. "It is a possessive thing, greedy. I look at you, Corinne Bishop, and all I can think is that you are *mine*."

"I am yours," she confirmed, stroking the proud jaw and muscled cheek of the male she wanted beside her eternally. "I am yours alone, Hunter. Yours forever."

With a growl, he pulled her into another, deeper kiss. "I want you to belong to me," he murmured against her mouth. "I want to know my blood lives inside you, as a part of you."

"Yes," she gasped, thrilling to the idea of binding herself to him now and for always.

Their eyes locked together, he raised his wrist to his mouth and sank his long fangs into the flesh. He brought it to her, the most precious gift he could give her. Corinne put her lips to his opened vein and drew the first taste of him into her mouth.

His blood hit her tongue like wildfire.

Thick and strong and roaring with power, it was the very essence of all Hunter was. And now that vitality was feeding her, enriching her cells, filling her senses . . . weaving into every fiber of her being. She felt the bond take hold, a radiant, glorious connection. She grabbed on to it and let it wrap around her, reveling in the total saturation of joy that engulfed her as she continued to drink from Hunter.

His blood obliterated the horror of all she'd been through. The torture was swept away, the degradation lifted, all of it scattering like dust under the power of the bond that was now growing, intensifying between them.

As she drew from Hunter's vein, she watched her magnificent mate's eyes blaze with passion and possession . . . with a love so intense it stole her breath. She was on fire for him now, her own need amplified by the intoxicating power of his blood.

She could hardly stand the wait as he carefully withdrew his wrist and sealed the wounds closed with his tongue. She was trembling as he undressed her, his own clothes gone in the next instant.

He covered her with his body and made love to her, sweetly, thoroughly . . . an ecstasy that burned as brightly as their love.

And while this moment of commitment and completion filled her beyond measure, there was still a corner of her heart that she knew would ache as long as her son was gone. But Hunter's promise to stand by her until they found him gave her faith. Perhaps he wasn't lost to her forever. Not yet.

With Hunter's love, and the blood bond that flowed through her, stronger than any storm, everything seemed possible.

A heavy rain had swept into the area by the time dusk finally settled.

Hunter shrugged into his leather trench coat, preparing to head back out to search for Nathan one last time before pushing on to New England. Based on his quick check-in with the Order a short while ago, things were going from bad to worse at the compound. As much as he hated to leave without Corinne's son, Hunter also could not ignore his duty to his fellow warriors.

More than even that, he needed to ensure that Corinne was somewhere safe and protected while he carried out all of his duties, not left to wait for him in the back of an unsecured delivery truck.

"I will be fine," she told him, reading his concern with an ease that should have unsettled him.

It didn't unsettle, however. It was reassuring how well she'd come to know him.

Incredible how visceral their bond was now, solidified by their mingling blood.

He caressed her beautiful, brave face. "I'll be gone only for a couple of hours. I can cover the entire area near the river and the state park around it in that time."

"Thank you," she said, turning a kiss into his palm. "Whatever happens—whether you find him out there tonight or not, just know that I'm grateful you're willing to try."

"Nathan is your family. That means he's my family too."

She gave a wobbly nod as he gathered her close. As Hunter gazed into her trusting eyes, he knew a deep wish to build a larger family with her—to give her more sons to love, once Nathan was safe.

Together they walked to the doors of the truck. Hunter opened them into the hiss of the steadily pouring rain.

Nathan stood outside in the deluge.

He was drenched, barefoot and half dressed in just the gray sweatpants he'd been wearing when he'd bolted earlier that day. Water sluiced off his shaved head and down the lean muscled plates of his *dermaglyph*-covered chest. His hands hung loosely at his sides, fingers dripping water into the mud beneath his feet.

Corinne went very quiet next to Hunter, as though not trusting her own eyes and afraid the boy was just an illusion that could shatter if she so much as breathed.

Nathan stared at them. "I don't have anywhere to go."

"Yes, you do," Hunter replied.

He held out his hand.

It took a long moment before the boy made any move whatsoever. Then, with a faint nod, he reached up and clasped Hunter's hand, stepping up into the truck.

Beside him now, Hunter heard Corinne's lungs expel a soft, shaky sigh. Her pulse was pounding, beating as hard as a drum, her blood racing so hard he could feel her excitement—her hope—in his own veins. But she held herself back, doing everything in her power to resist throwing her arms around her child in relief and elation.

She stood unmoving, waiting, watching her beloved son slowly make his way over to her first.

"Is everything you said true?" he asked her.

She nodded, tears overflowing her eyes. "Everything."

Hunter removed his coat and draped it over the boy's soaked shoulders. Nathan glanced over at him, still not entirely certain of them. "If I go with you, where will you take me?"

"Home," Hunter answered.

He glanced at Corinne then, understanding in just that moment how powerful the word truly was.

Home.

It struck him with the same staggering force as a weapon hammered out of steel, as unbreakable as a diamond, as steady as a mountain.

Home.

It was something neither he nor this lethal teenage assassin had ever known. Something they both had found in the beautiful woman who had somehow, miraculously, opened her gentle, stalwart heart to both of them.

Hunter put his arm around her slender shoulders, gazing at her with all the love that was overflowing in his own heart. He leaned in close to her and whispered for her ears alone: "Thank you for bringing me home."

CHAPTER
Thirty-four

Are you going to pace all morning, Lucan? Some rest would do you good, you know."

Gabrielle patted the empty spot beside her on the massive bed in their quarters at the compound. It was midmorning according to the clock on the nightstand, but he had been on his feet nonstop since the day before.

Too many fires to put out. Too many lives resting in his hands—not the least of which being the infant son newly born to Dante and Tess.

And then there was Sterling Chase, currently cooling his heels under lockdown in the infirmary. Lucan and the rest of the Order had been on high alert since he'd shown up on the estate grounds more than twenty-four hours ago, bleeding from multiple gunshot wounds and sporting a rather massive target on his ass.

The news stations were still having a field day with the eyewitness sketch they'd obtained of him. It was being played on every broadcast—local, national, and cable—and had been a permanent fixture on the various Internet news sites since the incident at the senator's party took place. Lucan wondered just how long it would take for the heat on Chase from human law enforcement to subside.

Not good, that the Order was harboring an individual wanted by several local police entities and the goddamned feds as well.

As pissed as he was at Chase not only for letting Dragos get away but also for getting himself shot and ID'd in the process, he had to admit it had been a good thing—a bloody admirable hunch—that had put Chase at the senator's party. Regardless of his personal issues of late, Chase's instincts had been solid, and royal fuckup on the execution notwithstanding, his public disruption had managed to thwart whatever Dragos had up his sleeve.

And there had been something going on, Lucan was certain of that. The conniving son of a bitch sure hadn't been there for the canapés and conversation.

He hated to consider what Dragos might have intended, considering the fact that some of the United States's top government officials had been in attendance.

Lucan walked another hard track in the rug. "Something big is about to blow. I can feel it in my bones, Gabrielle. Some shit is about to go down, and unless I get my hands around it quick, it's going to explode not just in my face, but in everyone else's too."

"Come here," she said, frowning now as she threw back the sheet and comforter to make room beside her naked body on the bed. She was gorgeous, and too tempting to resist, despite the gravity of his thoughts. "You're doing all you can," she told him as he settled in next to her. "We'll figure this out. All of us, together. You are not alone in this, Lucan."

He felt himself relax as she spoke, his troubles seeming to ease just by the fact that she was near. It was a power she had over him that never ceased to amaze him. "How did I ever manage to convince you to be my mate?"

Her soft laugh vibrated against his ear where it rested on her breast. "There was kissing involved, if I recall. Maybe even some kicking and screaming. On your part, primarily."

He pulled back and stared darkly into her eyes. "I don't kick, and I most definitely never scream."

"Maybe not," she conceded, a wry smile tugging at her full lips. "But you didn't go down easy, you have to at least admit that much."

"I'm thick-headed, according to rumor," he said. "Half the time, I don't know what's good for me."

Her auburn brows quirked. "Fortunately for you, I *do* know what's good for you."

She pulled him up for her kiss, sealing her mouth over his in a slow, penetrating claiming that had him going stiff as granite in his fatigues. With a snarl of pure masculine approval, he caught her around her tender nape and plunged his tongue between her teeth.

He already had her pressed beneath him when the phone line from the tech lab started ringing.

Lucan's warning bells went off like sirens as he tore himself away from Gabrielle's warm body and put the receiver to his ear. "What's going on, Gideon?"

"You don't, by chance, have the television on, do you?"

"No."

Gideon's voice didn't have its usual levity. Not even

close. "All hell's breaking loose downtown, Lucan. You'd better come quick. You need to see this."

Chase brought his head up from the pillow of his bed in the infirmary, straining to get a better look at the television screen mounted in the corner of the room. It had been parked on one of those pointless morning chatter shows, where a pair of hosts kibitzed and chuckled over vapid news items while sipping tall cups of coffee and flashing a lot of veneered white teeth at the camera. Even on mute, the thing had annoyed him, but he'd left it on just to give his eyes something to focus on, other than the four clinical walls that caged him inside the compound.

It had been either that, or let himself go mad and give in to the hunger that was still clawing at him from the inside out. The addict in him had wanted out of there in a bad way—needed it more than anything—but he knew if he stood even a rat's ass chance of breaking his dangerous slide, he was going to have to starve the blood thirst out of himself. He could think of no better place for him to try than back here, in the compound, among the only friends he had.

Friends he'd given every right to desert him.

And yet they'd taken him in.

Strapped him down and locked him up inside the infirmary, but what the hell, he wasn't going to look a gift horse in the mouth.

But now, as he peered up at the monitor, his stomach sank as he watched the show being interrupted by a live news report. He reached for the remote on the wheeled tray beside him, only to be reminded of his restraints as the shackles rattled but held fast. He could have yanked them loose, but fuck it. He could handle the sound without it.

Willing the volume up, he listened in abject dread as real-time footage of a massive explosion somewhere in Boston filled the screen. A female news reporter's voice described what they were broadcasting.

"*—at the UN building downtown. Police are just arriving on scene, and Channel 5 has news crews en route now. Initial reports seem to indicate this was a bomb situation of some sort. We're getting reports of significant damage to the building, and all surrounding streets in a ten-block radius have been sealed off by law enforcement.*"

Holy shit. Chase watched the roiling cloud of smoke and dust and flame billowing up toward the camera of the news helicopter that circled the area overhead. Although it seemed impossible—completely lacking in sense, except for the purpose of creating terror—his gut was telling him this too had Dragos's name all over it.

"*Further reports from sources on the scene tell us there is a vehicle pursuit under way by law enforcement at this time. It is believed the alleged suspect or suspects in this possible terror act are in that vehicle and were spotted by eyewitnesses leaving the scene in the moments before this explosion took place. Channel 5's news copter is reporting to the scene of this pursuit, and we will update you live as we have more information.*"

Chase put his head back down and muttered a ripe curse at the ceiling. If Dragos was involved in this stunt, what the hell was he up to?

Chase wanted to rip loose from his forced recuperation and head down to the tech lab, where he was certain all the rest of the Order would be watching the same troubling report by now. Gideon constantly monitored human news outlets, and shit like this—terror acts in the middle of the week, rolling toward the holidays— tended to make a big splash.

But he didn't belong around that long table in the lab anymore. He'd walked out on the Order, and he didn't deserve to ask them to take him back until he was sure he had his shit together.

As he kicked himself for the string of failures and fuck-ups that had been the bulk of his recent missions for the Order, the news reporter came back onscreen.

"We're breaking now to Channel 5's eye-in-the-sky, which is bringing you the latest from just outside the city, where police are currently in pursuit of the vehicle they believe is linked to this terrible incident at the UN building this morning. Again, if you're just tuning in, Channel 5 was first on the scene, bringing you news of a large explosion, a bomb of some type, that was set off downtown just moments ago . . ."

While she spoke, Chase watched in astonishment— then in mounting suspicion and abject dread—as a fleet of police cruisers and SWAT vans pursued a late-model red pickup truck from out of the city, toward an area of large, tree-filled estates and sprawling private properties.

Right toward the Order's domain.

Chase tried to sit up and felt his restraints bite into his wrists and ankles. The steel-reinforced leather band around his torso groaned as he strained to get a better look at what was happening on the monitor.

It wasn't good.

The pursuit turned the last bend, heading right up the sunlit street toward the outer perimeter of the Order's estate. To his horror, not an instant later, the red pickup roared up toward the front gates of the mansion.

Ah, Christ.

Mother of fucking God...

Sparks erupted as the vehicle hit the electrified gate and crashed through. Several men poured out of the truck and started pounding up the snow-filled lawn on foot. Running toward the mansion with a dozen or more cops hot on their heels.

Dragos sent them here.

He knew it.

He knew it the same way he knew now that this was an act of retaliation, not merely some bizarre coincidence. This was Dragos taking his revenge for what Chase had done the other night.

He brought this on the Order... on his friends.

With an anguished roar, Chase ripped loose from his restraints and fled the infirmary using every ounce of preternatural speed at his command.

Lucan stood with the rest of the Order, all of them gathered in the tech lab watching the news report incredulously.

Their disbelief had been nothing compared to the sick sense of dread—the first true sense of fear that Lucan had experienced in a long time—when the red pickup truck carrying the suspected bombers rammed the mansion's gate.

A silence filled the tech lab in that terrible instant.

It was full daylight outside. No chance for escape. They were trapped now, with no choice but to watch the skirmish take place above the compound and hope law enforcement left without deciding to nose around the property or question the owners.

And in the pit of his heavy heart, Lucan understood

that this was Dragos's intention all along. This was why he'd planted the tracking device in Kellan Archer. This was how he meant for the Order to go down.

Not by his hand, but by the humans.

"Seal all portals to the compound and lock them down," he told Gideon. "If any of those criminal fucks or the cops do something stupid like bring this thing inside the mansion, we don't want them getting curious about what might lie below the house."

If they did, the Order would have no choice but to kill them all on sight.

And that would be damned hard to sweep under the rug, especially since the whole bloody chase was being captured on live news coverage.

"Shut it down now," he said, slamming his fist onto the table and sending a big crack running down its center. "This is Dragos's doing. He sent them here. Right to our goddamn doorstep."

"Compound portals are sealed," Gideon reported. Then he hissed a curse, something Lucan did not want to hear at that moment. "Ah, Christ. I don't believe this."

He pivoted his head toward Lucan and gestured to one of the interior surveillance feeds from inside the mansion.

"Holy fuck," Nikolai breathed from his place among the others. "It's Harvard. What the hell is he doing up there?"

"He's saving us," Dante answered, no inflection in the warrior's voice at all.

They watched in dumbstruck silence as Chase strode calmly toward the front door of the mansion. He opened it on to the yard full of uniformed cops, SWAT members, and Secret Service agents. As he lifted his hands to his head in a show of surrender, sunlight streamed in all around him, a nimbus that lit him up in silhouette like an avenging angel.

The humans rushed up to intercept him, more than one speaking quickly into his radio as they got a good look at Chase, no doubt every man out there recognizing him from the sketch that was circulating in every station and precinct house between Boston and D.C.

Lucan watched, humbled and grateful. If not for Chase's sacrifice, those men likely would have torn the estate apart. They might still, but the Order had just been granted a stay from that particular execution. Instead of a potential daylight raid, the Order might have a chance to collect themselves and clear out at nightfall instead.

All thanks to Sterling Chase.

"Man, this is fucked up," Brock murmured from beside Lucan. "We can't just let them take him away like this. We have to do something."

Lucan gave a grim shake of his head, wishing there was a way to help. "Harvard just took that option out of our hands. He is truly on his own now."

Thirsty for more?

Don't miss the next novel in Lara's
hot and thrilling
Midnight Breed series

Darker After
Midnight

BY

LARA ADRIAN

Coming from Delacorte Press in Spring 2012

"The charges are set, Lucan. Detonators are ready whenever you say the word. On your go, it all ends right here."

Lucan Thorne stood silent in the dusk-filled, snow-covered yard of the Boston estate he had acquired more than a hundred years ago as a base of operation for himself and his small cadre of brothers-in-arms. For more than a hundred years, on countless patrols, they rode out from this very spot to guard the night, maintaining a fragile peace between the unwitting humans who owned the daytime hours and the predators who moved among them secretly, sometimes lethally, in the dark.

Lucan and his warriors of the Order dealt in swift, deadly justice, and had never known the taste of defeat.

Tonight it was bitter on his tongue.

"Dragos will pay for this," he growled around the emerging points of his fangs.

Lucan's vision burned amber as he stared at the pale limestone facade of the Gothic mansion across the expansive lawn. A chaos of tire tracks scarred the grounds from the police chase that had crashed the compound's tall iron gates that morning and come to a bullet-riddled halt right at the Order's front door. Blood stained the snow where law enforcement gunfire had mowed down three terrorists who'd bombed Boston's United Nations building then fled the scene with a dozen cops and every news station in the area in close pursuit.

All of it—from the attack on a human government facility to the media-covered police chase of the suspects onto the compound's secured grounds—had been orchestrated by the Order's chief adversary, a power-mad vampire called Dragos.

He wasn't the first of the Breed to dream of a world where humankind lived to serve and served in fear. But where others before him with less commitment had failed, Dragos had demonstrated astonishing patience and initiative. He'd been carefully sowing the seeds of his rebellion for most of his long life, secretly cultivating followers within the Breed and making Minions of any humans he felt could help carry out his twisted goals.

For the past year and a half, since their discovery of Dragos's plans, Lucan and his brethren had kept him on the run. They had succeeded in driving him back, thwarting his every move and disrupting his operation.

Until today.

Today it was the Order pushed back and on the run, and Lucan didn't like it one damn bit.

"What's the ETA at the temporary headquarters?"

The question was aimed toward Gideon, one of the two warriors who'd remained behind with Lucan to wrap things up in Boston while the rest of the compound went ahead to an emergency facility in northern Maine. Gideon glanced away from the small handheld computer in his palm and met Lucan's gaze over the rims of silvery blue shades. "Savannah and the other women have been on the road for nearly five hours, so they should be at the location in about thirty minutes. Niko and the other warriors are just a couple hours behind them."

Lucan gave a nod, grim but relieved that the abrupt relocation had come together as well as it had. There were a few loose ends and details yet to be managed, but so far everyone was safe and the damage Dragos had intended to inflict on the Order had been minimized.

Movement stirred on the other side of Lucan as Tegan, the other warrior who'd stayed behind, returned from the latest perimeter check. "Any problems?"

"None." Tegan's face showed no emotion, only grim purpose. "The two cops in the unmarked stakeout vehicle near the gates are still tranced and sleeping. After the hard memory scrub I gave them earlier today, there's a good chance they won't wake up until next week. And when they do, it'll be with one hellacious hangover."

Gideon grunted. "Better a mind scrub on a couple of Boston's finest than a very public bloodbath involving half the city's precincts and the feds combined."

"Damn straight," Lucan said, recalling the swarm of cops and news media that had filled the estate grounds that morning. "If the situation had escalated and any of those cops or federal agents had decided to come banging on the mansion door . . . Christ, I'm sure I don't need to tell either of you how fast or how far things would have gone south."

Tegan's eyes were grave in the rising darkness. "Guess we've got Chase to thank for that."

"Yeah," Lucan replied. He'd lived a long time—nine hundred years and then some—but for however long he'd walk this earth, he knew he would never forget the sight of Sterling Chase strolling out of the mansion and squarely into the aim of a yard full of heavily armed cops and federal agents. He could have died several ways in that moment. If the adrenaline-rife panic of any one of the armed men assembled in the yard hadn't killed him on the spot, spending longer than half an hour under the full blast of morning sunlight would have.

But Chase apparently hadn't cared about any of that as he allowed himself to be cuffed and led away by the human authorities. His surrender—his personal sacrifice—had bought the Order precious time. He had diverted attention from the mansion and what it concealed, giving Lucan and the others the chance to secure the subterranean compound and mobilize the evacuation of its residents once the sun set.

After a string of bad calls and personal fuck-ups, most recently a failed strike against Dragos that had inadvertently landed Chase's face on the national news, he was the last of the warriors Lucan would have turned to for answers. What he had done today was nothing short of astonishing, if not suicidal.

Then again, Sterling Chase had been on a self-destructive path for some time now. Maybe this was his way of nailing that coffin shut once and for all.

Gideon raked a hand over the top of his spiky blond hair and exhaled a curse. "Fucking lunatic. I can't believe he actually did it."

"It should have been me." Lucan glanced between Tegan and Gideon, the warrior who'd been with him when he'd first founded the Order in Europe and the one who'd helped him establish the warriors' home base in Boston centuries later. "I'm the Order's leader. If there was a sacrifice to be made to spare everyone else, I should have been the one to step up."

Tegan eyed him grimly. "How long do you think Chase would have been able to keep his Bloodlust at bay? Whether he's in human custody or loose on the streets, his thirst owns him. He's lost and he knows that. He knew it when he walked out that door this morning. He had nothing left to lose."

Lucan grunted. "And now he's sitting in police custody somewhere, surrounded by humans. He might have spared us from discovery today, but what if his thirst gets the best of him and he ends up exposing the existence of all the Breed? One moment of heroism could undo centuries of secrecy."

Tegan's expression was coldly sober. "I guess we'll have to trust him."

"Trust," Lucan said. "That's a currency he's come up short on more than once lately."

Unfortunately, right now, they didn't have a lot of choice in the matter. Dragos had demonstrated quite effectively just how far he was willing to take his enmity toward the Order. He had no regard for life, human or his own kind, and as of today he'd shown that he would take their power struggle out of the shadows and into the open. It was dangerous ground, with impossibly high stakes.

And it was personal now. Dragos had crossed a line here, and there would be no going back.

Lucan glanced to Gideon. "It's time. Hit the detonators. Let's get this done."

The warrior gave a slight nod and turned his attention back to his handheld computer. "Ah, fuck me," he muttered, the traces of his British accent punctuating the curse. "Here we go then."

The three Breed males stood side by side in the crisp, cold darkness. Above them the sky was clear and cloudless, endless black, pierced with stars. Everything was still, as if the earth and heavens had frozen in time, suspended in that instant between the silence of a perfect winter night and the first low rumble of the destruction unfolding roughly three hundred feet beneath the warriors' boots. It seemed to carry on forever, not some great bombastic spectacle of furious noise and spewing fire and ash, but a quiet, yet thorough, annihilation.

"The living quarters have been sealed," Gideon reported somberly as the thunder began to ebb. He touched the screen of his handheld device and another series of deep growls rolled from far below the snow-covered ground. "The weapons room, the infirmary ... both gone now."

Lucan didn't allow himself to dwell on the memories or the history that was housed in the labyrinth of rooms and corridors being systematically exploded with a touch of Gideon's finger on that tiny computer screen. It had taken more than a hundred years to build the compound into what it had become. He couldn't deny that it put a cold ache in his chest to feel it being pulled down so neatly.

"The chapel has been sealed," Gideon said, after pressing the digital detonator another time. "All that remains is the tech lab."

Lucan heard the slight catch in the warrior's low voice. The tech lab was Gideon's pride, the nerve center of the Order's operation. It was where they'd assembled and strategized before every night's mission. It took no effort at all for Lucan to see his brethren's faces, a fine group of honorable, courageous Breed males gathered around the lab's conference table, each one ready to give his life for the other. Some of them had. And some likely would in the time still to come.

As the soft percussion of explosives continued to rumble belowground, Lucan felt a weight settle on his shoulder. He glanced beside him, to where Tegan stood, the warrior's big hand remaining a steady presence, his cool green eyes holding Lucan's gaze in an unexpected show of solidarity, as the last of the thunder faded into silence.

"That's it," Gideon announced. "That was the last one. It's over now."

For a long while, none of them spoke. There were no words. Nothing to be said in the dark shadow of the now-vacant mansion and its ruined compound below.

Finally Lucan stepped forward. His fangs bit into the edges of his tongue as he took one last look at the place that had been his headquarters—his family's home—for so many long years. Amber light filled his vision as his eyes transformed in his simmering fury.

He pivoted to face his two brethren and when he at last found the words to speak, his voice was harsh and raw with determination. "We may be done here, but this night doesn't mark the end of anything. It's only the beginning. Dragos wants a war with the Order? Then by God, he's damn well got it."